Dear Reader,

I am very pleased that *Dawn's Early Light* will see
the light of day again! Many readers loved the book
when it was first published under my pen name,
Caryn Cameron, nearly a decade ago. It is a timeless
story of powerful emotions and those old-fashioned
virtues like honor, sacrifice, patriotism and
freedom, all anchored in a world-changing love.

I have visited the beautiful settings in this novel—
Baltimore and Bermuda—since I wrote the book,
and I fell in love with them all over again. That's the
way I feel about the independent but vulnerable
hero and heroine. Brett and Alex's trials and
triumphs still live in their author's heart, and
I hope they will find a place in yours.

I enjoy hearing from my readers, and I do answer
letters. You can write me c/o MIRA Books.

Fondly,

Karen Harper

Coming soon from MIRA Books and
KAREN HARPER

LIBERTY'S LADY

KAREN HARPER

DAWN'S EARLY LIGHT

MIRA BOOKS

ISBN 1-55166-278-7

DAWN'S EARLY LIGHT
First published under the name Caryn Cameron.

Copyright © 1988 by Caryn Cameron.

MIRA and the star colophon are trademarks of MIRA Books.

Printed in U.S.A.

My love to Don,
as ever

Part I

"On the shore dimly seen
    through the mists of the deep,
Where the foe's haughty host
    in dread silence reposes..."

—Francis Scott Key
"The Star-Spangled Banner"
Baltimore, 1814

One

April 6, 1814
Baltimore, Maryland

"How dare they shoot at us clear in here!" Brett Benton cried.

To the cabin boy's dismay, Miss Benton darted along the deck toward the crash of cannon from the ship behind them as if she meant to shake her gloved fist at the culprits. He could barely keep up with her, despite the narrow skirt and low silk slippers she wore. At least the holystoned pine deck was fairly steady now, as the French schooner *Le Havre* carefully picked its way into port through the shoals of the misty Patapsco River.

The boy caught up to the tall, thin woman and gripped the taffrail beside her. "No, Miss Benton, not firing at us, no," the thirteen-year-old Jacques assured her in the English she'd worked hard to polish during their rough five-week crossing from France. "Captain Piquet, he say—he says," he corrected himself before she could, "Baltimore ships fire off guns if'n they gets safe home through the enemy British blockade."

She exhaled a sigh of relief even as she instinctively corrected Jacques's grammar. "One must say, *if* they *get* safely through the blockade, my friend."

Still, she sniffed in annoyance and tapped her foot on the

deckboards, not at Jacques, but at that ship back there. She hadn't come all this way from London to Baltimore through storms, chills and some sort of lung cough to be turned back from her Yankee inheritance at the last minute! Not even if she was a British subject headed straight for what the *London Times* had called "that nest of pirates, Baltimore, Mobtown America." Not even if the only man who had ever proposed to her—or even looked her way twice—was a high-ranking officer in the very British navy blockade they had just run. It might be war between this mutinous country and her own beloved England, but her Great-uncle Charles had just died, and his half interest in a Baltimore shipping firm was now the only thing she had to her name in the entire world—even if that world was at war.

She jumped when the cannon on the mist-shrouded ship behind them bellowed again in the early dawn light.

"Come on, they shoot only into the air," the towheaded Jacques assured her, interrupting her thoughts. He darted off a few steps and gestured wildly, as if his arm were a spinning windmill. "Captain Piquet say bring you to the quarterdeck and watch them dock. *Certainement* we see better from there!"

Brett Benton gripped the handrail and lifted her narrow tube skirt carefully as she followed the boy's nankeen-trousered legs up the half flight to the quarterdeck. She was a most circumspect, conservative person, who before this trip had experienced no greater adventure than a stagecoach ride from Liverpool to London when she was seventeen. She had believed then, when Great-uncle Charles sent for her, that a glittering life awaited her in London.

But it hadn't been that way at all. There had been no fashionable Ton, no Season, no soirees or tête-à-tête at country estates for Brett Benton. No dinner parties or dances at the Prince Regent's Carlton House or at Brighton for her, despite the invitation to court that Uncle Charles had received once. But he had been too ill to go, and she had placed the rich vellum card with its ornate calligraphy and royal coat of arms in her Bible. She had brought it with her, still one of her most valued possessions.

For Brett London had meant at first private studies, rolling bandages for the endless wars against Napoléon and small, subdued supper parties for Uncle Charles's equally doddering veteran naval friends and the occasional younger officers. Then, after Uncle Charles's accident, she had nursed him for five long years until he died. All those things had swallowed her youth in one big gulp that astounded her when she looked back. London and the Londoners had never been hers. Except for Captain Dalton Kelsey's assiduous attentions, which had ended by puzzling her more than thrilling her, there had really been no excitement in her life at all. And how she longed for it, though she feared it, too, just as she did this new foreign city suddenly sweeping in too close.

"Ah, Mademoiselle Brett." The white-haired Captain Pierre Piquet greeted her on the quarterdeck, where he stood behind the helmsman and the pilot. "The guns saluting Fort McHenry, they did not give you alarm, I hope. Here is the ship, the villain. Look, see," he told her, and extended his brass eyeglass to her. She lifted it to skim the broad gray river behind them until a sleek ship and triangle of jaunty sails jumped into view. A rakish two-master, she shouldered blooming billows out of her way just behind them.

"A Yankee privateer," Captain Piquet told her. "Brave and bold and brazen like Baltimoreans themselves. No wonder your British hate Baltimore as much as our Bonaparte admires it, eh?"

She handed the glass back to the leather-faced old man with a sigh and waved farewell to Jacques as he scampered off to secure cabin gear. It was tragic, she thought, that her beloved Britain was at war with both America and France. Surely no nation, however powerful, had the right to claim or control God's vast oceans. She inhaled deeply of the seaborne scents she had come to love: damp canvas, resinous white pine decks, the tart sea air. She could almost smell from here the oil lantern swinging beside her hard cot in her tiny cabin.

The captain stood close to her and pointed out the sights,

using his charts, since he had never been to Baltimore before, either. Now the war had changed things and made it profitable for small French ships used to the more leisurely runs to the empire's sun-struck islands of Martinique, Mauritania and Corsica to ply the treacherous Atlantic on supply voyages. British blockades be damned, Captain Piquet cursed silently, and hoped Mademoiselle Brett, with her bold British patriotism and her disdain for profanity, never guessed his thoughts.

He noticed again that his sole passenger on this voyage was, as usual, charmingly unaware of the strength of her presence, if not the strength of her character. What a gift she had been to him on this trip! He had enjoyed hearing her insightful comments on Wordsworth and Coleridge, and had been astounded at her care for his scrawny cabin boy and at her desire to know of sailing ships firsthand. Even though she claimed salt blood flowed in her veins from her Royal Navy father and her great-uncle, Lord Nelson's famed Admiral Benton, for a woman she was quite remarkable. Sad she was so gangly tall and he so short. Regrettable she was a tart-tongued spinster of thirty and he a snowy-headed, amiable sixty, despite the tight ship he ran. She might seem prim and pale and plain, but when she laughed, ah, then she blossomed. A pity it was so seldom.

"Do not forget now, you promised I shall escort you to the Sanborn shipping offices if the old gentleman, your new partner, does not call aboard in person," Captain Piquet reminded her in his heavily accented English.

Brett thanked him for his continued kindnesses and went back down to the maindeck, while he shouted orders through his brass speaking trumpet to the sailors aloft in a web of spars and rigging. Brett marveled that even this close the shore was still a haze of muted red brick buildings and white steeples, smudges of dark roofs and wavering, vast, gray warehouses. Through the morning mists of Baltimore's basin, the masts of merchant ships bottled up by the blockade emerged like an eerie, enchanted forest.

Suddenly it cleared. Her new home sprang out at her, all

clear lines and sharp angles. Bells were ringing ashore. People rushed about shouting, looking from here like the puppets she had seen in St. James Park, with someone pulling their invisible strings.

Nervously she straightened her tall-crowned calash bonnet over the hoops that kept it from denting her mass of chestnut hair, which she wore pulled severely back on her head in tight braids and loops. She smoothed her warm olive merino redingote over her flower-sprigged muslin dress. She should have worn her poppy-red cashmere shawl up on deck, too, but it made her so conspicuous; after all, this was rebel America and those were her foes on the shore. She would have to win them over somehow.

She wished, not for the first time in her life, that she were not so tall and plain. From the time she had realized at the age of fifteen that she towered over all other women of her acquaintance, she had been self-conscious, and the naval officers she had met in her Uncle Charles's London home had never given her any cause to esteem her looks, not even Dalton Kelsey. Well, she thought, straightening her shoulders, where other women used charm and guile, she had learned to develop a quick brain and a biting tongue. They would have to do.

"My thirtieth birthday today, a new decade of life—a new life," she murmured aloud to buck up her courage. She gripped the smooth handrail and tapped her foot even harder. She hoped her uncle's friend, Alexander Sanborn, who owned the other half of Sanborn Shipping, had received her letter, which stated briefly that she would be arriving this spring and needed a place to reside. At least she knew how to deal with old men. If this Mr. Sanborn was anything like her uncle, surely they would get along well enough despite a few possible, minor differences.

A foreboding chill sliced through her. She clasped her elbows in her kid-gloved hands as if to embrace herself. Her stomach, which had been so trustworthy at sea despite swells and storms, churned beneath her long, boned corset. She prayed silently that Americans—especially old Mr. Sanborn—would at least be civilized. She bit her lower lip as her sharp, wide-set gray eyes skimmed the bustling waterfront for the elderly, white-haired man who would be her new partner in this great American adventure.

Alexander Sanborn, raven haired, nattily garbed and thirty-three years old, slapped his manager, Mason Finch, on the back and howled a cheer. "I just spotted a second ship behind that Frenchie, Mason!" he yelled. "The *Intrepid*'s back, bless her little female, privateering heart, and she's flying captured enemy standards in her rigging thick as laundry!"

Mason Finch echoed his young employer's raucous hoots as he grabbed the traditional bottle of precious imported French champagne from his locked sea chest and made for the door of Sanborn and Son Shipping right behind Alex. Mason had worked here for nearly thirty years, first for old Alexander, Alex's father, watching with pride as the stubborn boy grew to a determined man. Now, nearly five years after the old man's death, he had helped as Alex built Sanborn and Son to be a power in Baltimore. That is, until the war blew the shipping business to perdition. But now, Alex and other rich Baltimore merchants were fighting back with a privateering fleet.

Alex waited for Mason at the bustling corner of Pratt and Light as the older man loped across the rough cobblestones as fast as he could. Already, others who had seen the *Intrepid* putting in behind the French schooner were shouting congratulations and patriotic slogans. Their arms around each other's shoulders, Alex and Mason walked at a good clip toward the empty Pratt Street berth where the *Intrepid* had put in.

Aboard, champagne bubbled and beer flowed freely. Men shouted at sailors aloft who still stowed sails. Hearty handshakes, slapped backs and traded tales abounded. Alex roared with laughter when he heard that the *Intrepid* had even taken a howitzer and two mortars, as well as goods from the three British supply ships and merchantmen they'd boarded.

Nodding, smiling grimly, Alex sat astride two of the captured guns, lashed to the waist rail, while his burly friend Captain Joshua Windsor recounted this voyage's dangers.

"Blue blazes, Josh," Alex interjected, "I'd give my eye-teeth to be out there with you, chasing the limey bastards to take their booty. I'd love to sail with you the way I used to, but the blasted, boring business end of this war keeps me too tied down here."

Captain Windsor drained his glass with a quick toss of his silvered head. "You know we can't risk losing you out there with the Brits getting thicker all the time, Alex. And once Wellington bottles up old Boney and captures Paris, which I think he will very soon, the British will turn all their tender attentions our way. Things are going to get worse here, and you know it." He put a steadying hand on Alex's broad shoulder. "I thought maybe that French ship that put in ahead of us would be worth a visit to hear the foreign news. Which reminds me, any word on that new British partner of yours getting in?"

Alex shook his dark, curly head as he slid off his perch on the guns. "I'm not meeting every damn foreign ship with bated breath just to please Mr. Brett 'British' Benton. I hope he's been captured by the strangle noose of his own Brit blockade. Blue blazes, Josh," he admitted as his voice dropped and the two friends huddled shoulder to shoulder amid the hubbub at the rail. "I still can't believe my father did that to me."

"You know he was fading the last few years, Alex. Maybe he even forgot about the silent partner he needed years ago to expand everything here when times were tough."

Alex smacked the rail with a fist. "I don't see how you can forget to tell your only son, who thinks he's inheriting a firm free and clear, that half of it could be claimed anytime by some pompous jackass of a Johnny Bull Englishman he's never met, never heard of." He shook his head in angry bewilderment, as he had so many times these past three months since he'd learned the firm was only half his legally. "No way to fight it in court. I wrote Mother in Philadelphia, and she went through some of Father's old things. The original agreement from 1800 between Alexander Sanborn the elder and Admiral Charles Benton was there, all right. What really riles me is the Brits have captured our *Eastward Bound* and *Indian Maid*. Well, you can count on me to tell my silent partner when he arrives that those two ships are *his* cut of *my* business!''

He leaned his elbows on the rail and glared across the harbor at the newly anchored French ship. He had plans for Mr. Brett Benton when he finally arrived, all right. He would try to be civil—unless the bastard tried spouting off about the war. He was going to promise to buy him out after the war and then get him right back on whatever ship he arrived on. He could go back to enemy London, where he should have stayed—or straight to hell!

Alex's short-fused temper sizzled even more when he saw he'd smudged his hands on the guns where he'd sat. He looked, then cursed aloud. His new pale-yellow buckskin breeches were streaked, too. Who knew what he'd unwittingly done to the white cravat he'd just straightened.

He shrugged his broad shoulders in disgust at his disintegrating mood. Every time he even thought of some Englishman prancing in here to lay claim to half the fruits of his sweat at Sanborn's, it galled him as if he'd swigged acid. He'd been riding high over the *Intrepid*'s latest victories, but now his taste for further celebration was ruined. He almost wished he were home in bed with Simone to exorcise his frustration again. Now there was a woman who knew how to calm a man's moods. Not quite a saint like his own mother or as pliant as his sister, Pamela, but a woman he could trust to keep quiet in public about whatever went on in private.

Forcing a taut smile, Alex left the rail to circulate once more among the crew. He bid the still buoyant Joshua Windsor goodbye until later. ''I know you'll want to get home to Sally and the little ones,'' Alex told him with a sly poke in the ribs.

''I hope she's not still out matchmaking for you,'' Joshua responded with a rueful grin.

''Half the married women in town are. The other half are

still scandalized about my keeping a lady guest at the house—and a French one who smells good and orders new diaphanous, low-necked dresses every week at that."

They shook hands, Alex slightly handicapped by the several captured British banners he carried. The first mate had presented him with them to further adorn the walls of the Sanborn and Son's wholesale shop and offices.

"To all ladies who smell good," Joshua said, and lifted his empty glass in mock toast.

"And may the stinking Brits run into one another in the mists of our American deep out there," Alex intoned. Then he strode down the gangplank, the banners floating behind him, and disappeared amid the crowd of sailors who mingled with the cheering Baltimoreans on the wharf.

When no one had called for Brett Benton in the hour after docking, Captain Piquet and the cabin boy, Jacques, escorted her down the public wharf on Pratt to the Sanborn wharf and offices around the corner on Light Street. Brett's wide gray eyes and sharp nose took everything in. The pungent fish markets flaunting shiny pyramids of oysters and troughs of spring shad, roe and herring. Weathered rooming houses, tattoo shops, chandler stores and cafés crowded the busy wharfs. Piles of cotton bales and wooden barrels marked Jamaica Rum and Madeira were being unloaded from tethered vessels. Crates of sharp-scented tobacco leaves disappeared into waiting holds as overflowing hemp bags of coffee beans piled up on the wharf. Skimming the frayed signs that protruded over the cobbled street, she almost turned her ankle, but Captain Piquet had a firm grip on her elbow. Her jerk to right herself swung her steel-framed calico-cloth-covered reticule on its chain into his restraining hand.

"Oh, sorry, Captain."

"It is nothing, my dear. These terrible cobbles are ships' ballast. And the wharves are built on discarded oyster shells, see? The Americans are so clever and they make do with little if they have little. But when they have plenty, then—beware. They know how to take more than is theirs then, too, I fear."

Ordinarily Brett would have probed his comments with quick-witted questions, but at this moment she was speechless. She had stopped in her tracks when she spotted a dangling sign with a painted black-hulled vessel under a proudly puffed sail. Sanborn and Son, the sign read in defiant gold letters over the American flag, which her uncle had always referred to as the Yankee gridiron. Below, on a separately worded sign, the pedestrian was informed: Domestic and foreign shipping. Warehouse. Coffee and chocolate wholesale. Inquire within.

Over their protests, she bade farewell to the kind captain and the boy. Yes, she would come back to stay in her cabin until they sailed if old Mr. Sanborn did not provide a proper place for her to reside. Yes, she would send for her things as soon as she could. No, she was definitely not sailing back with them in a few weeks. She waved them off with more spirit than she felt and pulled the door open. A tiny bell tinkled over her head. The richly blended scents of coffee and chocolate enveloped her.

The small, deserted front room with its long maple counter opened to a paneled office beyond with its door ajar. Within she could glimpse flags and maps on the walls. She turned as she heard quick footsteps on the stairs from above.

"Exactly how many Johnny Bull ships did the *Intrepid* take then, Mr. Alex?" asked a high-pitched voice, and she saw black polished buckled shoes and buff kid breeches coming down the steps.

She almost cried out when she glimpsed the man's face, but she kept hold of her poise. Most of the man was normal, even good-looking. His open linen coatee half covered an immaculate and ornately embroidered waistcoat. The man's hair was brown and straight, and pale-brown eyes that glowed seemingly from within met hers. He was—well—bottom heavy for a fairly young man, as if he usually sat about with no exercise, but it was his face that had caused her alarm. He looked as startled as she, and quickly turned his good profile to her, hiding the left half, which was horribly scarred and puckered in tiny ridges of long-ago-seared flesh. There was a moment's awkward silence as he looked down to busily wipe inky fingers on a lace-encrusted handkerchief.

"Didn't mean to yell at you, miss, not at all." He half coughed, half cleared his throat. "I thought you were Mr. Sanborn come back from the dock. The men are out to welcome their privateer home, you see, and—"

"You mean that ship that came in popping off its guns and flaunting those British flags they looted was a Sanborn and Son ship?" she gasped.

He turned slightly more to face her, still keeping his ridged right cheek and puckered eyelid away from her. "You're not from here, I take it, miss?"

"I'm Brett Benton from London, via Le Havre, and off the ship of the same name," she explained. She realized her voice sounded too haughty and sharp, but this was an outrage. Old Mr. Sanborn wasn't here to greet her, was actually off congratulating that pirate ship! Then she noted that the shocked look on the man's stiff face had dissolved to a grimace of the mouth some might call a smile.

"*You* are the Brett Benton he's been waiting for, miss? But how—very interesting!" He coughed into his ink-smudged handkerchief. "Please, won't you step back into Mr. Sanborn's office to wait for him?" He consulted a gold filigreed pocket watch on an ornate ribbon fob. "He'll be in soon, I'm certain, and I'll just make you most comfortable till he does."

The man, despite his sad appearance, suddenly seemed the cat who had swallowed the canary as he escorted her to a chair across a vast mahogany desk in the inner office. He was Giles Cutler, the Sanborn bookkeeper, he informed her.

She assured him that was her background, too, and she hoped to be working with him soon in overseeing the firm. "My business experience is keeping supply records in an orphanage," she said.

Everything she said seemed to delight him, and she wasn't sure why. She was about to ask, when he insisted on fetching her a cup of coffee from upstairs. Alone, she nervously paced the room, frowning at the various captured ensigns, etchings of ships and maps tacked here and there in precise abundance.

Then, on the far wall, her gaze lit on the portrait of a handsome, square-jawed, silver-haired man. When she opened the brown velvet curtains wider to see it better, morning sunlight flooded the room.

The man in the portrait had steely light blue eyes and a firm jaw. Power emanated from the set of the features and firm chin. He was, no doubt, approximately the age Uncle Charles had been when he'd died. "This is Alexander Sanborn, I take it," she asked Giles Cutler when he returned.

"Ah, indeed," he told her. With sharply twisted mouth, he handed her a large china cup of steaming coffee and a handful of Berkeley's paper-wrapped English toffees.

"But how kind of you," she told him with her first smile since she'd disembarked. "Berkeley's. I had a friend who used to bring them to my uncle's home." Foolish tears crowded her eyes. Surely all would go well here. This man seemed to welcome her despite her indication that she intended bookkeeping to be her first entrée into learning the business. And he was not turning away from her, now that he saw she didn't flinch from his affliction. "However does one manage to obtain English toffee with this blockade?" she asked conversationally.

"I have my sources," he said only, as she popped a toffee into her mouth and bit into its dark sugar sweetness.

The distant bell in the outer shop rang; Mr. Giles Cutler darted back out with an actual look of glee lighting the normal part of his face.

"Mr. Alex, your Brit has arrived."

Giles Cutler's high-pitched voice carried crisply to her. She gulped and tried to clear her teeth of the chewy mass of toffee with a quick thrust of tongue along the roof of her mouth.

"Brett Benton's waiting in your office, and not real pleased about the *Intrepid*'s return from her happy hunting grounds, that's for certain," he added.

Quick footsteps, two or three pairs of them on the wooden floor. She tried to chew, to swallow. She turned stiffly to face the door. Two men, one old, one young, with Mr. Cutler hovering behind them, appeared in the doorway. Neither was the man in the portrait, though the younger one had his disturbing eyes and thrust of solid chin.

"Blue blazes, where is *Mr.* Benton, Giles?" the younger man demanded, his eyes hard on her. "It's not like you to joke."

She tried to respond, but her jaw felt mired in mush. Like a cork-brain, she merely nodded.

"A woman named Brett," the older man began. "Well, well, the good Lord knows we just never imagined that."

He was introducing himself, but his name blurred in her ears. She could not tear her gaze from the tall, dark-haired man. She stood fully five feet nine inches; few men topped her at all, let alone stood *that* much taller.

His eyes went coldly, assessingly, over her, slippers to neck, then studied her face as if she were some butterfly pinned under glass in his private collection. Their gazes clashed, as she returned his brazen stare. Straight, thick black brows crashed to obscure his slitted eyes. Rudely he closed the door on the two men with him and strode into the full sunlight in the middle of the room, where she held shaky ground. It was only then she managed to swallow the toffee before she choked on it.

"Have you nothing to say, woman? What kind of joke is this?"

"I might ask you the same, sir. I was expecting an older man, a *gentleman*—albeit an American, so perhaps I should have known better. I was expecting that man—there!" Brett insisted, and thrust a shaky index finger at the portrait on the far wall before yanking her hand back to her side.

He didn't even turn to look. He tossed his armful of stolen British flags on the desk and dared to lean back with his narrow hips against its edge and his arms crossed. She almost gasped at the impact of him this close. He was several inches over six feet, with big shoulders and chest that fitted his garments perfectly and tapered to the rest of him, which she dared not study. He had a long, taut-jawed face with firmly chiseled lips that looked cruel. His skin was almost as bronze as the Indian she'd seen on the docks. Ice-blue eyes pierced her. His nose had a slight crook to its bridge, and she reflected that a rotter like him had probably received it from a well-deserved facer in a brawl. His curly, collar-length, wayward black hair glinted almost blue in the slash of sun behind him, which also emphasized the shadow of a beginning beard even at this time of the morning. The man was almost sinfully handsome up this close, and she took a quick step back as if self-preservation itself depended on it.

He knew instantly she was not the sort of woman he was used to—or liked. The women in his life had always been pretty coquettes, like Simone, women who were aware of their charms and didn't hesitate to use them. This woman, if she had any looks at all, had done her darnedest to hide them. That dress, buttoned up high to the throat and in the oddest color of green; it surely could not have been bought to attract any man. And she was obviously not the type to be wheedled or honeyed or managed unless one used every wit—an endlessly exhausting task for a man who had found years before that women usually fell one's way for a smile. Her stare gave as good as she got with no fluttering or wavering. Plain and sour she might be, but he couldn't just dismiss her from his thoughts. He knew instinctively he'd have to handle her directly and firmly, or she'd be more trouble than he'd ever bargained for with a man.

"The person in the portrait is my father, Alexander the elder," he told her with a defiant tilt of his head. "He departed this Earth as surely as has your benefactor, Admiral Benton, so you'll deal with me. For starters, you should know I take orders from no one here at Sanborn's. I, Miss Benton— if that's who you really are—am Alexander the younger."

"And you intend to treat me as if you were Alexander the Great," she clipped out before she could yank the words back. Surprised, he jerked his chin up as he studied her again. Then, to her increased dismay, he burst into laughter.

It was all so ludicrous, so crazy, he thought, as he looked her over once again. He had been expecting a pompous, stiff-backed man and had gotten a pompous, stiff-backed woman. A thin, pale, tall one he didn't need or want or intend to allow in his life. He got hold of himself and narrowed his eyes to examine the rigid face in the shade of the big bonnet. He discerned brownish straight hair pulled up with none of the softening wispy curls he was used to with silver-blond Simone. Miss Benton had wide-set, dove-gray, challenging eyes in a heart-shaped face. Pretty enough, he thought, but challenging in ways that bothered him in a woman. Her mouth was firm, if a bit pinched, and when she parted her colorless lips he saw she had even, white teeth. It was even possible that if she would just dress properly she'd be passable looking, for he could catch just a glimpse of a swelling breast beneath the stiffness of her dress. But blue blazes, a British skirt to contend with on top of everything else in war-crazed Baltimore!

"Are you quite through guffawing and gawking at me, Mr. Sanborn?" she threw back at him. Her accent was sharp, and she seemed to spit out her words at a galloping clip.

"I wasn't really laughing *at* you, Miss Benton. I hope I may assume you are *Miss* Benton and not hiding some husband you've dragged to visit wartime Baltimore."

His voice was deep and soft and slow, rather as if he were some country-bred dolt. He said "Baltimore" as if it were "Bal'more." His tone set her teeth absolutely on edge. Those eyes, so heavily lashed for a man, seemed to slide right inside her, and she shifted her stiff legs together to take another step back. A wary glance told her that his hands were big and square with immaculate nails, although his heavy ivory silk cravat was soiled and awry and he had smudged the pale-yellow breeches that might as well have been painted on his narrow hips and muscular legs. She felt an unwelcome flush heat her neck and creep upward. Abruptly she turned away and sat on the edge of the chair, staring at the row of windows behind the desk.

"Now see here, Mr. Sanborn, we could argue this all day. Frankly, I was hoping you would honor an obviously legal agreement. I realize an outsider—a foreign one at that—can hardly expect to be taken totally into your confidence and the running of a shipping firm all at once—"

"The running of it? Now see here, Miss Benton. It's bad enough that your nation is ruining my profits, but women helping to run businesses just isn't done here in Baltimore, and I don't think it's done in jolly old England, either!" He stood, then stalked behind his big desk to grip the back of his red leather wing chair.

"*This* lady will, sir! I intend to learn this business. To help you profit it. The war cannot last forever and—"

"And the way the Brits would like it to end is to blow Baltimore off the face of the map, rape her warehouses—"

"Rubbish, Mr. Sanborn!" she insisted, and flushed anew at his crude choice of wording. "England is a civilized nation, though I wouldn't expect you to recognize that! The London papers may rant that His Majesty's Royal Navy should chastise the savages of Baltimore, but that hardly means all of us want that! However, if you continue to *act* like savages—"

He came around the desk so quickly that she jammed herself back in her chair in an effort to escape his towering menace. "If I were a savage, Miss Benton, you'd be out in the street on your pushy, pious backside right now, legal will and papers be damned! But I'm a tolerant, disciplined sort." He stood frozen, hovering over her, amazed at himself. He'd actually roared around the desk, intending to pick her up by her stiff arms, to dangle her before him, with what shakes and threats he was suddenly unsure of. A woman he'd never even met before had almost driven him to violence!

"I—I'd like to believe that," she muttered.

Her voice seemed suddenly small and shaky to him. He wondered if she'd known he'd actually meant to touch her in the heat of his emotions—the sort of churning passion only the war itself had stirred in him before.

He stepped back and tugged his lace cuffs farther down under his coat sleeves, and cleared his throat. "I can offer you a temporary room at my home for your visit," he told her. He took a deep breath and leaned back against his desk again, his thigh muscles rippling from the movement. "A single woman alone cannot just stay in some rooming house, not on this waterfront," he went on, as if to explain his sudden capitulation to himself. "Now I've got a lot to do here today, but I'll get us a curricle and take you there now. Later we can talk business and rationally decide how to handle all this."

How to get cash or promises to placate you before I send you back to Europe on that ship you came on, he thought.

How I can best work gradually in and learn the whole business as an equal partner, she told herself.

"I'd appreciate a place to stay until I can locate my own, but won't Mrs. Sanborn feel put out with a guest, Mr. Sanborn?"

"There is no Mrs. Sanborn, though you'll be well enough chaperoned and quite safe from the savage with a housekeeper who runs the place the way Napoléon runs France. And there's another lady guest who's there. A Frenchwoman. I hope you admit *they're* civilized, even if Mother England is at war with them, too."

"Thank you. Just until we've settled things. And I didn't mean to call you, specifically, a savage, Mr. Sanborn."

He looked surprised and smiled at her, albeit wolfishly. The impact almost tattered the remnants of her hard-won poise.

"Best save fine compliments like that until after we settle things between us, Miss Benton," he said, and closed the door much too loudly as he went out to fetch a carriage.

Two

Baltimore astounded Brett. She had not exactly expected hovels or Indian huts with camp fires behind the facade of the waterfront, but she had pictured the place as decidedly more primitive, even though it was the fledgling nation's third largest city. Mr. Sanborn the younger pointed out theaters, churches, newspaper offices, shops, taverns and the huge open-air Marsh Market, crowded with black women balancing top-heavy baskets of produce on their heads. War or not, Yankees or not, Baltimore bustled with civilized life.

She sat up even straighter on the padded leather seat as Alex Sanborn drove the sleek black curricle onto Charles Street. When her skirt brushed his hard thigh as they turned around the corner, she slid slowly as far away as she could with subtle hip movements and turned her head as if to admire the view to the side. Certainly, she thought, the grandly pillared two- and three-story rose or pink brick homes on this broad avenue couldn't quite compete with Grosvenor Square in London, but they were impressive. Velvet lawns etched with white dogwood and canary forsythia under newly budded chestnut trees—everything smelled of rich garden loam and green growth to a nose so long used to salt air. Alex kept up a polite recital of sights that almost made her believe there was some hope for eventually reasoning with the man. Savages hardly inhabited mansions as grand as the one he halted the sleek bay mare in front of.

He wrapped the reins, got out and reached up to help her down. His hand was steady and warm, even through both their gloves. The minute her slippers touched the bricked driveway, she tugged her hand back. She was grateful he seemed unaware of the way his touch had made her entire arm tingle. Their eyes met for the first time since the beginning of the ride. She noticed again that he seemed to be peering into her deep calash bonnet above her face as if trying to see her hair.

He pulled his eyes away and swept a gloved hand toward the mansion. "I give you Sanborn House, built by Alexander the elder, nearly ten years ago and now domicile to Alexander...the Great," he told her, his voice teasing but his mouth taut.

She lifted her gaze guiltily from his lips. "One must admit it's a grand home, Your Majesty," she offered, stepping a few steps farther away.

Once again, her quick wit took him by surprise; her retorts provoked but also stimulated him. And he noticed for the first time that when she relaxed her prim mouth it took on an enchanting bow shape. But he also noted that she nearly jumped out of her dull olive redingote when he touched her arm again just above her left elbow to guide her up the walk.

"No royal or noble titles allowed here in America, Miss Benton," he said in that slow, disturbing voice. "Merely Alex, lord and master of all he surveys, will do."

Out of the side of his eye, he saw her mouth soften again, though the corners didn't quite tilt up. Did the sharp-tongued shrew never laugh? He watched her large gray eyes roam the facade of the building. It made her feel as if he were seeing it once again for that first time when he'd returned from his four-year European tour. Twelve tall white Doric pillars guarded the marble-floored half-moon porch of the Georgian mansion. Above the black iron balustrade overhead, ten broad polished second-floor windows gazed eastward. Barrel dormer windows in the slate roof balanced two broad brick chimneys and the smaller kitchen stacks. He opened the front door himself and escorted her in, leaving her wondering if there were no servants in Baltimore to open the door for him.

Before them stretched a long central black-and-white marble-tiled hall with framed French mirrors, wall candelabra and oil portraits. He led her left into a tall parlor decorated in Empire style, with pilastered arches and columns. Gray-blue satin drapes looped over scrolled rods, and triple candelabra in wall brackets stood sentinel on both sides of the Italian-marble fireplace. Furniture in ebony and gilt wood with sloping, pointed legs was upholstered in soft blues that echoed the walls and flowered carpets. The place smelled of rich candle wax and lemon polish, of flowers in china bowls and, from far off, freshly baked bread. Despite her nervousness at just heedlessly stepping into a strange house with a man who was not a relative when no one else was in sight, she murmured in admiration.

"I'm pleased you approve, but I hardly expected a London-bred lady to be moved by any of what poor plebian Baltimore has to offer."

"I assure you my great-uncle's Grosvenor Square town house was lovely—but I didn't expect quite this elegance here," she admitted with a shake of her head.

He moved away and turned back to face her, feet slightly spread and hands behind his back. The sudden, bitter sarcasm in his voice took her unawares. "Of course not here. You had pictured rough wood floors with big splinters, and cracks to let the rats in, and bloody wolf pelts on the walls!"

Startled that he had read her thoughts and made them sound worse than they were, she stepped back to put more space between them. She felt caught at something naughty like a scolded child, yet a tart reply wouldn't come. Instinctively she wanted to placate him, and that alarmed her more than being alone with him like this.

"I am not London bred, Mr. Sanborn," she began with great unease. "I spent my first twelve years in a tiny house on a narrow street in Liverpool, adjacent to the docks, and five years after that in a crowded Presbyterian orphanage.

Both my parents had died, my father at sea fighting the Barbary pirates for England and my mother of a wretched lung fever—and loss of him." She turned her head away and stared down at the carpet's flowers of muted periwinkle and robin's-egg blue.

"I'm sorry."

She looked up at once, and saw that his stern face had softened. "Don't be. I adored the younger children in the orphanage, if that's what you mean. In a way it was the most normal family life I ever had. I kept the books there, too. You see, that's why I thought it would be a good idea if I began tomorrow—"

A scuffle of slippers in the hall, a woman's musical voice at the door. Brett turned expecting to see the housekeeper Mr. Sanborn had promised. But instead a stunningly beautiful woman—a vision of an angel, with spun blond hair and pale green eyes and lace and ruffled clothes—stood there with two wrapped packages in her hands and a black boy behind her with a stack of others. It was only when the vision dumped the wrappings she held on the boy's pile and shooed him away that Brett's sharp gaze actually took in her striking attire.

"Alex! Home in the middle of the day, *mon cher*?" the vision cried, and hurried in to throw her arms around his neck and flutter kisses along his jaw before his hands disengaged her.

"Business, Simone. Home on business," he insisted as if to warn her off, while Brett gawked.

The woman's petite but voluptuous body made her own look like a towering ship's mast, Brett thought. The blond curls the woman produced from under the feathered apricot bonnet she plucked off and sent sailing to the settee were wispy, cut fashionably *à la Titus*. She wore a buff-and-apricot satin striped Spencer over a splendid, if rather diaphanous, embroidered gown. Matching white satin slippers with apricot ribbons wrapping shapely ankles showed when she stretched to kiss Mr. Sanborn. Brett was both fascinated and horrified. This woman was obviously not the ordinary houseguest he'd led her to believe when he had so smoothly passed over her presence!

"Madame Simone Vilmons, may I present Miss Brett Benton from England," Mr. Sanborn began, and went on to make more formal introductions.

Brett's mind raced as she politely if coolly responded. She couldn't possibly stay here in the same house where this was obviously going on! Rubbish! She wasn't certain which alarmed her more—Mrs. Vilmons's clinging possessiveness with Mr. Sanborn or the essence of natural sensuality that emanated from her as strongly as her heady floral scent.

"Simone is a widow," he was saying when Brett heard his smooth rush of words again. "Simone, as long as I'm here, we'll all eat dinner together before I head back. Later, I'd appreciate it if you took a little respite from spending money to show Miss Benton the house," he concluded with one eyebrow cocked, as if he were signaling in some private language to the woman.

"But of course, anything for you, Alex, *mon cher*."

Her voice was as silky as her flesh-hued stockings. Even when she wasn't standing in a strong light, her limbs showed clearly through the skirt, and it was all too obvious she wore no corset or bum row under the gathers and flourishes. She was exactly the sort of woman Brett's mother and uncle would have been shocked to see grace their doorways.

"You will adore it here in Baltimore and at Sanborn House, Miss Benton," Simone assured her with a stunning smile. "May I call you 'Brett,' even if Alex doesn't? A lovely sanctuary, Baltimore and Alex's hospitality, from the wars of life, no? Come now, I shall take you upstairs at once to wash for dinner. And I will show you where to shop for new things, too, of course." Simone's eyes swept Brett's garments with a frown and a shrug. "Ah, you must have been at sea for a long while then, no?"

Before Brett could protest, the woman's perfume shrouded her and her exquisite lace-mitted hand clasped hers as if they had been best of intimates for years. Under the lord and master of the house's sharp eye, the petite, graceful Simone Vilmons tugged her from the room and up the curving sweep of stairs.

Dinner was most awkward, though Brett was starved. She wanted to talk business with Mr. Sanborn, and Simone wanted to talk everything else with him. Birdlike, the beautiful Frenchwoman merely picked at her food, while Brett had to force herself to slow down over the delicious clam gumbo, woodcock and green peas, beaten biscuits with jams and honey, and fruit and coffee, which was served by two Negro maids in the formal dining room.

"Alex will adore having you here to force me to eat," Simone said between sips of red wine. "Alex appreciates hearty appetites in a woman, no, my Alex? But," she said, and rolled pale green eyes, "he must admit Simone Vilmons has the appetite that pleases him most!"

"Simone," he remonstrated, actually more angry than amused for the first time at the table. His fruit knife accidently dinged his Sevres dessert plate like a chime. "Miss Benton doesn't need your flirtations flaunted at table!"

Simone gave a dramatic shrug, which Brett had to admit was enchanting. Despite herself, she studied the way the tiny woman simultaneously lured and put off the big man. Simone seemed to suck on a crimson strawberry before popping it between crimson lips in the tenuous silence. "So, do you intend to call each other 'Mr. Sanborn' and 'Miss Benton' all the time you are working together, so formal, hmm? Is it because England and America, they are at war, no?"

"You see, Madame Simone, business is business despite the war. Don't you agree, Mr. Sanborn?" Brett inquired, relieved to have an opening to get down to important things.

"Absolutely, and woman aren't directly involved in either. I said we'll discuss this later, and so we shall. I have a great deal to do this afternoon," Alex concluded decisively, and tossed his damask napkin beside his plate as if all discussions had ended.

Brett rose, too, and dared to step near the arched doorway as he moved toward it. "I'd appreciate a tour of everything at Sanborn's. I can be ready in just a moment," she insisted. He looked down at her upturned face with an expression she thought somewhere between frustration and fury.

He felt himself waver. Somehow it had annoyed him to discover her hair was a rich chestnut hue with both burgundy and golden highlights reflected in the window light behind her as she ate. "Later," he clipped out gruffly. Then he turned his broad back and was gone.

"*Ma chère* Brett," Simone observed as she stood and flounced out her skirt, "Alex, believe me, he is better handled with lace dancing mitts than leather riding gloves."

"I really don't think that has a thing to do with a business relationship between Mr. Sanborn and me!" Brett protested. But she felt herself blush. Rubbish, she fumed, but knew she'd had more hot skin in the few hours she'd been in Baltimore than Captain Dalton Kelsey had ever given her with all his hand-holding and goodbye kisses.

But she couldn't stay angry with the fascinating Simone. Scandalized, perhaps, but not angry. Simone Colette Vilmons was from an aristocratic family who literally had lost their heads in *La Révolution*—all but Simone and her younger brother, Jerome. With the aid of friends, they had fled down the Seine to Le Havre, the great seaport, and at age sixteen Simone had wed a much older man, Philippe Vilmons, so that she and Jerome would not starve. But she had grown to care for and honor the kind Philippe, who owned a fleet of trading vessels Napoléon soon appropriated for his navy. The Vilmonses fled France because Philippe did not approve of Napoléon's dictatorship, and during their flight Simone had lost Jerome. They lived in exile in Baltimore until Philippe's death the previous year.

"And then," Simone had concluded with another roll of stunning pale green eyes, "Alex Sanborn and I just rather, mmm, drifted together, if you know what I mean."

That neither surprised nor pleased Brett, but she might as well be civil to this woman if she wanted influence over Alex Sanborn of any kind. And she had been intrigued to find out how much Simone hated the detested British enemy Napoléon Bonaparte.

"Soon, one day, I will go to find Jerome. But I fear a little that Napoléon. A vile little upstart toad, hopping all over Europe, leaving his swarthy, slimy spawn of family on thrones everywhere!" Simone declared angrily with a toss of her head and flying hands. "Now Josephine, she is different, a woman of the world, worthy of the throne, no matter how they all used to talk about her before he divorced her. But of course you know, she used to change her fine batiste lingerie three times a day, just as I do. Ah, you English must learn not to wear those hoops with these narrow gowns still. And you, Brett, so tall and trim but for those full breasts you push about the wrong way in that silly English corset—*c'est bien dommage!*" she concluded, with blatant gestures to emphasize the hoops, the breasts and crushing corset.

Quickly the embarrassed Brett shifted topics, and delighted Simone by telling her that at this very moment it was possible Napoléon's enemies were at the gates of Paris. Startled by Simone's squeals and hugs, she actually hugged her back.

All in all, it was a fascinating day, but as night wore on and Alex Sanborn did not return, Brett became annoyed and hurt. She ate a light, late supper on a tray in her lovely bedroom after Simone went out to meet "friends." Brett assumed Simone was joining Alex somewhere and didn't want to tell her. But eventually she heard Simone driven up to the house in a carriage with at least three other occupants, then escorted into the downstairs foyer by a man before the group drove off. When she heard Simone come up and evidently go to bed in her own room down the hall, Brett breathed a double sigh of relief.

Brett had spent the evening retouring the house Simone had showed her earlier. She had chatted with Molly and Jessie Cooper, the housekeeper and her tall, thin majordomo husband, both of them freed Negroes. They were most kind and accommodating and proud to talk of their two sons. Mr. Alex had the boys "book-learned," as they put it, and they now worked for him at a shipbuilding yard at some place called Fell's Point. Out over the carriage house in back, the Coopers had their own quarters, finer than any Uncle Charles's servants had ever boasted, though the cooks, maids and Mr. Alex's valet had rooms on the vast top floor of the fine house.

Brett had bathed, then changed her clothes, but had refused to go to bed despite her exhaustion. If that man thought he could put her off by staying out until all hours, he was wrong, and she would wait up till doomsday for the conversation he had promised her!

Her eyes skimmed the lovely beige-and-yellow bedroom with its curtained Hepplewhite four-poster as she paced. The bed had tapering rounded footposts, decorated with an intricate scrolling floral pattern of laurel leaves, and a molded rectangular canopy and upholstered camelback-shaped headboard. The French wallpaper was gold flocked and the other furniture was rich satinwood. The chamber was so huge and light and airy after that little cabin aboard the *Le Havre*. And, blessedly, it was at the other end of the second floor from the large back twin suites Simone and Mr. Sanborn inhabited. Simone had made that quite clear on the tour—their rooms might be across the hall from each other, but they were quite separate. Brett hated to admit it to herself, but the woman's relationship with Alex Sanborn utterly intrigued her.

About eleven, in an attempt to keep herself awake, Brett took her oil lamp and went downstairs to the library Simone had pointed out. It smelled wonderfully of Moroccan leather and old vellum, and rich woods mingled with some sort of sweet liquor aroma from the big Sheraton sideboard laden with cut-glass decanters. The library in Uncle Charles's town house had often been her solace in the lonely years she had nursed him, for he had become a crippled invalid after someone had broken in and beaten him senseless. In those endless months he didn't know her, and as all his old friends fell away, she had come to feel that no one else did, either, despite Dalton's sporadic visits when he was home from the fleet. This Baltimore library, all shadowy and rich with knowledge and emotion, stabbed her with sudden homesickness for the town house on Grosvenor Square. At least the town house had had the merit of familiarity. But it had been sold more than two months ago to honor Uncle Charles's commitment to the navy orphans' charitable fund. She approved, but it saddened her that she would never see the house again.

She sniffed once hard and lifted the glass-and-brass lantern to see the books' titles better. She ran her fingertips lovingly along the gold-embossed bound volumes as if they were friends. Well, she was impressed with Mr. Sanborn for the first time, she told herself. Imagine Wordsworth, her favorite modern poet, among his books! Would wonders of the world never cease! She perched on the edge of the big chair at the desk, turned up the wick and flipped the slim volume open. Consulting the table of contents, she turned to the poem that most struck her mood tonight. She read aloud to the silent, shadowy room:

> I traveled among unknown men,
> In lands beyond the sea,
> Nor, England! did I know till then
> What love I bore to thee.

"Very touching, but you're in my chair in my private inner sanctum, British Brett. Is nothing sacred?"

She jumped to her feet, squinting to see him better as the lantern light flooded up into her eyes. His voice seemed slightly slurred. She wondered if he had been out all this time just drinking, when he obviously had an array of liquor here.

"I didn't hear you come in, Mr. Sanborn."

"Obviously. You're flaunting your true colors again, Miss Benton. Do you intend to recite your British poetry for our American customers or to the Baltimore merchants I mingle with daily?"

"It's not just British poetry," she flared, "it's Wordsworth. The best poet of our generation. So why did you buy this book if that's the way you feel?"

"I didn't," he said. "My father did. Just another of those

stupid things he did, like giving half his company to a Brit!'' He came closer across the thick maroon carpet with its gold stars within circles design. He walked steadily enough, though shadows under his deep-set eyes and the prickle of raven beard shadowing his lean face reinforced her first impression that he was slightly in his cups.

His eyes dropped to skim her lavender percale gown as he said, ''Your obviously rabid patriotism is only one of my little problems with letting you anywhere near my business in the flesh, you see.''

''*Our* business,'' she insisted, but her voice broke.

He came around the desk and she vacated the area as smoothly as she could to sit across the expanse of cherry wood. He smacked the book of poetry closed and tossed it aside, then slumped into his chair hard enough to make it creak. She sat bolt upright, her legs pressed together, her hands folded primly in her lap.

''You do realize what a liability it would be for me to have a British partner at this time in this place, do you not, Miss Benton? What would all *our* patriotic American customers think?''

''What would they think if it were published far and wide that you refused to honor a legally and morally binding agreement your father made? That hardly inspires trust in one shipping precious goods even here in Baltimore, I would assume,'' she countered, striving to keep her anger in check.

''Ah, blackmail,'' he said, his voice cold. ''All right, let's take off the gloves then and have our little talk. I'm willing to buy you out, but with this bloody British war, it's going to take time, be in installments, Miss Benton.''

''That would be unacceptable, Mr. Sanborn. I thought I was perfectly clear that I want in, not out of, the firm I own half of.''

He annoyed her further by flopping one big booted leg up over the arm of his chair and rubbing his nose as if they were on casual, intimate terms. He leaned his tousled head back against the chair to examine her again. Shadows and light snagged in the angles and planes of his face. She wanted desperately to know what he was thinking, but strove to keep her features calm and emotionless. Her fingernails dug into her palms in her lap, and her heart drummed a rapid tattoo she was sure even the servants on the third floor could hear. But she didn't flinch or break the challenge of his stare.

"Surely, Brett, if you want to help me make the business turn a profit, as you say, you will at least concede that the presence of a female and a British subject in this tradition-bound, war-crazy town would be a foolish mistake for Sanborn's. And not really safe for you. Even since the War for Independence against Britain—"

"I'm not afraid, and I believe you are referring to the colonies' war of rebellion, Mr.—"

Quick as a shot, he leaped up. Both palms cracked down on the desk. "Dammit, you see what I mean, lady? You don't know when to let up, when to concede even a little bit! When to be a woman!"

She stood, too, her knuckles jammed on the shiny desk across from him. His words brought back Captain Dalton Kelsey's cruelest cut. It had rankled her for years, and had been the reason she had told him she needed time to decide when he finally proposed marriage after Uncle Charles died. She was flooded yet again with all the pain and shame. "No one could really desire her, not with that damned unfeminine tall, lanky body and opinionated, quick mouth of hers," she'd overheard him tell his friends. And she had never really understood why, if he despised her so, he had continued to court her.

She was horrified to note that her voice came on the edge of tears. "Throw what sticks and stones you will, Mr. Sanborn, but that business is half-mine because Alexander the elder was once friends with my Great-uncle Charles. They at least trusted each other. And British Benton gave American Sanborn thousands of pounds to build up his business, and I expect you to honor that if nothing else! I repeat, I am here to help you build Sanborn and Son up, both during and after this dreadful war. I believe I can keep my personal feelings on a tight rein, if you can only do the same. I know how to keep books, you see, and I can learn anything else you'd like to teach me!''

Her emotional tirade singed the air between them. She had no idea that it was that last impassioned plea that touched and titillated him, that made him instantly decide to go back on the iron-bound refusal he had already planned. Neither of them moved from where they both bent slightly over the desk in defiance of each other. His shadowed eyes drifted to her mouth, and she could scent liquor on his breath as she watched, fascinated, like a moth captivated by a candle flame. His broad nostrils flared once and his hard lower lip dropped farther as he breathed through his mouth for a moment. She felt suspended. That rhythmic swaying of the ship she had experienced for the long weeks at sea swept back to almost make her dizzy.

''I'm not certain it will work for me to have a woman in the offices,'' he said at last, ''but we can try. Giles Cutler works upstairs with the books and you can have a go there.''

She released a slow breath, as tension ebbed from her body. She was appalled that her first impulse at his melting even a tiny bit was to dash around the desk as Simone might and throw her arms around his strong neck. Stiffly she crossed her arms over her breasts and stood erect. ''I'm sure there's a lot to see and learn. I would greatly appreciate it if you would have time someday to give me a quick tour of the warehouse. All I know right now is that it smells fascinating.''

That comment intrigued him, too. If the warehouse smelled of anything but more work and sweaty men, he hadn't noticed for years. ''All right,'' he was surprised to hear himself agree. ''Tomorrow afternoon. Wear something appropriate, as there's some climbing if you want to see it all.''

She nodded pertly. ''I do.''

''Will you have some Madeira with me to seal our temporary truce then?'' he asked, and sauntered to the sideboard to unstopper and lift a cut-glass decanter.

''Thank you, but I'd best not. It's late.''

The big head did not swivel back, but she could imagine

the flicker of annoyance on the stern face. "Surely you're not telling me you object to putting in late hours or having a business drink with a business associate," he said, and let the words hang in the air between them as a pointed dare.

"Of course not. A small one then, if you please."

He filled hers nearly to the rim, as he did his own goblet, and brought it over to her with his eyes on her face. As soon as she held it by its sturdy stem, he clinked his glass to hers and downed the contents without batting an eye. She immediately followed suit. The sweet stuff tingled her throat and she had the greatest urge to cough, but she smothered the impulse with a mere clearing of her throat under his watchful gaze. She wondered later, as she tried hopelessly to fall asleep, if it had been mere fantasy that his eyes had shimmered over her with a hint of admiration in their depths, but he spoiled it a moment later.

"And please stay out of my private library after this without permission, Brett. Let me know if you want something here, and I'll oblige. Blue blazes, at least a man's library and bedroom ought to be sacred from a business partner of the opposite sex."

"I understand and agree entirely, Mr.—Alex."

"Good night then," he said, and swung away at last to replace his glass on the sideboard. "Let's see, what is it that the foolish dandies and roués of Bond Street and the Vauxhall pleasure gardens of London town say to their lady associates?" He affected a stilted, stiff accent. "I remain your most devoted servant, ma'am." He chuckled and dipped her a stiff half bow.

She had an alarming impulse to laugh, though she well knew he mocked both her and her countrymen. "I wouldn't know what they say," she parried. "So I shall tell you only that any epithet suggesting you are anyone's servant is great folly." Surprised he had no comeback and embarrassed she was gesturing with her empty Madeira glass like a cork-brain, she snapped out of her own great folly. But she dared to nearly brush his arm when he did not move aside as she reached across the sideboard to put her glass on the silver tray. Under his slitted gaze, she hurried from the room and up the stairs.

Three

"I take it your church orphanage didn't use bills of lading then, Miss Brett," Giles Cutler inquired dryly. They sat side by side on tall stools at the long pinewood desk under the upstairs windows at Sanborn's the next morning. He had been laying before her all the duties of the bookkeeping realm here at Sanborn's, over which he ruled with an iron hand. His courtiers included a grizzled, hunched scribner named Clarence Omers; Todd Miles, a dirty-faced scuffling messenger boy Brett meant to take in hand as soon as she could manage it; and a paymaster for days a ship came in, whom she had not yet met.

"I'm afraid I know nothing of bills of lading, Mr. Cutler. Nor of salary accounts, nor all these indemnity procedures, either. But I do want to understand all this, if you'd be so kind as to explain, Mr. Cutler."

"Just 'Giles,' if you please, at least when we drudges are exiled up here on the second floor, laboring over our numbers. Once you learn all this, you'll be a great help to me. Or, I should say," he added hastily after a quick hack into his ubiquitous, ink-speckled handkerchief, "I shall be a help to you—if you're to be full partner with Mr. Alex."

She frowned out over the bustling wharf under their windows. "You say that as if you don't believe your employer's words on it to me are to be trusted, Giles."

"Not at all, didn't mean that at all," he insisted hastily. "But you really mustn't expect the others to be as accepting as I am—not even as much as the master himself appears to be right now."

She let that implication pass. She supposed it didn't do to fraternize too closely with any of the employees, as she had during those long-lost days at the Presbyterian orphanage. At least not until she had a better grasp of how people and duties meshed here, and that was as confusing right now as these various handwritten record books laid out before her. Bills of lading, insurance liability for lost or damaged cargo, salary listings for crews and workers, and banking receipts for loans or donations. Her head spun with the potential problems of learning all this, but her cleverness also seized on possibilities.

"That Exigencies Fund of yours you gave the messenger boy a coin from," she remarked to Giles. "Isn't that rather a large cash amount to keep about when no one's here at night?" Her inadvertent glimpse into the small lockbox crammed with stacks of coins and bills in his bottom desk drawer had astounded her. Surely if money was tight now, as Alex claimed, that was a great deal to have uninvested and simply lying about.

"Floating fund, Mr. Alex's orders, and only he and I have the key. I'd not broach it with him," he warned, waggling his finger at her like the sternest of tutors. "He doesn't care to have his methods questioned, you know."

"I do know," she conceded, and let that matter also drop for now, though she plunged on with yet another concern. "All these payments for supplies, marked 'F.S.,'" she asked. "Does that mean financial something or other, and why so much for it?"

"F.S.—the *Free Spirit*, Mr. Alex's new clipper ship he's pouring funding into. She's to be the fastest thing on the Atlantic and custom made to slip the British blockade," he told her with a strange feral gleam in his eyes. "She'll give them a good chase for the money. Once she's launched in a few weeks, your countrymen will never catch her unless someone actually knocks a hole in her sleek little hull." She studied his face, which was crinkled with some emotion she could not name, until he caught her stare and turned away from her. "She's being built in a closed yard at Fell's Point," he added, his voice normal again.

"I can't wait to see her, but I hardly approve."

They shared a mutual, understanding nod. It gratified her that Giles Cutler seemed not only to accept her opinions but to genuinely want her to get on here. Perhaps it was because she truly accepted him as he was, which was something few other people seemed to do. But, then, she had learned that hard lesson years ago in her struggle to love a mother who was so bitter, judgmental and strict. And she had also learned how to discern debits and credits in life. And so far, she felt Mr. Giles Cutler was as firmly in her credit column as Alex Sanborn was in her debit category.

Giles Cutler left her bent over her work, her hair glinting ruby and gold in the slant of morning sun, but he watched her slyly out of the corner of his good eye while he spoke sharply to both the scribner and the messenger boy to get them about their duties. Laggards were anathema to him. And it was no good to have them eavesdropping on anything he might tell the woman. He was determined to win her over, make her trust, even pity him.

But he also had to be certain she did no snooping about, as only a small portion of the floating Exigencies Fund he kept for Alex Sanborn went for its intended purpose of charity to the families of Sanborn sailors the British navy had impressed. A few coins a week were sufficient to keep them from actually starving, and they were grateful enough never to raise a peep, Cutler assured himself. They didn't realize that Mr. Sanborn believed he was totally housing and feeding them until their abducted husbands and fathers were returned or recaptured from the iron-bound embrace of some British man-of-war.

He didn't need this new female partner at Sanborn's discovering that for years he'd siphoned off Sanborn petty cash for his own purposes, even if he felt perfectly justified in doing so. Alex Sanborn owed him more than a paltry sum of money, he thought savagely; he owed him for a ruined face and a blighted life. But that didn't mean he wanted his little plots discovered by Miss Benton. Wiping his hands on his lace-edged handkerchief, he hastened to rejoin her.

He sat down next to her with his good side to her once again. She really was very attractive, he mused. And unlike most women, she did not appear repelled by him. Why, maybe she was even attracted to him. He longed for a woman who did not have to be coerced by coins to warm his bed, and pressed his crooked lips together to stem the lecherous smile he felt creeping to them.

"May I take this current warehouse inventory along with me when I meet Mr. Sanborn for the warehouse tour?" she asked, interrupting his convoluted thoughts. "Just to get used to how this sheet matches the order of things over there."

"If you wish," he said, and slid his gaze over her when she looked back down at the long inventory. "Never go near the place myself."

"The warehouse? Really? Never just to check on things, when it's right next door?" she persisted. She bit her lower lip in regret when she realized she'd overstepped somehow.

He drew himself up, and his puckered, damaged eyelid twitched. "I'm merely the firm's bookkeeper, Miss Brett, and Mr. Alex has long taught me my place. I'm not the warehouse overseer, as you'll learn soon enough when you meet him. I'd keep an eagle eye out for Kit O'Malley and his rabidly reactionary warehouse louts if I were you," he warned with a cough.

She meant to ask him what he meant, but the scruffy messenger boy clomped back upstairs to tell her Mr. Alex was back from dinner and ready to show her the warehouse. Gratified that he had kept his word, she seized the inventory sheet and hurried downstairs.

She was pleased to see Alex Sanborn and had to stop herself from rudely scrutinizing him the way he always did her. Perhaps such a boorish, provocative practice came from breathing American air, she told herself, biting back a smirk. He was immaculately garbed today in a double-breasted dark blue coat with high, turned-down collar, which contrasted with his stark-white starched neckcloth and high shirt collar. Black knee breeches plunged into soft, black boots topped with wide strips of turned-down brown inner cuff. She felt as excited as she had when, as a girl, her beloved father had taken her and her mother to the summer fair on the green that last time he had been home on leave.

As they headed toward the warehouse, she realized she was chattering. "If you met with other shippers over dinner, I wish you would have introduced me to them, Alex."

"Another time," he said gruffly. "The mere facts that you're British, here at Sanborn's and of the so-called gentler sex were enough for them to swallow in one day."

She let that go for now. She'd not be accused again of not knowing when to concede even a little bit. "I'm anxious to see that new ship you're building, too, even if I can't agree with your motives entirely," she offered brightly as they walked the wharf toward the main entrance to the tall, vast Sanborn warehouse.

Both thick dark eyebrows shot heavenward. "The *Free Spirit*? I suppose Cutler told you that. Then I hope he mentioned it's a closed shipyard, Brett. Top secret because of the clipper's radical designs."

"Surely not closed to me. I'd love to see her. I adore ships and feel I really know them—"

"The way you do bookkeeping?" he interrupted, his voice taunting. "Am I to assume you understood everything Giles showed you this morning?"

"And am I to assume you told him to throw everything at me to discourage me my very first day in?" she demanded, a stiff arm crooked on her hip.

"Hardly," he snorted. "You want to learn everything on your own here, partner. Your wish is my command," he said, and smothered the desire to grin at having temporarily bested her. He saw how she waged a battle to let that pass with just a toss of her bonneted head. How easily she kept pace with his long strides, he marveled. She was not one to walk with those mincing steps other ladies took in their tubular skirts. She had worn a high-belted split cambric tunic with a wide Paisley border over a relatively wide-skirted gown, which would at least help her climb ladders and steps. Blue blazes, he had no intention of coddling her if she insisted on playing by men's rules!

But he had already decided not to let her see his beautiful, sleek *Free Spirit*. Not until he was certain he could fully trust her. Several of his friends at the Fountain Inn this noon had pressed home the possibility she might even be a British spy in their midst. When she brought up the shipyard at Fell's Point again, he went quickly on the defensive, putting up a smoke screen he hoped would keep her off the subject.

"You expect to clamber around a warehouse in those heelless slippers?" he challenged her at the open door.

"I make my own. They're sturdy enough."

"Lovely, but no damn good here." Once the curse was out, he regretted it, but she didn't flinch or scold as he'd expected. "I'll order you some boots," he added, and stepped inside the cool, vast warehouse, with her right behind him.

He introduced her to the overseer, a red-haired, slope-shouldered giant with an ill-concealed scowl named Kit O'Malley. Giles Cutler's warning echoed in her ears even as she heard O'Malley's words ring out to his men, who stared from various aisles and perches: "Just y'all remember what the boss said 'bout cussing with a woman here to visit."

"Thank you for asking *others* not to curse, Alex, but I don't want them to feel they have to treat me differently than they do you," she murmured with mocking sweetness. It thrilled her that he only smiled guiltily at her barb as they left Kit O'Malley behind and started down an aisle between dim, aromatic stacks of goods.

"A nice sentiment, partner, but not very realistic," he shot back. "You are different from me, and the sooner you learn that it's not a bad thing, the better off everyone's going to be."

She decided not to probe that until she had Simone's skillful help. Alex led her out into a central open area and pointed upward.

"Oh, how clever," she admitted, the inventory list clasped, forgotten, in her hand. "It's really got two floors for extra storage."

She tried to take in everything he pointed out: the second partial half floor, which circled the ground level like a gallery; the two large horse-pulley-drawn shelves he called elevators, which lifted and lowered heavy loads; the winches hoisting huge iron hooks on ropes, which drew netted boxes and barrels aloft. He indicated mountains of cotton bins, stacked boxes of tobacco leaves and loaf sugar, barrels of West Indies rum and Madeira, sacks of dried indigo, coffee and cocoa beans, all awaiting sea or land transport.

"So much on hand," she remarked, awed.

"Thanks to the blockade your countrymen have thrown up," he told her. His hand came hard on her elbow as he steered her over to an empty plank elevator. "Not to mention the two Sanborn ships they've taken already."

"I didn't know that," she admitted quietly.

"I'm afraid that may have been the story of your life so far."

"Rubbish, Mr. Sanborn."

"Let's argue privately later, without the men gawking, if you don't mind, Miss Benton, since we're back to stiff formalities," he whispered, entirely too close and warm in her ear. His breath stirred the ruffles and ribbons on her Nile-green poke bonnet with its beaked brim in front, and she chewed her lower lip uneasily, but resisted the impulse to jump back. She had no intention of yielding any more ground to this man in any way.

He ordered the workers to hoist their planked platform. As it creaked upward, she looked excitedly about them. A few men bent to their tasks, but more stared her way curiously, expectantly. She tried to ignore the blatant, disapproving glares and whispers. She had no idea how other Yankee warehouses worked, but this one certainly seemed innovative and well ordered, she assured herself as they stepped off the platform. Up here, the profusion of hemp sacks stamped Indigo for Dye made the path quite narrow. She peered carefully over the edge at the expanse of floor below littered with goods and large, open bins of snowy cotton. As they walked slowly along twenty feet above the ground floor, she remembered her inventory list and looked down to skim it for indigo.

"A new family of kittens up here," Alex called back to her as he disappeared down a little alleyway between heaps of sacks. "I'll have to get the mother cat some milk and food. She's earned it with this fine contribution to keeping the mice population under control."

Everything happened so fast that his last words were still sounding in her ears. From somewhere a rope thick as a man's arm swung at her; the iron hook at the end of it thudded into her side. She actually heard a rib or two crack before she felt it. She crumpled the inventory against her stomach and doubled over as pain and shock roared through her. In that same instant, the momentum of the blow carried her over the edge, into nothing but air.

She heard her own scream as the room revolved around her, and a man's voice shouting her name again, again. Her stomach cartwheeled past her throat. She hit on her back with a thump, then bounced. Amid a deep pile of unginned, scratchy cotton bolls, she drew a ragged breath. Agony sliced through her side, and her ankle hurt, but she was alive. She looked up, dizzy and startled, as above her Alex Sanborn grasped the swinging hooked rope that must have hit her and quickly shinnied down it.

He swung over to her. "Brett!" His knees depressed the unsteady pile beside her so she almost tilted into him. "Are you all right?" he asked, and there was concern in his voice. "You could have been killed." He stood up and roared over the side of the bin, "Fetch a surgeon here now, O'Malley! And hold the son-of-a-bitching man jack who's responsible for this!"

It hit her then with more stunning force than the iron hook had: Alex could have arranged this either to warn her off—

or worse. He could have stepped away just in time and had them swing that hook!

Alex turned back to her. "No, don't—" she gasped when he ran a big hand up her arm. Even those two short words caused her ribs to sear fire into her middle again.

"Where do you hurt?"

She tried to pull back from his touch, but there was nowhere to go and too much pressing pain. "My side. Oh!"

She almost jumped straight out of the bin when he drew a slender knife from a hidden sheath under his coat. Before she could protest, he slit her tunic under her arm and then proceeded to slice through the side seam of her gown.

"No, you can't. Wait!" she gasped.

"It may take a while to get help. It will relieve the pressure. Don't talk!"

"Take your hands off—oh!"

Somehow he managed to run a finger under the thin green muslin as he slit it cleanly away from binding her breathing. Staggered by the impropriety, as well as the pain every time she drew a tenuous breath, she gazed up goggle eyed at him.

"Blue blazes! A corset! Simone says these damn things are passé."

"No, don't," she thought she said again, but finally surrendered to the grip of pain and his strong hands. She screwed her eyes tight shut and tears squeezed out to soak her lashes. A man—this man—bending over her with the knife—a man who could easily want her frightened off, even dead. She trembled as she felt him slice away her boned corset to free her bruised rib cage and sever the waist cord that kept her bum roll in place behind her. Then he stripped off his coat and covered her with it.

She forced her eyes open. His big form over her blurred to two Alex Sanborns, then wavered through the rush of tears she fought desperately to blink back.

"Tell the men—and that Kit O'Malley—of yours," she gasped out through gritted teeth, word by painful word, "that I'm fine and—I expect them to be more—careful next time. Or they'll be—looking elsewhere—for a job."

He heaved a sigh of relief that she took for exasperation. But he yelled his partner's orders over the side at the milling, nervous men just as she said.

Brett lay in her bed at Sanborn House and breathed carefully, slowly. Even if she lay perfectly still every inch of her ached. Only a twisted ankle and a few cracked ribs, the surgeon had said—quite remarkably minor for such a fall that could have been so much worse. She knew it, and unfortunately, she feared, so did Alexander Sanborn. She wished she knew him well enough to decide how desperate he was to be rid of her. Her thoughts drifted but she was too alarmed and aroused to sleep. He had lifted her in her arms from the cotton bin and carried her so carefully, apparently tenderly, down the ladder to the warehouse floor, where they tended her. He had done the same to get her into the carriage and bring her back to this bed he'd laid her in before going out again.

"Mmm," she murmured, more in remembrance of being in his arms than at the pain that reverberated through her each time she breathed. His body heat, his strength that had flowed through her when he held her to him. The warmth and rich essence of his coat he'd wrapped her in. The firm press of his powerful arms, the bulge of his chest muscles through his soft white shirt. Her cheek against his shirt, she had even felt the resilient spring of his curly chest hair underneath. She had heard and felt his heart thudding against her ear. The intimate aura of his masculinity had sapped the little strength she'd had left. He had emanated a heady mingled aroma of leather, wine and the brisk sea air, and something else so musky and marvelous. She moaned again at the unfathomable yearning it still evoked in her body and heart.

But when she heard Simone's quick footsteps in the hall, she pulled herself up slightly and tugged the corners of her poppy red shawl over her thin batiste night chemise. Her hair loosed wild down to her shoulders must look a fright, but Simone could not possibly think her more plain or unfashionable than she already did. Knocks fluttered on the door, which swung slowly open. Simone peered cautiously into the room, then exploded through with little black Clemmie behind her, loaded with wrapped packages as usual.

"Oh, good, good. The color, it is back in your cheeks now, English roses!" Simone greeted her with a charming smile. "Here, Clemmie, just leave these packages and off with you. It's nearly five o'clock, *mon amie* Brett. Has our Alex returned yet?"

Brett ignored Simone's willingness to share Alex, at least in her speech. "If so, I hardly would have seen him here."

"Don't be so certain of that or long faced for it, hmm? He was livid, furious when he charged off back to the warehouse on his horse like an avenging knight. Here," she went on as if in one breath, "I'll open these things, since you're indisposed." She tore into the largest parcel and produced a plum muslin gown with low-cut square ruffled neckline and pink puffed-and-gathered sleeves. "*Voilà!* Yours from Alex, to replace that old, dreary one he had to ruin today," she declared, and proudly held it up against her own petite form, so that its length nearly dwarfed her.

"It's lovely, Simone, but I can hardly have Alex buying my clothing the way he does yours—"

Simone sighed and rolled her pale green eyes in apparent pique. She sailed the gown across Brett's blanket-draped feet and came around the large four-poster to perch carefully on its edge by Brett's hip. "*Mon amie*, I do not know what you think of Alex and me, but I tell you some things, hmm? Alex, he does not buy my clothing. Oh, of course he has bought me gifts, but not my clothing. I have my own money, my own friends, my own life. Listen, I am not some woman who does not know that freedom is important, and that means not owing a man too much, no. I am in love with Alex Sanborn, yes—what woman who breathes would not be? But I do not love him, you see, and that is the great difference, eh? I think I have really never loved any man, even my dear husband, Philippe, though I cared greatly for him. But real love—you know, with all the passion for *and* loyalty to one man—that is most rare, and I have never found it yet. The passion with

Alex, yes, but the loyalty to stay forever, no,'' she concluded with a shake of ringlets and curls.

Touched and awed, Brett tried to sit up, but Simone's small hands pressed her shoulders back. ''The others in Baltimore, I do not care what they think or say,'' she went on. ''Someday I shall return to my France to find my dear brother Jerome when Napoléon, he is gone. But you, honest and bold, *mon amie* Brett, these things I wanted you to know.''

For the second time today, tears flooded Brett's eyes. Too tight-throated to speak, she gripped the Frenchwoman's hands tightly in hers.

''So you like the gown. *Magnifique!*'' Simone cried when tears threatened her own kohl-darkened eyelashes. She darted up to display the other wrapped packages until the teary moment passed. ''This one, matching pink kid gloves. That one, plum slippers with ivory ribbons. That long one, a ruffled parasol to keep the Baltimore sun from giving you nose freckles, eh? With your coloring and working beside the water, you must beware, you see. And from me to you some rice powder of roses, just like Josephine wears.''

''Simone, I cannot thank you enough.''

''Ah, but will you thank Simone when you see no corset here, no—what is it called—bum roll to push out your skirt flounces in back when your derriere is perfect enough to do it for you? I tell you the great LeRoy, Josephine's designer, would not allow it, and neither shall the great Simone Colette Vilmons!''

Brett joined her in a little laugh despite the pain it shot through her tightly bandaged ribs. ''You admire Josephine as your guiding light of fashion, and I shall honor Simone Colette Vilmons as mine!'' Brett told her. ''Imagine, I had to come to enemy Baltimore to find how to gown myself like the enemy French. And to find a dear friend.''

Simone took off her new bonnet and stayed for an hour, chatting, opening and displaying like a proud peacock each of the other packages. Brett was exhausted, but she had no desire to sleep. Occasionally, even as she listened to Simone's musical voice chime on, the warehouse whirled past her again. She felt nothing under her but emptiness, then the hard bounce when she landed. More than once as she and Simone shared things from their pasts and talked of women's woes, Brett breathed a silent prayer of gratitude, not just for her safe deliverance from the accident today, but for someone like Simone. Never had she been able to claim a friend her own age, and a worldly, sophisticated one her fiercely strict Presbyterian mother would have frowned on at that!

"Ah, his footsteps in the hall, and in a hurry as usual," Simone said as they both hushed to listen to the distinct click of boot heels on the polished floor. "I shall just go to my room now, hmm?"

Brett sat frozen, listening to his steps. If Simone meant she wanted to leave so she could be alone down the hall with Alex, that was fine. But if he thought to stop in here a moment, *she* had no intention of being alone with him. Most certainly not in a bedchamber, lying here with next to nothing on and her hair loosed like this!

As he knocked on the door, she wrapped her shawl over her breasts despite the sudden jerk of pain. "Simone, I cannot see him like this—" she began.

"Nonsense. You are covered. Come in then, Alex!" Simone called out.

He poked his head around the door. His face looked drawn, but he smiled to see them there together and Brett awake. He strode into the room as Simone darted to her feet. "I shall be back later, *mon amie*," she called blithely to Brett with a flutter of fingers. She pecked a kiss on Alex's chin, which he seemed not to heed, and sailed out the door, before Brett could protest.

Brett knew her eyes were huge as saucers as he came closer.

"I won't bite or anything else, Brett," he said quietly. "I'm glad to hear you laughing with Simone. Better then?"

"She was laughing. I'm still hurting," she managed.

"The surgeon said binding your rib cage like that will help it, and the twisted ankle should heal in a day or so." He knew he was gawking even if his words still flowed politely. She looked so different all tousled with that glorious head of hair fanned out around her heart-shaped face on the pillow. Simone's hair was closely cropped in back, as was the current fashion among many stylish young women. It had been ages since he'd buried his hands and lips in bounty like Brett's. The bedclothes outlined, too exactly for him not to look, a sleek, slender form with shapely legs and hips, a trim waist. Even her hands and the bright-red shawl she clasped over her breasts could not hide the mounded globes there. It annoyed him how the memory of her, hurt but defiant under his touch today, kept coming back to haunt him. His instinctive anger at her kept getting all mixed up with a strange urge to be her protector, too. While she often aroused him to violence, he seemed unable to stand by while others hurt her.

"Your knuckles are all black-and-blue," she said to break his intense scrutiny. She watched, fascinated, as his big, bruised hand dropped to the corner of the high mattress where she lay. Then she tore her eyes away back to his face.

His gaze jumped guiltily to meet hers. "Let's just say I did a little more than terminate the job of the man responsible for that loose, swinging hook at the warehouse today."

"Wasn't that a little extreme? I planned to lecture him about safety myself the next time I went back in there to verify the inventory sheet."

"So what happened today wasn't enough to show you the dangers inherent in this little crusade of yours, Brett?"

"Even if you're implying my accident was deliberate, I will not be scared off, Alex. Not by a swinging hook or new things to learn or a partner who doesn't want me around!"

"Brave words, but the warehouse and shipyard are no place for a woman!"

"They are if she owns half the warehouse and shipyard—and the precious clipper ship you're building so secretly there!" She winced in pain at having to suck air into her lungs to raise her voice.

"We'll continue this tomorrow after you've slept," he insisted as he dared to actually come right up to the head of the bed and bend down to cup her shoulder with his hand.

A crackle of energy jolted through her at his touch. It frightened and infuriated her more than the fall earlier today. "It didn't work, did it, Alex?" she said defiantly. "I'm not backing off, and I intend to return to Sanborn's the moment I can walk if not breathe! I'm not one to be kept here in your house in your bed while—" she got out before she realized what she'd said, then gasped and glared at him as his face broke into a huge, taunting grin.

"I said the shipyards and warehouse were off limits, but not my house and my bed," he murmured.

"You said last night the library and your bedroom were," she managed feebly, before she realized she was only provoking him more. She blushed at her blunder. Still, she couldn't stem her next words, which seemed fed by her embarrassment and the way she felt all prickly warm and dizzy like this when he was so close. "I suppose you're used to women falling into handy beds whenever you've so much as winked, but I won't be mocked, Mr. Sanborn!"

"Today I'm only used to women falling into cotton bins, and I was teasing, not mocking, Miss Benton. Perhaps you'll learn the difference someday. And I really prefer it when you call me 'Alexander the Great,' because I'm about ready to start calling you 'Your Majesty' in return. Molly!" he roared in the same breath. The stocky Negro housekeeper stepped in almost immediately, as if she'd been hovering out in the hall, awaiting his summons. He did not take his eyes from Brett's flushed face as he said, "Miss Benton has foolishly vexed herself when she needs her sleep. Would you please bring me a glass of Madeira and some valerian drops to calm her?"

The old-fashioned mobcap on the curly silvered head bobbed and Molly swished from the room with a mere single roll of eyes in her dark face.

Alex Sanborn leaned one hand on the bedpost above Brett's head and propped his bruised knuckles on one cocked hip. "Of course, I might actually have just sent old Molly for arsenic with a secret code to rid myself and Sanborn's of you. Blue blazes, isn't that what you meant today with all the accusations—that I tried to do away with you?"

"And did you?" she dared.

"Not yet. But you may yet drive me to it. My fellow shippers today warned me to be certain you're not a British spy. Cozy thought, that neither of us trust the other when we have to." His eyes traveled her entire length before brazenly recapturing her narrowed gaze.

"You may go to the devil, Alex Sanborn!"

As Molly bustled back in with a silver tray, he chuckled maddeningly and sauntered toward the door, somehow vastly pleased with himself. "I'd be afraid to go to the devil, Brett Benton," he threw back over his shoulder. He turned at the door. "I'd be terrified that when I got there, I'd find a stubborn, suspicious chestnut-haired woman who owned half shares in the place. Good night."

Brett downed the Madeira with the sedative, which Molly solicitously held to her lips. She half hoped it was poison. She didn't know how she was going to last another day near a man she distrusted and detested, yet who still made her go weak with longing more painful than this other thorn in her side!

Four

A week after the accident, Brett was back at Sanborn's. Alex seemed reasonably resigned to her return and absolutely buoyant when another ship returned safely. She pounced upon that moment to receive his promise that he would introduce her to his shipping cronies at the Fountain Inn tomorrow. After all, he went there almost daily for lunch and admitted everyone was curious to meet her.

The next day when they set out, she was touched that he walked slowly, though her ankle was completely healed. She noted with silent amusement that they had accidentally dressed in the same rich plum hue, though she knew better than to bring it up even in jest. Partway there, through the crowds of noontime Light Street, he stopped to give the street hawker a penny for a copy of the *Baltimore Patriot* newspaper.

"No Bay ships sunk this week!" the lad chanted over and over. "Balt'moe's count of looted Brit vessels over three hunert now!"

"Music to my ears," Alex told her smugly. "And if it's not to yours, best not say a word unless spoken to at lunch. I'm warning you, Brett, if you embarrass me today, it will be noon meals with Giles and his little crew for the duration."

She chose not to confront his subtly couched threat, a practice she was at last perfecting. She amiably avoided small skirmishes so her big battles could be more effectively fought. Alex had finally agreed to bring Giles's accounting books home to her at night, and she had pored over them the week she had been indisposed in an effort to master the Sanborn record-keeping systems. Thus, step by circumspect step, she intended to wage her private war to be full partner with the stubborn Alex. Eventually, when she knew as much as he did, he would be surrounded and have to surrender! She knew that was not quite what Simone had meant that first day about handling Alex Sanborn with lace mitts rather than leather gloves. But she had her pride and intended to keep using her brain against him rather than the feminine wiles she rather suspected she considerably lacked.

She stood in the warm sun, peering around his shoulder at the headlines. "British Raid Innocent Civilian Homes Claiming Soldier Barracks," one read. "Mr. Madison's War Bound for Worse Times!" another shouted. When he noticed her nose nearly on his coat sleeve, he tucked the paper under his arm and they went on. But at the next corner another ragamuffin newsboy flaunting the radical, antiwar *Federal Gazette* grabbed her attention. "Brits threaten to clean up Yankee insurrection as soon as Napoléon defeated!" the small hawker shouted, only to be hissed, booed or shoved by passersby.

News from home! A pro-trade-with-Britain paper! And how dared they treat a boy that way! There were entirely too many unsupervised children on Baltimore streets to suit her, and as soon as she came into some profit from Sanborn's, she intended to do something about it! She fished a half-dime coin from her calico cloth reticule to give a huge tip. Ignoring Alex's hard stare, she whispered to the lad not to let the crude citizens harm him. "I just purchased this to keep up with both sides of the war," she assured Alex, brandishing her rolled paper like a sword.

"Perhaps I'd best leave you out in the street to read it with ruffians like the boys who hold horses," he groused. "Certainly no partner of a Baltimore firm would be caught dead in a shippers' meeting with one of those appeasement papers!"

But she saw him trying to scan its headlines, and folded it pertly under her arm just as he had done. Despite Alex's apparent care for her when she was hurt, she hadn't yet dismissed the possibility he might want to be rid of her any way he could, and that kept her warier and more defiant than she liked. She couldn't resist baiting him, but she would hold her tongue today—as he said, unless spoken to—and show him that he, at least, could trust her. Besides, he was taking her and Simone to the theater that evening and she thought it would be most awkward if they weren't speaking to each other for that.

Brett found the Fountain Inn narrow, crowded and redolent with intriguing smells of mingled foods and the occasional local pipe tobacco. The exterior of the building was all brick and clinging ivy, the interior polished wood and sawdust on the floor. She was expecting a fountain, but found no hint of one. There were only two other women on the premises and they both toted trays with tankards. Alex introduced her to many men, who seemed polite enough, if curious. Only a few insisted on staring as everyone sat at long benched tables to partake of terrapin soup, olio salad, a huge joint of beef the inn's owner carved at the table, bread with jams, cheese and rich strawberry *gâteaux* washed down with tankards of wine punch.

Alex tried not to watch her. He wished he could be less aware of her, wedged in on the bench between him and the wall. At least it kept her from having someone else on her other side to chat Brit patriotism to during the meal. She seemed to relish the food, though he'd tasted better. When she thanked the man who thumped her plate of dessert down before her, he recalled how appreciative she always was for things the servants did for her. He admired how she enjoyed the daily little moments of living he'd long ignored in his rush to get bigger things. And, dammit, he admired how the week of eating and resting since she'd arrived had filled out the sharp angles of her face and body. In her new dress, her form seemed almost lush, and he found it hard to keep his eyes off her roses-and-cream complexion and the radiant hue of her hair.

It annoyed him that his thoughts almost betrayed him: he jumped when she inadvertently bumped his thigh with hers while squirming for a better position to hear someone down the table. As soon as the dishes were cleared and a few more clay or wooden pipes lit, the headier discussions of the day began.

"Blasted cost of living's going to do us all in if we can't get more ships through." Round-faced Chase McVey's voice rose above the hubbub. "I don't give a hang what the *Patriot* says about this week's lack of sinkings, it's only 'cause we don't dare risk our ships out there! I've got flour rotting in my warehouse. And the net's bound to tighten as soon as Wellington mops up on Bonaparte and extra Brit troops are freed to be shipped over here. That could be happening even right now."

"But Marsh's brig *Defiant* and Sanborn's *Pamela Mary* are due in about ten days from now from the West Indies and should both be laden to the gunnels with goods," another man far down the table put in.

"I didn't know we had that ship out," Brett whispered in Alex's ear with a pluck on his sleeve.

"You do now," was all he said, and wished people wouldn't blurt out arrival schedules for ships in public meetings.

"Maybe more of us better risk more capital for faster ships," Daniel Dills, sitting next to Alex, said. "You know, like Sanborn's *Free Spirit* that none of us has been allowed to see." He gave Alex a zestful slap on the back that bounced him into Brett. "How's your damn secret mistress of a ship comin', anyway, Alex? And, pardon me, ma'am," he added politely to Brett to excuse his cuss word, although she was almost immune to them by now in this pagan paradise.

"Her launching's within the month, gentlemen," Alex announced, but Brett noted his voice was nervous. "Of course you're all invited to see her at the launching party, if not before."

Mr. Dills was right, Brett fumed. That ship was almost like a mistress or lover for Alex. He always spoke of it as a "she" and jealously guarded her. He poured hundreds into her, the way one would spoil a mistress. He went out many nights to spend time with her and even planned a party for her! His feelings toward the *Spirit* seemed akin to passion. Maybe that's why things between Simone and him were not wholly what she had expected them to be. But this entire situation with his wooden mistress angered Brett. Alex had been adamant that she wasn't to go near the Fell's Point shipyard. She'd even tried to get old Molly and Jessie to tell her anything that their sons, who worked there, might have revealed about the ship. But Alex must have sworn everyone to some oath of secrecy!

Brett seethed, but she let the ebullient patriotism of these men slide right off her back as the braggarts bragged and the complainers complained. She fixed a serious look on her face and tried not to say a word. If she just got through this, Alex might not be so possessive of his beloved ship. Or, at the very least, he'd bring her back here for lunch, where she'd learn something else!

Her chin jerked up. The burly, bull-necked Quinby Marsh, directly across from them, was addressing her. "So, do the British know their Admiral Cochran and his lackeys running this blockade are regarded here'bouts on the same level as Satan hisself, ma'am?" he was asking, his small eyes boring directly into hers. Beside her, she felt Alex draw a warning breath.

"Actually, I met Admiral Cochran years ago at my great-uncle's house," she told them, and gazed boldly from man to man at their table as she went on—every man jack of them but Alex. The room hushed instantly. "But I don't recall he had horns on his head, nor a pitchfork or tail. Sir George Cochran is no doubt only an honorable man trying to do his duty as he understands it, just as all of you would under similar, trying circumstances."

"'Sir George,' she calls him!" Quinby Marsh hooted amid protests and denials that any of them had anything in common with "The Scourge of the Chesapeake." "I mean, Alex, you told us her uncle fought under Lord Nelson, but here your new partner knows old Satan Cochran hisself. We told you you gotta watch harboring internal foes to our city." Marsh pivoted his bull neck back toward Brett. "How 'bout Cochran's demons then, who been burnin' Chesapeake Bay towns and cartin' off goods to feed their soldiers?" Marsh demanded, his already florid face growing more livid. "I s'pose, Miss Benton from Britain, you been real tight with his Captains Ross or Kelsey, too!" he accused.

Her heart thundered at the mention of her being "tight" with Dalton Kelsey! So these men all knew exactly who was commanding the American war under Admiral Sir George Cochran. Jumbled feelings overwhelmed her, made her stutter as she tried to answer. Their table—perhaps the entire place—erupted, with roll after rumbling roll of brusque comments and shouts as Alex's deep voice rang out in her place.

"Lay off now, men! Blue blazes, if Baltimoreans judged guilt by association, we'd all be swinging from yardarms as pirates, you know! I give you my word, the lady is only embarrassed by her first close-up display of two-fisted Baltimore political discussions. I think you'd best back off and treat her as a lady who is our guest and not a full partner yet!"

"As you do, Sanborn?" a man named James Hartman challenged. "Can't say I'd get much done myself with a young, fetching woman about, English or not!"

She could tell Alex was even more annoyed at that turn of talk. A little muscle set up the rhythmic ticking along his hard jaw that she'd learned was a warning sign of an impending display of temper. But he only profited from the nervous chuckles to take her and their two newspapers, which he'd been sitting on, and smoothly extricate them from their bench next to the wall. Chatting, nodding to a few, stopping only to slap coins on the counter, he steered her outside.

She heaved a sigh. All she'd done was truthfully answer a question back there, and they'd exploded like that. This whole town was a powder keg. No wonder Alex was the way he was sometimes, she mused as he guided her away from the waterfront with a firm touch at the small of her back.

"Aren't we returning to Sanborn's, Alex?"

"Not yet."

"Where are we going?"

"Just walk. I need the air."

They strolled several blocks without speaking, west on Redwood, then sharp south on Eutaw toward the harbor. The commercial buildings thinned; small private homes began, then became sparser.

"Are we strolling clear to Washington?" she ventured at last. "I don't know about you, but I have a great deal to do back at the firm." She darted a glance at him. His profile was glacial. "Alex, I'm sorry about back there."

"It was bound to happen. It wasn't really your fault. It can't be helped," he told her, his words chopped and his voice gruff. She wondered how long he'd been rehearsing those kind platitudes in his mind as they'd walked along.

When he indicated they were going to take a path that cut across a narrow wooded strip toward the distant bay, she balked. "It's just a little longer way back, Brett," he insisted. "Momentary communing with nature. Peace and quiet."

She turned to face him at last. "I'd rather not."

"A lady who gets all moony eyed over Wordsworth?" he taunted. "You're not still thinking I'm out to get you, I hope. Word of honor, I won't pitch you in the water or touch more than your elbow. Or is your ankle hurting?"

"No," she admitted, still hesitating to follow him down the shaded path. The woods did look lovely, and she hadn't been anywhere on dry land so enticing since her last stroll in Hyde Park the day before she'd left London. She scolded herself for being such a coward. Obviously, he wasn't going to do something dire and desperate to her in broad daylight. Or, the little voice she tried so hard to keep smothered demanded, was she afraid to be alone with him for other reasons?

Her long strides caught her up to him swiftly. Then the two of them slowed to a saunter amid trees and bushes shivering with bird songs. Tiny daisies dotted their path. She could smell brackish land from here, so the tide must be out. The breeze invigorated her and brushed bright blossoms into her cheeks under the thin dusting of scented powder Simone had given her the week before. On a little grassy ledge above a narrow, tide-abandoned ribbon of beach, he sat on a broad boulder and spread his handkerchief for her beside him. He dropped both the newspapers he still carried to the ground and put his booted foot on them. She half sat, half leaned, her legs pressed stiffly together to keep her steady on the slant of rock.

"You see, don't you, Brett, it just isn't going to work."

She swiveled to face him. She had no idea this was coming. "No, I don't. Just because those men got a little vexed."

"A little vexed! They don't trust you and they're not going to. Dammit, you've actually met Cochran, 'The Scourge of the Chesapeake,' we call him!" he said, his voice almost little-boy sulky.

"They called him 'Satan' back there," she goaded. "I can't help who my uncle was, Alex, or that I helped with his dinner parties when he needed me years ago."

He sighed so hard his big shoulders slumped. She amazed herself by reaching out to touch his coat sleeve. "I am not a British spy, Alex."

He shook his head. "Even if that's true, you're a target for them. You're putting yourself in danger from rabid Baltimoreans who see their fortunes rotting unless they can send out fast or lucky ships. And you're a sitting duck to be contacted by some slimy, sneaky British informant who wants to know everything you've found out for God and country about Baltimore shipping and city defenses!"

She hadn't thought of that. Could it be true that someone, even someone sent by Dalton Kelsey, perhaps, could contact her here? She'd written him through the Admiralty when she'd decided to leave England, so he must know she was in Baltimore by now. But if she told Alex now that the second in command to the "Great British Satan" had asked her to marry him, he would surely pitch her into the water.

She lifted her eyes to Alex again, unaware she was blushing gently. The sea wind tugged sun-struck tendrils loose despite her broad-brimmed bonnet. He noted that her lips had actually pouted provocatively at whatever that last thought was that had darted through that sharp brain. Her full, high breasts, now no longer corseted, had heaved and pressed taut-budded nipples against the gown and thin redingote.

He reached for her shoulders before he knew he would move. "Swear to me you'll never do anything to harm Sanborn's," he insisted, his voice much colder than his body felt.

She dared to be defiant. "Shall I swear on your copy of the *Baltimore Patriot*, since we don't have a Bible?"

"I'm dead serious, Brett. Swear it."

"You're hurting me." She tried to wriggle off the rock, to stand. His hard-won patience wavered. It frightened him that a woman could make him lose control like this. He tugged her closer to him, using the muscles of his arms to show her how much stronger he was.

"No, Alex!"

One arm hard around her squirming shoulders, one hand grasping her chin, he ground out, "When are you going to stop fighting me on everything that's between us?"

She froze. She sucked in a breath. His rough embrace made her go shaky, not with revulsion, but with a swift, drowning sweep of desire. Her thoughts and protests scattered. "I—I don't know," she murmured. "I just—"

He tipped his head to get under the bonnet and covered her half-open mouth with his. His touch stunned her as if she had fallen again, and she pressed her lips tight closed. His mouth, which had first felt so hard, softened instantly, beseechingly. Her knee, then her thigh slid against his hard ones. Her will was deserting her, and she faltered under the devastating impact of her awakened senses. This bore no resemblance to Dalton Kelsey's closedmouthed, dry-lipped kisses.

Alex kissed her lips again and again in little forays, as if coaxing her to open them. She did at last, only to have the tip of his warm tongue taste her there, brush her lips, outline them wetly, then intrude deeper. She opened herself farther to his skillful touch. He skimmed her teeth and, when she tried to gasp a breath, invaded totally. Though she was dizzy, that shot her eyes wide open. His were closed, and so near that she could see each separate black lash along his cheeks. Shaky to her very core, she closed her eyes again and surrendered to the rush of sensation.

Leisurely his tongue examined, cajoled, teased. Hers emulated his caressing movements, until she could only cling to his shirt and waistcoat in mindless rapture. At that capitulation, he hugged her even tighter and moaned deep in his throat. His big hand dropped from her chin to her waist, then lifted, ever so gently, to stroke her rib cage just under the swell of her breast. It didn't hurt a bit, but it jolted her out of this mad folly.

She pulled back so abruptly that he almost tipped off the boulder, and twisted away, pushing hard at his chest. Off balance, he let her go and watched her stagger back a few steps until she regained her own balance. He propped one foot up on an outcrop of boulder so his breeches would not flaunt the reaction his body had to hers. He steadied himself to drape one arm nonchalantly across his raised knee.

"Calm down, Brett. Don't tell me you didn't like it, too, and—"

"And nothing!" she gasped. It annoyed her how quickly he seemed to recover his poise, when she felt so shaken. She was panting as if she'd just run miles. "Is that the new tactic, Alex? If you can't force her one way, convince her the other?"

His features changed swiftly from smug to furious. "Seduction, you mean, Brett? Hadn't thought of it until you rather crudely put it in that light after what I thought was a spontaneous affectionate interlude. But perhaps the only one thing we do well together is fight. Besides, if we'd gone farther today, it's obvious you'd have needed careful tutoring, just as you do at the firm, and I really don't have the time or inclination."

"Rubbish! That's just like you, and all the rest of your

cronies!" she spit at him. She knew she wasn't making sense, but she lacked a better insult.

"The rest of my cronies?" he demanded, and dared to shout a laugh. "Blue blazes! If you think any of them can get you to go all breathless and shaky with one little kiss that didn't mean a damn thing, you're certainly welcome to try. Only I doubt if any of them could stomach a pious, pushy little Brit in their arms any more than I!"

Devil take him, how she hated this man, hated him, hated him! she raved silently. She stormed away down the path toward town. She lifted her hem to take even longer strides, but it didn't help. She heard, felt him at her side before she saw him. He reached for her again, spun her around to face him. She tried to kick, but heard a seam rip as the skirt stopped her leg.

"Now listen to me, Brett!" he shouted. "I'm having to trust you, but so help me if you ever do anything to endanger Sanborn's or Baltimore, I won't be responsible for what I might be driven to!"

"Just so you don't force a kiss on me again!"

His ruggedly handsome face went stony again. "I don't think anything short of breaking your British friends' blockade could make me so stupid again," he clipped out, and loosed her so fast she almost fell.

She brushed her arms off where he'd touched her as though he'd had muddy hands. "Then it's business only," she said. "That's all I ever wanted." She faced him squarely, realizing she had lied to him for the first time. She wasn't able to return his glowering stare for once and looked away. She'd be willing to die before he would ever know what thoughts of him did to her.

"That's a deal, British. But it does not include seeing the *Free Spirit* until she's launched, and that's that."

She almost fired another salvo, but pressed her lips tight shut. The next time she faced him down on that, she didn't intend to be out in the middle of the woods alone with him, or have her legs still trembling with desire. His touching her that way had turned her stomach upside down and made her feel all tingly, even between her legs. It was an entirely new, staggering feeling, and she didn't trust her own thoughts or voice any further.

She just nodded stiffly and straightened her bonnet. Not even walking side by side, they hurried back toward town.

Brett ignored Alex as best she could each time he came out into the retail store area where she was observing Mason Finch's handling of customers that afternoon. When the messenger boy, Todd Miles, came in all ragged and dirty looking still, she called the child over to her. Up close the ten-year-old ragamuffin had a cherubic face, if pinched and smudged.

"Hello, Todd. Have you been playing at all today?"

He frowned at her. He was brown from the sun, but it hardly hid the dirt on his face. She wished she had a washrag at hand. "Naw, miss. Don't have time a bit for that, workin' for Mr. Giles and Sanborn's," he told her. He wiped a soiled sleeve across his runny nose. "Don't you tell Mr. Giles none I'm a laggard."

"No, certainly I wouldn't," she assured him with a pat on his shoulder, which she hoped was not infested with lice or fleas. "I'm sure you're not a laggard. I just wondered how you got so dirty. Do you have a mother?"

"'Course," Todd muttered as Mason Finch's voice cut in.

"Miss Benton, Todd has a mother and six brothers and sisters. He has a father, too, but unfortunately he was taken off the Sanborn ship *Eastward Bound* last October and forcibly impressed into the Royal Navy. The good Lord knows that Mrs. Miles, trying to keep body and soul together as she is, has no time to check the boy's face several times a day, let alone make certain he has time to play."

"Then perhaps we can help out here," Brett suggested.

Mason Finch rose from behind the counter and came over to ruffle Todd's unkempt coal-black head. "We already do. Off with you then, lad, with that last message," Mason urged, and the boy scooted gratefully out the door with his letter.

"I didn't mean to upset him or intrude, Mr. Finch."

"Of course not. I recognize honest concern. But you

mustn't think Sanborn's ignores the needs of such people," he told her with a shake of his salt-and-pepper head. "Alex Sanborn, just like his father before him, allots large sums to care for the families of sailors lost at sea one way or the other. Todd may work up to being Captain Windsor's cabin boy on the new vessel sooner or later. At any rate, the good Lord knows, the boy has a job, so his mother doesn't feel she's just living on our charity. And with over sixty of our men impressed by the illustrious Royal Navy of late," he concluded, his usually neutral tone gone prickly, "it does rather tax the profits of Sanborn's in tight times."

"I'm pleased to hear all that—about the charity, I mean. Thank you for sharing it, as Mr. Sanborn hadn't seen fit to explain that yet," she said, not flinching from the man's stern gaze. "But that doesn't mean I can't try to help Todd. I'm sure Captain Windsor would rather have a clean and articulate cabin boy."

"But not one who articulates with a snobbish Johnny Bull accent," Alex put in where he suddenly stood in the door to his office. "Besides, Todd's been allowed to see the *Spirit*, and I don't need a Brit pumping him about it."

That did it! she told herself as she and Alex glared at each other across the fidgety Mason Finch. He meant to be nasty and to flaunt his refusal to share the clipper ship with her, the thing he probably loved most in the world right now. It was nearly ready to be launched, and even the firm's messenger boy had seen it! But she refused to rise to his bait and let him see her hurt or angered by that brazen Yankee tongue of his. She knew what devastation it could wreak in all kinds of ways!

"Excuse me, please, gentlemen," she replied in her most calm and honeyed tones. "I believe I need to see Giles Cutler about that charity fund Mr. Finch was just kind enough to explain to me." Slowly, smoothly, she turned and climbed the steps from the room.

"Are you quite all right?" Giles Cutler asked at last, after watching her sit gazing out the window without moving for several minutes. She hadn't said a word since she'd come up from downstairs just now. "Forgive me for asking, but I hope Mr. Alex hasn't been brusque again. I believe in loyalty to my employer, of course, but I can't abide rudeness, Miss Brett."

She pivoted to face him. "I appreciate that, Giles. Actually, I was just marveling how an apparently self-indulgent man such as Mr. Sanborn is willing to spend the firm's meager profits right now for indigent families of captured employees. That is what your Exigencies Fund, which you didn't want to discuss, mostly goes for, isn't it?"

His heart pounded. He stalled for time by coughing into his handkerchief. If she challenged him on records for those funds or somehow checked into how much he actually gave to the families compared to how much was allotted, his embezzling would be discovered and his plans ruined! He had to gain her sympathy, even make her beholden to him in some fashion, so that she would not credit any wrongdoing if she should discover it.

"Ah, excuse me," he choked out, then coughed again. "Permanent lung damage from the fire, you see."

"The fire? I didn't know," she said instantly concerned. "I mean, I assumed a fire had hurt you once."

He sat on the stool on the far side of her to display his disfigured profile to her. He bowed his head, even added a sniffle and touched his handkerchief to his nose again. "Never like to speak of it even after all these years, but I trust you, Miss Brett. You are kind enough to treat me for what's under these horrible scars and—forgive me for being blunt—there are other ones on my body that my garments cover."

"Giles, I didn't know. If it's too painful to speak of, please don't feel—"

"No," he persisted, the pitch of his voice rising even more. "Perhaps if you'll listen, it will help."

He laid before her, quite skillfully, he thought, his story as he had come to see it. How, as a ten-year-old, he had lost his parents to spotted fever and how his only brother, Will, had sent for him to come here from York in Canada. "My brother was eleven years older, so you can imagine what a lonely boyhood I had with him grown-up and gone, Miss Brett."

She nodded. She could indeed.

He explained how he had looked up to Will, who was then working as an assistant bookkeeper for old Mr. Sanborn right here on this site. He was thrilled to be with his adored brother, but the Sanborns kept Will so terribly busy for the pittance they paid him. Sometimes, just to be near his brother, Giles followed him to work and hid out along the docks or slept in the much smaller old Sanborn warehouse until it was time to go home. "But," he admitted with another sniff while he savored the pitying look on her face, "when Will became friends with young Alex Sanborn, he never had time for me at all. Mr. Alex always had him out carousing till all hours. I don't blame Will for any of it, of course. We needed the Sanborns' goodwill even to live."

"Of course you did. Just as Todd Miles and his family do now," she put in.

"Yes, ah—that's it. And so, you see, one day when I was sleeping in the warehouse on some sacks of tobacco, one of the workers must have started a fire somehow, and I was trapped. Will heard my screams and tried to fight his way in to save me." Giles shook his head and thrilled when she reached out to pat his arm. Ah, how perfect this would all be if he could have her for his own, too. In one blow, he'd ruin Alex Sanborn and the firm and gain her lovely body in his bed. His mind raced at the thought of it. She would not be like the other sluts he'd forced to bed him at all.

"And that's why you never like to go over into the warehouse. The tragic memories," he heard her whisper, and he nodded again.

"I was horribly burned—obviously," he went on. "And Will died in his heroic effort to make it all up to me at last. At least after that, old Mr. Sanborn took some pity on me and saw that I was schooled in letters and mathematics—of course I'm eternally grateful to Sanborn's for that."

"I'm so sorry, Giles, about all this!"

He shrugged grandly and reveled in the tears he saw in her eyes.

"Here I was smarting over the fact Alex won't let me near his new ship, and you had all this on your heart!" she continued, her voice tender. He shuddered with desire even as the next step of his plan came to him.

"If I could swear you to secrecy, Miss Brett, I could get you in to see the *Free Spirit*, and he'd never know a thing of it," he said with a glance around the empty room, his voice low. "That is, if you'd vow that even if you were found out you'd not tell Mr. Sanborn I arranged it. I know the Fell's Point shipyard like the back of my hand," he boasted before he realized that he'd almost given himself away. He added quickly, "As I used to do accounts there on the site before he closed the place to visitors."

Her face lit. He watched in awe as she became not merely tender but absolutely stunning with radiance and vitality. "You do? But with all those people working there, when would we go?"

"At night—tonight if you'd like."

Her quick mind raced. She could claim she wanted to stay home and Alex and Simone would go to the theater together. She had been looking so forward to it, but she and Alex were hardly civil, anyway. Yes, Mr. Yankee Sanborn, she told herself, I am your full partner. I desire and deserve to see our new clipper ship, and what you don't know won't hurt anyone!

She smiled as she accepted the wrapped piece of Berkeley's toffee Giles extended to her, as if it were the finest glass of champagne, to celebrate a victory. "Yes, I promise it will be our secret, Giles! Now tell me what time to meet you and what I'll have to do!"

Five

"You sure you should go riding in men's breeches to-morrow, Miss Brett?" the old housekeeper, Molly, asked as she handed the garments over at the door of Brett's bedroom. "It seems to me there's 'nough of a fuss already 'bout you in this town. An' this shirt of my boy Jacob's—it's much too big."

"No, it's perfect for what I have in mind, Molly, really. And please don't mention this to Mr. Sanborn. After I've learned to ride better, I intend to surprise him, you see."

"Sure 'nough you been a surprise to Mr. Alex all along, right from the beginning!" the woman exclaimed. A chuckle rumbled up from somewhere inside the calico gown and expanse of crisp white apron, which never showed a speck of soil. "Nobody surprised Mr. Alex 'bout much when he was a boy. He done all the surprising himself. But now, my, my, how times do change," she said with a smug roll of dark eyes.

"Now please, Molly, take this money. It will replace these clothes with new ones," Brett insisted as she had before, and tried to press the half-eagle coin into the woman's big square palm.

"No, miss," she said, and put both hands up. "When you give 'em back I'll just get 'em washed again and no one the wiser at all, less'n Mr. Alex sees you, an' we both catches it from him!''

After Molly left, those last words echoed in Brett's brain. If Alex did see her in this garb—let alone if he found out what she meant to do—it would be worse than Molly ever envisioned. But she had no intention of being caught or "catching" anything from Alex Sanborn! She was proud of her masterful job of convincing Simone and him that she felt too tired to go out tonight. Simone had fussed and Alex had narrowed his blue eyes in that dangerous way of his, but they were both in their rooms, preparing to leave without her. As soon as they were out the front door, she would be out the back, dressed as a lad. She would saddle a horse from the stables herself. She'd watched her uncle's groom do it more than once in those early years in London when Uncle Charles had taken her for a canter in Hyde Park. But when he stopped riding the horses had been sold, and no one else had ever taken her again.

She sighed as she scampered into the big cotton shirt, then yanked up the breeches. She stuffed the huge shirttail in and belted it tight, tucked long wool socks up in the breeches, then pulled on the new boots Alex had bought her the week before. Rubbish! she thought. Why didn't they ever make boots to fit just one foot? Her feet had as many curves as her body and she'd get blisters, certain, from these! But she had to admit that the squeaky leather smelled wonderful.

This plan would work, she assured herself again as she paced back and forth across the golden rug to soften the stiff boots. She was to meet Giles Cutler in front of the Zion Lutheran Church at the corner of Holiday and Lexington. They would ride together out to the tip of Fell's Point, where Giles had a special lantern hidden, one that threw only a narrow beam of light through a metal shield. He claimed he knew how to slip past the two guards who patrolled the perimeter of the grounds but seldom went inside the warehouse at night. She would look the forbidden *Free Spirit* over and be back at the house before Alex and Simone returned. And someday, when Alex Sanborn was particularly goading, she would tell him she had visited the birthplace of his precious mistress when she was still in her cradle!

She continued to pace the room, waiting to hear Alex and Simone go by in the hall. She was ready to dive beneath the covers of her turned-down bed if Simone knocked to say farewell. The mid-April wind outside was balmy, but it howled as if in warning. She heard their voices, their footsteps pass. A sharp sense of exhilaration shot through her. She would show him! And show herself she could handle a challenge in this man's world. She twisted her shoulder-blade-length hair into two thick loops and secured them on top of her head with combs and whalebone pins, then knotted a Paisley handkerchief around her head as she had seen some sailors on the docks do. She turned down the wick of her lantern until it hissed and gutted out. Then she tiptoed out into the deserted hall.

Alex Sanborn sent the puzzled, protesting Simone off in the curricle by herself to meet friends at the theater. Tonight she would announce that she was returning to France soon, now that Napoléon was on the run, and he regretted that neither he nor Brett would be there with her when she told everyone, but it couldn't be helped. He would miss her, but he had known she would leave Baltimore sooner or later.

He stuffed his gray kid gloves inside the brim of his tall, curly beaver hat. He wished he hadn't worn his striped gray satin breeches, but otherwise he would never have gotten Simone as far as he had. He loosened his elaborately wrapped and tied satin cravat with one big finger as he strode around the side of the house to where he could look straight up at Brett's windows.

If someone came to the house to see her, which he doubted, he could watch their approach from here. If she dared to go out, he could follow. Only if she stayed in would he admit he might have been wrong that she was up to something. He wedged his hat in the supple branches of the forsythia bush. The pushy wind would have it off his head in a trice out here.

Besides, no use wearing it, since he was probably going out among British spies rather than Baltimore society tonight.

His neck was about to break from staring up, when her light went out. His pulse pounded. If she did turn out to be a British informant, it was best that he know now and do what had to be done. Only every time he even thought about touching the woman—in anger or any other way—the intensity of his emotions shocked him.

He stood on one foot, then the other, trying to listen for both the back and front doors. She was taking her time if she was coming out. Then he heard the whinny of horses in the stable. In the shadows of the moonless night, he moved stealthily toward the back of the big brick house.

There was a light in the stables where there shouldn't be! He edged closer, half tempted just to lunge inside. Before he could even peer in, the lantern died. Almost immediately, a horse and rider brushed past him in the dark. The horse broke immediately to a trot down the brick drive. A strange lad sat astride Sea Bird, the smallest horse he owned. Alex gasped. His senses told him what his eyes could not. Cursing, he fumbled his way into the darkened stables to grab another horse.

"But why do we need two lanterns if we're both going in?" Brett whispered to Giles a half hour later, as they huddled under a weeping willow across the street from the shipyard at Fell's Point.

"In case we get separated inside," he hissed. "It's a big place. And beware of all the sawdust and kindling around on the floor. The entire shipyard," he went on, turning his half-scarred face to her under the cover of the dark, "could turn to an inferno if someone were careless with fire."

She nodded, wide-eyed. She could certainly understand why Giles feared the possibility of fire. The thought of anything at Sanborn's going up in smoke probably terrified him, and she thought him very brave to risk all this for her. He obviously knew the place inside out just from having done accounts there before.

"The guards are just where we want them now," he muttered, his mouth close to her ear. "Before they come back, we go."

His hand clasped her shoulder as he started off, rather too familiarly she thought, but it was no time to protest. Half crouched, they darted across the hard-packed dirt street. He avoided the front entrance and scurried around to the side of the long wooden building. Her eyes had become more accustomed to the dark, but Brett still squinted to see where they were going.

"The chute where they take in supplies that come by the bay," he murmured close to her ear. She heard him fumble to light both lanterns. Light leaped into her eyes, momentarily blinding her before he turned both wicks down, and she saw that only his lantern was a shaded one. He had dressed all in black and she realized immediately that she should have, too. Her loose white shirt stood out like a flag of surrender. He motioned with his head, his damaged profile to her. Light etched each jagged ridge and puckered scar and cast his features in demonic shadows. Her heart began to pound even louder. His half-contorted mouth moved entirely too close to her again. "Sit down, slide in," he whispered, and disappeared.

She cradled her lantern carefully and did as he said, half scooting, half sliding right behind him down the nearly level chute where long wooden planks entered the building. He grasped her arm and helped her stand. "This way. If anyone should come in, we'll have no choice but to gut both lanterns and feel our way out in the dark."

Brett approached the great ship with awe. She stared up, up at the ship from keel to deck. No masts and rigging yet, as those would be added after the launching. Their lanterns were pitifully meager to do her smooth white oak skin justice. Scaffolding and ladders leaned against her hull like pieces of metal filings drawn to a powerful magnet. Out of the water like this, she was the most magnificent thing Brett had ever seen.

"Two hundred twenty-five tons and ninety-seven feet

long,'' Giles hissed in her ear. ''She'll carry six big guns and
a crew of forty.'' But it wasn't the numbers that moved Brett.
The sharp scents of mingled woods and sawdust and tar
caulking assailed her nostrils. She could imagine the sounds
of the great vessel lunging through the sea: cables rattling
through hawseholes, the crisp clap of canvas and hum of the
wind in the rigging, the sibilant rush of water along this giant
keel. Sleek and shapely, a woman a man could love, she
mused, and blinked back tears. She started from her reverie
at Giles's next words.

''Just think. All this planning, hope and pride could go so
easily up in flames,'' he said, his voice crackly with emotion.
He scuffed a little pile of sawdust with his toe, then kicked
a few pieces of broken wood into it just under where he held
his lantern. How easy it would be to just drop the lamp, he
thought, and see the flames rise. He'd had dreams of fire, had
lusted after it all his life. But somehow his obsession had
grown worse after the fire he'd started had trapped poor Will
and scarred himself. It wasn't his fault, however; it had been
Alex Sanborn's fault for separating Will and him, for not
giving him the care and attention that a young boy needed.
Everything Giles had ever desired—good looks, submissive
women, power, wealth—were by rights Alex Sanborn's, and
he hated the man for it. But Giles had power, too. He would
start a fire and see Alex's precious ship go up in roaring
flames.

''Whatever are you doing? You told me to be careful!''
Brett whispered in shock.

He jumped, came back to his senses. ''And so we shall,''
he agreed, and grinned his crooked grin. ''Doesn't ever do to
play with fire, does it, Miss Brett? I'm going to check the
position of the guards, and I'll be right back. Don't wander
far from here, and keep your ears cocked.'' He turned his
back and melded into the shadows.

She almost called after him that she wanted to go, too, but
she was in no hurry to leave the ship. She wanted to climb
the scaffolding to see if the decks were done, but she recalled
all too well her recent fall at the warehouse. She was happy

simply to have been here. Let Alex Sanborn taunt and boast of his *Free Spirit* all he liked, for it was hers in a way now, too.

Walking under the spindly-legged scaffolds, she strolled along the keel toward the stern, gazing upward, running her hand tenderly along its curves. But she froze when she heard a footstep. She doused the light and stood breathing heavily in the dark, straining to hear, the gutted, smoky lantern clasped to her. She'd just stand here until Giles came back; she'd see his light. She'd panicked, put her lantern out too soon. Perhaps there were cats in here that made noise, just as at the warehouse.

She heaved a sigh of relief as she saw Giles approach, lantern in hand, though he was coming from the opposite direction in which he had gone. But then he lit a lantern hanging on a post, and she knew it could not be Giles at all. The man hung his own lantern up, and she hunched to the floor, then crept back under a scaffold as wan light washed the area. It was not a guard! Alex Sanborn himself stood with a pistol in his hand, his big, dark form unmistakably outlined by the lanterns on the post.

Carefully she put her lantern on the floor and shuffled backward until her shoulder bumped the hull. She edged sideways as she saw his head pivot to search the area. He called out, "Watch the doors, men, but they might have gotten away!"

His voice so sudden, close and real, panicked her. She stood to run for the chute, hoping Giles would be there, or that he at least had escaped. Her head bumped a crosspiece of wood; the tiny thud seemed to reverberate forever. She zigzagged blindly into the dark.

"Halt! I have a gun!" Alex shouted.

She heard his feet thudding behind her. An iron arm came hard around her and her legs just folded. His pistol hit, then spun away. Alex smacked into the floor with her on top of him. He rolled them over until he pressed her hard to planks and sawdust. He held her there, breathing hard, his knees between her spread legs, his hands pinning her wrists above

her head until she stopped her mad thrashing. She realized
her exertions had pulled off her scarf and ripped her hair free.

"I thought so! You bloody little British traitor!" he spit
out. "Who helped you here? Don't tell me you're alone!"

Then he didn't know about Giles. She'd promised him she
would not give him away. But all that was nothing to the fact
that Alex held her captive under him, crushing her down with
his powerful body to hold her nearly immobile. The feel of
him against her made her dizzy in the darkness.

The rage in the voice seemed not her own. "Get off me,
damn you, Alex!"

His face merely inches from hers, his breath scalded her.
"Such language," he muttered. "But, then, there's a lot I
don't know about you. I had no idea you'd make such a pretty
boy, though even this big man's shirt can't hide that you're
a woman."

He made no move to get up. She tried to wiggle sideways
from the hard thrust of his thighs, but he only settled in more
intimately against her. She stopped struggling and strove instead to calm herself, taking in long, shuddering breaths,
fighting how they moved her stomach and breasts against his
hard body.

"Whatever language I use," she gasped out, "whatever
things I do, I have learned from you! Now let me up! I have
every right to be here!"

He lifted himself off her, stood and hauled her immediately
to her feet. Then, in the same swift movement, he bent to
bump his shoulder into her belly and pulled her over his
shoulder with his hand hard on her bottom. She squirmed and
beat his back with her fists.

"Stop it, Brett!" he ordered through clenched teeth as he
stalked over and unhooked one of the lanterns from the post.
"You'll kick this and we'll have a fire. Or was that your plan
all along?"

He carried her up a few wooden steps and deposited her
like a sack of grain on a hard, curved-backed chair in a little
room with windows overlooking the dark expanse of roofed
shipyard. When she tried to get up, he shoved her back into

the chair, then sat on the edge of a desk to tower over her, his knees hitting hers.

"Just settle down for once," he threatened with a stiff finger jabbed toward her wide-eyed face. "I could have you arrested and imprisoned, maybe worse in this town, the way it is right now. No one's going to help someone I accuse of being a British spy. And I could accidently have shot you in the dark."

She glared at him through her mass of loosed hair. Then, with both hands, she thrust the rampant tresses back from her forehead. Her chin lifted boldly. "How did you find me? You're supposed to be with Simone at the theater."

"You're damned hard to follow," he admitted. "I lost you at the house. Blue blazes, I went clear to the firm, first thinking that you'd let someone in there now that you have a key. I'd like to think this is just another of your little schemes to defy me and you're alone in this, but—"

"I am alone, as you can see," she insisted with a half-hearted fling of her hand to the cluttered room. "I told you I'm no spy. But I am a full partner at Sanborn's, and you refused to let me see our greatest asset for the future, war or not. I own half this building and that ship you adore, and I have a right to be here!"

Her mouth dropped open as he answered her by lifting her to her feet against him. His voice was as hard as his hands. "I don't want to be put off, Brett. I want to know how you got in, how you knew the way! And I want you back on that French ship you came on. You can go with Simone. She's returning to France next week—"

"No!" she shouted, uncertain what she was refusing. Simone—she didn't know she was leaving. But she was not going back with her, not going to let this man control her and touch her like this! Whether he was gentle or rough, she feared the way her knees went weak as water, how badly she wanted him to touch her any way he would.

Panicked at the realization that she actually desired his caresses, she bucked against him, then kicked him once. He grappled her hard to him and plunged one hand into her thick hair to hold her still. "Take your hands off me!" she gritted out as he tilted her head back as if she actually offered him her mouth.

"But you need handling badly, and I'm the one to do it," he responded, his voice gone dangerously rough and slow and deep.

She pressed against him with all the intensity she had meant to fight him with. His mouth took hers again, and she answered in kind. Her breasts pressed flat to his hard chest, loose cotton shirt to embroidered silk waistcoat. Her entire body ached with heaviness for him. At last, when she could no longer breathe, his lips deserted hers to rain soft kisses down the slant of her cheek, along her trim chin line, down her throat, as she arched mindlessly back for him.

"Alex, oh, Alex!" she moaned throatily.

His mouth moved lower to thrust aside the soft collar of her shirt. His slick tongue glided past the hollow of her throat and out along her fluted collarbone. He held her pinioned against his hard body with one iron band of arm behind her waist. His other hand cupped, then gently cradled one trembling breast.

She thought she would explode inside with billows of long-smothered yearning. She had wanted his mouth and hands forever. And where her thighs tilted into his, where his hipbones and muscles and the thrust of him pressed against her softness, she wanted to be his. She closed her eyes desperately against the assault on her senses when he merely flicked one big thumb gently over the peak of her nipple through the yielding cotton and knew her worst fear was true. She was falling in love with Alex Sanborn!

"Alex, mmm, Alex," she mouthed against his ear to answer his rhythmic caressing of her breast.

He pivoted so that he leaned against the wall to support them. "Brett, so desirable, so provocative, and she doesn't know it. Doesn't know what she does to me like this," he murmured as his mouth dropped to follow the path of his darting, teasing finger.

Her eyes opened languorously, then widened abruptly. She

was staring straight into the frozen painted gaze of a figure of a wooden woman that had been leaned casually against a wall in the corner of the room. It had flowing silver-blond hair, pale green eyes and naked, rose-tipped breasts. Brett jerked in Alex's arms. The figurehead, standing wide-eyed as if shocked by their actions, looked just like Simone. If she needed any proof, she now knew for certain that Simone had been his mistress, had been naked with him, had no doubt reveled in his kiss and touch! It jolted her to her senses as if Simone actually stood but inches away.

She pulled back, first embarrassed, then angry. "Alex, stop it! Don't!"

Starry-eyed, he just lifted both arms stiffly beside her head to pin her in and leaned against the wall, watching her confusion. She knew her body shuddered and smoldered. Their breathing raced, then seemed to slow in unison. She pressed her crossed arms over her breasts as if she, too, had stood here naked from the waist up for him. She felt confused and desperate. Simone was leaving and she would be in the house alone with Alex. She wasn't leaving Baltimore, but she had to find another place to stay. If not, things like this could happen all the time—only more and worse, in his room, in her own four-poster, instead of against a rough wooden wall!

"What is it, Brett?" he asked after a moment, his voice calm and resigned.

"That figurehead. It looks like Simone."

"It was painted months ago. If I had it done now it would have flowing chestnut hair with golden-red highlights in the sun and stunning dove-gray eyes."

"Don't joke with me. And I won't be your next mistress, Alex!" she spit out as she darted under his raised arms and stepped quickly away.

"Haven't you thought that would be one way to win me over?" he challenged, as in apparent composure, he leaned one big shoulder against the wall where he stood.

"You must be mad. Never, never, never!"

"I guess I dreamed what just happened between us then."

Desperate to get them off this dangerous subject and back

on more formal footing, she said the first thing that came to her mind. "I have just realized you could have shot me back there in the dark, claiming you mistook me for a thief. It relieves my mind about us, Alex. You see, tonight I realized but for this sort of thing—I could trust you now."

"But can I trust you, my dear, coldhearted little Brett? 'But for this sort of thing,' of course. Now you listen to me. I think it's best for both of us if you go back to France with Simone. I'll pay for your passage and send you money when I can to buy you out."

She turned her back and straightened the shirt collar he'd pulled awry. "Rubbish! I'm not leaving, Alex." She tried to sound calm and businesslike, just as though none of this had ever happened here between them. "Besides," she added, "I'd hate to see money that's half-mine be captured by some blasted British brig just off the bay."

He couldn't deny he admired her pluck and aplomb. And she had evidently learned something from him, he told himself as he strode over to the desk and flopped in the chair to take a piece of paper from the drawer. She had learned to hide the fact that she'd just been racked with passion, and he had to admire the skill with which she did it. But, if they were to go on, they had to make a written deal. She'd put her half of the business against a pledge that she was not a British spy and he would pledge his half that he would never intentionally harm her physically. He looked into her clear eyes, gone dusky gray in the half light, as she turned slowly back to face him.

"Sit down then," he said, hoping he sounded only gruff. "I've a business proposition to make to you, if you agree, and then we'll start over again on neutral terms."

"Neutral terms, that suits me," she insisted, and sat down properly across the desk from him as if they had just met for the first time. But now she knew that each time Alex Sanborn touched her she responded like some pagan madwoman, and nothing—nothing—would ever be the same again.

It was just after midnight when Simone tiptoed across the hall to Alex's bedroom door and tapped her fingers lightly against the wood in their little signal. He had been back when she'd returned from the theater. She heard him pacing in his room like a caged animal even now. "Come in," a brusque voice answered. Wrapping her rose satin wrapper tightly to her, she darted in.

His bedroom was richly masculine—like the man himself, she had always thought—in browns and golds with touches of maroon. A heavy satinwood bureau, wide Napoleonic bed and table with two chairs were the only sparse furnishings, as though the room were a captain's cabin on a ship. Here were none of the sorts of decorative things she loved to have sitting about. He had fine tastes, but that streak of the stoic or Spartan in him was anathema to her indulgent, whimsical personality.

But she had no leisure tonight to consider such matters. She had come in to Alex with the express idea of clarifying certain matters in her mind, and she must not let herself be distracted. She knew Alex well, and she knew when he was disturbed or angry. Captain of his ship or not, Alex Sanborn was not the sort to know how to treat a woman who defied him. Women—including her, she had to admit—had tumbled in so many ways for the handsome, strong Alex that he was a veritable babe when someone fought him the way a ship might in a storm. Alex had met his match in Miss Brett Benton, and Simone meant to find out now how deeply his feelings ran.

"I heard you come in earlier," he admitted lamely as her cool green gaze examined him.

He was still in his dress breeches, but his waistcoat and cravat were gone and his shirttails were out. His hair looked horribly mussed, as if he'd raked his fingers through it repeatedly, but, then the breeze outside was stiff. "*Cheri*, a terrible evening, no?" she said.

He shrugged and walked over to where she leaned against the door, which she had closed and bolted. "How was it for you, Simone? Everyone in the doldrums since the life of Baltimore says she's going to set sail soon for home?"

"In the doldrums to lose their laughing friend Simone, but the women so pleased they will have their chance with the most eligible bachelor in all Baltimore again, no? Your Captain Windsor's wife will be back to finding you a bride the moment I board ship. And Claudine Cantrell's prune-faced mother tonight, she almost broke into—what do you call it— a jig when she heard."

She was pleased that she had at least coaxed a smile from his solemn, rigid face. She stepped forward at his approach and wrapped her arms around his narrow waist, leaning her head against his chest. "*Cher* Alex, you see, they do not know, as I do, that there is another woman already who takes your eye and thoughts."

He hugged her back hard, but she felt his head jerk up. "Brett? Only because she's turned everything I care about to chaos in the mere eight days she's been here," he muttered. She lifted her beautiful face to him and he saw the smug doubt there, so he added, "And I'm willing to prove it to you in any bed, anytime, including right now."

"Mmm," Simone murmured, and cuddled closer, her chin propped on his breastbone so she could look straight up into his eyes. "I would adore it, of course, if you are not just trying to prove it to yourself. What happened tonight then? Why did you send me off alone and stay here—if you think my little woman's brain can handle it to know?"

"Your 'little woman's brain' could outfox me and most of the men on land or sea, and we both know it, Simone. And what happened tonight was that Brett lied to us about being fatigued. The moment we went out, she rode off to see the clipper ship, apparently just because I forbade her to." He told her the sketchy details, omitting how they'd touched and how he'd felt.

"So, then, there is not much time for you and me before I sail," she said, eager to change the subject. She cared greatly for Brett Benton, but she adored the way Alex made her feel in bed. "We have less than a week then, you and I," she went on, and provocatively ran a tip of pink tongue between her pouted lips. But she had to be certain that if they lay together tonight, it would be only the two of them in bed. She had to know that, she told herself, and fought to keep her head. "And you are so very sure, of course, you do not care for *mon amie* Brett Benton in—in the way we share."

"Very sure," he vowed, but as he leaned down to kiss Simone's softly parted, glossy lips, he knew it was not true. The way he felt, he might as well have been kissing that painted wooden figurehead waiting to be mounted on the prow of the ship. The sweet, familiar scent of Simone in his arms, and her darting tongue, did nothing to arouse him. He found to his dismay that he could think only of the way Brett had felt in his arms only hours before. Desperately he tightened his embrace on Simone; he bent her head back as he returned her molten kiss. But he longed for the taller, more slender woman to press down into his big bed, and as Simone wriggled from her satin wrapper and pressed herself against him he knew he no longer desired her.

He jerked his head up and grabbed for the sliding material as it cleared her shoulder, tugging it up to cover her. Then he pulled back, even as she did.

"So you admit," she said shakily, "what I was telling you, no? We have had wonderful days and nights, *cher*, but I will not spread my legs for you when there is another woman you desire."

"Blue blazes, Simone! It isn't that!" he protested so loudly that she jumped as she rewrapped her luscious ivory skin in the rose satin again. He smacked his hand against his thigh several times to punctuate his fierce denials. "She's not half as beautiful as you," he protested. "And she's a damned, dangerous nuisance with that tart tongue!"

"Mmm, but tart can be so sweet when it is right for your taste, I think. Good night, *mon cher* Alex. We are both tired and I must begin to pack tomorrow. So much to take back for my new life, but Captain Piquet, he promised that cabin boy, Jacques, will call every day to take some of my things aboard before we sail." She held up her hand to halt the protest she saw coming from Alex again. "The captain and the boy, I can tell, they care for Brett Benton, too. And, my

Alex, I will come to you my last night here if you wish for a lovely farewell. But if you do, be certain that you take only me to your bed and not someone else in your head, eh? Sleep well.''

Lost in his thoughts, Alex Sanborn stared at the door, which she closed quietly behind her, a long, long time.

Tears in her eyes, Brett stood with the household staff and waved goodbye to Simone as Alex helped her up into the large Sanborn barouche. They had agreed Brett would bid Simone farewell here at the house, for the ship was sailing at first light tomorrow. Despite nearly a week of sending Simone's baggage piecemeal to the ship, the barouche floor and seats were piled with last-minute parcels. Alex had declared he'd paid the *Le Havre* as much extra duty to carry one woman's things as if he had shipped an entire holdful of cargo to France. Brett found herself hoping more than anything that the *Le Havre* would safely slip through the net of British ships and get her dear friend Simone safely home to a new life in France. Napoléon Bonaparte had been vanquished and was to be sent to exile, so many things would be different now.

As the carriage clattered off, Brett ran impulsively down the drive and along the lawn. ''Goodbye, my friend! Someday I'll come to Paris to see you, I promise! Thank you for all your advice!'' she shouted, despite the fact that Alex, his face alert and curious, sat next to Simone in the barouche. The carriage picked up speed, and for a moment, Brett stood forlorn as Simone's lace handkerchief fluttered at her. She watched the barouche turn the corner onto Lombard Street and disappear.

She drifted back upstairs, unshed tears still prickling her eyelids. She would miss Simone very much—miss this house, too, as she was moving next door this afternoon to live with the Widow Featherstone. Henrietta Featherstone seemed kind, but she hardly had Simone's bubbly personality, a *joie de vivre*, as Simone put it. Brett would feel the lack of Simone's amusing stories and outrageous advice on fashions. But for

Giles Cutler, she had no other ally against Alex, and Simone had been rather remote this past week.

She gazed down the length of hall toward Simone's open door across from Alex's. Last night she had seen Simone go into his room with only a silk wrapper around her. She knew the same thing had happened at least once before, the night she and Giles had gone to the shipyard. She wondered how many other nights they'd been together while Simone had led her to believe she did not really love him, that she had "other friends." At first Brett had chosen to hope that Simone and Alex were not bedding together, but she'd been forced to believe her own eyes now.

Drawn like a magnet, she walked slowly down the hallway, lined with oil paintings of Sanborn ships, to peek into Simone's pink, flowered bedroom. The maid, Annie, a rake-thin Negro girl, darted about with a feather duster already. The bed was immaculately made; it looked untouched. Wouldn't it just be stripped if it had been used at all last night? Brett agonized. She cared only because she felt betrayed by Simone, she assured herself. Where or with whom Alex Sanborn slept was certainly his own business.

She meandered back to her room. She was certain a thirty-year-old virgin could hardly imagine how it must be between a man and a woman in bed in the dark of night, and yet she'd wondered until all hours about it lately. At dawn today, she wasn't certain she'd even slept. Her memories, her fears, her most intimate longings kept merging in the most alarming ways at night. The way Alex had touched her, first on their walk along the sea and then at the shipyard, gave her a glimpse into the cataclysmic feelings such an encounter could invoke. She closed her eyes and leaned in her doorway as the mere remembrance of those wild emotions coursed through her body and mind. Her breasts tingled, her thighs ached as if he had touched her again. Her lips pouted as she pictured him kissing Simone farewell on the deck of the ship, perhaps in the intimacy of her little cabin. How unfair that such longings could do this to a woman, especially when the man who caused them had been so proper and aloof this past week. She had insisted on business only with him, but hated both him and herself when he perfectly complied.

But at least she had convinced herself that she didn't really love Alex Sanborn. She had thought for a moment when he'd touched her and held her in his arms at the warehouse that she did, but careful thought when she was alone and calmer had convinced her that he would never be the proper, kindly gentleman of her maiden's dreams. He was too different, too brazen, and the only thing she loved was the way he made her feel at times. Surely he only pursued her because he could not abide not being instantly obeyed and openly adored by every woman he met. It was pure, mad folly that a civilized, educated woman could love a man she most often detested.

"Miss Brett, you sure you feeling all right?"

Her eyes shot open. Molly stood inches away in the hall, and she hadn't even heard the big woman clomp upstairs. "Yes, fine. Just thinking about how different things will be now. Oh, what's all this? Simone didn't forget some of her things, did she?" Brett asked, noticing a pile of wrapped goods in Molly's stout arms.

"No, ma'am, but they been bought by Miss Simone all right. Mr. Alex, he done called her queen of the shops of Albemarle Street more'n once, that sure. These for you, and I wasn't to give 'em to you till Miss Simone's carriage out of sight."

Brett allowed the woman to drop the parcels on her own bed, between her meager piles of possessions she had been laying out to be carried next door. Molly stood with eyes alight and arms akimbo. "She say have Miss Brett open them alone so she not have anyone to scold or tell to take them back, 'cause she be long gone by then. An' she say there's a note to you tied to one of them. Sure enough, here it is!"

"But I can't believe she'd do all this!" Brett murmured as she sat down on the corner of the bed and leaned forward to take the envelope from Molly's big hand. She did not even notice when Molly slipped from the room and quietly closed the door to leave her alone. The linen paper of the one-page note smelled of Simone's floral scent so strongly as to bring her presence back. Brett almost felt she stood there in person, all ruffled and curled and scolding yet.

Ma chère amie Brett,
I am sorry the *Le Havre* sails before the big War Relief Ball next week, so, as my protégée, you simply must go for me, and in the Simone Vilmons's style! Gown, gloves, a necklace, reticule, stockings, silk shawl, and no wretched English corset or bum roll! I expect you to stand stodgy, war-crazy Baltimore on its ear for me.

My friend, you have made these two weeks we knew each other a joy. I will think often of you as I return to my beloved France to find my brother. Take care of Alex for me, *chère* Brett, in whatever way seems the one you must follow. On that I say no more, but pray you will find a man who inspires not only the passion, but the loyalty forever, too.

Wishing joy and love in your life,
Adieu,
Simone Colette Vilmons

Six

Alex had long ago sent the barouche back from the harbor, but he didn't return until dusk. Brett was making a last trip with some of her things between Sanborn House and the Widow Featherstone's rose brick mansion across the adjoining lawns, when she saw his tall, quick-striding form emerge through the pearly-gray spring evening. He saw her, too. Their eyes held, and her stomach cartwheeled as he made straight for her.

"Simone's all settled aboard then?" she asked, the boots he'd bought her in one hand, a small, shallow Chinese porcelain bowl of floating camellias in the other. The distinctive fragrance of the waxy, white blooms scented the air between them.

"Yes. Hours ago. Brett, why aren't the servants taking those things over for you?"

She decided to ignore the blatant change of topics, despite the way her imagination had been running as to why it should take so long just to bid Simone farewell. "They have a lot to do," she said only.

"Surely Great-uncle Charles had servants in London, and the lot my servants have to do is care for the family," he retorted.

She could tell instantly that their first argument of the week was brewing, and she welcomed it. Heat was better than the stilted, formal, icy demeanor they'd both hidden behind since she'd gone to the shipyard. But she didn't intend for the fight to be about servants' duties, or even where he'd been if he'd settled Simone aboard the *Le Havre* hours ago.

"Let's just say I learned to do for myself the first seventeen years of my life, Alex," she said crisply. "And I appreciate it if anyone, including servants, does a kindness for me."

"Admirable. And if a business partner does you a kindness?"

"Then it's strictly business. That is what we decided with that silly contract, isn't it?" Before he could rise to his next rejoinder, she plunged on. "Did Simone tell you about the lovely gifts she left for me—for the War Relief Ball you conveniently forgot to tell me about?"

He shrugged exaggeratedly, but his rugged face had an almost guilty expression for once. "Yes, she did. But it's not for a few days. I needed to decide some things. I was going to tell you."

They stood facing each other along the property lines, he with his arms crossed over his muscular chest, she cradling the boots and bowl of camellias closer to her. "You mean you really expect me to attend a function that actively promotes this war against Britain?" she demanded. "I'd like to sit this one out, Alex, stay neutral. It goes against my grain to—"

"Fine. Her Majesty thinks she can pick and choose. 'Alex, take me to the office,' she demands, 'take me to the warehouse, the Fountain Inn—the shipyard! But I just couldn't go to some shoddy American ball where the crude people of Baltimore will all be anti-British,'" he mocked. "'Why, they'll be collecting money to fight my civilized friends out there on the blockade, who want only to ruin our business and starve and burn Baltimore into oblivion.'"

"Rubbish! That isn't fair! That isn't why!"

"No? I've finally admitted to myself that you've got to go to the ball, Brett, and look like you mean it, too. Simone realized that before I did. And you have to come to terms with the fact that if you insist on staying in Baltimore you must choose America over your precious England, at least during the war. That's the only way you—and *our* business, which *you're* continually compromising with these stubborn stands—are going to come through this mess!''

She jerked one arm up so fast, she spilled water and tumbled camellias down her skirt. ''I suppose that if situations were reversed and we shared this shipping business in England,'' she exploded, ''you'd turn pro-British then!''

''Blue blazes, either that, or get the hell back to my own country!'' He spun away, abandoning her to her own inner turmoil.

For once, she knew he was right. At last she had no desire to lecture him for his cursing or strike out at him for her own confusion. When she just stood silent, stonelike, his strides slowed. He stopped and turned back.

''You're right, of course,'' she said, her words so quiet the evening wind almost tugged them away. ''But the old self dies hard—just as my doing things the servants could do,'' she added, and lifted the boots and bowl in a helpless gesture.

His first impulse at her honest capitulation was to run back and embrace her. How could she be so strong, yet so vulnerable? She looked boldly feminine and alluring to him in that moment—a staggering revelation. But he swallowed hard and forced himself to hold his ground. ''Then when I take you to the ball, Your Majesty,'' he said slowly, ''please wear the flowers but not the boots.''

He felt her smile, though the dusk hid it at this distance. Once again he steeled himself not to hurry back to her. ''But I don't dance, Alex. Good Presbyterians never do,'' she protested, before she realized she had echoed exactly her mother's bitter words to her so many times so long ago.

She heard his low chuckle. ''Then I hope to hell I can find a bad Presbyterian somewhere to escort to the ball,'' came his lilting words to her across the stretch of lawn. For once she only chuckled, reveling in the way he teased her.

''My, my, but that's a lovely ball gown,'' Henrietta Featherstone observed as she popped her silvered head into the bedroom while the maid, Glenda, finished hooking Brett up the back. "It's a bit wispy, but it almost reminds me of the old days, when men were men and women were women."

In the four days Brett had lived with Henny Featherstone, she'd learned that the old lady had opinions on everything, most of which began with "In the old days" or "When I was younger." The plump, snappy-eyed, seventy-nine-year-old woman was pleasant and sprightly, but she seemed to live almost entirely in a past peopled with her husband and two sons, who'd died in the Battle for Long Island under General Washington. She had a daughter, Marilee, who was married to a barrister and lived in the nation's young capital, Washington. "How dared they build that place on wretched swampland, when it's named for such a man as General Washington!" Henny opined. "Now *there* was a man, just like my Thomas!" Henny knew every minuscule detail about events forty years before, when the British were first the enemy. And she'd told Brett in no uncertain terms that she'd accepted an Englishwoman as her houseguest only when "young Alex" had explained clearly that he was hoping Brett could be taught to change her ways.

Brett nodded to Henny, only half listening. She stooped for Glenda to lift over her coiffure the double strand of lustrous pearls Simone had left her from her own collection of jewelry, admiring the way they matched the white gauze gown with its rich silk appliqué. Seashell pink puffed sleeves echoed the pink ruffles at the daringly low-cut, square neckline and double scalloped hem of the skirt. She had laced her pink silk slippers tightly over white silk hose, though she had no intention of dancing this evening. Slowly she tugged her elbow-length white kid gloves up her bare arms, then stooped again to stare in the mirror at the white camellia blossoms Glenda had scattered through her upswept hair. She had used to hate mirrors, but tonight she was fascinated.

"And what do you see?" Henny Featherstone prompted as she perched on the edge of Brett's bed. "I see a beautiful British woman ready to make peace with Baltimore."

Brett turned to study the wrinkled face framed by the white

lace butterfly cap. Henny dressed in old colonial fashions; Simone would have had a frenzy dressing her *à la mode*! Besides full, heavy skirts and frilly trim everywhere, Henny wore her silver hair puffed up under a black velvet bow, with a single long curl down to her collar in back. But Brett wondered if she really lived in the past or if that was mere pretense so as not to have to face things today without her husband and two sons. "You know, Henny, I'd like to make peace with Baltimore," Brett admitted, "but I just don't know if Baltimore—"

Alex's voice below in the hall prevented Brett from completing her thought, although at Henny's insistence she kept him waiting a moment before descending the staircase. She went down slowly, head up, but halted two steps from the bottom. She saw his eyes widen. His nostrils flared. He looked incredulous. She stared back, defiant and nervous. He looked so elegant in gray satin breeches and richly embroidered waistcoat. His ivory silk cravat was ornately tied, his garments immaculate, and his hair brushed slightly forward at his temples and forehead to make him look—well, the part of a rugged dandy.

"Just like the young set to be tongue-tied," Henny groused. "Alex, did you never learn the proprieties of greeting a lady?"

They exchanged formal pleasantries to appease the hovering old woman. Brett accepted her fringed silk shawl from the maid. Despite that and the warm night, gooseflesh skimmed her skin when he tucked her gloved hand under his arm next to his warm ribs to escort her out.

He turned back at the door, his tall, curly beaver hat in his free hand. "I wish you had decided to come along with us instead of just sending your generous contribution," Alex told Henny.

Evidently, Brett noted, Henny could live in the present well enough when it suited her and Alex.

"Stuff and nonsense. There's nothing happens in this town anymore worth my going out. Now if the enemy comes our way again, I'll consider it. I've still got Thomas and my boys' muskets upstairs, primed and set to go!" She waved goodbye to them from the door. "I don't suppose they still do the minuet to Mozart," she was chattering as they went down the steps and Alex helped Brett up into the curricle. "I danced with my Thomas till all hours in the old days—"

"I certainly hope Henny won't take those old muskets she has upstairs and shoot me as the enemy by mistake," Brett observed as she gathered her wispy skirt closer to give him room on the leather seat. "I'd be devastated to miss all the patriotic lectures you told her to harangue me with."

Smiling smugly, he sniffed her delicious smell, all freshness and scented powder and the spicy odor of the camellias in her hair. Funny, but he'd never paid much heed to smells until lately. And she'd touched some sort of darkener to her eyelashes and lip rouge to her shapely mouth to make it look luscious enough to kiss. "You remembered the camellias and aren't wearing boots," was all he said, but his tone and eyes caressed her.

She knew he still examined her minutely. She gathered her silk shawl slightly higher. She had actually felt his breath on her bare skin there when he had turned her way and spoken those warm words so close.

When he spoke again, she'd almost forgotten the last thing she'd said. "No more lectures tonight from Henny or me. I'm trusting you, Brett. And business partner or not, you look absolutely beautiful."

She turned to meet his eyes and almost tilted into him in gratitude and longing. Her face heated and she blessed the dusky carriage. No one had ever told her that before, not Great-uncle Charles, not even her only suitor, Captain Dalton Kelsey. But, then, it had never occurred to her that anyone should; she had never thought of herself as beautiful. She wanted to believe Alex, now, but knew he must mean that the gown was beautiful, a compliment to Simone's taste. Brett yearned to be beautiful herself, for him, to reach out to him some way they had never yet managed without conflict and pride. As his equal partner, yes, but not only for Sanborn and Son. She turned away for a moment to stare out into the darkness sweeping by. She shot a quick prayer heavenward and willed that, just for this night, she should be beautiful.

Mount Clare Mansion, a Georgian-style plantation home set on a stretch of green west of town, blazed with lights and laughter. Crystal chandeliers dripped rainbow prisms. Polished silver, Waterford glass and the women's jewels reflected myriad wall candelabra like mirrors. The heady smell of the tall boxwood hedges, tulip trees and dogwood wafted inside through half-open windows. Conversations buzzed and swelled, and couples pirouetted on the dance floor to waltz music, the women's pastel skirts like blossoms spiraling on a polished wooden pond.

Alex and Brett stepped into the crowded room after greeting their host, and were immediately hailed enthusiastically by Captain Joshua Windsor. "Alex and Miss Benton, good evening." Brett was glad to see a familiar face; Captain Windsor often came in to the firm to see Alex. "My Sally's been dying to meet your new partner, Alex."

Alex hugged the perky, red-haired Sally Windsor and introduced her to Brett. Sally, Captain Windsor boasted proudly, though the fact was already obvious, was going to bear their seventh child this autumn.

"These two ruffians," the mint-green-gowned Sally confided to Brett with a pert nod at the men, "have entirely too much in common since the *Free Spirit*'s being built. I take it, Miss Benton, you've seen the wood-and-brass object of their affections at the shipyard, even if I haven't."

"Please call me 'Brett.' Yes, I've seen her—briefly," Brett admitted with a toss of her ornately coiffed head that was meant for Alex. "She's sleek and stunning. I'd be jealous if I were you, Mrs. Windsor."

"Especially since I'm rather beginning to resemble a barn!" the woman joked. Then she added, "And call me 'Sally,' please do, as Alex and Josh are such firm friends."

Brett returned the woman's smile warmly and began to relax. Here was a native Baltimorean who knew she was British and yet was kind and friendly. Perhaps tonight wouldn't be so bad, after all.

"Actually," Alex offered, "I was planning for Brett to go through the shipyard more thoroughly later this week. Since Josh will be the *Free Spirit*'s captain, you're more than welcome to come along, Sally."

Brett bit back her surprise behind a taut smile. Yes, she thought, as the four of them headed over to the buffet table together, perhaps this evening would be delightful, after all, if she just gave these people a chance.

Brett sat later with Sally on a satin settee in a corner of the cream-and-canary ballroom while Alex fetched more wine punch and Josh talked with another ship's captain. Sally said she hadn't the breath in her to dance at this point, and Brett was grateful to have an excuse to sit out with someone. It seemed that simply everyone else was dancing. Her slippered foot tapped in time to the music. She studied the smooth, circular movement of the waltz as graceful couples whirled by, then came around again to make her slightly dizzy. Suddenly she realized that two women were blocking her view. She stared up at what had to be mother and daughter, the similarity was so great. But one woman's skin was shrunken, mottled and webbed with wrinkles, while the younger mirror of those same features was stunning. The daughter's shiny ebony hair framed a porcelain-china face with pouted lips. The sumptuous apricot India-silk ball gown complemented her coloring beautifully.

"Brett," Sally Windsor said, her voice tinged with warning, "since they do not seem inclined to introduce themselves, may I present Mrs. Myra Cantrell and her daughter, Claudine. The Cantrells are the largest sugar importers in Maryland."

"I've heard about you," the shapely Claudine said to Brett, twisting her long silk gloves, which she had removed, as if they were someone's neck.

"Then I'm at a disadvantage, Miss Cantrell," Brett retorted, "as I haven't heard of you."

"Just like Alex to say nothing, Mama," Claudine insisted to her mother with a toss of topaz earbobs.

"Really," Mrs. Cantrell observed to herself as much as anyone, "having a Brit here tonight is quite an insult to the Signer's home."

"The Signer?" Brett asked.

Mrs. Cantrell sniffed in blatant disdain. "Your host tonight is John Carroll, whose father was one of the revered signers of the Declaration of Independence, Miss Benton. Independence from Britain!"

"What a double honor to be here then and to meet you and your daughter the very same night!" Brett retorted with the controlled expression she had mastered when Alex baited her. "You see, Mrs. Cantrell, I, too, believe in America's independence, especially economically, so that our Sanborn ships can trade freely. I hope you'll explain that to any others you may have cause to tell about me."

"Now you look here!" Claudine Cantrell cut in with a stamp of her silk-slippered foot. "You're ruining Alex's firm, his chances to get new business here in town."

"Hello, Mrs. Cantrell. Claudine," Alex interrupted as he returned to hand Brett and Sally their cut glass cups of wine punch. "We are *all* here tonight to have a good time and raise what money we can for the cause. Don't you agree?" he asked the Cantrell women with such fervent amiability that Brett could tell he'd guessed the tenor of the previous conversation.

Claudine's stiff face suddenly transformed to smiles and blushes. She darted a pink tip of tongue between vermillion lips. "A wonderful suggestion! Alex, you naughty thing, I've been looking all over for you! We haven't danced yet and I wanted to tell you I'm number four in the bidding for the cotillion reel later."

"Number four, I'll remember. But right now, if you will excuse me, ladies, I came over to ask my partner, Miss Benton, to dance. Shall we, Brett?" he inquired, and offered her his arm.

Brett sat frozen a moment as Sally removed her cup from

her unresisting fingers in an effort to urge her on. He knew she didn't dance, didn't know the first thing about waltzing, Brett seethed with inward panic. But the offer had crumbled Miss Cantrell's smug face, and for that small victory, she stood up to join him. "Excuse us, please. So interesting getting to know you better," she threw airily over her shoulder at the glowering mother-daughter duo, and let him escort her to the floor.

"Thank you for saving me, but let's just step out of the dancers' way somewhere, Alex."

"You hardly needed saving back there, but stepping out's a tempting offer I'll take you up on later. Right now, we're going to waltz. Come on, Brett, 'your devoted servant wants to sport a toe!'" he teased in his best imitation of the Bond Street British dandies.

"Alex, I—" she got out, before he stepped closer to her and lifted her right hand in his left. His right arm rested firmly on the back of her waist.

"I've found you to be an exceptionally fast learner," he went on when she didn't budge, "and I can't tell you how that pleases me for future endeavors."

"Compliments abound tonight," she said dryly. "Alex, I just can't dance."

"Can't or won't, my pious, proper little Presbyterian. One-two-three. One-two-three. Come on," he prompted, and nodded at their feet while he stepped off a little triangle. Stiffly she let him pull her along. It was not so bad, until he started to turn them, to dip and glide.

He watched her frown in concentration, almost as if she were in pain at first. But then her tense brow unfurled as her svelte body relaxed in his arms. "Beautiful," he told her as she smoothly matched his steps. "And certainly more original than Claudine. Besides, I prefer to be the one asking ladies to dance and not vice versa."

"Who is she to you?" Brett ventured, despite the fact it threw her one-two-threes off.

"Someone her mother thinks I should marry," he answered so forthrightly that Brett almost missed another step. "But I keep thinking she'll look like her mother in a year or two. She already sounds like her. Actually, I favor women who think for themselves, though that does have obvious drawbacks.''

But she didn't rise to that bait. She was dancing, waltzing, flowing to the sweep of the music as he held her in his arms. The room revolved around them; other couples swept by. It stunned her to know it was the most wonderful, exhilarating thing she'd ever done next to sailing. A broad smile transformed her entire face, and she threw back her head slightly as they went around again. To think that she'd missed it all these years, she mourned. She was devastated when the music stopped too soon.

"What is it?" she asked Alex as people pressed toward the dais, where the musicians sat.

"The cotillion reel bidding," he told her, and took her hand to tug her farther toward the front. "More money for the cause."

"The cause of buying powder and cannonballs?" she couldn't help asking tartly.

"The cause of rebuilding Tidewater homes that British troops have burned," he told her, and she argued no more.

But she was horrified when she realized what he intended. Along the front of the satin-swagged dais, unmarried women were lining up with shy smiles and coquettish looks, waiting to be bid on for partners. "Brett, I won't insist, but I thought it would be a good way for us to make a statement to this town," he whispered in the crush of people near the front.

"How dare you just haul me up here before you tell me!" she mouthed at him. "Just when I started to trust you!"

"Think about it. And I promise I'll buy you so you don't have to learn the reel from anyone but your waltz teacher."

"Buy me!" she protested. "You always were adept at crude talk, not to mention deeds!" She glared at him as the bidding began. She had no intention of putting herself on display like that simpering Claudine Cantrell up there. Besides, the women on the dais were so young—in their early twenties, most of them—and true-blue Baltimoreans. Rubbish, they didn't have a conscience that demanded loyalty to a father and uncle's beloved Royal Navy!

But the matter was soon taken out of her hands. The auctioneer was Quinby Marsh, the thick-necked bully who had scolded her at the Fountain Inn luncheon. Just after he sent a furious Claudine off with some skinny boy after she'd glared pointedly at Alex during her bidding, Marsh spotted Brett in the crowd.

"And next," he bellowed, "we all have us a real special treat. One of the enemy has come to live among us, and we can only hope she's learned the error of her previous ways. Sanborn and Son's new partner, London's own Miss Brett Benton!"

Brett stood rooted next to Alex on the crowded floor. Some hissed or booed. Necks craned; frowns accused. Alex didn't move, but she felt his gaze hot on her. That turned her shock to determination. She moved so quickly to lift her skirt and hurry up the two steps to the dais that Alex's assisting hand on her elbow came almost too late. She turned and looked out over the sea of excited Baltimoreans with a shaky, little smile. They hushed at last, and she realized that they expected her to speak!

"As a member of Sanborn's, I'm proud to be here tonight to be able to contribute to Baltimore's effort to end this war," she began. Her voice rang out clear and sure. "None of us wants this war. And I'm pleased to have this moment to tell you I hope everyone's ships get safely through every blockade until things can be settled. Sanborn's and all American ships must be completely free to sail God's beautiful seas again!"

A few cheers, from Alex loudest of all. "Hey!" someone yelled. "Just don't you tell a British spy nothing, lady, even if he asks!"

The bidding soon covered up whatever protests the crowd might have had. Brett could tell she had temporarily bested Quinby Marsh. Claudine Cantrell and her prune-faced mother looked daggers at her from across the room. And Alex kept loudly topping the bids shouted out by people who wanted to show they could use an enemy to fight the enemy. Brett stood, head high, trembling slightly, wondering what Simone would say if she could see her now. She knew well enough what her parents would have said, or the church people at the orphanage, or Uncle Charles, or Dalton Kelsey, if they could see their plain, sharp-spoken Brett being haggled over like a piece of goods on Petticoat Lane. She heaved a sigh of relief when Alex won at last for the astounding bid of two hundred twenty dollars!

"Sanborn's is behind Baltimore in every way!" he shouted to the crowd when he stepped forward to claim her hand. "And you're all invited to our clipper launching in two weeks. We'll give the Cochrans and the Rosses and the Kelseys of the world a run for their money in their precious blockade then!"

Everyone cheered as he tugged her off the dais and out of the crowd. She felt stunned by the rush of events, by his shouting Dalton's name to the crowd like that. They'd lynch her sure as tomorrow's dawn if they knew she had been proposed to by one of the men commanding the hated British blockade and that she hadn't actually, formally, refused yet. Alex walked her clear outside to the back lawn. The cool, sweet air of the country calmed her.

"I thought we'd better learn the reel out here first," he told her. "Can't see spending that sort of money for a dance partner, or any other kind of partner, who has to be taught everything."

She didn't respond to that as he steered her farther along the brick path into the parterred garden. The house lights faded; there was only silvered moonlight to show the way. "Alex, they'll think for certain we've run off to inform the British if we don't go back inside," she remonstrated gently.

He laughed. "I'm only here to inform the British I'm proud of her tonight. And for this—"

He raised a loosely balled fist to lift her chin. The warm backs of his fingers caressed her throat. He lowered his mouth toward her so slowly she knew he was giving her every opportunity to protest and escape. But she wanted none. She wanted his kiss, his touch. Her rattled thoughts slowed, though her pulse raced. She parted her lips slightly as their mouths met.

His fingers slid up and down her bare, arched throat, chin to pearls, as the kiss deepened. She lifted gloved hands to his big shoulders to steady the swaying world. He took a step closer, and she welcomed him by leaning gently against him. His hands dropped to rest lightly but firmly on her waist through the wispy gown. Their tongues played together; their breaths entwined; their body heat mingled. Finally he lifted his head, only to brush his lips against the corkscrew curl on her temple. "Better British and American relations," he murmured. "As you said inside, they're badly needed."

She astounded herself by laughing musically. She felt a bit giddy from the wine punch or the dancing or the delicious kiss. "Teach me the cotillion reel," she asked, pouting, lowering her hands to grasp his gray velvet lapels gently. There was a new woman in her body, she marveled—she felt partly afraid of her desires and power, but most of all she felt wonder.

"I'm reeling over you," he whispered. "Let's just do this again." He had bent to kiss her eager lips, when they heard shouts from the house. They stood apart, moved out of the shadow of the clipped hedges and squinted back at the mansion, ablaze with light. "Something's happened," he said, and took her hand. "Come on."

She held her skirts with her other hand as they hurried up the brick path. They could see people gesturing inside, fists raised in anger or protest. "Stay here," he ordered at the door to the back hall.

"No, I want to know!" she insisted, and hurried right behind him.

Josh Windsor saw them under the carved arch to the ballroom and strode toward them. "Word just came one of the Dills schooners got in," he told Alex. "The captain says he was in a pitched battle with a British man-of-war called the *Raven's Wing*, Commander Kelsey's ship."

Alex ignored Brett's gasp. "And?" he demanded.

"Kelsey scuttled Marsh's brig, *Defiant*, and your own *Pamela Mary* after stripping everything off them."

"Damn that bloody bastard!" Alex cracked out. "It almost seems as if someone in town is feeding the greedy Brits information. They seem to have known every time a loaded ship was due back lately!" His big fist cracked into the wall. "Blue blazes, we got too cocksure when every ship came through last week!"

"I wouldn't go back in with Miss Benton right now," Josh warned, and urged Alex and Brett back out into the hall. "You know how crazy they get when dollars go down into the soup. They're hot for British blood."

Both men stared at Brett. "I'm sorry, Alex," was all she could think to say.

He just stared at her, astounded, as his mind raced. He'd finally begun to trust her, even to want her as a man wants a woman, when this happened. Damn her! She'd known that both those ships had been due back now—she'd heard it at the shipper's luncheon that day he'd taken her to the Fountain Inn! But many others had heard it, too. He desperately needed to make sure of her. Perhaps he could tell her something only she would know, then watch to see whether the information got back to the Brits somehow. Damn the woman! Why couldn't he keep his feelings straight about her from one moment to the next?

Brett's heart fell as Alex glared straight at her. Had he really just bid two hundred twenty dollars for the chance to dance with her? Had he really danced with her and kissed her in the garden in the moonlight? Suddenly it all seemed the merest fantasy. She looked down at her flowing pink-and-white gown. She was no fairy-tale princess, even if for a few hours she had believed she was. She was just the tall, thin, gawky girl her mother had always called her. She tried to blink hot tears back from her eyes as Alex seized her hand and hurried her down the long, glittering hallway and out the waiting door.

Part II

"What is that which the breeze
  o'er the towering steep,
As it fitfully blows,
  half conceals, half discloses?"

—Francis Scott Key
"The Star-Spangled Banner"

Seven

By daylight the Sanborn shipyard at Fell's Point was not as awesome to Brett, yet it was even more exciting. Portions of the large, flat roof were hooked open to let in light and air. The horsepowered derricks that had hoisted the massive keel timbers in place stood idle now, but everything else moved and clanked in the rush to complete the vessel. Big ovens hissed and rumbled as they steamed the last planks to fit the contours of the hull. Yard hands bent noisily to their tasks everywhere as Alex and Captain Joshua Windsor began Brett and Sally's tour of the *Free Spirit* at the stern.

"Even without masts and sails, you're so right, Brett, she *is* a beauty," Sally said. She punched her husband playfully on his arm. "I thought perhaps Joshua had exaggerated her charms, though I suppose there's a thing or two she can't do for a full-blooded man."

Alex and Josh laughed, while Brett avoided Alex's narrow-eyed perusal. In the three days since the dance at Mount Clare they had returned to their old antagonism toward each other. She knew he was seething over the loss of another huge chunk of Sanborn's fortune and America's pride when Dalton Kelsey's war frigate *Raven's Wing* stripped the *Pamela Mary* and sent her to the bottom of Chesapeake Bay. But Brett knew she was innocent of that no matter what these spy-suspicious Baltimoreans feared, and she didn't intend to continually beg

Alex to trust her. But at least he'd still brought her here today as promised.

Alex pointed out the huge temporary wooden brace that would keep the rudder from breaking off at the launch next week. Stern first, the clipper ship would slide down her loosened wooden cradle blocks into Fell's Point Harbor to be towed a short distance to a wharf nearby. There she would be fitted with two masts, miles of rigging and finally her canvas sails. As they walked fore, they stopped to watch men completing the only part of the sleek wooden hull not ready for that rush of water at the launch.

"The men flattening the planking snugly to the curve of the hull are called dubbers," Alex told Brett and Sally. "Those with the big augers for drilling holes are borers. Then the mallet men come along and pound these wooden treenails in to hold the planking to the curve. Brett," he said, and reached for her elbow, "I've got something for you here. Jacob," he called to the tall Negro leaning into his drill, "come here a minute, will you?" He turned back to her as the man strode over. "Brett, you recognize Molly and Jessie's son from the house, don't you? He usually oversees the supply room here, but in the push to finish, he's pitching in, too."

She did indeed remember the man whose clothing she had borrowed from old Molly the night she and Giles Cutler had sneaked in here. At Alex's request, Jacob explained how he used his auger, then he extended it, handle first, to Brett. The drill was over two feet long, with a smooth wooden handle for rotating the big bit into the planks.

"Alex," she said, hoping her voice sounded light, "I said I wanted to learn the business from the ground up, but I didn't quite mean building Sanborn vessels, too."

"Tradition," Alex explained. "Baltimore has traditions for launches and for building the fleet. Before the ship hits the water, the designers and owners all do at least some small task to help build her. Since the yard hands are caulking with oakum and tar up on deck and you're hardly dressed for that, I thought, as a Sanborn partner, you'd best take a turn with a drill."

She was so pleased she could not help but bathe him with a radiant smile, which he returned with a big, boyish grin. Shipyard sounds seemed to hush for her. The others standing here, the weight of the big auger Jacob placed in her hands—nothing seemed real but Alex smiling, his sky-blue eyes caressing her. Then Sally's skirt brushed hers as the other woman shifted from one foot to the other. Josh Windsor cleared his throat. Dazedly Brett turned away and let Jacob help her drill one hole, then did another by herself, driving the bit deep into the pine planking.

She frowned in intensity at her efforts, but inside she was rejoicing. She felt connected to this big ship now. It was more than partly hers; it was a part of her. Alex had at last offered her freely a part of Sanborn and Son, something vast and beautiful they shared. And it was as if she drilled into her own mind and heart to know she could care so deeply for him, too.

"All right now, ma'am, if you'll step back." Jacob's voice interrupted her musings. "We'll have Clem here pound in the treenails to hold it."

Alex smiled down at her again as the stocky mallet man importantly drove long wooden pegs in the two holes, and his voice came so quiet only she could hear. "Remind me never to take you on when you have one of those sharp things in your clever little hands," he teased with a nod at the big metal drill.

She smiled at him as Jacob retrieved the drill, and the crowd applauded and cheered wildly. The men went back to their jobs, and the four of them climbed the temporary gangplank up to the deck. Brett amazed herself again. She felt as warm and close to Alex now as she had felt cold and aloof toward him just a few moments earlier. Being near him, trying to understand him, she decided, was somehow like steering such a ship through crashing breakers in a raging storm.

Amid the strange "boink, boink" sound of the hawsing beetle that drove the strips of oakum and tar between the boards to seal the deck, they chatted and strolled forward. Sally and Brett had to lift their skirts, and everyone watched where he stepped to avoid the splatters of tar, which would be later sanded off with holystone. Near the prow, Josh hung back a minute to help the plump and pregnant Sally.

Brett and Alex watched companionably as carpenters rushed belowdecks to complete the captain's cabin. The biting smells of tar, paint and wood shavings mingled with the sweep of fresh Tidewater air and sun pouring through the roof windows overhead. Brett blinked back happy tears as she marveled at the way men and material meshed to make this great vessel. She couldn't wait for the launching, and she couldn't wait to stand at Alex's side among cheering Americans when they heard the *Free Spirit* had slipped the British blockade again and again.

"Brett," Alex said, "one more surprise. I hope you like it." At the very prow of the ship, he pointed outward.

Brett stared. She gasped. Sally and Josh came up behind them, and she heard Sally gasp, too. The painted figurehead of the woman was now mounted on the prow. Her white garments still flowed back from her shapely body; her hair still streamed as she stared wide-eyed but unafraid into her future. Her full, lush breasts were still bare and pointed and rose tipped. Only now her eyes had been painted soft gray and her hair was a rich chestnut hue with both gold and garnet highlights!

"Alex!" Brett cried. "How could you!"

Her hands shot to her hips as she spun to face him. Behind him Sally fanned herself with a gloved hand and gawked. Josh was all too obviously trying to stifle a grin.

Alex had the audacity to actually look surprised at her fury. "But I knew the other way made you feel uncomfortable—" he began.

"At least 'the other way,' it told the truth! Flaunt your half-naked mistress Simone for all the town to see, if you must, but leave me out of such innuendos! No wonder all the yard hands are smirking at me today!" She started away from them, back across the perilous, tar-speckled deck. In her hurry, she paid no attention to where she stepped, despite squawks of protests from the workers. Alex tore after her.

She was partway down the gangplank, when he pulled her around to face him and seized her by both upper arms.

"There's just no pleasing you, is there!" he thundered.

She tried to break his hold on her, but his grip wouldn't budge. "Rubbish! Other than Henny, Sally Windsor's practically the only friend I have in this wretched town, and she's back there appalled by what that naked woman tells the world!"

"It only tells the world you're a part of this venture, too! Isn't that what you've wanted? Blue blazes, my sister's likeness was on the *Pamela Mary*. Before your friends out there sunk her."

"But was your sister's likeness half-naked?" she demanded. She knew she was ranting like a fish vendor and people were staring, but she was beyond caring. "Was she?"

"No. But it's just the way the carver interpreted the concept for this ship. Everything about the *Free Spirit* evokes freedom, and now you're ruining it all!"

"*I'm* ruining it all," she challenged, her voice dripping sarcasm. She pulled away from him when he released his grip. "It's lovely the wood-carver interpreted it that way, but just think how the Baltimoreans who already detest me will interpret it, Alex!" She strode huffily to the bottom of the gangplank, then turned back to glare up at him.

"I only hope we can afford the paint to put her back the way she was," she said bitterly. "Simone's the free spirit— she deserves the honor."

"It stays this way on *my* ship," he ground out, his face and voice furious.

"Then please inform your friends the Windsors that I'm sorry for that if you're not. And now I'm taking the Sanborn curricle back to town, as I have a great deal to do at the firm I keep pretending I have some say in."

He charged down the plank a few steps after her. "Do that. Just stay away from here and do something to earn your keep!" he shouted, and threw his hands up to dismiss her in utter disgust.

"*You're* the one who sorely needs a keeper!" she managed

lamely for lack of a better insult. Her eyes narrowed to slits as she stormed out amid the hubbub of workers around the great ship.

Rubbish, she vowed, she was through caring about Alex Sanborn. They were worse off than that first day she'd arrived. Only she hadn't in her wildest nightmares of Americans expected such a stiff-necked, bullheaded, crude, caddish, selfish, doltish, brutish, Yankee rotter! She had to get away and stay away from a man like that! When she spotted the one-horse curricle at the side of the building, she clambered up and set off by herself at a quick clip.

In her frustration and anger, she kept the horse at a trot up Fall's Avenue to Market Place. There the innocuous bustle of shoppers and vendors at the crowded Marsh Market calmed her. It would be better if she didn't rush back to the firm like this to have Giles or Mason pry out of her what had happened. The entire town would be gossiping about it soon enough. At least she had moved out of that vile man's house. If Henny Featherstone hadn't come down with chills and fever, she would move clear to the other side of town to get away from him. She slowed the horse to a walk as her eyes took in the busy stalls, open air tables and shops. Finally she climbed down and left the curricle among the others at the long iron public hitching rail.

She strolled along as her thoughts slowed, and decided to buy something for Henny to lift the old woman's spirits. Something that would remind her of her beloved past so she would accept that she had to take better care of herself in the painful present.

The prices hawkers shouted were exorbitant. Rampant inflation was another terrible result of the British blockade. A soothing tea, that was it, Brett thought as she read a sign that proclaimed Fine Teas and Herbs, Best Prices. She'd buy Henny some chamomile to perk her up and ward off that fever.

Inside the fragrant little shop, she waited while an angular-faced woman with a fat black mammy behind her had her tea weighed out. The woman seized the little package from the shopkeeper and thrust it, without looking, at the turbaned slave. After Brett had placed her order, the woman still stood there. It took Brett a moment to realize the stranger was actually addressing her. "The likes of you are to blame for these soaring prices, that's sure."

"I beg your pardon," Brett said nervously as several other people stepped into the store, including two men. "And do I know you?"

"I know you!" The woman sniffed with disdain and glared down her long, pinched nose. "Quinby says you're rotten British to the core, even if you wormed your way into Sanborn's."

There was only one Quinby whom Brett knew, that oaf Quinby Marsh, whose vessel Dalton Kelsey had sunk with Sanborn's *Pamela Mary*. "Mrs. Marsh, if that's who you are, I regret the prices, but I'm hardly running the blockade. I think that's unfair as you and—"

"Horse dung!" one man who'd just entered shouted. He hardly looked as if he'd have the money for one teaspoon of tea, Brett thought. Quickly she paid the half-eagle coin for her quarter-pound of chamomile.

"Step aside, please," she said, and nearly had to elbow her way to the door. Just outside a little crowd had gathered.

"See, that's her, the one what's a Brit spy," she heard someone shout.

Holding the small package of herbs to her, she edged back along the shops toward the curricle, which she'd left halfway across the square.

"You oughta be payin' for our tea, too, as half of it's in British hands and bellies!" a woman's voice shrilled behind her.

She turned to reply, but she was being followed by an increasing rabble. Someone dared to snatch her reticule, but she yanked it back.

"Somebody's got to pay, and pay dear!" another voice bellowed.

Brett quickened her steps, but several dirty-looking louts

were already leaning against her carriage as if waiting for her. Someone ripped her package away, and tea leaves floated to the ground.

"I heard she personally knows the Brits running the blockade!"

"The *Patriot* says the same bastard what sank the latest ship's just been promoted to commander, and we can barely afford to eat!" a familiar voice screamed.

Brett's frenzied gaze took in Mrs. Marsh again, shaking her fist nearly in her face. Dalton Kelsey, Brett thought, and felt anger at him for all this. The ambitious Dalton Kelsey had been promoted to commander for sinking ships she owned. This was his inflation! These demented people were his fault, not hers!

Cornered, Brett spun to face the crowd. She tried to stare them down, to calm them with an upraised palm. "Please listen to me. Sanborn's lost a ship last week, too. Mr. Sanborn and I know how it feels—"

"This ain't against Alex, lady," some burly man yelled. "You're the one came pushin' in here, forcin' him to give up half his daddy's hard-won Baltimore business! I say, let's get us some tar and feathers and send her out to the fleet to show 'em what we think a English spies, eh?"

Something whapped against her hip and slid down her mint-green muslin skirt. A fish! Another followed, then a handful of soft strawberries splattered across her gown. She tried to push the men aside to climb into the curricle, but they shoved her back. The faces in the crowd jumped and darted as fists bounced aloft and voices roared. People threw garbage and shouted at her. One ruffian actually held her arms back while she kicked and screamed. Her bonnet fell off; her hair spilled loose to become a target for slime and ooze. It seemed to go on and on. They shouted terrible things about England—about her. Her captor's hands were hot and sweaty on her body; his touch revolted her more than the things they threw.

She should never have come to America, never believed she could win Alex over, she thought. She should have told

Dalton Kelsey she would wed him, stayed safe in England to bear his children. At least they would love her while he came over here to punish these animals! But it was Alex she needed, the panicked little voice in her head shrieked. She wanted Alex!

Sounds buzzed; sights blurred. Was she back at the shipyard? She was certain she smelled tar. She kept her eyes tightly shut and stood there so quietly she thought at last the abuse began to lessen. She wanted just to crawl away and hide. But it was one voice loud over the crowd that quieted them. She was dreaming that Alex's voice was shouting at her. She dared to slit her eyes open despite the gooey glaze of molasses someone had dumped over her head.

Alex Sanborn stood alone, unarmed, facing the crowd, which had backed off a few steps. The people closest to him held plump pillows and two men balanced a bucket of steaming tar between them on a pole. Brett's legs buckled as her captor released her at last; she crumpled hard into the puddle of sticky, smashed food at her feet.

"The whole brave city of Baltimore against one lone woman who has asked only for our hospitality, is that it?" Alex roared.

Despite her trembling, she looked up. Her eyes widened as he cracked a fist into one man's jaw and shoved another back on his bum. He actually cracked the men's heads together who held the tar bucket, then tipped it over on them. They screamed and thrashed as the crowd backed off farther.

He ran to her, almost slipping in the pool of muck, then lifted her and held her to him, despite the smear she made everywhere they touched. People between him and the curricle fell back as he shouldered through the crowd. He hoisted her into the carriage and climbed up beside her. She saw the messenger boy, Todd Miles, and the newspaper boy she had once given a coin to run toward them. Todd pulled Alex's big, sweating horse by its reins. She jerked her eyes away from the tumultuous scene and stared straight ahead.

"I never thought there'd come a day when I'd be ashamed to my very soul of Baltimore!" Alex shouted as he leaned down to unwrap the reins. People were breaking away from the fringes of the crowd to disappear into side streets. "I think it's a disgrace you give the London papers the right to call us 'Yankee Mobtown'!"

He turned to brace Brett with his free arm but saw she was sitting ramrod straight, uncrying, head up, knees together and grimy hands folded in her splattered lap, as if they were out for a Sunday afternoon drive in the country. He felt stunned. Blue blazes, what a hell of a bold and beautiful woman! Then he charged the horse directly through the remnants of the crowd as they scattered, yelping, out of his way.

He took her back to Sanborn's, since it was closest. He would let her bathe there and send Todd to Featherstone's for a change of clothes. "Anyway, Henny would attack them with her husband's old musket blazing if she saw you, and we don't need that," he said, hoping to break through that stoic, dazed look on Brett's face. He seemed to have a huge lump of anger and despair—and some deep awe of her he couldn't name—in his throat and stomach. He helped her in the door and directly to his office, while Mason shouted questions and Giles thundered down the steps from upstairs. Only when she inadvertently caught a glimpse of herself in the narrow mirror he kept behind the door, did she finally collapse into gasping sobs. He lifted her in his arms and sat down in his big desk chair with her cradled across his lap.

"Sweetheart, you were so brave, so brave," he muttered helplessly against her slick matted hair while she gasped for breath, shuddering against him. He held her even closer.

"Horrible. It was horrible," she said. She pressed her face to his big shoulder, letting him hold her, clinging to him. She moved closer to loop her arms around his neck.

"It's all right. You're safe with me now." Tears burned his eyes. He could have taken on this whole town of bastards with his bare hands for her at that moment. When he noticed both the astounded Mason and Giles Cutler peeking around the door, he told them only, "Get hot water and a tub from the warehouse. Lots of water for her hair!"

They knew that tone. They both darted away.

"Mother always said I was so homely, so plain," she muttered. "I never used to look in mirrors." Her face, half smothered against his muscled neck, smeared him brown and red there.

"Stop, stop, sweetheart, I'm so sorry," he crooned, and rocked her. He felt her stiffen in his arms; he sensed from the inner power she emanated that she was struggling for control. He watched with mingled relief and sadness as she sat up straight on his lap, then wriggled awkwardly off to gaze down at her ruined gown and flop her filthy hands helplessly against it.

"I'm sorry, too, about—this mess," she told him, her voice quiet and not her own. "And you mustn't call me that, Alex."

"What? My sweetheart? We'll see."

He stood. He took her gooey hands in his own as they studied each other openly. They exchanged sudden taut nods of recognition that were not for their ludicrous, ruined appearances. If it wasn't so awful that she'd destroyed his clothes as surely as hers now, she thought she almost might have laughed. His face looked as dirty as the little messenger boy's who'd been with him. "Todd Miles," she said suddenly. "Why was he there?"

"He and his brother saw what was happening and ran to Sanborn's to fetch me. Thank God, I was just getting back on my horse. A few more minutes and you might have been the most defiantly beautiful woman ever to be tarred and feathered."

But neither of them laughed at that. She meant to tell him he must not ever use endearments on her or say she was beautiful when it wasn't true. She wanted to say she would be eternally grateful for his rescue. He meant to make it all up to her by telling her he was wrong not to have trusted her at the firm. He wanted to share the launch celebration with her and tell her the well-guarded first voyage date for his beloved *Free Spirit*. But Mason Finch rapped on the door and carted in a big brass tub, so they only stood in awkward, aching silence.

Mason's shocked gaze went over her, then darted to Alex. "Curse Baltimore!" he said only, and stomped out, leaving the door ajar for the buckets of water to come.

Outside Alex's office door, Giles Cutler halted with a bolt of cotton in his arms that Brett could use to dry herself and her hair the Yankee bastards had ruined with their garbage. The boy Todd and his brother had spilled out the entire story to him. Now he had another reason to even the score with Sanborn's and this plaguey town. And, perhaps, after looking a shocking mess so that people gawked, horrified, Brett would have yet more sympathy for him. It infuriated him that it had been Alex Sanborn who had comforted her and not Giles Cutler. But he would have her in the end, and when he did, he would both break her to sobs and soothe them away until he was ready to begin with her again. He fumbled for his watch on its ribbon fob. Pity he had to run, because spying on them together, struggling with their passions, raised a wonderful, throbbing lust in him. It would make taking Brett and ruining Alex sweeter in the end, but he had to meet his man in a half hour.

He had lifted his hand to knock, when he heard those next astounding words from Alex to Brett on the other side of the half-opened door. "Brett, despite all that's happened today, I'm promising you'll be at my side for the launch and when we take the *Spirit* out for her maiden run. It's to be May 15. And you're the only one I'm telling that date to until the day before we sail."

She murmured something in return, but that hardly mattered to Giles Cutler. So easily the piece of information he most prized had fallen into his grasp! He dumped the bolt of cotton on Mason's desk, where he'd surely find it. Not even stopping to get his hat, he darted out the front door just as Mason marched men in the back, laden with buckets of water.

Impatiently Giles Cutler paced the steps of the red brick Zion Lutheran Church. No one was going in or out this late in the morning, but people bustled by. He'd hated the meetings in public places at first, but had become resigned to them. It was wiser than skulking off to some dingy alley, which might arouse suspicion. He never looked into the faces that drifted by. He never looked as if he expected a thing until his contact spoke.

"Pardon, but would you care for a Berkeley's toffee?" the clipped voice inquired.

Giles turned slowly toward the man. Both their faces registered surprise. The man was not Sparrow, his usual British contact. And obviously this new man was startled to see someone with half his face leathered by livid scars. Giles coughed into his handkerchief before replying, "Berkeley's is my very favorite."

"Then have some, as I've far too many." The man concluded the password exchange and offered him a small cloth sack of what he knew would be toffee wraps—some containing candy and some holding the beautiful, shiny, golden, eagle American coins the Brits no doubt took off captured Baltimore-based ships.

They strolled north together on residential Holliday Street. "You're not the usual toffee man," Giles observed.

The man wore an old-fashioned tricorn hat and a dark-blue coat that pulled at the seams around his barrel chest and bulky shoulders. He had sharp features and an aquiline nose; the full, soft lips seemed incongruous on the wily, almost cruel face. A black velvet eye patch, which was probably part of the disguise, gave him a distinctively piratical air. A very expensive signet ring, whose scrolled initials Giles could not read, glittered on the hand resting on a brass-headed cane. The man's limp wasn't very convincing, Giles told himself smugly. Yet he evoked an air of disdain and superiority that rattled Giles's usually aloof demeanor. And the man's one eye that he could see alarmed him—palest brown with no visible rim. From a little distance his eyeball seemed only the piercing dot of pupil and nothing else.

"I wanted to come myself, Flame," the man clipped out in what Giles assumed was an educated accent. "I'm just

Sparrow's superior, no one special," he added hastily. "You may call me 'Raven' and say straightaway what you have for us then."

"A little piece of information worth more than the usual bag of toffees, I'd say," Giles dared with a twist of his handkerchief.

The head pivoted sharply and the eye sliced down, then up him, before looking away. Who did this horrible, disfigured monkey of a man think he was to play games with him, Commander Dalton Kelsey groused silently. But, of course, the cheeky son of a bitch was their best Baltimore contact. Cutler could hardly know he was speaking with the man who had sent more Yank ships to the bottom than any other blockade captain. Nor did he know he stood in the presence of the man who had been third in command in destroying Bonaparte's fleet at Alexandria!

Besides, Kelsey mused, Sparrow had said this ogre worked at Sanborn's and that was the same firm Brett Benton had gone to claim half of. Dalton Kelsey wanted to get his hands on her as never before, now that both of them had more to offer—and to lose. He was approaching the pinnacle of power! One way or another, whatever it took, whomever he had to destroy, he'd be an admiral soon. All he had to do was capture, loot and torch this pompous, privateering city. And by damn, he'd make Brett Benton his captive if she refused to be his wife, and then let her try to defy him and what he wanted from her!

Kelsey tapped the bothersome cane he carried on the brick walk and darted a sideways glance at the turncoat Cutler. Perhaps he was a man after his own heart, despite his looks. After all, he obviously used deceit at his convenience to get a good bit of the wealth that was his today, and Kelsey could admire that.

"So, Flame, spit out this prize piece of information," Kelsey ordered. "By damn, I'll make it worth your while—and worth your life when we finally take this city and grind its so-called patriots into this red dirt!" he declared, and scuffed a square-toed boot at the ground.

"All right then, just so you remember, sir. Alex Sanborn, the one I told Sparrow heads up the privateer fleet that's so slippery, you know."

"Yes, yes. The one who's building that speedy clipper ship you've described. Well, man, go on!"

"Finally found out when she sails. And you could just be there waiting for her in the lower bay on May 15. I'm planning to be aboard her one way or the other to make sure she's yours. And I won't expect another plugged penny after that if I can just be there when you hang Sanborn and watch when you get ashore to burn everything he owns here. My nickname Flame—I took it for a reason, you see."

A man of revenge after his own heart, indeed, Kelsey thought. They shook hands on it, and when they started off again, Giles noted Raven had forgotten to limp. Even more carelessly, the man took out an enameled, gilded snuffbox with the initials D.K. clear as anything on the lid. Giles thrilled to think whom he was dealing with at last. That knowledge emboldened him more than anything else.

"And, sir—I mean Raven, there's a woman involved whom I'm interested in, too, and—"

The Englishman shouted a sharp laugh through a snuff-induced sneeze. "Isn't there always a woman causing trouble, my man?" Women were good in bed, but he had little use for them elsewhere. They were like spaniels, he thought—amusing, good for breeding or to warm a bed or be kicked out, depending on one's whim. "Women!" he muttered. "Got a few of the hot little bitches stashed in cozy ports here and there myself. If you help me to hang that rogue Sanborn you can name the woman you want, Flame, and I'll have her wrapped and ribboned naked for you, by damn!"

Giles chuckled low. But his blood ran cold when the man said suddenly, "I need to know one more thing. There is a Miss Brett Benton from London in Baltimore, who owns part of Sanborn's now, isn't there? I've made her acquaintance in London and just wondered."

Giles's wily brain darted, but he dared not lie. The least said the better, he decided. "That there is, Raven."

"Is she well then? Plain and pious as ever, I take it."

Giles swallowed hard and nodded, though he was sure neither term described Brett Benton anymore. At least these questions showed Dalton Kelsey hadn't put a watch on her or heard how the crowd had treated her this afternoon. Already he was wondering what use he could make of the knowledge that Brett once knew Commander Dalton Kelsey. Would that be enough to blackmail her if worse came to worse between them? He could hardly threaten to tell that bastard Sanborn, as it would tip his own hand that he consorted with the enemy. But he evidently was not expected to offer any more information here on Brett Benton.

"By damn, it's turned out to be a better day than I'd hoped," said Raven, and he clapped Giles on the shoulder. He knew now that he had the opportunity to get his hands on the very ship that would make his reputation and break the back of this Yankee dog town. He'd make an object lesson of patriot Alex Sanborn by stretching his neck. And eventually he'd get his hands on the whole of Baltimore, maybe the entire damned country, as soon as those extra troops arrived from Europe. What's more, he thought, though he said no more about Brett Benton, if she owned half of Sanborn's now, he would have to impound ships flying the Sanborn standard rather than scuttle them. He had no use for Brett's stiff, skinny body, but if he could coerce her into marriage, he'd get what her uncle had left her. And now that included an American shipyard, too!

"You know, my man, I suddenly find this Yankee dog hovel quite a lovely sight!" Commander of His Majesty's Royal Navy, Dalton Kelsey told the scar-faced man. They laughed delightedly together as they surveyed the enemy city of Baltimore, sprawled at their feet.

Eight

Whatever Baltimore thought of Brett Benton, they turned out in droves to see the *Free Spirit* launched on May 5, 1814. The docks and shoreline of Fell's Point Harbor were lined with cheering citizens as the big shipyard doors toward the water were opened. Brett stood on deck, braced against the wheelhouse to counteract the tilting slide of the great vessel. A skeleton crew, headed by proud Captain Joshua Windsor, scattered up and down the decks at various last-minute tasks to secure things. But Brett's eyes watched only Alex. He seemed to be everywhere, peering over the bulwarks, shouting to the men who were preparing to smash the blocks of wood supporting the keel. He had explained how the weight of the hull would be thrown onto the cradles. Piles of beams built up along the hull's underbelly would fall and roll on another greased layer of beams. And the ship's birth would end in the baptismal waters of the Patapsco River, which led to bay and sea.

"Ready, men?" Alex bellowed over the rail. He turned back and shot Brett a jubilant smile. "Hang on, everyone!" he yelled as he gave the go-ahead to yard hands below.

He joined Brett, shoulder to shoulder, pressed against the mahogany wheelhouse. Nothing happened at first. But her heart almost launched itself in sheer joy as he covered her hand with his where she pressed it against the wheelhouse wall. Waiting, they both gazed upward at the square of sky through the shipyard ceiling. At the flagpole on the stern and in both mastholes they had mounted huge American banners. The colorful fifteen stars and stripes lay limp right now, just waiting, as they were, for the rush of breeze.

Brett felt the blows echo far under their feet as the men loosed the keel blocks with a clatter. The ship seemed to sigh as she settled heavily into the slick trough.

"We're moving!" Alex shouted, and dashed a quick kiss on Brett's cheek.

Everyone on deck cheered wildly as the rumbling ride began. Faster, faster the stern plunged downward toward the water. Full sunlight slapped them as the *Free Spirit* left her dim wooden womb behind. Brett shrieked with excitement and delight at the plunge. Their own cries were echoed by the crowds waiting outside. How different it all was, Brett thought, from the horrible screams of that other crowd last week in Market Square. How badly she wanted to be one of them, not their hated enemy. She grasped Alex's hand harder as the star-spangled banner directly above their heads fluttered out to flap in the stiff wind.

"Brace yourself!" Alex shouted just before the huge stern hit, then the entire vessel settled with a jolt and rush into the sea she had been born to conquer.

Men ran everywhere, checking the rudder, peering over the sides, running down into the hold to check for leakage, waving to the crowds, motioning to the two small vessels that would tow them to the rigger's wharf just two docks down. Wine punch flowed freely with boasts and talk of the ship's great voyages to come. People congratulated Alex on his bold belief in America's future to risk so much for a venture in these perilous times.

Brett was totally swept away by excitement and pride. She laughed and vowed with the others that the *Spirit* would slice through the British blockade like a hot knife through butter. But she lifted her pewter mug a bit more soberly at the toast that Dalton Kelsey's mighty war frigate, *Raven's Wing*, be sent to the bottom of the sea by the *Spirit*'s six guns.

The high color drained from her cheeks. Her eyes caught Alex's as her smile faded. He shot her a look as if to ask if she was all right, but Josh Windsor pulled him over to the wheelhouse. Hastily Brett downed the last of her wine punch and turned away from the cavorting crew. She knew now that she had to tell Alex about Dalton Kelsey's part in her past. And she had to tell him soon, so he would be over his huff before the maiden voyage to Bermuda he had promised to take her on in ten days. He would be vexed, of course, but things had been so good between them since the crowd had attacked her. If she admitted everything to him, he could hardly accuse her of being sent over here to spy by Dalton Kelsey, or some such rubbish!

She stood at the prow as they tethered the *Spirit* to the wharf with ropes as thick as a man's arm. Here, beginning at first light tomorrow, the riggers would mount her masts and set her towering web of spars and schooner rigging. Brett leaned far out to stroke the figurehead as one might a pet dog. It had not been completely repainted, but its base had been recarved and touched up with more white so that the bare breasts were covered with flowing drapery. Having her own image looking forward into a new life, even as she did, was just one more thing that tied her to this wonderful, sleek ship.

"Brett!" Alex's voice slashed through her thoughts as he hurried up to take her hand again. "Over here for the last part of the launching! Tradition for owners, builders and crew."

The crew and foremen from the shipyard had already made a double circle on the midships deck. Eager as a boy, Alex tugged her into the middle with him and Captain Windsor. Her eyes nervously skimmed the circle for familiar faces. Mason Finch was here, but Giles Cutler had disappeared somewhere.

"All right, now I'm not insisting you do this, Miss Benton," Alex announced so all could hear, "but it's solid Baltimore tradition that the captain and owners splash themselves with a bucket of seawater." He saw she looked surprised, and grinned at his challenge to her. "No one knows where the custom came from, but it's good luck around here," he urged, his voice more quiet. He motioned toward three wooden buckets brim full of water, which were sitting on the deck now sanded to pristine white. "Never had a woman owner or captain in Baltimore—maybe the whole country," he declared loudly, "so you can start your own tradition and just watch if you want. Josh."

Captain Windsor picked up the first bucket with a cheer the circle of men echoed. He raised it straight up with stiff arms, then tipped the water directly over his head. With a wild whoop, Alex did the same. Both men stood dripping wet, laughing. Alex shook his big curly head like a dog. She knew everyone was looking at her now. Alex's clear blue eyes were alight with devilment. She hesitated. Did he think she wouldn't take his dare? What was the ruin of yet another good gown, hat and coiffure to her in this tumultuous town?

The bucket was heavier than she'd expected. The circle of men clapped and cheered her on. Her arms shook as she lofted the bucket. How warm and different their cries were from that other crowd's. Perhaps, someday, some way, she would be able to call this rabid, often cruel city her home. With a squeal of surprise at how cold the water was, she doused herself, plumed, straw-brimmed bonnet and all.

She sputtered and coughed while everyone cheered raucously. Alex hugged her, then Josh. Somehow, but for the nagging, fearful thought that she had to tell Alex about Dalton Kelsey, she had never in her life been so happy.

Two hours later Brett watched the rosy remnants of daylight shimmer in the western sky that etched the outlines of the docks. She sat comfortably, feet up on the cushioned transom seat under the wide stern windows in the captain's cabin. Her splattered gown was almost dry now but for the shoulders and bust, where she had taken most of the water; she'd removed her drenched hat and loosed her hair to dry better. After the festivities, the crew had gone about some tasks, but she knew by the lessening sounds that few were still aboard. Josh had bade her farewell when he went home. Now she sat wrapped in a blanket, waiting for Alex to take her back to Henny's. Strange, but she couldn't wait to see him again, however dangerous and hopeless such feelings were.

The new smell and look of this captain's cabin exhilarated her. Everything was neatly built in, from shelves for books to a sideboard for decanters to the narrow bed along one wall. Two large lamps were securely mounted on the center beam, though neither had been lit. If she had been born a man, she would have loved a life like this—if she were unmarried and had no family to leave the way Josh Windsor would soon leave Sally and the children behind again.

She sighed and looped her arms around her bent knees to rest her chin there. How she longed for a husband and family of her own. But would being married to the cold, self-important, imperious Dalton Kelsey root out this void she had for years tried to fill with duty and discipline? He was an ambitious Royal Navy man; he would desert her for the sea as her father had her mother. Would children only be enough? Her mother had turned more bitter each time her father left. After the things Brett knew Dalton had done against the Americans—even in the line of duty to England—she wasn't certain she could ever be his wife. He'd been so adamant about marriage after Uncle Charles had died. It had taken courage to insist she needed a year to decide. But even then, she had felt nothing for him to even wanly echo the powerful feelings she had for Alex Sanborn. And she had never been certain what Dalton Kelsey really felt for her, especially once she'd overheard him tell a friend once she was too unattractive and tart tongued ever to rouse passion in him.

She recognized Alex's footsteps on the companionway outside. He rapped sharply on the door. She didn't have time even to swing her feet down before he entered.

"No, sit. Sit. I'm exhausted," he admitted as he closed the door and strode quickly across the cabin toward her. "Mind if I sit, too?"

Before she even gave him permission, he plopped down very close, facing her. But such manners didn't even faze her anymore. He stretched out long, booted legs that blocked her in against the mahogany ledge and sweep of windows. She leaned comfortably back, but kept the blanket up around her damp shoulders and breasts like a big shawl.

"You were wonderful up there," he said. In the dimming light he shot her a smile that shivered through her with its sweetness and allure.

"Did you think I wouldn't do it?"

"I knew you would. I know you better than you think, Your Majesty," he said, using the old, teasing nickname.

"Don't bet this ship on it, Alexander the Great," she responded lightly. But she felt the little warning flutter of butterflies low in her belly. She knew she had to tell him about Dalton, yet she abhorred ruining this intimate mood they shared. She felt absolutely aglow in the warmth of his attentions, but she knew what could happen if she just sat there gawking at his rugged, handsome face and form in the dark. Before she could swing her legs over his to stand, he scooted forward to pull her gently against him.

"Alex—"

"That's my real name. No protests, Brett. Let's just celebrate a little more, as we've wanted to all day. I know I've wanted to touch you as much as launch this ship, and the way you've looked at me—"

He didn't even finish his thought. She clutched her cocoon of blanket to her as he enfolded her in his strong arms and kissed her cheek, her earlobe, her chin, her throat. The rich curtain of her hair swung free between them to get in his mouth. He tenderly swept it back from her face with both hands, while she sat there as if suspended. He studied the white face tilted up at him in the dark, its sweep of curved cheek, the tilt-tip nose, the softly parted mouth. And the huge, fathomless gray eyes framed by lush lashes.

"Delicious hair," he murmured, and ran a quick tongue along his lips where her strands of hair had caught. "Just like the rest of you."

She knew blatant flattery when she heard it. But somehow she was nestling against him, returning his hot kisses while he stretched the two of them out and rolled them over on the cushions. He pressed her down gently, lying warm against her. His weight was not on her, but one leg over her knees stilled them. The kissing went on and on, until her will flowed into his. She anchored him to her with bold hands that caressed his neck and dared to ruffle and pull his thick black curly hair. She swept her touch lower to grasp his broad back muscles, then clasp his narrow waist even as he tugged the intruding blanket away from between them.

"Still wet here," he murmured, his voice gruff against her shoulder. "The material clings. Here, let me dry you."

The rational part of her tried to scream no! as his sure hands reached around her under the blanket. He unhooked the gown, while she said nothing. She held his shoulders, kneading them to stop the swaying of the ship. She gasped as he threw off the blanket and tenderly peeled down her square-necked muslin gown to her waist. The damp material caught on her arms, gently imprisoning them at her sides. "No," she managed in a voice from far away when he dared to slip the straps of her thin batiste underchemise away, too.

"I had to see you, touch you," he told her, and took her lips again. She felt her damp nipples bud even harder into the chill air. She wanted his touch, his kiss so desperately that she didn't care if she looked like a naked-breasted figurehead this way. That other woman who liked to waltz and laugh and tease had taken over her body again, and she wanted to share it all with this man. She watched wide-eyed, trembling with desire as his eyes and hands dropped to her bare breasts.

"I'm glad no one else has seen you like this," he told her solemnly. "No one else has, have they?"

Thick, damp tendrils of hair brushed her bare shoulders as she shook her head. Dalton Kelsey flashed through her stunned brain, but she knew she would have flattened him on her uncle's drawing room floor if he had ever dared such a thing. Her vow to tell Alex everything about her only suitor fled as he lowered her to the cushions and leaned over her for more lingering, deep-tongued kisses.

She moaned. Her hips moved of their own accord in little yearning circles. She welcomed it when his mouth trailed lower down her throat to her breasts. She actually arched up to meet his lips when they replaced his skilled fingers caressing her tiny thrust of nipples. It had grown completely dark in the cabin now, darker than outside the windows. She closed her eyes and abandoned herself to him.

She could have sailed off the cushions, sailed aloft to the stars as he touched and kissed her. His tongue circled each pink peak beseechingly, then darted over it before he suckled. Now she finally understood how women could risk everything for a man—how Simone could search the world for the one man she would both feel passion for and loyalty to. How a plain spinster who'd come to a bold nation could revel in lying half-naked with a man.

Her eyes shot wide open as his hand drifted down from her breast. It caressed her flat belly through her gown, cupped her hip, drifted down between her knees, pulling the gown with it. Slowly he moved it up between her thighs. She pressed them together with every last ounce of sanity she possessed.

"Alex, we can't!"

"We won't then. Just let me touch you!"

"It's mad folly."

"The best is always mad folly," he promised, as he sat her up and cradled her with one arm around her shoulders. She only remembered her arms were trapped at her sides by the gown he'd pulled awry when she tried to reach out to seize his marauding hand. His warm fingers stroked her thigh, skin against bare skin, and a flash of light coursed through her brain. No—it had been real.

Alex shoved her down on the floor and scooted off the window seat beside her. "Damn, there's someone on that wharf flashing a light," he said. He pulled her clothing up and thrust the blanket at her. "I've got to see. Stay down!"

Again, even as he crept for the door, a strong, focused beam swept once more in a narrow arc through the window. Brett huddled lower. She heard Alex shuffle down the darkened passage, dart up the steps, then run across the deck overhead, shouting to someone. Stunned and still shaky from the tumultuous jostling of her emotions, she huddled in the corner and straightened her clothing.

Sanity flooded back. She had been demented to let him handle her like that! She was not some dock tart to be tumbled in some captain's cabin at a man's whim! She felt hot all over. She could not deny that she had wanted it, had protested only halfheartedly. Whatever was the matter with her, she scolded herself, and blessed the person with the light—unless he had seen what they were doing!

When Alex returned a few minutes later to report that the wharf was now deserted, she was dressed and sitting at the captain's desk in the dark room, her hair twisted up under her sodden hat. She was grateful he did not try to resume his seductive assault. Even as he led her up on deck his voice was lightly teasing, as if none of this had happened. She could only assume he regretted the embarrassing incident as much as she.

"I suppose it's a little late for waltzing under the stars," he told her.

Her voice caught in her throat. "Much too late."

"I've got to go to Philadelphia for a week to get some things for the maiden voyage, Brett. I plan to see my mother and my sister's family while I'm there. That will leave you in charge of Sanborn's here—with Mason's and Giles's help, of course."

If he was leaving and entrusting things to her, she thought, then telling him about Dalton Kelsey could certainly wait until his return. He could hardly go off to Philadelphia with a clear mind if she sprang her secret on him right now, so she told him stiffly, as if they'd never embraced or kissed—or more, "I can handle things. I welcome the challenge."

"I'm banking on it," he said, his voice so warm she knew he meant more than just watching the firm.

He helped her up into the curricle like the most proper gentleman. Silently he cursed the flash of someone's lantern that had stopped him. He wondered if the person had meant to spy on them or just wanted a closer look at the radical design of the ship. But all that world of business had been the farthest thing from his mind when he had touched Brett. She did something to him no other woman ever had. Beneath her controlled proper surface raged some hidden spring of emotion and passion. She became transformed to a radiant, stunning woman when she smiled, when their eyes held, when they touched.

But he knew he was crazy if he thought he could really possess a woman like this outside of wedlock, and he needed no such complications. Especially not with a hardheaded business partner, and a British one at that. She was no Simone, no light of a man's fancy. She was formidable, troublesome, stubborn Brett Benton, and he told himself that she was not worth the price or risk. And yet, he couldn't keep his eyes and hands off her.

He sat straighter up on the seat of the curricle to ease the tautness of his doeskin breeches at the juncture of his thighs, suppressing his wild notion of tethering the horse along the dark of Fall's Way and making passionate love to her again, even if their bed would be the narrow seat of the curricle.

He was glad he was going to Philadelphia, he told himself. He should never have invited Brett on the maiden voyage of the *Free Spirit*. He didn't know how he was going to control himself, let alone her, if they ever found themselves totally alone again. He darted a glance sideways at her. She sat erect, pressed stiffly into the far corner of the seat. Her profile looked carved from ice. He clucked loudly to the horse to urge him to a quicker trot.

To Brett's dismay, she missed Alex horribly the week he was away. But it had taken her that long to steel herself to tell him about Dalton Kelsey before they sailed on the *Free Spirit* in two days. She had invited him to stop by Henny's the first evening he was back and made Henny promise she would not just barge in on their interview. But Henny and her servants would still be in earshot in case Alex yelled too much or she needed help. He came, most annoyingly, to sit beside her on the narrow Georgian settee the moment Henny left the parlor.

"You've missed me desperately and wanted to tell me so in private," he began with a smile to jangle her nerves even more.

She stood and paced to the other side of the big gateleg table, cluttered with a lantern, assorted needlework and the big Featherstone family Bible. "Don't be ridiculous," she said. "This is something very serious, something I find hard to say. But I know you'll understand."

The pleased little grin evaporated instantly from the corners of his mouth. "You said everything's been fine at the firm, so it can't be that. I'm listening."

"All right. You heard me admit I'd met Admiral Cochran that day they asked me at the Fountain Inn. I told the truth right out."

He frowned. "And?"

"Alex, I can't help who my great-uncle's friends were, whom I met at his house in London before any of this war happened," she cried.

"Something else about Cochran?" he probed, and sat forward on the settee. Even in her perturbation she noticed that his big body seemed to dwarf it to mere doll's furniture.

"No," she said. She met his stern gaze squarely. "There was another guest at the house off and on who's rather well-known in these parts." She took a deep breath, then blurted out, "Dalton Kelsey."

He jumped to his feet, then thumped right back down. "That bloody bastard who scuttled the *Pamela Mary*?" His voice cut, knife edged. "Blue blazes, Brett, great, just great! He's done more direct damage to us and Baltimore than Cochran, you know!"

She nodded, her face tragic. "I know."

"Is that it?" he demanded. "Tea at teatime with Kelsey, is that it?"

"Not quite."

"Then dare I ask what 'he was a guest at the house off and on' means? I don't even know what Kelsey looks like, how old he is. Was he a guest more on than off?"

She leaned forward and propped her palms on the table

before her. She had to tell him, but for the first time in a long while she was really afraid of what he might do. "He—I guess you would say, after his wife died, he—courted me," she said, her voice a monotone. "When Uncle Charles died, he proposed to me."

Alex's lower lip dropped and his slitted eyes widened, but the explosion she was expecting didn't come. He raked his hand through his already windblown hair to make shafts of it stand ludicrously on end. If his eyes had been daggers, she would have been dead, but his voice came calm.

"And you obviously turned him down. When was this?"

She wanted to say that she hadn't exactly turned Kelsey down, but Alex seemed so calm. "More than a year ago," she responded. "He sailed off to Egypt. Then I found out that Uncle Charles had left me half of Sanborn's, and decided to leave for Baltimore."

He stood and approached her. She straightened and stepped back, but he captured her hands hard in his. "Did you love him?"

"No," she declared instantly, her voice strong, her eyes unwavering.

His taut features relaxed. He looked amazingly relieved. "Have you heard from him or contacted him since?"

"No."

"Do you want to?"

"Only to tell him to keep his hands off my fleet—at least my half of it!"

To her utter amazement, he laughed. "You're even more dangerous than I thought," he told her. "Consorting with the two top Johnny Bulls out there. I don't suppose you'd care to admit to serving up tea and sweet biscuits for the entire Royal Navy."

She pulled her hands from him. "Alex, how can you joke about this? I thought you'd be furious! I've been agonizing over having to tell you for weeks!"

He reached for her by one wrist and gently seized her chin in the other hand. "You'd have been a fool to tell me if you were a spy, and you're anything but that—a fool or a spy.

Besides, I know Kelsey didn't make love to you the way he should have. He must have been a real milksop not to teach you to kiss better than the way you started out—now calm down. I said 'started out'!''

"You're despicable."

"You're going to think so if you don't now, Brett." His hands on her wrist and chin tightened. "You did a fine job of overseeing things while I was in Philadelphia, and you're going to have to keep it up while I go to Bermuda on the *Free Spirit*."

"But you said I could go! I told you so this would blow over before we sailed!''

He shook his head, his face sterner than it had been since he'd come in. "Impossible now. You'll stay here, and don't bother arguing. I expect to sail circles around your dear Commander Kelsey's ships, but I can't take the risk of having you along after what you've just told me. Besides, it's better—safer for you in all kinds of ways—if you stay. You see, unlike that lily-livered British bastard, I have a real problem keeping my hands and mouth off you."

She started at his forthright way of putting what she knew was only the truth. He let her step back before he went on. "But you are going to swear to me right now on Henny's Bible here that you will not pull another stupid trick like that night jaunt to the shipyard just because I've told you no. Josh and I don't take kindly to stowaways. When I get the *Spirit* safely out and back the first time, we'll settle everything between us. Agreed?''

She was still stunned from the sweep of events. He hadn't exploded at all. He hadn't reacted at all the way she had pictured it. And she had just started to think she knew him! So this time she would bow to his wishes. But she had no intention of capitulating to him for everything in the future. Especially if she understood what he meant by "we'll settle everything between us."

It felt so good not to fight him, though she longed to go to Bermuda. Still, he was trusting her here. He didn't blame her. He was not angry.

"Agreed," she said quickly.

She had no idea he nearly put both fists through a hundred-year-old tree trunk on Henny's lawn when he walked out into the night a half hour later.

The day the *Free Spirit* would sail dawned bright and new. Goods were still going aboard the vessel as Brett looked out the accounting room window at the ship's high, slender masts, set at a rakish backward slant to bend like whiplashes under the huge sails. She knew they would look as if they were toppling backward when the clipper came close to flying speed. The vessel looked so graceful with her flush, wide decks, despite the fact they were built that way to handle guns. A "wet ship," Alex called her: she could take breakers over her prow and still make over three hundred miles in twenty-four hours, a modern marvel. She was sharp bowed and sleek and ready to go, and Brett felt crushed she was not going, too.

Yet she had not complained. She had kept as busy as the rest of them these past few days and that helped. The ship wasn't sailing until noon, so she intended to take some gifts to Todd Miles's family to thank the two boys for helping Alex rescue her. She'd been stockpiling children's clothing and toys for over a week and would be back in plenty of time to wave the clipper off.

She had had stiff words with Giles about her leaving the firm for even a few minutes on such a momentous day. When he heard where she was going, he almost looked as if he'd swallowed the handkerchief he coughed into. She assumed she thought she was dressed too well to go into that part of town. But she planned for Alex to remember her standing on the wharf clad in her plum muslin gown with its pink puffed and gathered sleeves. She'd even worn Simone's pearls for the occasion, though she'd wrapped a light cashmere shawl around her shoulders to cover them. When the *Spirit* sailed, she'd be prettily dressed, waving and shouting good luck with a serious, yet happy face. But she had to keep busy right now, so she just marched off downstairs under Giles Cutler's flustered glare.

She summoned Todd, mussed and grimy as ever. Head down, shoulders hunched, he scuffed away from the dock toward her. But when she told him where they were going, his little face lit like a lantern. "My ma, she'll like that real good," he told her.

"You mean really well," Brett countered.

"Sure, like I said. Come on, I'll carry more of that stuff. We gotta run so's we can get back quick."

She knew they would be going into a rather tawdry area of town, so she'd decided to walk instead of taking the curricle. She set off at a good pace behind the bouncing boy. Soon the wide cobbled or brick avenues shrank to one-horse, rutted dirt streets. Smells of day-old fish and onions replaced fresh-baked bread and garden smells here. Most windows were not even glass; refuse littered the street. "Down here on Brandy Alley!" Todd called back to her with a proud little grin that knifed her heart.

She learned from him that the family had moved to smaller quarters since his father, Sam, had been impressed by the British Navy off a Sanborn ship last September. He had six brothers and sisters and their names all began with *T*: in order, Tabitha, Thalia, Todd, Terence—who sold the newspaper she bought—Ted, Tom and Teresa. All were under thirteen years of age. Since last winter, his ma had missed his pa real bad and cried a whole lot.

He darted down a cluttered alley between two brick buildings, shouting, "Ma, Ma, see who come ta see ya!" while people poked heads out windows overhead and babies wailed from the depths of dingy rooms.

She followed him across a crumbling, peeling doorstep and into a rank-smelling gray hall. He pushed the first door open with a thin shoulder. "Ma? You here?"

A slim, sweet-faced woman sat slumped in a rickety, straight-backed chair, the only piece of furniture other than the crude table and straw pallets that edged the bare-boards floor. She turned her head lethargically toward her visitors, and Brett saw immediately that while her brown hair was disarrayed and caught back with a piece of twine, it framed a perfect oval face and china-blue eyes. But the mouth was as lank as the hair, the eyes as listless. She held a squirming toddler in her lap as if she did not realize he was there. As Todd's excited words of introduction and explanation tumbled out, she rose slowly to her feet.

"The boy told me about you," Lissa Miles said. Her olive-green gown hung on her like a coatrack when she stood. "I'm real proud him and Terence helped the other day. What those folks done was real cruel. You dint bring Mr. Cutler, or tell him where you was coming, did you?" she asked, and her eyes darted again behind Brett toward the door.

Brett surrendered her packages to the eager Todd, who dumped them on a cluttered table and ran back outside, screeching for his sisters. "No, it's not the time of month for Mr. Cutler to bring the Sanborn donations, if that's what you mean. But he does know I'm here."

"Oh, dear," she said, and moved away from her chair to lean her hip on the window ledge. "Please sit, ma'am. And I dint mean to ask for more money."

The woman's voice was beautiful, rich and low, despite its blend of defeat strangely mixed with agitation. Brett could tell she must have been a lovely woman once, though she could not place how old she was. Her heart wrenched at what she knew the young mother must have been through, left alone with seven half-orphan children by a husband gone to sea and not returned.

"I know you didn't ask for more," Brett assured her. She sensed she had to take the chair, or the woman would be offended. "May I hold your baby?" she asked, and pulled the little wriggler onto her lap. "But the money—it's not enough, is it?"

The woman's eyes swam with tears. "Oh, dear, of course it's real fine. Todd's wages, too. Only with all these mouths to feed, you know—I wouldn't want you to tell Mr. Cutler we're anything but...satisfied." Her words ended on a huge, trembling sigh.

"Please, Mrs. Miles, is there something about Mr. Cutler? He does pay Todd's wages, doesn't he? And I certainly plan to tell Mr. Sanborn that with seven children, you just need more until your husband comes back."

"No, no! I don't want to make a fuss, ma'am. Please tell Mr. Cutler I dint say nothing!"

It took much more time than Brett meant to spend there as the Miles children scampered in to ooh and ah over the clothing and toys. They held the balls and stuffed horses as if they were precious religious relics, then thanked her and darted outside again with worried looks at their mother. Brett was relieved to see that none of them was as dirty as Todd, and she'd tend to that in the weeks to come. But when she was ready to leave and said she'd be back the following day with more money for food out of Mr. Cutler's fund, the woman became instantly hysterical.

"Oh, ma'am, Miss Benton, you shouldna told him you was coming here! He'll be worse—worse—" She sobbed.

Brett put the baby on the floor and her arm around the shaking woman's shoulders as the whole story fell out in jagged pieces.

She and many of the other Sanborn sailors' families with men lost at sea had found their allotments steeply diminished lately. Mr. Cutler told them it was the war taking all the funds. But she'd been so desperate, and he'd suggested another way he would give her more from his own funds. Last winter, when the children were hungry and she knew the boys were starting to steal food, she agreed to Giles Cutler's plan to meet him at his rooming house.

"I just hated myself, ma'am! Still do! To think I'm a trollop and broke my vows to Sam! But I never done it before or since, really I dint. Now I can't stop crying all the time. When Mr. Cutler drops by here, he always says I have to let him do all that again—"

"I'll have that rotter's head—his job!" Brett promised as she comforted the sobbing woman. "His own afflictions give him no right to do this! I tell you, Mr. Sanborn didn't know, but he will now!"

Lissa Miles raised her tear-glazed face to Brett's flushed, angry one. The woman grasped her hands in a viselike grip. "But just don't tell Mr. Cutler! You don't know him! Don't know him at all!"

"I know what I have to do!" Brett insisted, and stepped away to plunk coins from her reticule on the tabletop among the other things. "Your children need food, not toys, but I didn't know. I'll be back tomorrow, and you won't ever have to worry about Mr. Cutler again!" she vowed on her way out the door.

"Stay here with your mother and help her go shopping for food, Todd," she ordered the boy, who waited, wide-eyed, in the alley. The other children huddled around him, holding their toys. They had evidently been listening to what went on inside. "And you stay away from Mr. Cutler. You can see the *Free Spirit* sail another day. After this war is over, my lad, as Mr. Alex told you, you'll get to be her cabin boy someday!"

She could tell by the look on the dirty face that for once he'd understood everything she said.

Nine

As she stood at the foot of the *Free Spirit*'s busy gangplank, Brett spotted Mason Finch helping to oversee the final stowing of goods aboard. Everything still looked rushed. Alex was pushing to cast off before the tides in the bay changed, but she didn't see him.

"Mason," she called up with her hands cupped around her mouth. "I need to talk to Alex!"

"The good Lord knows, he's been looking for you, Miss Brett!" Mason bellowed down at her. "Probably dashed back to the office one last time."

She hiked her skirt ankle high and ran. She wouldn't mind facing down Giles herself with accusations of embezzling funds and defiling Lissa Miles, but Alex had to know first. She knew full well that the records in the Exigency Fund account book showed Lissa Miles to be receiving enough money to support her family, but the amount she said she had actually received from Giles Cutler was far from that. And Brett fully expected that interviews with the other dependent families would show the same discrepancy in funds. No wonder Giles Cutler dressed so well and had imported candies despite the blockade! She intended to give him the sack and tell everyone why. She'd like to see him in the Bridewell prison here before he even knew what hit him! He'd done as much to damage Sanborn's reputation intentionally as she had unintentionally!

She asked several people on the dock, but no one had seen Alex in the past few minutes. Crowds clustered along the bustling wharf to watch the clipper cast off, which should probably be within the hour, judging by the height of the warm spring sun overhead. She banged open the back door of Sanborn's and made straight for Alex's office. The door was slightly ajar. She knocked hard.

"Alex. Alex! I need to see you right now!"

The door swung open. She stepped inside and quickly scanned the office she'd shared with him lately. It would be hers while he was gone the two weeks to Bermuda, and she meant to do a wonderful job for him and Sanborn's here, whatever it took.

The office was deserted. Rubbish! Alex wasn't even there to tell that Sanborn's had harbored a viper in its bosom, one that had more than once beguiled her to take a bite of his shiny apple of deceit—or the Berkeley's toffees he glibly offered. She spun around to look elsewhere, and smacked right into Giles Cutler.

"I—oh! You!"

He pushed her back into the room and slammed the door behind him. "Get out of my way! Let me pass!" she clipped out before she saw the pistol he lifted from behind his hip. Her voice died in her throat.

Heart pounding, she backed away until her thighs hit the big desk. "Giles, why the gun? Please put it away."

"I thought you'd be smarter than to play games with me at this point. Always meddling, always prying where you don't belong." The leathered, livid half of his face displayed a demonic expression while the normal half still looked only angry. "You don't belong here, but you do in my bed!"

She gasped. "I won't allow that sort of talk! Now you look here, Giles—"

"Oh, I am, I am. I've always wanted you. But now you've forced my hand, running off to comfort that sluttish mother of the boy and then coming back here all disturbed like this. So Lissa Miles fed you her lies, I see."

Her mind darted for a way out. She knew the woman hadn't lied. Part of Giles actually looked jubilant; part of him leered. Gone was the proper, circumspect stare. He pointed the gun at her and looked her over greedily, the way he must have poor Lissa! Her skin crawled and her sense of outrage exploded.

"It's all true, isn't it, Giles? All the things she told me. And you've been pocketing money from the charity fund while children starved and mothers were forced into prostitution—and you used that poor woman to—"

"That poor woman!" he roared, his free hand thumping his flat chest. "What about me? No one pities me anymore! Alex Sanborn as good as killed my brother, scarred me for life! He gets everything he wants at the twitch of his little finger! Bedded that beautiful, blond French whore. I used to follow her around when she shopped and curse him for it. And now he's got you!"

"Giles, stop it. That's not true. Just put the gun down and you can go. Clear out of Baltimore, just go!"

"Oh, I'm going, and you with me, Miss Brett," he said mockingly. "Proper Miss Brett, writhing half-naked in his arms aboard the *Free Spirit*, displaying herself right in the window for me like a trollop for sale. Well, I'll accept that from you."

"The light!" she gasped. "It was you! You saw us?"

"Just enough to whet my appetite. You'll do that for me and more! You'll beg me!" he raved, his voice slick with menace. The barrel of the pistol wavered in a strangling grip so tight his fingers had gone white. "You see, you and I are stowing away on the *Free Spirit* this morning."

"Giles, please, listen to me. You're not going aboard and neither am I."

"I know you want to so you can lie naked with him again. If only I had the time with you here I'd teach you who your master is, whom you will obey!"

She moved at last, though she felt his eyes as mesmerizing

as a snake's. She was afraid he would strike, but she edged carefully along the desk to get past him and gain a path toward the door.

"Stand!" he hissed. "It would be such a waste to shoot you." He lifted the gun straight-armed at her chest, then strode quickly past her to yank four ties from the velvet drapes. It plunged the room into semidarkness. "Bend over the desk and put your hands behind your back," he ordered as he approached her again. When she stared defiantly at him he jabbed the gun in her middle until she obeyed. Quickly he wrapped her wrists with the ties from the drapes. Even as he pushed her to the floor to bind her ankles together, her mind raced.

Surely Alex would come here to say goodbye when she didn't go to the ship as promised. Mason would tell him she'd been looking for him. Alex would rescue her and she would explain everything she had learned about Giles Cutler. The man was demented! They could have him in prison before the *Spirit* sailed.

Despite the gun in his hand, she opened her mouth to scream when he dared to run his hand up her stockinged leg under her skirt. But he crammed his ink-stained, lace-encrusted handkerchief in her mouth. She thought she would retch from it, from his eyes, from his hands, which he slid as possessively over her as one might a brood mare. How had she been so completely taken in by him? Where was Alex?

With a huge sigh of regret that time was fleeting, Giles darted out of the office, and returned with a wooden chest balanced on a two-wheeled dolly. "And here I was afraid you wouldn't get back in time today," he babbled, while her frenzied brain sought to grasp his words. "A box in the hold with a stowaway may not seem as good to you as sharing that bastard Sanborn's bunk in his cabin, but you'll learn. You'll learn well."

To her utter horror, he opened the trunk lid and half lifted, half shoved her inside. Finally he uncocked his pistol and put it in with her behind the crook in her knees. "Don't struggle and don't make a sound, or you'll use up your air before I can get you out, my precious. I've drilled only a few small holes in the side. You see, we're going sailing on the first voyage of our life together—and the *Free Spirit*'s last!''

He slammed the lid shut on her terrified face and chuckled to himself. Down in the hold, she'd be so grateful when he let her out that she'd cling to him and cry as she had to that bastard Sanborn after the townspeople had abused her. He belted the trunk closed with its two wide leather straps. He'd already stashed aboard the other things he'd need until Commander Kelsey and his Royal Marines boarded the vessel, which he hoped would be by nightfall that evening. And the first thing he intended to inform Kelsey he was owed for all this was a single cabin for Brett Benton—and himself.

He laughed aloud as he tilted the trunk up on the dolly and rolled it from the office and out the back entrance.

Brett soon gave up even moaning in her tiny black tomb. Her knees were bent up to her chest; her bound hands pressed painfully between the back of her hips and the wall of the trunk. She forced herself to breathe carefully, slowly. Sounds outside told her they were on the dock. At least he didn't intend just to dump her in the harbor to drown like some trapped, unwanted kitten. The trunk tilted up the plank. She could still hear the bustling of activity on board and a cacophony of voices as the ship was made ready to sail. If only he hadn't wrapped her skirts around her feet to muffle them, she could at least kick to make a noise. Her muscles went rigid as she heard Giles greet several men by name. Then she caught Alex's voice, though it sounded far off.

"I hope that's your last of the lists and account books, Giles!" Alex shouted. "Miss Benton's not back yet?"

"She probably lost track of time!" the demon called to Alex. "Besides, she told me earlier she could handle it better if she didn't actually see the vessel sail. She didn't mean to disappoint you, but didn't want to make a scene," Giles added.

Brett silently cursed Mason Finch for not telling Alex she had needed him. Needed him—it always came down to that, she thought, and tears matted her thick eyelashes. The trunk tipped, rolled, jolted. Alex's voice giving orders faded. "Put that down into the hold quite a ways, lads," she heard Giles say. "Bookkeeping business Mr. Sanborn won't need till Bermuda."

She almost fainted trying to scream through the disgusting gag. She lay desperate, jostled as sailors noisily bumped the trunk down into the hold while Giles chatted loudly to them all the while. All voices departed, then Giles's quick steps came back. She was certain she heard the distant hold door slam. She fought down her panic, counted between breaths. After an eternity she was so dizzy that the ship seemed to be swaying. She was drifting in the dark sea of fear, so swept away, so sick with this gag. Giles Cutler meant to let her die like this in the hold of the ship she had shared with Alex. They had both loved this ship, both loved—

Light pierced her eyes. Giles bent over the opened trunk holding the same narrow-beamed lantern he had taken into the warehouse that night to see the ship in her cradle. "We're under way, my precious," he said. "Welcome to our little world belowdecks, and we won't be going up till our British friends come calling."

Alex still seethed inside that Brett hadn't come to bid him farewell before the *Free Spirit* weighed anchor out of port on her maiden voyage yesterday. And here he'd been pondering whether to kiss the little witch farewell on deck! He'd known how disappointed she'd been that she couldn't come along, so this was probably her final protest. But he'd admired her the past week. She'd been pleasant, businesslike and supportive—a tremendous help at the firm. Blue blazes, only one day off the coast toward Bermuda and he missed the woman already! When he got back to Baltimore, they were going to have that serious discussion about their relationship. It was time for a permanent truce between them in this private, little off-again, on-again war they waged!

Yesterday the *Spirit* had slipped by the Chesapeake blockade, outrunning three British ships that had seemed to be lying in wait for them. But Alex Sanborn had no intention of just darting past the blockade the stubborn Miss Benton had made in his life. Damn, but he was ready to strike his colors and court her, if she'd only let down her guard a bit to allow him nearer. Ever since those passionate moments they'd shared in the captain's cabin the day the clipper was launched, she'd been careful not to be alone with him but in their office with the door ajar. It just made him desire her all the more, feeling an unquenchable thirst for her as if some fever raged in his blood.

"Sail, ho!" the lookout clinging to his dipping, swaying perch overhead shouted down to him and Captain Windsor.

Josh stood by the helmsman at the door of the wheelhouse. Alex had taken a trick at the wheel earlier and reveled in controlling the plunge and pull of the finely crafted vessel. "I'll go up for a look, Captain!" Alex shouted to his friend, then swung up into the shrouds. Hand over hand, he climbed to the main-topmast cap. The lad shoved his spyglass at him. Alex held it to his eye, fought to steady it. Three triangles of stark white sail shot into his view: one ship, a bold three-masted frigate, high out of the water. Her fat black flanks bore a white band checkered with two rows of gunports bristling cannon. A British warship, and it looked like one of the three they had left in their wake yesterday! He clambered back down.

"She means to fight, Josh, but she'll never catch this trim lady!" he boasted while Joshua Windsor examined their pursuer through his own glass. Behind them the white wake on the heaving gray ocean seemed to link the two ships, hunter to quarry.

"True," Josh replied, shouting his words into the spanking wind, "but she's sure an English man-of-war! Probably thirty guns to our six. I'm going to break out the Spanish colors to see if we can fool her if she gets in range, Alex."

"She couldn't possibly catch this ship!" Alex protested. "Never! But just in case," he agreed grudgingly, "we'd better stand alert to fight."

"Crew, clear deck and prepare to stand your guns!" Josh

ordered. The first mate repeated his captain's command over
and over through his long, brass speaking trumpet. The chase
went on. Twenty minutes later, Alex seized the eyeglass
again, as he had repeatedly. It was definitely not his imagination that the big vessel was more than keeping up with
them, shouldering her pushy way into the wind, when the
Spirit should be clipping along to leave the enemy vessel in
her wake. If he didn't know better, he'd think this pristine,
solid, trim little ship must be taking water belowdecks to drag
her down.

Alex cursed under his breath as he hurried to the captain's
cabin to strap on his heavy fighting belt with pistols, cutlasses,
ax and his sword.

A half hour before, Brett had watched with growing dread
as Giles Cutler clapped his hands in glee. Clear as anything,
the "prepare to stand to guns" battle order up on deck had
drifted down to them in their little world Giles had made in
the hold. The last day and night had been like being in the
depths of hell for her, held personally captive by a grinning
Satan. She shuddered even now at the thought of his scarred
face against hers. The mere memory of his hands touching
and stroking her racked her again. She was only grateful that
Giles, too, had been kept on edge by the tramp of the changing watch overhead and by bells and orders that sifted down
to them. Otherwise she was certain he would have forced
more on her than kisses and lewd caresses despite their
cramped, stale quarters.

But she would have welcomed anything compared to what
she saw him do the moment he heard that first call to battle
stations. She yanked to no avail against the wrist bonds he'd
tied to an iron ring in the hull. Right beside her, chuckling
while she watched in horror, Giles Cutler produced a big drill
from the other chest he'd secreted with his supplies. In a
grotesque mockery of the happy day she'd drilled holes in
this very hull to help build the *Spirit*, he heaved his weight
against the drill to spring holes in her side. It struck her then

with stunning force that the man was as horribly scarred inside as out.

Despite her gag she protested and shook her head wildly. He had tied the handkerchief around her lips outside of her mouth now; for that much she'd been grateful. She rattled her iron ring. But he ignored her frenzy as he calmly, deliberately, proceeded to drill a second hole four inches to the left of the first. Ocean water spouted in both holes, though not, she was certain, enough to sink the *Spirit* quickly.

He looked up proudly as if to flaunt the destruction he was creating. Then he laughed at her terror and reached out once more to touch her breast. She recoiled as if his hand seared her flesh.

"Wish this wood was the bastard's heart, but it's the next best thing," Giles chortled. "He adores this ship—probably more than he ever could a woman, so you're better off with me, my precious. I'm afraid there may be a little fight coming. And as soon as they board her," he said, and coughed so close in her face he speckled her with saliva, "I'm going to climb aboard that lovely body of yours, hopefully above-decks." He chuckled again. "I must say it's going to be rather damp down here soon, anyway. Come over here. I'll let you help so we can tell the invincible Mr. Alex we worked on this together!"

She watched frozen in dread as he loosed her bound wrists from the wall ring. With a knife he kept in his belt, he sliced through only her ankle ties. He dragged her over between the two spouting holes, which immediately soaked her disheveled gown with cold saltwater. Then, clamping her back tight against his chest so she could see every move he made, he produced a clawlike iron tool that bit into the hull to open a gash as big as his spread hand between the two drill holes. Water gushed in like a fountain, and he fell back with her on top of him with a splash.

Water temporarily blinded him. She cracked her elbows hard into his ribs. In her efforts to get up, her foot hit the softness at his crotch as he sprawled there. He gasped, doubled over, swallowed a mouthful of water and began choking.

Surprised at her success, she scrambled up and splashed away in the ankle-deep flow of water.

She hadn't walked anywhere for nearly twenty-four hours except behind a barrel to use a crude chamber pot, and her knees felt like a rag doll's. But at least she had gotten a chance to pull her gag down. She stumbled, bounced off crates stacked close in the narrow aisle. She could hear him gasping and splashing after her, as she grabbed for a ladder rung, but her tied wrists made it so hard to climb out of the clinging wet. A barrel floated by, bumping into her legs.

She screamed once for help, but Giles yanked her back by her feet. His head cracked a crate as they fell heavily. He lay very still as the insidious slap of water licked her skirts where she knelt beside him to right herself.

She didn't know if he was dead. She almost hoped he was. Alex! She had to warn Alex the ship was leaking down here. She fumbled underwater for the dagger Giles had stuck in his belt and carefully sawed through her ties. Blood coursed down her wrists and tingled her fingers. She had just begun her climb out of the swirling black waters, when Giles's lantern gutted out, plunging the hold to darkness but for random splinters of light in the deckboards overhead. She felt her way up the ladder, but the hatch overhead wouldn't budge. In the chaos on deck, someone must have bolted it or placed something heavy on it. Between the bellow of guns overhead, she began to scream Alex's name.

As the British man-of-war closed, it had become evident to Josh and Alex that the ploy of the red-and-yellow neutral Spanish flag had failed. Defiantly they'd run out the American Stars and Stripes. The Union Jack and a British commander's ensign, which the first mate identified as being Commander Dalton Kelsey's personal flag, had answered, standing straight out in the stiff breeze. The *Spirit*'s decks had been cleared of loose gear and the six carronades run out. All hands awaited Captain Joshua Windsor's orders to fire.

As the ships came abreast, running side by side at forty yards, Alex Sanborn knew what the man he had sent to the hold would find. His sleek, fast *Spirit* was wallowing, floundering, slowing more and more. Somehow, something had sprung belowdecks. That did occasionally happen on maiden voyages. But they had been so damned careful with this ship! She had seemed tight, so seaworthy! The carpenter he'd summoned had at first claimed the problem might be the anchor haweshole to port, but they'd found that undamaged.

"They're closing!" Captain Windsor's excited voice sliced through Alex's frenzied thoughts. "Stand to your guns, men! Prepare to fire! If they employ grappling hooks, repel all boarders!"

Cannons crashed; billows of smoke boiled. At each belching shot, the *Spirit* leaped and shuddered beneath their feet. Answering grapeshot screamed overhead to slice rigging and splinter masts. Alex agonized for his beautiful virgin ship; it was as if he suffered each ball and blow she took. "Vent! Sponge! Load! Aim! Fire!" echoed in his brain. In the reverberating lull between shots he heard a high-pitched, muffled scream that sounded like his name. His sharp eyes scanned the deck; no man was down yet. His mind was playing tricks in this chaos. "Fire again as you will!" Josh Windsor's shriek sounded in his ears.

Two sailors went down nearly at Alex's feet in the next volley and two more leaped to take their places. Ducking, threading his way through the sprawling wounded, the carpenter Alex had sent into the hold scampered to him as both ships thundered fire again. "Bad flooding under the forecastle, and the pumps not keeping up with it, sir!" he shouted. "And a woman, sir, a stowaway. She may have caused the leakage, Mr. Sanborn. We found this drill, as well."

At first Alex barely heeded the second part of the man's information as he gave the orders to man the pumps in a clear voice. But then the import of it sunk in. A stowaway—someone had sabotaged his ship. He looked down dazedly at the drill the carpenter was thrusting at him. Anger swept through him in an overwhelming wave. How dared anyone harm his lady, his *Free Spirit*? The thought of holes being drilled in her perfect sides sent him staggering backward with rage.

Then with a wild cry he heaved the drill over the heads of the gunners into the sea.

Completely devastated, he was still standing motionless when another cry went up. "She's escaped us! Mr. Sanborn, it's that lady partner of yours. She's a traitor."

As another hailstorm of British grapeshot peppered shrouds and rigging overhead, Alex saw Brett. She was soaked, disheveled, a mythological goddess of wrath with streaming bronze hair and tattered garments in the wind, the ship's bold figurehead come to life. Cannon convulsed the deck under their feet. Smoke smothered his view as Brett careened over to him and gripped his arm, while he stared down at her in horror. She'd defied him again, stowed away. She had drilled holes in the ship he thought she'd treasured as much as he did! It must have been her; there was no one else. Now she'd come up on deck to revel in this attack by her British lover, that bloody bastard, Dalton Kelsey. Damn her to hell, the man was welcome to her!

He shoved her back so hard she collapsed to her knees. "Get away from me, British traitor! Get below!"

"Alex, it's not what you think!" she cried up at him. Her wild eyes kept darting to the carnage around them, then back to his furious face. "Let me explain—Giles Cutler abducted me."

He ducked beside her on the littered, blood- and sea-slick deck as the crash of cannon nearly deafened them. He grabbed her shoulders hard and shook her until her inner world exploded, too. Stunned, she watched his lips move in a grotesque pantomime of a nightmare.

"Liar! The way he abducted you and took you to the shipyard that night, I suppose? Were you looking for a way to sabotage my ship even then? I'm sick of your lies, whore!" he screamed. "Now get below before I throw you to the sharks!"

She sprawled on the shifting deck; he crouched over her as if he would kill her with the cutlasses or sword in his belt. They both stared up openmouthed as Giles Cutler staggered over to them. His forehead bore a livid bruise. He was soaking wet. Alex ground out a string of curses, but only shoved Giles aside. He hauled Brett to her feet and held her hard by one hand on her wrist amid the tumult of noise and smoke. "Get below, Brett, or so help me, I'll give you beaten black and blue to that British bastard!" he yelled again, and gestured wildly toward the enemy ship, now a mere twenty yards off. "You've as good as sunk the *Spirit*, ruined Sanborn's! And the Brit ships were waiting for us, knew we were coming out. You're the only one who knew ahead when we were sailing, you filthy, spying bitch!"

Brett stuck Giles's hand away as he dared to reach for her. "Come on, Miss Brett. You can't fool him anymore!" Giles shouted. "He knows you hate him, hate all Americans. I didn't want to help her, Mr. Alex, but she vowed to make up lies about me actually embezzling money, when I never took a penny. Said she'd sack me if I didn't, Mr. Alex. I'm sorry that I—"

Brett screamed in rage. No words could come out, just stark raw anger at the man's brazen lies and the traps he'd sprung on all of them. Alex slapped her once to quiet her hysteria. Enemy shots ripped through the *Spirit*'s rigging, as Alex's eyes ripped her apart. But she had to make him listen, had to! She hadn't done it, hadn't known a thing. She hit out at the sailor Alex ordered to drag her below. Alex had never believed her, never trusted her, never given her a chance.

But other cries besides her own shredded her sanity.

"Prepare to board!" echoed from the enemy ship, now so close she could see distinct British faces. With a huge groaning jolt, the two ships rammed, the frigate's bowsprit forcing through the smaller clipper's fore shrouds. Brett fell against Giles, then onto Alex, flat on the deck. She thought for a minute that in the roaring confusion either man might kill her.

Josh Windsor fell wounded near them in the next spray of close-range grapeshot. Brett scrambled to him beside Alex, but Alex shoved her back. Blood poured from Josh's shoulder, and neither his hand nor Alex's seemed to stem it. "Alex, save the clipper," Josh gritted out as waves of pain racked him. "She's such a beauty. Surrender! They may want her, not sink her. We might get her back someday—"

The ship's surgeon bent over his captain as Alex nodded, whispered something to his friend and gripped his hand. He stood and yanked Brett to her feet beside him. Hurt, battered, she did not try to pull away. His brutal touch sustained her, even though fury distorted his wild features. His breeches and shirt, cravatless and open at the throat, were stained and torn. Smoke-smudged, sweating, blood-speckled and defeated, he looked more wonderful to her than any man she had ever seen.

"Josh is right," Alex muttered to himself. "Surrender. Damn, who'd believe it? But who would believe sabotage? Damn!" Brett hung nearly suspended before him in his savage grip. "Prepare to strike the colors!" Alex Sanborn shouted over her head. He straightened to his full height. Behind him Giles Cutler hovered, his face suddenly no more shocking in his glee than Alex's in his devastation. Brett would have given anything in that moment to stand proudly beside Alex. She feared now that no matter what she said, she might never have the chance.

"Have you struck the colors?" a tinny voice trumpeted from the British ship.

Brett started at the shock of hearing a clipped British accent after these six weeks of Bal'morese. Iron hooks grappled the vessels together, marring the clipper's once pristine, polished mahogany deck rails.

Alex nodded his accord to the first mate. "Aye, colors struck!" the first mate shouted through his speaking trumpet, though they hardly needed to do much but whisper at such close quarters.

"Cease fire!" came from the British man-of-war, which Alex could see now was definitely Kelsey's *Raven's Wing*. He yanked Brett closer; her shoulder slammed into his hard chest as he turned her to him. His free hand seized her chin in a viselike grip to contort her face. He wanted to ruin it, to punish and obliterate this woman who had led him on to trust her, to want her. He felt so betrayed he wanted to tear her sodden clothes from her and hand her over stark naked to Commander Dalton Kelsey. She didn't deserve to walk the *Spirit*'s decks! He'd believed her—he'd almost loved her!

"You're Kelsey's war chattel now, evidently always have been!" he ground out between clenched teeth. "Just be certain you're never alone with me again, or I swear I'll use my sword on you—and not to surrender!"

Pleas and protests died on her lips. She watched paralyzed with grief as he drew his long sword from the scabbard on his belt. If he had sliced her to ribbons at that moment, she could not have felt more pain. He loosed his hold on her, shoved Giles Cutler out of his way as if he were a wisp of air. Head high, forced self-control making the muscles so rigid he almost shook, Alex Sanborn shouldered forward, ready to present the conquering Commander Kelsey of His Majesty's Royal Navy with his sword, hilt first.

Aboard the *Free Spirit* the wounded writhed and moaned. They were tended to as fast as the surgeon and the surgeon's mate could dart from one to the other. Shackled fast to the larger ship, the floundering clipper awaited formal boarding by British officers. At the bulwarks Alex Sanborn stood alone, waiting. Brett stood half hidden behind Giles Cutler and the clipper's first mate, but she could see the scene clearly. Finally the ramrod-stiff, barrel-chested English commander she had not seen for over a year climbed down and stepped aboard the *Spirit*'s deck. Yet in Brett's eyes, Alex's bold bearing completely eclipsed Commander Dalton Kelsey's glittering presence.

The aquiline-featured, impeccably attired Kelsey looked as if he'd just stepped from the elegant foyer of the Prince Regent's Carlton House in London. His formal blue uniform and wide, plumed cocked hat flashed with gold trim and braid in the sun. His spotless white kid breeches and thick silk shirt and cravat dazzled the eye amid the muted, darker colors of the captured crew crowding the rails. His boots shone like mirrors of polished ebony. Other officers in blue and an array of vibrant, scarlet-coated Royal Marines spilled aboard after him. Despite Alex's cruel rejection, Brett astounded herself by wishing she had one more burning wick to touch to a cannon and blow the British to a man off the deck of her ship!

"I am Commander Dalton Kelsey, sir, of His Britannic Majesty's Royal Frigate-of-war, the *Raven's Wing*," Kelsey announced properly to Alex and the hovering Americans as if he planned to just invite them over for billiards and port. Precise formality no matter what the carnage; Brett recalled he'd once described to her the *Royal Navy Regulations* book, which governed so-called civilized men at war at sea. With a curt nod and click of polished heels, Commander Kelsey accepted Alex's sword and immediately passed it to an officer behind him.

"I am Alexander Sanborn, owner of this merchant vessel of the independent nation of the United States of America," Alex's voice rang out, despite the British commander's snide pursing of full lips at that bold declaration. "The captain of the vessel lies wounded, Commander, and we would appreciate time to tend him and our crew struck down by your unjust attack."

"Unjust attack!" a lieutenant standing to Commander Kelsey's left snorted. "I say, but there is no such thing in dealing with Yankee rebels and Baltimore pirate ships of this order!" However much his underling raved, both Alex and Brett noted that Kelsey had heard not one word after the announcement of Alex's identity. Brett took a step forward to plead with Kelsey against a tirade she sensed was coming. Giles pulled her back around the splintered mast as Alex Sanborn's angry voice rang out again.

"I'm certain you'll be only too pleased to provide safe passage somehow back to dear old Mother England for the British spy who gave us over into your hands, Commander, and even drilled holes in this vessel to allow our capture."

Kelsey jerked up his head to thrust out his pointed chin even farther. He had expected to find the turncoat Giles Cutler among the crew here, but he had no idea the man was British. And, by damn, he'd clearly told Cutler not to reveal his spying to the Americans, even when they boarded! "A spy you've no doubt been in as close contact with lately as when she was your lover back in England," Alexander Sanborn said brazenly under Kelsey's eagle-eyed stare. "Men!" Sanborn cried, and turned to scan the crowd, "haul the traitorous baggage up here!"

Giles Cutler darted back out of their way as the *Spirit*'s first mate seized Brett's wrist and a burly marine took her arm to pull her forward. Dalton Kelsey's already jubilant face broke into a wider smile. He rubbed his hands together, while his two big rings winked in a stab of sunlight. He could not recall being more excited, even when he'd burned and scuttled ship after Yankee ship. Three prime pigeons, if one counted the ship itself, in one throw of the net, he congratulated himself! Giles Cutler was more to be praised than he had originally thought!

"By damn, my dear girl, but it's a delight to see you again, even if in such wretched circumstances," he crowed at Brett Benton. One look at her tragic expression told him all he had to know about her attitude to these cheeky rebels they'd snared. She was glaring at him! At him, the little bitch, her uncle's one-time protégée and avid suitor for her hand!

Kelsey's pale brown eyes darted again toward Alexander Sanborn, who was pointedly ignoring Brett's beseeching gaze. By damn, Kelsey thought, she was hardly the same woman he'd last seen waving a wan farewell to him from her great-uncle's front door, draped in its black crepe swags of mourning. Despite her bedraggled state, this woman was all vibrant life, color and passion. Lush, glowing flesh had filled out the hollows and angles of her body and face since he'd seen her last. She looked magnificent with her hair tumbled loose like this, all gilded and free in wind and sun. Even her eyes seemed a warmer gray, the hue of the seething, daring ocean itself. He realized then with another start that the bold figurehead he'd glimpsed during the fight was made in this new, daring Brett Benton's likeness.

In his utter astonishment at it all, Kelsey sucked in a loud breath. "I see the crude Americans haven't treated you like a lady at all,'' was all he could manage at first. "Take her aboard the *Raven* to my cabin, Lieutenant—for questioning and safekeeping. And, by damn, clap Mr. Sanborn in the hold in irons until I have time for him, too. And man the pumps on this war prize of a vessel at once!''

Brett let herself be led away. She couldn't bear the look of sheer hatred crushing Alex's brow. She had to make him understand, but this was hardly the time. She'd ask Dalton to let her speak with him later. Alex would have to believe her to understand. She'd insist that Giles Cutler be questioned before him. She went boldly, head high without a glance back at any of them as her three escorts lifted her over the *Spirit*'s railing and helped her up the ladder to the higher deck of the *Raven's Wing*.

Once there, she stared dazedly about. Puddles of blood with trails of frenzied footprints soaked the sand that dusted the bleached white deck. Men still scurried about, helping the wounded, stowing guns and shot. Her escorts pulled her onward as she put foot ahead of foot on the gritty sand. But at the top of the steps of the dim companionway to the captain's cabin, she propped stiff arms on both sides of the door.

"The Americans," she asked the young lieutenant in charge, "will they be impressed or imprisoned?"

"The able ones impressed, ma'am, Admiralty orders."

She nodded numbly at that familiar phrase from her youth and let him help her down the steps. But in the narrow passageway she overheard what one marine following muttered to the other.

"Blimey, there'll be a capital hangin' in the morn, sure as shootin'. That Sanborn there's been the number one privateer Kelsey's been gettin' spy news from Baltimore on. I wager you a fortnight's pay that one'll be hoisted at the end of a rope from his own ship's yardarm by the dawn's first light tomorrow.''

Brett heard a woman's shrill cry before she realized it was her own. She hit out at the men, clawed at their startled faces in her efforts to get back up on the deck and warn Alex. I took the three big men to still her, to drag her into Kelsey's cabin. Her cries and thrashing only stopped when her head hit the corner of the bunk and she tumbled into limp oblivion.

Ten

‑‑‑○‑○○‑○‑‑‑

Brett swam upward through the foggy, velvet darkness toward the sound of a man's voice. The sharp blast of ammonia salts in her nose yanked her to consciousness. "They said she just hit her head, sir. She's awake now," the man's voice said, and moved away. With great effort, Brett lifted her eyelids. The startling salmon light of an ocean sunset flooded through the stern windows over her. Memory crashed back. She was in the captain's cabin aboard Dalton Kelsey's British man-of-war and Alex was in irons somewhere aboard.

"Mr. Sanborn? The ship?" she cried, but the man went out and closed the door.

Dalton Kelsey filled her view as he bent over the narrow built-in bed where she lay. He took her hand. "My dearest girl, you mustn't fret for the enemy. You do realize Alexander Sanborn is our enemy, do you not? And the ship is now His Majesty's prize—under my control, of course, as all is aboard my flagship."

That cleared her head faster than ammonia salts. She pulled her hand back when she realized he held it and struggled to sit up, despite his protests. She had to be careful if she was to be allowed to see Alex and save him and the *Free Spirit*. She thought first of insisting that Giles Cutler be dragged in but he would only say awful things to Dalton about Alex. Dalton might even reward him for testifying against Alex.

Besides, Giles was probably in chains with the rest of the crew, and that would have to do for now. Best she not even mention Giles Cutler until she talked to Alex alone. He had to believe her when she told him she was not a British spy!

Her hand shot to her forehead. Pain crunched her brow. She ached all over. She shoved down the blanket that trapped her legs in the bed. Her eyes took in her dishabille, the torn and dirtied gown that made her look like a street urchin, or worse—the display of leg one long rip in the skirt flaunted. Her bodice was still damp and clung too tightly. She quickly tugged the blanket up and wrapped it around her like a bulky shawl. She swung her feet over the side under Dalton Kelsey's all too avid gaze.

Pity, he thought, that there were navy regulations to abide by and some dealt with proper care of captured women aboard. He wasn't certain whether Brett Benton was ally or enemy right now, but he did know what he wanted to do with her. As she stood before him so gloriously tousled he found it hard to believe that he had once dismissed her as sharp tongued and skinny, useful only for the things she had inherited from her great-uncle. Maybe he should just take her; he'd ignored or skirted naval rules with aplomb more than once before when it had suited him.

By damn, if he had things his way he'd have the injured Americans they'd captured tossed overboard to the sharks, including the ship's wounded captain. He'd have Sanborn hanged right now! And he'd enjoy this woman in a trice as a war prize, as she thrashed under his thrusts in this bed. No formal trials, no leniency, no foolish gentlemen's manners, no quarter or mercy—that's how he'd run this blasted war! Unfortunately there were restrictions to contend with, which included the civilized courting of this woman until he got what he wanted from her one way or the other.

"Don't stand if you're dizzy, Brett," he murmured solicitously. He steadied her at the elbow as she ignored his command and took a few steps. "I've ordered some gruel and tea for you."

She wanted to smack that counterfeit look of concern from his face, to jump away from his touch. She did neither.

"I can't thank you enough for your kindness to me, Dalton. This place and these circumstances are a far cry from the town house on Grosvenor Square, you must admit."

Over the steaming food a pigtailed seaman carried in on a wooden tray, Dalton kept reminiscing about the days when her uncle was alive. He wanted to know what she had done with her uncle's things—even his papers. His insistence on small talk infuriated her. She wanted to demand Alex's freedom. Arguments she could use against the impressing of sailors like poor Lissa Miles's husband and demands the wounded like Josh Windsor be released flooded her brain. She struggled for calm, finding herself frighteningly trapped between her old loyalties to Britain and her love for the new challenge of America. She could have ranted and debated with this powerful British commander like the best Baltimore shipping merchant.

Dalton Kelsey's wily brain teemed with possibilities as he watched Brett choke down her food. He could tell she was on edge, but she still responded to his conversationally phrased inquiries as politely and formally as if they'd just met on a stroll through Hyde Park. She tried to affect a certain nonchalance about her new life. She was hiding her attachment to the Americans, and Sanborn especially. That deceit and her smoldering emotions made her a temptation she had never been before. He marveled again at the transformation of her thin body and pinched, pale, stoic face to this compelling, blooming beauty. The price he must now pay to possess her seemed infinitely more reasonable. He kept studying her, fascinated and yet afraid she was not to be trusted now.

Yet none of that would matter in the end, he thought smugly. He could force a promise of marriage from her, perhaps even wed her aboard ship before they parted again. Her great-uncle's precious papers included an entire document accusing Dalton Kelsey of crimes that could mean his ruination and execution even yet if they came to light. That damning evidence must still be secreted with the old admiral's papers.

Brett had admitted she'd stored them away in London until her return, when she would have more time to go through them and decide what to donate to the Admiralty.

But if Brett Benton were his wife, he would control all her property. By damn, he would destroy those papers—destroy her, too, if he must. He had as good as killed old Admiral Benton when they had argued that day at the town house over the evidence the wily son of a bitch had collected. Brett had been out to church. When the old man refused to surrender the incriminating papers and dared to lecture him, he'd struck him such a blow that it had caused a stupor from which the old man had never awakened. And now, to protect all he'd worked for these years, he had a series of other blows to strike.

"Well, then, dearest girl, we've spoken of nearly everything but that which is most heavy on my heart," he went on. He selected and polished each word, every nuance of voice, to attain the desired effect.

Her teaspoon rattled as she put it down in her saucer. She could not halt her barely perceptible trembling. Alex was what was heavy on *her* heart. She had to weigh every move carefully to rescue him. But she was staggered by her formidable opponents: this vengeful commander, the British navy and two great countries at war. Still, she managed an encouraging nod to urge Dalton on.

"When last we parted I asked you to be my wife and you insisted you needed time," he continued. He twisted his gold signet ring around and around his finger as he spoke. "You needed a year, I believe you said. It's been that, and here we are oceans and continents from where I expected to find you."

"Sometimes life deals us a hand we don't expect," she said. Holding the blanket about her shoulders, she rose and took a few steps away before turning back. "You know, I'm sure, Dalton, a great many things have changed in my life since London. I have business interests now, even though they are not British."

"They are clearly anti-British, dearest girl."

"We—they, the Americans, I mean—obviously don't see it that way. They only want to be free to trade without foreign interference." She took a deep breath. "I have interests and concerns in common with Alex Sanborn now, and your arrest of him therefore threatens my future."

"I've duly noted your interest in the man!" his voice cracked out before he could blunt its sharp edge. How dared the little bitch even suggest she cared for a Yank dog rebel over Commander Dalton Kelsey, he seethed.

"It's strictly a business interest!" she insisted to match his volume and vehemence. "He and I are co-owners of that new sleek clipper ship you've confiscated and of a Baltimore business that thrived before this unfortunate war with its British threats and blockades!"

He rose to his full height, regretful he was but an inch taller than this woman even in his heeled boots. She'd always needed bridling badly, and a bit in that quick, clever mouth. He itched to take on the task. Already he saw that gentle, deceptive courting would not do the trick, so he plunged ahead with new strategies accordingly.

"Then may I be the first to congratulate you, Brett," he clipped out with a mock bow. "By damn, I'm hanging your so-called business partner at first light tomorrow, and perhaps *that* will leave you *full* owner then. You'll not be seeing him again. It's most unnecessary and unwise. But when you wed me, we'll own your little piece of defeated America together—after this 'unfortunate war with its British threats and blockades,' that is, hmm?"

He reached dramatically for his enameled-and-gilded snuffbox in his waistcoat pocket. He watched her absorb the blows he'd dealt her. She seemed to waver, and he wondered if she would get the feminine vapors. By damn, he'd like her teary eyed and pleading, but not over the loss of some other lover! And he burned to know whether she'd kept herself chaste for him, or had she spread her legs for that brazen, bluff Yankee dog Sanborn!

But his mouth fell open when she blinked back tears so fast he wasn't certain they'd been there at all. She composed her face, squared her shoulders and sat back down across the table from him. She snaked an arm out of her blanket cocoon and scooted her plateware and cutlery away from between them. Then with a shrug she threw the blanket on the chair behind her. She leaned toward him across the table on both elbows with her chin in her hands, facing him boldly with a riveting gaze.

Dalton Kelsey's fingers in the snuff stilled; his thick lips pursed in surprise even as he ran a quick tongue between them. The snuffbox, with his hand still in it, hit the table to rattle china there. He crossed his knees to control the rush of desire in his loins for this bold, sensual woman he had obviously never known.

"I admit I don't want you to hang Alex Sanborn, but not for the reason you evidently think," she began. She argued coldly, logically, amazingly, he thought, about how she needed to have Alex Sanborn back in Baltimore to finish teaching her to control and expand her business. Sanborn's would be wildly profitable after the war, she assured him. She would be willing to give him half—even three-fourths—of all her profits if he let her return with Alex Sanborn to Baltimore so he could finish teaching her all she needed to know.

"I intend to hang the man," he responded with a crisp shake of his head. "Regulations, after what he's done. Necessity and duty. Your great-uncle would have done the same. The man's fast, armed ships and rabid patriotism have been a thorn in my side and a blow to my—the navy's reputation!" He, too, leaned forward over the table, expectantly awaiting her next move.

As the time and arguments went on, Brett knew her voice rose, her breasts heaved. But she'd learned to remain cool under fire from Alex that day at Henny's when she'd told him this very man had once proposed marriage. She'd seen then how effective changing one's methods could be, especially when it was unexpected. She had to save Alex. She loved Alex for the things he had allowed her to share among his people in his city. She loved Alex for his protection of her when others turned against her. She loved Alex, devil take him—for Alex!

With obvious relish, Dalton Kelsey countered her arguments and refused her pleas that he spare Sanborn. Then he added, "But after the war I'll see about getting that sleek little clipper we're pumping out returned to you. Until then, she'll be my personal supply ship. But," he said, and lowered his voice even as his eyes drifted down to her bodice, "I vow you can have her back now if you marry me. That way you and *I* will share Sanborn's, not you and that *dog of a rebel Yankee*!"

She almost lunged across the table to tear his tongue out. She could have attacked him with her nails, her teeth! Her raging emotions terrified her; she'd never felt the power of such savagery before. She couldn't let Alex die! She couldn't let this night go by without explaining her innocence to him! She had to comfort him! And yet she needed all her wiles here, not her feeble physical powers against Dalton Kelsey and his ship full of armed men. But he'd inadvertently just given her the idea for another ploy.

She sighed loudly. "I see I've got to admit my real plan," she said, and fought to keep her voice steady. "I've told no one else. I can't abide the man, but I'd been trying to get Alex Sanborn to marry me so I could become his sole heir in the business. I knew a loudmouthed, flag-waving Yank bully like him was bound to get himself killed in this war one way or the other and leave me his fortunate—and rich— widow."

She narrowed her eyes and hit her fist hard on the table so that her teacup rattled. "He thinks I'm plain and a scold, and I can't stomach his crude manners. But Sanborn's is all Great-uncle Charles really left me, Dalton, and I'm hardly getting any younger. I was hoping to get him to wed me, thinking that would give him control of all the Sanborn shares. Of course, he's hardly a gentleman like you and has made it plain he wants nothing to do with me—like that."

She glanced back toward the door and leaned even closer across the table to whisper to the flabbergasted man. "I will admit it only to you, but this whole capture—and Alex Sanborn's imminent hanging—is very—well, convenient for me. But if you hang him before I marry him, his heirs will get half and I'll be back where I was, struggling with the rude, provincial Americans for control of my fortune. Now if I were left his widow—'' She let the thought hang. She had no idea how Alex would react to this, but she had to see him. Beyond that, she would try to set him free somehow! It was a plan born of utter desperation, but it seemed the only way to her.

When Dalton Kelsey merely sat dumbfounded at her proposal, she reached across the table to cover the hand that still held the open snuffbox. ''I've always loved hearing about ships and the sea, you know that,'' she said, and forced a smile. ''Now I've got my chance to own a big shipping firm on my own—to be richer than Uncle Charles ever was. I'd planned to move back to London after the war, when you'd finally be back, too. Dalton, I'd adore for a man like you, a British naval hero my uncle admired, to own half of my firm through marriage. But this way I'd get the entire Sanborn fortune for myself, and now since you're going to hang him, anyway—''

Suddenly she had the oddest sensation that the irises of his pale brown eyes had disappeared and his dark pinpoint pupils pierced right through her. ''By damn, it is an intriguing idea,'' he managed to choke out. He got up to pour himself a goblet of port from a closed, barred cupboard, sloshing some on the floor in his hurry. He offered none to her, but downed it in one loud gulp.

''All right,'' he said, and swung back to face her. ''From what you say, we'll have to force the marriage on his part, but I can handle that. And then we'll have to give the two of you an hour or so together tonight. You'll have to consummate the marriage in case the courts ever contest your complete right to his fortune.'' His mind raced now. His narrowed eyes met her wide, suddenly surprised ones.

Consummation of the marriage—she had never thought as far as that! Consummation with Alex, making love with Alex! And if she then conceived his child—

Dalton Kelsey saw she sat as if transfixed. He swaggered over to her, then pulled her to her feet against him, his arms crushing her to his barrel chest. "Then, Brett, by damn, you will vow to wed me by dawn's early light tomorrow as soon as I hang the Yankee son of a bitch."

Brett's only gasp was inward. She managed to stand still in his embrace. She felt numb to further shocks now. If she couldn't reconcile with Alex, if she couldn't find a way to save him, she almost didn't care what happened to her. If worse came to worse and Alex died, maybe after she married Dalton, he'd let her go back to Baltimore. She could carry on Alex's work for him if the wild Baltimoreans would let her. But she just couldn't bear to think of losing him. Comforting Alex, telling him she had not betrayed his trust, that she loved him—that was all that mattered now.

"I'm waiting for the answer I need, Brett," he said, interrupting the torrent of her thoughts.

"Yes, that's a plan that solves all my problems and will make you a rich man someday," she told Dalton Kelsey, her voice one dead monotone pitch he seemed not to heed. "I owe you so much, Dalton. I agree—to both marriages."

"Then I have a lot to do," he told her. He loosed her and strode for the door. She was grateful he had not tried to kiss her. After Alex's passionate, skillful embraces, Dalton's would be weak, pale imitations. With a silent prayer for strength, she watched him walk away.

At the door he turned back. "I'm going to lock you in for your own safety until I arrange everything. And you'd best change clothes. There's a green gown and bonnet on the chest I found for you. It will do for a hasty wedding and brief conjugal visit. After our marriage tomorrow, I promise you, you won't be wearing a thing."

The door slammed. She heard him lock it and talk to a guard in the passageway. Stunned at the sweep of events she herself had set in motion, she walked slowly to the sea chest and lifted the gown. It felt slightly damp, but it was a lovely mint-green percale with ruffled, square-necked bodice. Dazedly she held it up to herself. Her exact measurements, the exact color of her gown she'd had ruined in the market that awful day. Then she realized it must be the one Giles Cutler had mentioned he'd brought along for her. Had Dalton Kelsey really just found it in a floating trunk in the *Spirit*'s flooded forecastle hold, or had Giles somehow given it to him? And if they knew each other before all this—

She gasped as she saw the pewter dish just beyond the straw bonnet. Proof flashed through her brain like jagged lightning strokes: Giles's hatred of Alex, his desire to be on the *Free Spirit*'s maiden voyage. His knowledge of how to get in the closed shipyard where the clipper was built. This gown and now these!

Her shaking hand reached out to lift one of the candies from the dish by its twisted paper wrapper as if it would burn her. Giles's favorite Berkeley's toffees in Commander Dalton Kelsey's private cabin! She remembered now that Dalton had often brought her the same gift when he visited the London town house. And she'd heard the marine whisper to his mate earlier that some Baltimore spy had reported Alex was the number one privateer. So Giles Cutler's debauchery was deeper than embezzlement and the defilement and abduction of women! But she'd discovered much, much too late Giles's sinister source for contraband British goods in wartime—and Dalton Kelsey's source for classified information. Giles Cutler had sold his soul to the British to betray Baltimore and the entire nation. And she'd just made her own devil's bargain that put her squarely in those same evil British hands! She could only pray that Alex would actually believe her when she told him of the real spy in Sanborn's midst.

Down the corridor from his cabin, Dalton Kelsey nearly bumped into Giles Cutler in his hurry. "You said to wait up on deck, but you took so long," Giles began.

Kelsey glared. No one disobeyed his orders aboard without a severe flogging and dousing with stinging saltwater. But this grotesque monkey of a man had done him a great service. He stemmed his instinct to give Cutler a curt dressing-down and forced himself to pat him once on the back.

"I'm afraid your good work for us ashore will be compromised if you're the only one to return to Baltimore from this capture, man. You'll be staying aboard at least until we can put you off in some other pro-British port."

"No danger the captured clipper's crew will tell," Giles countered, and hacked a quick cough into his handkerchief. "Impressed men sent to sea on British ships and the dead owner of a shipping firm will tell no tales back in Baltimore. And I wanted to let you know that I'll be glad to take Miss Benton off your hands now as you promised—"

"Miss Benton?" Kelsey cracked out. "By damn, I promised nothing about Miss Benton. The lady's been my fiancée for over a year, man. She's agreed to marry Sanborn straightaway, before I hang him, so we can get full control of his Baltimore business. But she loves me—and will be marrying me before I send her to Canada for safekeeping." He began edging past Giles in the narrow passage. For the first time the man's face horrified Kelsey rather than just disgusted him.

"Look, Flame—Giles," Kelsey began, trying to recoup, "I appreciate all you've done. You will be further rewarded." He shuffled another step away. "But you need either to sign on aboard the *Raven's Wing*, or at best let me set you up in some city like Washington or Annapolis, where you won't be questioned if some Yank dog spills his guts in Baltimore. By damn, I swear to you, I intend to torch those two other hovels, as well as Baltimore come autumn." He frowned as he turned away. The normal half of Cutler's face showed shock, the ogre's side pure fury. "And I'll see about having the Baltimore doxy you asked for saved for you until after the war," he added hastily over his shoulder as he clambered quickly up the steps of the companionway.

Stunned by this twist in fortune, Giles Cutler propped both stiff arms against the wall under the lantern, which licked his face with its wan flame. Beyond, where Kelsey had disappeared, black night poured down the steps. Giles's clenched fist smashed the wall. Once, twice, again. Each time he only grunted as the lantern in its wall bracket shuddered and rattled. He had a nearly overwhelming urge to grab it and race down the corridor scattering hot oil and flame to burn this vessel out from under that pompous bastard Kelsey! After all he'd done for him and the British—as good as delivered the *Free Spirit* and Sanborn into his hands to make his reputation! All he'd wanted out of it was Brett Benton, thus completing his revenge on Sanborn. And now Commander Kelsey insisted she was his!

So Brett Benton had fooled him. Was she Kelsey's spy in Baltimore, too? Is that why she'd been so anxious to see everything—shipping manifests, the layout of the warehouse, the closed shipyard? If so, Giles Cutler deserved her more than ever, and he meant to have her. He stared as if mesmerized into the wavering flames of the lantern behind its glass barrier. A clever plan—the only possible plan—burned in his wily brain. He composed both sides of his face with difficulty and darted up the steps after Commander Kelsey.

Alex refused to take Brett's hand even at the ship chaplain's request. Brett stood trembling while the portly, balding man read the words of the Anglican rites of marriage, feeling in her bones their cruel mockery of both Alex and her. Here she stood being wed to a man who hated her, dressed in a gown the traitor costing Alex his life had bought her. Only her pearls from her dear Simone comforted her even a little. *Take care of Alex for me, ma chère Brett,* Simone had written in her farewell note. *I pray you will find a man who inspires both your passion and loyalty forever.* Brett had found that man, but everything had gone so terribly wrong. She clenched her hands at her sides to control herself. She tried so hard not to listen to her own frenzied thoughts or the import of the chaplain's words "'Till death us do part...'"

Her bridegroom stood stiffly beside her in his own clean shirt and cravat, boots and gray kid breeches. She could feel the tremendous physical impact of his presence even now, when he was someone else's pawn and prisoner. Her nipples leaped to taut nubs against the softness of her chemise and gown. Her body ached to have Alex's iron arms around her.

"'With my body I thee honor; and all my worldly goods with thee I share...'"

Alex had not said a word, hardly looked her way when the two armed guards had escorted him in. Not even when she'd insisted they remove his leg irons had his eyes met hers. "'May they ever remain in perfect love and peace together,'" the chaplain intoned. But Alex was seething. She noted the telltale pulse at the side of his throat beating a rapid tattoo before she forced her eyes back to the chaplain.

Her voice quavered as she repeated the words to love, honor and obey. "'Those whom God hath joined together let no man put asunder,'" the chaplain pronounced.

"Join hands, please," he requested even more pointedly, an obviously wary eye cocked at the big American's stonelike expression.

Brett heard Dalton Kelsey behind them clear his throat and half slide his sword from his scabbard in ominous warning when Alex still didn't budge. Her heart thudded in her throat. Her legs and backbone turned to cold liquid. Perhaps she hadn't done the right thing. But she had a knife she'd taken from Dalton's cabin laced tight with her slipper ribbons against her inner calf. Lying just under the swell of each breast, held to her skin by the ribbon at the high Empire waist, lay two keys she'd found in Dalton's desk drawer. What they opened, she had no idea, but she was desperate. Why couldn't Alex trust her just a little, give her the benefit of the doubt long enough that they could be alone? Why wouldn't he even meet her eyes?

She nearly jumped out of her skin when Alex seized her hand. His skin was warm, his grip brutally strong, but she didn't flinch once the dizzying shock of his initial touch passed. Her head spun as the chaplain's final words washed over them: "Now, by the power vested in me through His Majesty's Admiralty, I do solemnly pronounce that they be man and wife together. You, ah, may kiss the bride, sir."

The force of Alex's fury pivoted her to face him more than his sudden seizure of her elbows. "The bride," he said only, his voice cutting with contempt. Then, obviously turning her in such a way that Dalton Kelsey could have the benefit of a full side view, he pulled Brett hard against him and his lips descended.

The kiss was crushing, almost brutal in its utter mastery and power. Although at first she went limp in his arms, his anger coursed into her to stiffen her backbone. Even if he turned physically abusive—and she knew he might—she must talk to him alone.

His hands slid heavily up her arms to grip her, until she thought there was no blood left in them. His tongue raped her mouth. It was then, as Dalton Kelsey sprang forward to pry them apart, she fully realized what she could be in for if she still insisted on a private visit with Alex Sanborn.

"This man's a beast, Brett!" Kelsey clipped out. She fell against Kelsey's barrel chest as Alex instantly released her. Despite the painful tingling where Alex had touched her, she stepped immediately back from Kelsey's protective touch. "Enough of this little scene. We'll go no further with this farce—" Dalton began threateningly.

"No?" Alex demanded, whirling to face down the much shorter man. "No consummated wedding night as you promised me earlier, then no further cooperation, commander. It's bad enough I've been both sold out and bought by this woman like a piece of goods, but I expect to get something out of this little charade. Half my firm, which my father and I worked for most of our lives, is a pretty steep price to pay for a tall, skinny, cold, sharp-tongued bitch any way you look at it!"

Brett gasped. Even in their rough beginnings he'd never spoken to her like that. Nor had his words or eyes cheapened or insulted her like this. Tears prickled behind her eyelids, but she blinked them back. His nostrils flared as if he breathed fire. His chiseled lips were set in a hard line, their corners turned down in complete contempt. His slitted eyes raked her brutally up and down, as if she were some slut he'd picked off the docks. She'd gotten used to his intimate, teasing, challenging visual examinations, grown to expect them, even long for them. But this! She would be mad if she went off to the first mate's cabin alone with this man as they'd promised. But she had to tell him the truth. When he saw she'd brought keys and a weapon, surely he'd then believe and understand her.

Paper in hand, the chaplain bustled back to stand between her and Alex. "Now please, please, no such violence of words or otherwise on such a sanctified day."

Alex wheeled on Kelsey again. Brett was sure he would have lunged at him but for the two guards with pistols drawn. "Sanctified, indeed!" he snorted. "A merchant vessel seized, innocent Americans killed and wounded and one—just one— thanks to this forced sham of a marriage—to be hanged at dawn. Don't lecture me about violence, sir," he told the chaplain. "Now *that's* the British idea of 'such a sanctified day.'"

"Enough, Sanborn. You will sign the agreement now," Kelsey ordered, his hand on his dress sword below the gold epaulets and array of medals he sported as if it were his wedding. "And then, if Brett is still willing, you may have some time alone to make your peace with her."

Alex ignored the click of cocked hammers on the pistols behind him as he stepped past Kelsey to take Brett's arm again. He turned her to him with both hands and tipped her back until her thighs tilted into his iron-hard ones before them all and she stared straight up into his face. "On the contrary, Commander Kelsey, *if* I am to sign, I demand your word of honor—" here his voice dripped sarcasm "—that I will have time alone with my new wife whether she is willing or not."

"By damn, Sanborn, I said it before, and the lady did, too. It's a legal marriage. Just sign. But I swear to you if one hair on her head is harmed, I'll flog you within an inch of your life before I hang you!"

Brett supposed Dalton wanted her to look at him with gratitude, but she was mesmerized by Alex's piercing stare. Though his touch was brutal and mocking, her loins seemed to meld with his. The chaplain extended a quill to sign the document with and called her by her new married name. Still, none of that moved her. She saw no one but Alex. She felt suspended in his grasp, chained to his hot, devouring gaze.

He loosed her so fast she almost crumpled at his feet.

"Sign, dear wife. Time's fleeting. And I intend to make more than peace with you this night. And without leg irons on my ankles, Kelsey."

She didn't look at Dalton as he grudgingly agreed, or at the hovering chaplain pointing at the spot she was to sign. The guards with guns behind her didn't exist. Dalton Kelsey didn't exist; neither did this entire wretched war. There was no one else in the whole vast universe but her and Alex. But they had come to such an impasse. She loved him desperately and he wanted only to hate and hurt her.

Her tears blurred her shaky signature as she signed *Brett Anne Benton Sanborn*. Nationality—*British*. She watched, stunned, as her new husband signed in bold script on the line next to her name: *Alexander Sanborn the Younger. American*.

Her feet moved, but the rest of her seemed to drift at Alex's side as they left the captain's cabin without so much as a toast or a final chaplain's blessing. Down the corridor, down four steps. She refused to look at either Alex or Dalton. A turn in at the first mate's room. Her eyes adjusted to the single meager lantern there. Her cheeks flamed hot with shame when Alex haggled with Kelsey for another lantern to "see his prize better." Still, she felt it could not be her here in this predicament. Not even when Kelsey handed over another lantern with some grand pronouncement about a guard in the hall to hear her if she called. He informed them the door would be firmly bolted. Everyone went out but Alex and her. The door banged shut; the bolt grated closed.

Now, when the time had come to tell Alex the truth, she could not bear to face his anger. Besides, Dalton might still have his ear pressed to the door. She shot a wary glance around the little room. A single rope hammock hung from the rafters; the rest of the small space was crowded with stacked bolts of calico wrapped around wooden planks. She didn't know whether to breathe a sigh of relief or cry at the impossibility of two bodies in the swinging rope hammock. Swiftly she jumped back at Alex's sudden movement behind her.

"Bridal jitters, sweetheart?" his cold voice taunted. "A guilty conscience? Come a bit late, perhaps?" He bent to plow his shoulder into a stack of wooden bolts of cloth nearly as tall as she was, then slid them heavily across the door. "Doesn't do to have unwanted visitors crashing into our little honeymoon idyll without fair warning," he muttered.

"Alex, I can explain everything," her whispered words tumbled out. "I'm not the spy, but I know who is. Look," she pleaded, her voice shaking. "I've brought you a knife and two keys."

"For an attempted escape so they can shoot me in the back?" he derided. But he stood intent with hands on his lean hips as she lifted her skirt to pull the dagger from the ribbons around her calf. He could not control avid interest, though he silently cursed himself for it, when she reached into her bodice and beneath her breasts to extract two keys. He just crossed his arms over his chest as she extended all three items to him with outstretched hand from six feet away.

"I warned you not to risk being alone with me, Brett. They may have taken my sword, but you're offering me a fine replacement in that dagger. And the few hours I have left leave no time for your clever tricks or arguments." He leaned back against the stack of bolts. "You may, however, continue to unlace those shoes and rid yourself of every other stitch you have on. I thought you were about to open your bodice for me. I'll have more of that."

"You bastard! This was all just so I could get to see you!"

"Excellent, as I intend to see all of you. And—" he threatened and lifted one big finger to point it at her stunned, angry face "—I don't want a word out of you tonight, no matter what happens in here. You've ruined everything for me, but now you're going to make at least some of that up to me flat on your back. It will help me not to think of what's coming tomorrow, you see."

In a sudden move, he untied and unwrapped his cravat and skimmed his shirt up over his head. He tumbled several bolts of cloth across the floor, and kicked them in a pile. All the while, she stared wide-eyed at the expanse of his firm muscled flesh flecked with dark hair, at the rippling of his clearly defined back and midriff muscles. Broad shoulders narrowed to a solid rib cage, and his flat belly disappeared beneath the gray kid trousers with an ominous bulge in front. While she gawked, he began to unbutton the front of his breeches.

"We—we can't. There's no bed!"

He laughed. "My treacherous little lying innocent. Don't you think I know now that Kelsey's had you? He's pampered you badly if it's always been in a bed. And he gave me the charming news of your nuptials—your second, real nuptials—tomorrow. But tonight's tonight," he said, and moved slowly, menacingly toward her. "You've finally taught me all about the real Brett and why she came to Baltimore. And tonight you're going to learn all about the real Alex and what he thinks of traitors who bargain with their bodies. I'm very sure the floor will do for all the things I have in mind."

Wide-eyed, the dagger gripped convulsively in her hand, she backed toward the wall as he stalked her.

Eleven

Brett stood trapped between Alex and the wall. He took the knife and keys from her tight grip. She remained unmoving while he unwrapped her fingers one by one and lifted the items from her damp palm. Her nostrils flared at the scent of him, all sea wind and musk with a hint of brandy. When he had bathed and changed clothes, Dalton must have allowed him a drink to steel himself for his wedding ordeal. Alex's presence this close overwhelmed her. She dared not look into his face or she would gladly have sacrificed her love to his anger and lust. She had never dared imagine a wedding night with Alex Sanborn. Now she dared not let herself think what he might do during it for revenge.

"Who knows how long the British bastard will give us," he muttered. "He's playing with me, but I swear tonight you won't."

He bent to stuff the keys and daggers into the top of his boot. His big hands lifted to her shoulders to face her away from him, and she stared at the dingy wall while he deftly unhooked her gown. She closed her eyes and fought to compose herself for whatever he might do. He gave her no time to protest, argue, not even a moment to adjust to the rough touch of his hands. Rudely he peeled the gown down and pushed it over her hips to the floor. Her thin batiste chemise followed in a rush, until she stood nearly naked in a pool of her garments. She held her breath, waiting for his next move, not daring to think what he would do in his thinly leashed fury.

She gasped when his hands circled her arms to cup her naked breasts more completely than the tight bodice had done. The movement toppled her back into his rock-hard embrace. Sensations staggered her as the smooth skin of her back came in contact with his hard chest.

"A good wife does anything her husband asks." He dipped his head to breathe the whispered words against her silken shoulder. "Practice arching your back for me."

Standing in only her green-gartered white silk stockings, ribboned slippers and pearls, she did exactly as he asked. She was beyond independent thinking. She knew only that she had come to this tiny room for Alex's touch. All her thirty years of muted longings had been for this, and she hadn't known it until now. This was a dream, surely nothing harsh or cruel could even touch them unless they willed it.

Cupping her breasts in his big palms, he stroked their pink rosebuds in delicious, agonizing circles, one way, then the other. Her knees were like water; she braced them against his hard muscled legs to stand. She felt the chamois softness of the material covering the thrust of him against her bare bottom. The feel of the pliant, slick leather of his boots against her naked calves sent shivers up her spine. His open mouth slid heavy along her neck and shoulder to shift her pearls and nibble a line of little bites there. He tweaked her nipples, brazenly rotated them between warm, callused fingers until she thought she would scream out her desire.

His open hands slid down her rib cage to splay themselves against her satin stomach. "We should have a full mirror on this wall so you could see how beautiful you are this way," he rasped out. "And how beautifully willing. Did he tell you to keep me amused like this?"

She gasped when he rotated his middle finger in her navel. His hands marauded lower again to shape themselves firmly to her angled hipbones, then meet in a possessive grasp between her legs, which she had mindlessly moved apart for him.

"Mmm, stop," she protested in a sound more like a wanton murmur.

"Stand still." His voice was suddenly harsh and rough. "You've always defied me. Tonight you do it only at your own peril."

That half sobered her. Rubbish, she scolded herself, she'd fallen instantly victim to his seducing touch. Perhaps he meant to pin her hard against these rough wallboards in this little storeroom when he took her. But his touch had gone as delicate as lamb's-down.

She gasped as his fingers moved skillfully between her legs, and she tried desperately to clamp them together. Too late. The minute she fought him he changed his tactics. He lifted her, then spilled her flat on her back on the soft disarray of calico cloth, with him standing spread-legged at her feet. Quickly she closed her legs again and pulled a swath of material over her midsection. He scowled as he yanked off both boots and, under her saucer-eyed stare, divested himself of his half-buttoned breeches. He was a big man, but she hadn't expected that part of him to be so...alert and ready! Though there was nowhere to go, she tried to scramble away when he lunged at her stark naked.

He shoved her back down, tore the cloth away from her body. "Enough of pleasing you," he said. "That's been my big mistake ever since you first stepped off that French boat. Were you missing Kelsey every time you let me kiss you? Did you just act the touchy virgin innocent? The clever British spy sent over by her high-ranking navy lover. And both of you laughing at the poor Yankee dupe with his tongue hanging out to bed you!" he mocked. "Blue blazes, tonight I *will* bed you, as often and any way I want!"

His admission that he desired her—wanted to bed *her*, Brett Benton—somehow staggered her anew. "Alex, please, I didn't know. My spying—it's not true. I didn't go to Baltimore for him. I don't love him!" she blurted, as her jumbled thoughts spilled out.

But he wasn't listening. He literally shredded her garters and stockings from her legs in the rush of his rage. "You're much too dressed, British. You know, if you're really low enough to wed that bastard the same day I hang, I'd love to stick you with my child! But who knows what your type would do to an innocent baby! All those teary-eyed stories coming from an orphanage and caring about street children! Was anything true about you?"

"Yes, yes. Alex, please, please, just listen."

"No! Keep your mouth shut from now on, traitor. You were the only one I told the *Spirit*'s sailing day to far enough ahead to tip the Brits, and there they were, waiting for us. I swear, I'd have let your lover Kelsey flog me to death as he threatened if that was all that was at stake. But he swore to spare Josh's hanging if I went through with this! And I'm only touching you now to sully Kelsey's goods before you deliver my firm to him just as you did my ship!"

His hands were rough, his kisses brutal. His powerful body, which she had only glimpsed and gasped at seconds ago, mastered her. With one hand he easily pinned her arms up over her head. Then he knelt over her and forced his knees between her thrashing legs. She fought him silently, desperately, but she knew it was too late to fight her love for him, and that turned her more frenzied than her fear.

"I wish," he gasped out as he separated her legs by spreading his own huge, muscular thighs, "I had the time—to show you what you'll be—missing when you're Kelsey's!"

His hot, wet mouth covered a breast with stunning impact. To her amazement, it robbed her of desire to resist. She wished he'd release her wrists so she could stroke his mussed dark head where it bent over her so close. She wanted to pull him closer. She wanted to wrap him in her arms to comfort him, tell him everything about how he had changed her life.

He settled his weight in closer. His hardness probed her soft center. He steadied her and pressed her down. The heat and power of his body radiated to her trembling flesh. She felt both shame and rapture at his brazen, intimate touch.

"I only wish I could say how much I love you," she murmured, half to herself. But her words were drowned in the impact of his simultaneous probe into her slick tightness.

She gasped even at that merest entry. The idea of their being joined so perfectly and intimately racked her with the earth-shattering uniqueness of it. It didn't hurt. If felt both imprisoning and liberating. Every inch of her skin flamed as she realized even this wasn't enough of him for her.

But he had stopped; his big body halted over her. He released her hands and propped himself up just inches off her on his elbows. His features looked ragged as he studied her. His sky-blue eyes were wide in shadow. His mouth was slightly parted.

"What?" he asked.

She was so stunned she could hardly remember what she'd said. "I don't care how much you hate me or hurt me," she managed as her eyes swam with tears, reflecting his image in the hovering lantern light. "I love *you*, damn you, and not Dalton Kelsey."

"Liar! You're marrying him."

"It was the only way to see you! I had to try to help you. I had to tell you—"

"I'd be the world's biggest fool to believe that. Don't say it again."

"I will!"

"I want to break you, hurt you, I should hate you, but I can't, Brett, Brett, Brett," he half moaned, but if he said anything at all after that, she didn't hear it.

He began to kiss her everyplace he could reach without breaking the tenuous union they'd forged. Their tongues touched, darted, danced. He nibbled down her throat while she raked wild fingers through his rumpled hair. One big hand skimmed her smooth flesh while he propped himself slightly to the side to watch her writhe against him. His fingers found her core and caressed her there endlessly before they rolled once completely over in the tumbled calico. She could feel her initial tautness slackening to welcome his bold intrusion now. His quick fingers took her to the edge of a precipice over the churning sea, then pulled her back again, then pushed her toward it, again, again.

"Brett, Brett," he breathed heavily in her ear as she shifted her legs to accommodate his first full thrust as it plunged him deeper into her. He stopped when he met the firm resistance of her virginity there. For the first time aboard the enemy ship, his hard lips lifted in the essence of a smile at what that meant. And then, even as she tried to pin his big body to her with her fingers splayed along his hard shoulders, he shoved, she gasped, and they were fully one.

His mouth covered hers to stifle any cry, but she made none. She only kissed him back, swept away by a sensation she could not name and had never fathomed. He rested heavily a moment, and then, just when she was lured to believe this was their pinnacle, he began to move inside her.

"Oh, oh. More?" she asked, astounded.

"Much, much more," he said, and grinned in joy at her charming naïveté. He made good his promise as he slid powerfully in and out of her quaking body to set a pounding pace that seemed to shake the ship. And then, in perfect unison, as mere exploding fireworks of cannons had never done, they shattered the vast universe together.

When it was over in a flash of sound and color, she cried and clung to him at the beauty of such dazzling joys. He held still for a moment, heaved a trembling sigh, then rolled off her. She wanted to tell him how wonderful and special it had been. But when she reached out her hand, she grabbed only air. He stood on wobbly legs and bent to reach for his discarded breeches. A fine sheen of sweat gilded his powerful torso and limbs in lantern glow. She lay still, stunned for a moment, both fulfilled and utterly bereft as the real world crashed back over her like a wall of cold seawater. Dizzily she sat up and wound a swath of green-and-brown calico around her perspiring body.

He said nothing while he pulled on his boots and shirt, then stuck the dagger in his belt and studied the two iron keys with frowning intensity as if she weren't even in the room.

He tiptoed over to the door, shoved the pile of calico bolts halfway over and listened intently. She stood on legs like water and noted blood on the white-and-brown patterned material where she'd lain. Embarrassed, though he obviously didn't see or care, she kicked the ruined material away with her foot and joined him at the door. Her heart fell when he pulled her to him only to clamp a big hand over her mouth.

After all this, he still didn't trust her! She needed this time to explain everything and he was gagging her as surely as Giles Cutler had done, though not so brutally. And that damned Dalton Kelsey had always thought she talked too much. Rubbish! She hadn't talked half-enough to any of them. Furious at it all, she elbowed Alex in the stomach. And lived to regret it.

He gasped, but had her hands manacled to her chest in a fierce, one-handed grip in the same instant. He half tripped, half tipped her on her back again and had a gag tied over her mouth and her wrists bound together in front with a ribbon of cloth. Anger imbued her limp body with strength. She kicked and bucked until the calico wrapped around her split and gaped to expose her naked midriff and hips.

"Believe me, British," he gritted out as he leered down to taunt her, "if I had the time right now, I'd be willing again. But you're going to have to just wait a minute."

He smacked her bare bottom smartly once, but did not repeat the blow when it resounded in the room. He rearranged and tightened the wide ribbons of calico over her and went back to the door. She knew better than to get to her feet, though he hadn't bound them. Seething, she watched, slit eyed, as he carefully inserted each key in the wide iron bolt's keyhole. He cursed under his breath and tossed both keys into the pile of calico above her head.

"I should have known those were for show. Any more tricks up your naked sleeves to beguile me with?" He came back to stand over her, spread legged. He looked down at her from his amazing height. "You know, dear wife, I'm no braver than any other man facing death and the loss of everything he's ever loved or worked for." His tough tone disintegrated as he went on. "And if I thought for one minute that by either loving or raping you I could make myself forget what your future husband has in mind for me tomorrow, I—"

As he swung away she saw tears glimmer in his eyes. He turned his back to her, leaned a big shoulder against the wall in the corner of the small, crowded room where the bolts of calico had been stacked. She got to her knees, stood slowly. The rocking movement of the ship seemed part of her now. She approached Alex slowly, but she was not afraid. She wanted to tell him she would gladly continue Sanborn's for him, that she would fight for America in the war—anything to try to make it up for him, anything if only he would believe she loved him more than life itself. At that moment she would have gladly died with him, but she knew Dalton would never allow such a defiant show.

Though she risked his anger and strength, she leaned her cloth-wrapped cheek tenderly against his upper arm. He jerked at her touch but did not move otherwise. He sniffed heavily, and she knew, indeed, that he, too, could cry for lost causes. Swiftly he turned to her and buried his face in her wild hair, while she stood still bound and gagged before him. His touch trembled with raw need and aching tenderness.

"Maybe, just maybe, when I die," he muttered, "I'll at least have the warm memory of what might have been if I had ever really married." He pulled her gag down to make a crude necklace around her throat. His lips took hers repeatedly with a consuming, desperate passion she answered until both of them were whispering fervent love words through their mutual astonishment.

She arched up against him. He made no move to unbind her wrists, if he even remembered. He skimmed the calico from her body until she stood stark naked again. His eager mouth followed rampant hands down her quaking flesh. She moaned deep in her throat as she offered herself as comfort. She felt him fumble with his breeches buttons. Before he even freed himself, he lifted her up with a band of iron arm around her waist. Her legs locked on either side of his lean hips. She lifted her bound hands around his neck. She had to trust him, and she did. He had just pressed into her, when the quiet rap sounded on the door behind them.

They froze, listening. He grappled her to him yet. The knuckles sounded again, sharper this time.

Alex set her down so fast she almost fell. Swiftly he arranged his garments and rewrapped the calico at their feet around her to bind her arms down to her waist in front. The bolt slid slowly, heavily in the door. To her dismay, he pulled her gag up in place again. He pushed her against the wall behind him, then drew the dagger from his boot top and crouched behind the door.

It opened slowly because the stack of wooden bolts and cloth still partly leaned against it. "Mr. Alex? Miss Brett? It's me, Giles Cutler. It's all clear now for our escape."

Alex waved the knife back and forth as Giles stuck his head in, saw Alex, then stepped in. "I've got two loaded pistols and supplies for a few days at sea," he told the astounded Alex in his high-pitched whisper. He did indeed have guns, and both were drawn. His eyes, politely enough it seemed, darted to the bound and gagged Brett, but he averted them in exaggerated surprise. "I've hit this fellow out here over the head, and I'm really going to have to drag him in," he went calmly on.

Alex sprang to action. He and Giles hauled the unconscious marine in on the floor and bound and gagged him with more strips of material. Brett's heart thrilled for Alex at the possibility of his escape. Anything was better than his certain hanging. But she knew Giles Cutler was capable of killing him, also, and she needed to say so. Ignoring Giles's blatant stare from behind Alex's back when he saw how little clad she was, she padded over to Alex. He only thrust her back against the wall.

"You and I may get shot at in the process, but any risk is better than certain death, Giles. Give me one of the pistols and let's go."

"We've got to take Miss Brett," Giles argued, not offering either gun. "Who knows what Kelsey will do to her. Besides, I want to set fire to the ship to divert them when we go."

"You're the one who's mad!" Alex argued. "Our own men are aboard, and I won't have the *Spirit* go up tethered to her! And Brett stays! An open longboat adrift at sea somewhere hundreds of miles out from the Bermudas is no place for her. Besides, Kelsey can't marry her if he's not even sure she's a widow." Alex felt desperate, torn. He didn't trust Cutler, who had a lot of explaining to do as to why he was stowed away with Brett on the *Spirit*, but there would be time for that after they escaped.

"All right about the fire, but I still say Miss Brett goes, too," Giles Cutler clipped out, and leveled both guns at Alex. "And I'll have your word on it. Both of you or neither. Time's wasting."

In answer, Alex grabbed Brett's gown and slippers and hustled her to the door just as she was. When she shook her head and muttered through her gag, he shook her so hard her teeth rattled. "You may want to stay with Kelsey, but Giles is right. Kelsey is less likely to blow us out of the water if he spots us with you tied across the bow, British. And, besides, we hardly got a good start on our loving, little honeymoon, did we?"

With an iron grip on her arm, he shoved her ahead of him. In his mingled exultation and fear, he didn't see, as she did, the twisted loathing on Giles Cutler's demonic face.

They gutted out the single corridor lantern and huddled in the dark under the companionway until they heard the watch change overhead. The number of bells sounded told Brett that she and Alex had been in the first mate's cabin barely an hour. Although it was late May, the crisp Atlantic night air sweeping down the steps slapped her to full consciousness. Her heart pounded at the danger of their bold escape.

"Half the usual number of sailors aboard because they've been deployed to pump and guard the clipper," Giles hissed at Alex in the pitch-black.

Brett felt Alex nod.

Giles still held both pistols as Alex hurried her up the steps. Her ears seemed to scream the ships sounds at her. A sad, lonely sea chantey on a distant flute or pipe. The ding, dong of a swinging chain somewhere. The occasional flap of slack, shifting sails. And the sibilant, perpetual slap, slap of water along the hollow hull.

Half crouched, they darted into the narrow waist area on deck, which was encompassed by guns and the bigger longboats with smaller ones nestled within. Here another companionway led to the seamen's berth deck below. The gunwales were high; deserted gangways dangled over their heads, which had just earlier today spouted sailors into battle against the *Free Spirit*.

Somehow Giles already had a small longboat with three pairs of oars swung out over the gunwales. They clambered in on the side away from the tethered *Spirit*. Alex shoved Brett down on the seat in the prow; her toes stubbed a small wooden keg stowed there. He threw her gown and slippers at her feet. Quickly Giles and Alex ran the pulley that lowered them down the wooden hull of the great ship. With a jolt and a tilt, they hit the water. They quickly cast away into rolling waves as both men fumbled for oars to row.

Dazed at the sweep of events, Brett watched the lights of the binnacle lamps aboard the shrinking *Raven's Wing* twinkle and fade. Could any of this be real? She had been taken prisoner and was now escaping. Dalton Kelsey had crashed back into her life. She had actually forced Alex Sanborn to marry her. A consummated marriage, though it might be short-lived if she didn't warn him about Giles. Had her new husband taken her body in revenge and hatred or in love? Had he stroked her skin alive and fired her heart with brutality or tenderness? Exhausted, shivering, stunned, rocked by the great, gray waves of vast night, she wasn't sure. One wrong move, one shout over the water, and the hunt would be on for them. Entranced as the huge form of two linked ships faded and finally disappeared, Brett braced her bare feet in the boat and watched the men pull hard on their oars.

Sometime in the night Giles had stopped rowing, and held the pistols on Alex to force him to keep on. Despite staggering fatigue, Alex rowed until daylight glimmered over the eastern fringe of the horizon. Finally a bloodred ball of flame leaped into view and slowly simmered to golden. Only when Giles sneezed did Brett jolt awake on her precarious, rocking perch. The bright sun hung a handbreadth high on the horizon to startle her eyes. Boundless gray waves marched in all directions. No sails, no ships. Had she actually slept? Her eyes widened with dismay when she saw Giles holding both guns on Alex, who sat between them. At least, perhaps, Alex would believe her about Giles now.

"Put the guns down, Giles," Alex said, his voice calm but ragged. "I've done all your hard rowing for you, and I didn't let you bring me out here just to shoot me."

"Little enough you have to say about it, galley slave. Row, you bastard."

However exhausted and bereft, Alex had no intention of letting Giles cow or quiet him. "Your true colors run out at last," Alex goaded. "Was I wrong about Brett then? Are you the Baltimore spy?"

Brett leaned around to see Giles clearly, since Alex blocked her view. "It's all right, precious," Giles told her, his voice sickening sweet. "Yes, to the second question. I'm Kelsey's spy and proud of it. But I took my orders these past few weeks from Kelsey through your supposed wife here."

Brett protested loudly through her gag, but the men ignored her. She quieted when she saw Alex's big back muscles flex once through his spray-damp shirt as if in warning. Otherwise he didn't move.

"Then you won't mind if we untie the lady and let her speak for herself, Giles," Alex went on, his voice deadly calm. "There's no reason for her to deny anything, now that you're in complete control here."

Suddenly she knew Giles would not shoot her. It was not part of his careful plans. She had to do something to help Alex. She stood shakily in the prow. Her knees almost buckled as she bent her legs to take the rock and pitch of the boat.

"Sit down, Brett!" Giles cracked out, and lifted both guns at Alex's middle. In the exact moment that Alex half stood and turned to grab for her, Brett gave the boat a vicious tilt. Unfortunately it was Giles who clung to his seat, while she and Alex both pitched out into the waves.

Cold, heaving water grabbed her, pulled her down. It burned her eyes, choked her through her nose. She kicked instinctively to right and lift herself. She had no idea how to swim. Her wrists tied—her gag. Would they let her drown?

Hard hands on her buoyed her up. She cleared the rocking surface as Alex ripped her gag down, and gasped lungfuls of air. She shoved the heavy, sodden curtain of her hair back from her face with her bound hands. She and Alex rose and fell together on the waves, bobbing almost parallel with the longboat. She saw Giles brace himself with one foot on its side, as he crouched to lift an oar from an oarlock. To help them or hit them, she wasn't sure. Alex's hands on her felt so good; she wanted to cling to him forever. With the flash of a dagger before her face, he somehow slit her ties to free her hands. She flopped them in the water and paddled hard. Behind her, he sucked in great breaths of air. Then, to her surprise, he tossed the dagger up into the boat beside Giles.

"You win, Giles!" Alex shouted. "Help her up! Whatever you do with me, don't let her die. You want her, take her."

"No!" she cried when Alex actually ducked her under. He turned her to him as Giles extended the oar nearly within their grasp.

"Our only chance," Alex choked out the whisper as his face streamed water. "Trusting you—should I?"

"Yes, yes," she mouthed before he pushed her away toward Giles's outstretched oar.

She grasped it and he hauled her steadily toward the boat. She dared not look back at Alex. She felt so alone now that his hands had left her. The oar, the solid side of boat and Giles's dry hands to her were nothing compared to Alex's touch. She kicked and scraped her stomach on the side as Giles hauled her up. The unwrapping calico trailed behind her over the side and into the sea to afford Alex a full view of squirming bare bottom and thrashing legs. She sprawled across the bottom of the boat to bang her chin against a shallow box of sand. Then, before she could right herself, Giles lifted a gun and aimed at Alex bobbing in the waves.

"Noooo!" Her scream exploded with the gun. She clawed at Giles's leg even as he turned the other gun down at her.

"Quiet," he yelled, "or I'll get you, too!"

She grabbed a handful of the sand and flung it up into his glaring, leering double face. She scrambled to her knees even as he pulled the trigger at her. She smelled the puff of powder, and actually heard and felt the bullet whisk past her left ear. She shoved at his knees, hit his hip until he toppled heavily over the side with a splash.

Panicked, she scrambled to her feet to search the sea for Alex. Gone. Only Giles sputtered and thrashed. Gone!

"No, dear God, no don't let Alex die!" she cried. She stood naked in the boat, ignoring Giles's garbled screams. Then, even as she stared aghast at the empty, rolling sea, Alex exploded upward through a wave near the boat. In four strokes he was below her. She yanked madly at his sopping shirt, nearly ripping it from his body.

"Get back! You'll tip the boat!" he ordered as he managed to heave himself over the side.

"I thought he shot you! I thought you were gone!" she chattered. Sanity fled with her elation. She threw herself against him, hugged him so hard she almost choked him. He clamped her briefly to him as they knelt facing each other in the rocking boat. Only when his hands clasped her buttocks, wet cold flesh to flesh, did they both realize she was stark naked.

"Get that dry gown on," he muttered, and sat her down hard amid Giles's carefully packed boxes. "We'll tie Giles with your calico."

But when he stood and grabbed the oar to fish out the man he could have gladly killed with his bare hands, he was nowhere. Alex spun to the other side, squinted with his hand over his eyes into the rising sun. He turned back again.

"He's gone," he said, unbelieving. "He was only in a minute or two."

She stood beside him, clasping the green gown Giles had

bought in front of her. "He can't be. He's staying under the way you did, thinking we'll shoot him. He's hiding near the hull."

Alex darted looks over the sides. Nothing.

"Wouldn't he float if he—even if he went under?" she asked. Had she actually killed him? She wanted him to admit his lies about her to Alex! Alex had to know she had never betrayed him! "I didn't want him to die," she said at last.

"I know," he admitted, and slumped limply into the seat where he'd rowed all night. He stared at his knees as if mesmerized. "I'm going to believe you about everything as best I can."

It was something, but it wasn't enough, she thought. She yanked her gown on and stood in the boat, searching for Giles long after Alex sat just staring bleary eyed at her. Finally, when he sat down in the boat in a stupor of shock and exhaustion, she collapsed facing him, too stunned for tears or words. They sat like stone statues, letting the sea take them wherever it would.

The sun was nearly straight overhead when Alex awoke. He started at first at the blinding light, then at the sight of Brett, sitting asleep, straight up, with both hands propped on the oars she must have pulled inside the boat. Despite their perilous predicament he smiled grimly and shook his head to clear it. This woman—his wife—look dressed for a party. She still wore the pearls Simone had given her for the War Relief Ball. She sat in the seat above him almost primly, legs properly crossed at the trim, ribbon-tied ankles. But the wrinkled gown, salt-caked skin and wind-whipped, gilded chestnut hair suggested her true, buried wild nature. And that he would always treasure, no matter what happened to them out here.

"Brett!" He sat on the seat across from her and woke her with a steadying hand clasped over her knee. "Brett, it's midday, and we've got a lot to do!"

She jolted awake, saw him. Then her eyes jumped past him to stare out over the heaving, green-gray waves as if Giles Cutler might rise from their writhing embrace. Her gaze darted back to Alex again. "It's been a nightmare from the moment he took me aboard the *Spirit* in a trunk." The words tumbled out. Her voice sounded crackly.

His big hand on her knee tightened reassuringly. "There's time to tell all that later," he said. He was afraid to hear her story, terrified now that he'd find some hole in it to prove her affection for that bastard Kelsey or her betrayal of him and the Americans. "We've lots of time ahead together. But survival comes first. I've got to figure out where in blue blazes we are and which way to go. Keep a watch out for sails and cover your face, or you'll turn pink as a steamed lobster."

She did as he said, while he tried to calculate their position, then decided he'd get it more exactly by the stars that night. He had her go through the boxes Giles had packed for what he had—no doubt—thought would be his escape with Brett after he shot Alex. Sand he'd swept off the battleship's deck in a box for a tiny cooking fire aboard. Powder and bullets for the two pistols, which had gone with him over the side. A wine bottle filled with water, and a small keg of rum. Six biscuits and a slab of half-moldy yellow cheese. A canvas tarpaulin to cover the longboat in case of rain, fishing line and two hooks, a cutlass and a tinderbox.

"That last's the best news yet," Alex told her as he rigged the tarpaulin for a crude sail. "I don't fancy cold, raw fish any more than I do a cold, raw wife."

The corners of her mouth perked up at his first hint of humor after all they had been through and still faced. Being lost at sea suddenly didn't seem so bad to her if they could be lost together.

"I've got to admit," he said a while later, "I grieve more for the loss of the *Spirit* than Giles Cutler after all his treachery." They watched the small sail, which he'd fastened to an oar with ripped and braided pieces of calico cloth, belly out with wind.

"Then you do believe me."

He squinted into the sun, then looked her over so thoroughly that his gaze made her pull her knees tighter together and nearly squirm on her hard seat. "I'm trying to, Brett. But

I'd almost rather burn the *Spirit* myself than have her converted to Kelsey's British gun vessel to fight my countrymen with.''

"But she won't be. Dalton told me," she assured him brightly before she realized what she said. "The *Spirit* will be his private supply ship until everything's over."

His warm glance chilled. "How sweet of dear Dalton to share that tidbit with you, since you weren't his spy. Of course, his idea of everything being over is Baltimore and all America in ruins and you in his bed."

"Look, Alex Sanborn," she said, "I don't care what his ideas are, because I want no part of them. Yes, I agreed to marry him, but only to try to save you. And in a way I did!"

"Good going, Brett," he mocked, as his big hands yanked knots of calico so tight she thought they would tear. "Another finely executed plan on your part, just like everything else you've touched since you set foot in Baltimore. And out here you only spilled both of us into the water so Giles could pick us off like sitting ducks. We're adrift somewhere in the Atlantic with about two days of food, and that big man-of-war your dearly beloved fiancé commands probably combing the area for us. And speaking of executed plans, I'm holding you personally responsible if your dear Dalton hangs Josh Windsor in my place back there! I don't trust Kelsey's word of honor worth a damn, though he swore he wouldn't hang him, too. That was the price offered to make me marry you, in case you're curious."

Despite the increasing cruelty of his words, her mind darted to Josh's wife, her dear friend Sally Windsor, heavy with child. And to the other Windsor children, awaiting word of Baltimore's great flying clipper, the *Free Spirit*.

She decided she had nothing further to say to Alex's taunts. He obviously mistrusted and hated her, and that wasn't going to change, marriage or not, mutual survival at stake or not. She accepted a sip of water from him when he thrust the wine bottle at her, but she refused to eat the bits of biscuit and cheese he held out, until he threatened to hold her down and force-feed her the ration himself.

She turned her back on him to eat, adjusting the strip of floppy batiste chemise she'd fashioned for a sun bonnet and had tied under her chin by a strip of calico as she slowly chewed the dry biscuit. She'd give him no excuse ever to touch her again if he felt that way—no matter how she longed for him. She'd show him she didn't need him. She'd assure him he was free to do what he wanted without her whenever they got to shore. If they did.

Around them the waves tilted and rolled as Alex flapped the sail around their makeshift mast to keep the breeze at their backs.

Twelve

What Alex called their "civil truce" lasted three days. By then their water was nearly gone, and they were stretching it with rum, but they were half into the tiny keg. There was not a cloud in the blazing blue sky that could portend a freshwater shower. By then they were immune to the up-down, up-down of their little boat on the big ocean. It was a part of Brett, just as the up-down, up-down of their rocky relationship was. She began to fear that the honeymoon that never really began might indeed be over.

She obeyed Alex's orders unquestioningly, including sitting in the shade of the sail to keep her pale complexion from frying. Still, the reflected sunlight off the water had begun to burnish her ivory skin. The meager rations that remained of the stale biscuits and moldy cheese left her continually hazy. And with the necessary sips of rum in a nearly empty belly, she was even more light-headed than Alex's brooding, watchful eyes made her. Up-down, up-down. She desired him, yes, still loved him desperately. And yet he made her so angry, too, and she'd tell him that if she wasn't so thirsty and tired. She leaned heavily against his arm when he sat beside her to steady the spout hole of the keg against her parched lips for her afternoon ration of rum.

She savored the warm wash of sweet fluid, held it in her mouth as long as she could bear to. After she swallowed, she ran her tongue everywhere inside as if to caress where it had touched. He took his little swig from the spout, then corked it and wedged the keg carefully under her seat. Still she leaned against his arm when he sat back up beside her in the cool shade of the sail.

Deliberately, loving the softness of her in this harsh world, he pressed his arm even more into the soft swell of her breast. He spoke for the first time in hours. "Here I've got a lady unchaperoned and tipsy on rum, with no bed to take advantage of her." His eyes, narrowed against the glitter of sun on water, skimmed over her in an exaggerated leer.

She laughed for the first time in days. "Don't flatter yourself, Mr. Sanborn. I'm just tipsy from going up and down all the time."

"We could arrange that, too, if we had a bed, Mrs. Sanborn."

He smiled grimly, but the jest sobered both of them and neither laughed. After three days of avoiding all that lay between them, they stared into each other's eyes. His rugged face under the rough start of dark, raspy beard looked as bronze as some Indians' she'd seen on the docks. She was a gentle pink, which gave color and life to her beauty. She swam in the warmth of his gaze. When he looked at her that way, nothing but being near him and loving him mattered. Then Alex looked suddenly away out over the rolling vastness, and she realized she could read his turbulent thoughts.

"We're really lost, aren't we, Alex?"

His quiet words came back to her on the perpetual push of wind. "Some would say so. But I think we're about two hundred or so miles southwest of the Bermudas." He frowned and little creases that had not been there before webbed the dry, salty skin around his mouth and eyes as he turned toward her again. "I'm afraid, British, the Bermudas are full of your hostile countrymen, as well as my smuggler friends. And there are still shipwreckers on the outer islands who live off craft that fall victim to the reefs. There are no streams or rivers, so they have to catch fresh water just as we have to out here. Some call them the Isles of Devils, so you'll probably think me right at home there when we arrive,'' he said, trying to reassure her with another poor joke.

She sensed he struggled with his own composure. ''Rubbish! I'm certain we can find your contacts, who will smuggle us safely back to Baltimore!'' she offered, and squeezed his arm to buck him up. She was longing for the comfort and security of his touch. They had even slept in different shifts and he hadn't so much as brushed against her in their tiny wooden up-down world until now.

''So we agree we're not lost. We'll get to St. George's Town eventually,'' he said, his voice deadly calm, his eyes holding hers again.

''Oh. Then our problem is running out of supplies. With not much rum left and the trouble we've had hooking fish—''

''My practical, clear-sighted partner, Brett,'' he got out, before she threw her arms around him and clung hard.

He embraced her warmly, so strong. She melted against him; her wind-tossed chestnut hair forming a shifting curtain around both their heads. ''I swear to you, my mermaid, we'll make it one way or the other.'' He held her slightly away to take her chin in his big hand, and brushed his callused thumb back and forth over her chapped lips as he spoke. ''I've had a rough few days out here coming to terms with everything. We've got a lot of living to do, Brett. Fighting, too, and I don't mean with each other! Somehow we're going to make it off this ocean and back to Baltimore!'' His raspy voice almost broke. ''Now how about an 'I forgive you, Alex' wifely kiss? And man the fish line while I try to keep this *Free Spirit II* on course to our next scenic honeymoon spot.''

Tears glimmered in his blue eyes, but they might have been from the sting of wind. She thrilled that he still thought of her as partner—and wife—although she'd given him no choice on either. They kissed, slowly, sweetly at first, as if to reassure each other they would be all right. But that kiss soon swept to one of raw intensity. Up-down, eternally, up and down, with Alex. Now their truce was at least an armistice, but she wasn't certain who had won. And, despite all they faced, she found in his arms a peace way down inside that she hoped nothing would ever touch.

The next two days, after their food was gone, they stayed alive by netting tiny shrimp in a calico-cloth strainer at night. Streams of fire had flashed under their boat in the dark, and they'd learned that barnacles and shrimp gave off the glow. Food they couldn't catch by day could be netted in the dark without any bait. But twenty finger-size shrimp hardly filled their knotted stomachs or halted their food fantasies. They pictured the big dinners at the Fountain Inn in Baltimore or those Molly put on the groaning table at Sanborn House. Crab gumbo, fried chicken, beaten biscuits with jam or honey: the longings were endlessly haunting. The next night the waves were higher and the flashes of light that meant food were gone. Their water was gone and their rum—the last potable liquid they had—was running very low.

Despite it all, they went through periods where they talked endlessly to keep their sanity. Alex told her his side of the story of Giles Cutler's early years. How young Giles had followed his brother, Will, everywhere and kept him from completing his bookkeeping work, until he was forbidden the Sanborn-office premises. How he refused either to go to school or to take the warehouse job the Sanborns offered him. How the boy hung about shop windows at all hours, just gazing in, when he couldn't be with Will. Alex denied Giles's accusation to Brett that he'd taken Will carousing, though he admitted he'd done enough of it with his own friends. But the boy turned even more demanding of Will's time when Will began to court a seamstress's daughter. Shortly after that, Will was trapped inside the mysterious warehouse fire. Smoke inhalation killed him, although Alex managed to pull the badly burned, lung-damaged younger brother out in time. Sanborn's rebuilt the warehouse. Alex and his father took Giles firmly under their control and thought they had rebuilt him, too. Obviously they had been deadly wrong.

"You know, Brett," Alex's hoarse voice went on, "I wondered for a while if the lad set the fire himself. But he was so horribly scarred I couldn't bear to bring it up. And when he turned out to be obsessively driven to succeed as our book-keeper, I shelved the idea.''

"Perhaps you shouldn't have," she said, and told him everything about the night she and Giles had gone to the ship-yard to see the *Free Spirit* in her cradle. "He scuffed a pile of kindling together and kept warning me that the entire place could go up in flames. Alex, I shudder to think what could have happened that night. And you would have blamed me.''

He draped an arm around her shoulders and tugged her against his side. She could feel what the five days at sea had already done to him; ribs once wrapped in muscle bulk were more distinct. "And he wanted to burn Kelsey's ship when we fled, even with everyone on board," he went on. "It's obvious now, with all you say about his embezzling from Sanborn's at the cost of people like Lissa Miles, that there was a lot I was too damned busy to find out about Giles Cutler. I only wish I would have listened to you sooner about him. And I thank God he's the only spy linked to Dalton Kelsey.''

"I never would have helped Dalton that way—never," she insisted. "Not even though I love England. Not even if I had loved Dalton.'' She reached a hand up to rest it on Alex's lean, brushy cheek. "I never did love him, not even when I considered wedding him, Alex. I thought he was a great naval hero my father and uncle would have been proud of. I was lonely. I wanted a family. But I wanted to be loved *for myself*, and Dalton never did that!''

He lifted his hand to cup hers to his face. Then he slid her palm deliciously down over his stubble of dark beard until it covered his lips. He pressed a warm kiss into her palm. Despite the salt on everything out on the ocean, her skin was sweet on his tongue when he darted it out to lick her there.

"And now what do you think of Dalton Kelsey?'' he murmured into her palm.

"I can't think at all when you do that!'' she protested as little tremors feathered through her loins and lower belly.

He leaned forward on his seat to capture both her hands

and pressed them to her knees. "I have to know, Brett! I saw how he looked at you. The man desired you, and that infuriated me more than anything."

Her heart thrilled at that admission. "I—I know. But it never used to be like that. I think he saw I'd changed. He's always believed I'm a pushy, cork-brained chatterbox. I overheard him tell a friend so once, that no one would ever want to marry me. I thought at first he must want me because Uncle Charles's influence could advance his career. When he pressed his suit even harder after my uncle died, I came to think maybe he did care for me somewhat. But he never made me feel the way you do all over," she blurted before she realized what she'd said.

He heaved a sigh of obvious relief and managed a nod. Then he slid her hands heavily up her thighs until his knuckles rested at the very juncture of her legs. She was glad the sun blush on her skin under her makeshift bonnet hid the rush of blood to her cheeks and neck. She tingled at his look, his touch, this controlled but very deliberate caress.

"And no one has ever made me feel—and go all wild inside and out—the way you do, Brett," he told her. "No, not even our friend Simone."

He had read her mind exactly, too. He kissed both her hands and released her. She sat stiffly, foolishly longing again for his touch while he turned away to drop the fish line over the side. Though his voice became a mere rasp and she had to move closer to hear, he kept talking. How she wanted to believe the things he said, just as he had believed her about Giles and Dalton.

"And so, despite the fact that my relationship with Simone was very, well—amorous at first," he admitted as he watched the silver stretch of line trail hopelessly behind them, "it wasn't true later. After you came, she realized I had stopped thinking of her even in our private moments, so she refused me. Blue blazes, Brett," he said, and wheeled suddenly back to face her, "she knew I wanted you before I did! She was very sensitive about these things, you see—"

"Sensitive, but not sensible, at least at first, to bed with

someone who didn't love her, someone who just desired her,''
Brett put in, and fingered her pearls nervously. She knew she
had done the same. Alex surely didn't love her, but how she
wanted him to say he did. "I was thinking of you. I wanted
you," he had said only. She knew that for a man that was
hardly love!

"What's the fun of being sensible, Simone often said,"
Alex explained. "Simone was interested in amusement and
fun."

"And you, Alex?"

"My interests?" he said, and his rugged face took on a
hint of that little-boy smug look she hadn't seen for days.
"Before the war, my interests included a great deal of business and a great deal of fun. But I never realized the two
could be so well mixed up until you crashed into my life."

"Mixed up? Crashed in!" she began to argue, but thought
the better of it. "But you did name the clipper ship for Simone, didn't you?" she asked, instead.

"The *Free Spirit*? Now there's a lady I always loved from
the first and knew it. No, Brett. The figurehead *was* made to
look like Simone at first. But my ship was named for the very
thing that's made my country fight yours twice in the past
forty years. The free spirit is America's. And you and I are
going to get back somehow to Baltimore as fast as we can
and continue to fight, Your Majesty."

"Aye, aye, Alexander the Great," she murmured.

They exchanged tenuous smiles, and their eyes held. She
was, she thought, falling in love with him all over again when
they talked and shared their feelings this way. But the circumstances they found themselves in were far worse than they
had faced before—in fact, deadly.

She sighed and gazed out over the rolling deep as turbulent
as her thoughts. She wanted to tell him how he alone had
made her feel like a sensual, beautiful woman. But she knew
she looked a mess now, all wind blown and salt sprayed in
her bedraggled gown, with only her pearls to remind her of
the life of luxury she had once taken for granted. Anything
compared to this was luxury! She had no doubt that she

looked just as her mother had always said—awkward and gawky and wretchedly plain. And she knew the one thing she and Alex hadn't talked about was their marriage. A patriot like Alex Sanborn wouldn't abide by a forced wedding to one of the enemy! *He* was the free spirit his clipper ship had embodied! Once back in America he could easily cast her aside. She fought back the nearly overwhelming desire to throw herself in his arms and beg him to love her forever—for the few days they had left out here now their food and drink had run out completely.

"'Water, water everywhere, nor any drop to drink,'" she muttered so she wouldn't cry.

His voice came rough and scratchy, but he sounded somehow his old, teasing self. His hard mouth tilted up on one side. "Another damned Wordsworth quote, I suppose."

She shook her head. "Coleridge, his best friend," she said, her voice almost inaudible.

"Cheer up, *my* best friend," he countered, and nodded at the sky behind her. "For the first time I see a little gray cloud on our horizon, and it's to windward. If it rains, we'll knock the top off the keg and fill it."

Her heart leaped with hope. "We'll fill the whole boat and take a bath! And I'm going to wash my hair!"

Days ago, even yesterday, he knew he would have laughed at her inherent exuberance, but today he was so weary and worried about their very survival he could only admire it silently. How he longed to hold her again, to make hot love to her, but even thinking of that was pure torment out here. He patted her knee and turned back to watch the length of dangling, empty fish line.

Their single, beautiful cloud turned into a noisy threatening mob of thunderheads by nightfall. When howling winds yanked the sail, Alex took it down and wedged it and everything else in under the seats in the boat. At the first big, pelting drops they hooted and cheered and threw their arms around each other in a frenzy of rejoicing. They drank their fill and slicked encrusted salt off their own bodies, then playfully each other's. But soon the rocking pitch became too much for them, and they held on to the seats and sides even to stay in the boat. Then, as the vessel began to fill, they bailed wildly with cupped hands in the swirling darkness. The waves churned so high he lashed the tarpaulin over them for a cover. He wedged his long body in under two seats and held her to him as their fragile little craft crashed up and down in each steep roll of black water.

He held her tight while she molded her quaking body to his big one. Her head fitted perfectly under his chin. One arm bent against his chest where she could actually feel his pounding heart; her other arm grasped his waist, bare skin to skin where his shirt had long torn away. Behind the boards at her back she could feel the slap-pound of crashing water. Her thighs pressed to his, she anchored her calves and ankles between his powerful legs. He had connected his wrist to the boat with the fishing line in case they pitched out into the sea. At least, she thought, trembling in his embrace, if the waves battered the boat to splinters, they would go out into the wet vastness together.

Under their little tent of canvas, they could talk, mouth to ear, when the drumming of the rain momentarily halted. "What I wanted to say the other day," he shouted in one lull, "was that I never slept with Simone after you came. Never!"

She hugged him harder. Tears that could well be raindrops blinded her eyes. "I meant what I said on our—our wedding night," she told him. "That I love you. I didn't know any other way—to see you," she screeched in an attempt to outdo the roar of the storm. "So I came up—with that—marriage idea!"

"And I didn't mean to be so rough then! I never meant to force you. Or to hurt you. You've always made me go crazy inside. Like this storm!"

They huddled even closer, one body in the smack of rain and waves. Thunder rumbled; wind shrieked. Brett closed her eyes and held to him with her last shreds of strength and courage. He hadn't said he loved her, but his other words and his holding her this way was enough for now.

If she died, she thought, she had at least finally found what she had longed for all these thirty years. All that time to get to this single stunning realization: she had found someone she loved, even in the face of howling death. Not even in her adoration of her father had she so much as sensed what love could be; never with her harsh mother, who had taken her husband's dutiful desertions of her out on his child. She had been appreciated and cared for at the orphanage, and for many long years Uncle Charles had needed her, but not until Baltimore, somehow dear to her despite her troubles there, had she seen even a glimpse of what love could be. Vivid pictures jumped out at her: herself in Alex's arms at the shipyard, on the clipper on launch day, the rescue from the crowd. Wanting to please Alex, arguing with Alex. Loving Alex. Her whole life careered in vivid vignettes through her brain. She had to stop her life from going by!

Under the roaring heavens, she began to kiss Alex. She kissed his rain-slicked neck, the solid thrust of his chin, the hollow under his high cheekbones. His beard had begun to soften now. His earlobes, his nose, she kissed them all. But it was he who found her mouth first and met her frenzied passion with his own. He held her so tight she couldn't breathe, but that didn't matter. They forged a mutual grip cast in iron. They clung madly in kisses that challenged the twist and roll of the sea. His tongue plunged; she answered boldly. Their desire for each other and life itself heated their chilled skin and made their limbs quake from within. At last he pulled back, held her still, his mouth an inch from hers.

"Listen to that," he rasped out. He sucked in a quavering breath. "Listen!"

"What?" she cried. "Nothing but the storm."

He actually shouted a triumphant laugh. "Two storms, but the one outside is slackening!"

She listened. It was true. Their little wooden cocoon rolled as hard, but the wind no longer shrieked. The rain only danced on the canvas now and thunder rumbled away. The storm outside, he had said. Yes, but not the one within. Like idiots they hooted with delight and kissed each other wildly all over again.

A saucer of light preceded sunrise two mornings later. They lay together, limbs entwined, and let the morning breeze push their little craft southeastward. They felt washed clean with rainwater, and their driving thirst was slaked from the storm that had driven them, but they were still hungry. Always hungry. A single small fish Alex said was a bonito, which they had hooked amid the flowing sheets of deep, rich, green-blue plant life, had been their only food since before the storm. Ravenous, they had eaten it half-raw, unable to wait until Alex could cook it over the meager fire they had made with big slivers of an oar he had hacked with the cutlass.

Carefully Brett pulled from Alex's jumbled embrace in the bottom of the boat. Since the storm, they'd slept side by side at night. She sat up dizzily and stretched. She blinked in amazement and looked again before she dared to wake him. More than once yesterday, she'd thought she'd seen things on the horizon that weren't there at all. But this was much nearer! And surely she couldn't imagine things she'd never seen!

The great, dark bodies of twelve whales spouting and diving surrounded their boat a short distance off. Two sleek leaders seemed to be herding the others. Some had little ones! And around them slithered a thick shoal of thousands of silver fish, glinting in the sun. And around and above all that, hand-size fish flapped tiny wings to soar from the water. Again and again they fell back into the waves, then flipped out once more as they cavorted. It was better than the Prince Regent's glittering military escort through the streets of festive London!

She was so moved and dazzled at first that no sound came out when she tried to talk. "Alex, wake up!" she croaked. "Big whales and little ones! And fish that fly!"

Awestruck at the power and majesty around them, they just

gawked at first. Chills raced through her at the sight. Then Alex's excited voice nearly jolted her out of her skin.

"Sardines for the taking, Brett! Get the calico! Take off your gown and use that if you have to!"

They scooped in calico nets of skinny, flipping sardines. And then, as if a gift from heaven, a flying fish vaulted right from the rows of foam-capped waves into Brett's lap. "Oh! Oh, Alex, we didn't even have to catch it!" she cried, and held it up proudly by its tail.

"Can't blame the poor little bastard for leaping into your lap!" Alex actually roared with laughter. "Blue blazes, I'd bite on your bait and line anytime!"

With trembling hands at the sudden bounty, Alex fumbled with the tinderbox until he got a start of flame on the meager pile of sand the storm had spared them. He hacked more splinters from the oar they used for fuel wood, and in no time had a cleaned fish roasting on the end of the cutlass, while Brett hovered, savoring the delicious aroma. The whales and flying fish leaped in their own feeding frenzy. And with a grateful prayer to God for temporary deliverance, Alex and Brett feasted with His creatures of the deep.

On the seventh day they realized that the water had turned iridescent, and they left the deep, gray-green roll of regular wave troughs behind. Emeralds and sapphires seemed to glitter just under the wake of their boat. Alex said the depth of the water was changing. They spotted floating tree limbs, which he hauled aboard in case they needed more fuel. And the first birds since Baltimore soared over them, white-bellied gulls and brown pelicans.

"Land's nearby, Brett. The signs are all here. I can almost smell it."

He warned her that they might have to row to keep the boat steady on the way in, and fashioned a crude tiller from the second oar of the extra pair in case he needed to steer to make a landing. They lashed down what they could and waited. Their eyes streamed tears from the glare of sun and strain of staring at the cerulean horizon. The Isles of Devils,

Brett recalled he'd said. At least there would be people Alex knew to contact in St. George's Town. Excitedly they planned what they would say if they were rescued by British loyalists. She couldn't wait to get a drink, to take a real bath. To eat food besides fish and walk dry, solid land. But, her thoughts tormented her, how would Alex feel to be back among his friends and have a British wife he'd never chosen? The knot in her stomach tightened painfully. He was staring so raptly leeward. What would happen back on dry land to the partnership for survival they had forged at sea?

"Listen," she cried. "What's that?"

"Waves crashing onto something. We must be near a reef, maybe where the color changes again there. Things could get wild, but our draft's too shallow to snag it. I think Josh said the Bermudas' reefs are six to ten miles out from landfall."

Clinging to their racing, cavorting craft, they soon swept over the reef. Beyond, the waves actually increased in height as they sighted a thin black thread of land etching the horizon. Behind them the bloodred sun began to set, staining the whitecaps crimson.

"Damn, I wanted us to go in with daylight," Alex complained. "In the dark, everything will be harder."

He lowered the sail and lashed that down, too. They felt a giant hand of surging tide pulling them in. Darkness descended. His tiller was useless. When whitecaps began to crest higher, they sat together on the floor of the boat and bailed with the halves of their empty water keg, which he'd sawed in two with the cutlass.

She wanted to tell him again that she loved him, but he was so tense. Still, she knew she loved him and was wed to him for now, she told herself stubbornly. That had to be enough.

He wanted to hold her, to comfort and care for her, but he was afraid he would actually break down if he did. Her pluck and courage had helped him keep going this past hellish week. And now, dammit, he could hear the crash of waves on a bigger reef before the shore, and she couldn't swim. In the dark, he lashed the four remaining oars together to make a crude raft, and, over her protests, tied her to it with a length of the fishing line that had been so worthless. At least, he prayed, let it be worth something now.

"But what about you?" she cried. "Maybe the boat won't tip us out. We can just ride it in together."

"I'm tying myself to the boat. I can hear the breakers, sweetheart. Do as I say. If you get tossed out of the boat, keep your head up, hang on to these and just kick your way in. The waves will do most of the work and I'll find you."

"What about the sharks we saw yesterday?"

"They won't be looking for tasty morsels in these high breakers," he shouted to her. "Now just do as I say for once."

Holding hands, their bodies rigid, they sat on the floor of the bucking boat. The tide ripped them inward; resurging waves shoved them out. Up and down. Smash and slap. They tilted, nearly tipped. She had to say it. She had to tell him she loved him again. If only he had loved her, too!

"Alex, I—" she managed just as a wave like a giant's wet hand simply lifted the boat over and shook them out. They grabbed, clung to each other. The boat smacked down next to them, just missing Alex. Then they were off to the races as the undercurrent dragged Alex, then her, with it. She went along easily at first, then her ties to the floating raft of oars yanked her nearly out of his grip. She clung hard, desperately. She couldn't lose him out here! She grasped his waist as they went under, then broke the surface. In the sliding trough between waves, she sputtered for air through the heavy curtain of her sopping hair. Then she realized Alex wasn't returning her grip. Had she done all the holding since they'd spilled in? Had their boat hit him when it had overturned?

He was so limp! Perhaps he'd taken in too much water. She held him in the flowing wet dark, fighting the surge of waves, fighting for breath, fighting losing him. The boat dragged them both onward. Mountainous, inky waves peaked to foaming white and broke over their heads. Then, in the pull of violent opposites, the boat ripped him from her grasp, while her little raft of oars tore her another way.

Suddenly there was nothing in her embrace but warm, pulling water. She held her breath, kicked wildly. The oars he'd lashed to her yanked her to the surface again. They came right at her, almost hit her. "Alex!" she tried to scream, but she swallowed another slap of saltwater. She thought she heard his voice, but it might be the crashing rumble of the surf. She kicked, pulled, embraced the oars and half hauled herself atop them. She clung hard and tried to pierce the darkness. If the boat still floated, she couldn't see it. There was nothing but building, cresting whitecaps out there. "Alex! Alex!" Relentlessly the roll of water sucked her toward shore. "Aaaalex!"

The waves stretched out, shot her forward on her little raft of oars. Darkness, her hair, saltwater blinded her. He would be ashore waiting for her. Of course he would! The boat would take him in better than four skinny oars. The water would revive him. He had only seemed limp in the water, but ashore he would be just fine!

She actually skimmed, belly down, way up on the sand. It scraped her skin, gritted through her lips so she chewed it when she gasped. Land! Solid land! She shoved both palms into it to support herself. She struggled to her knees, fought to stand. The sand seemed to pitch as hard against her as the sea had. She yanked at the cords that still bound her to the beached oars. He'd tied such knots to her body and her heart!

Like a madwoman, she bit through the cord and staggered again to her feet. The sand was hard. She ran jaggedly, one foot and then the other, lurching down the beach. Up and down the shoreline, scanning the endless crash of sliding, foaming waves on waiting sand.

"Alex! Alex!" Dear God, he had to be there, be there somewhere! The boat. It had to wash in on this same beach, this same island, wherever she was, didn't it?

She turned and ran back farther the other way again, passed her clutch of oars in the sand. Then, against the white shimmer of waves, she saw the hump of boat like a beached whale.

She tore to it, ran around it knee deep in the next wave. He lay on the other side, unmoving, sprawled facedown with one leg under the upturned boat, while the water washed over him and receded.

"My love! My love!" she shouted.

She knelt beside him, tried and failed to lift the boat off his leg. She clawed desperately at the sand to free his leg from beneath. Terrified, she carefully turned him faceup and dipped her head to his bare chest to listen for his heartbeat. In the continued thunder of surf, she could hear nothing.

"Please be alive, Alex. Please! I love you! Please!"

She bit his cord loose. With her last wasted strength, she put her hands under his armpits and dragged him slowly, jerkily, higher onto dry sand. She collapsed beside him, cradled his wet, cold head to her breasts.

And then she felt the wisp of his warm breath against her cold skin there. Daring to hope, she pressed her palm down on his chest and felt the thud, thud of his heart outdoing anything the sea could threaten. Still cuddling him in her arms like a heavy, big baby, she screamed her relief and gratitude to the heavens. Then, for the first time since the mob at Baltimore had wreaked their wrath on her forever ago, she cried.

Part III

"O say, can you see
    by the dawn's early light,
What so proudly we hailed
    at the twilight's last gleaming."

—Francis Scott Key
"The Star-Spangled Banner"

Thirteen

~~~oᗞᑶᗞᗞᑶᗞ~~~

Huddled on the beach behind a grassy knoll of sand, Brett cradled Alex's head in her lap and waited for the dawn. They were coated with sand and dried salt like a second rough skin. He moaned and moved from time to time, but, despite her efforts to rouse him, slept heavily on. He began to feel fiery to her touch, even in the cool night breeze. She formed thoughts, prayers and fears through a thick fog of exhaustion. From time to time her stomach twisted and she wretched up saltwater she'd swallowed on her rough ride into shore. She was sore and stiff all over. He had a big bump on the side of his head that she could feel, and she knew his ankle was severely twisted or even broken. But they were together. And, she told herself at the first glimmer of silvery light along the lonely, endless stretch of beach where they were stranded, they were alive. When the sun's warmth touched her, she finally slumped over Alex in a stupor of sleep.

Noonday sun, ravening thirst and hunger woke her. With the weight of Alex's head still pressed in the juncture of her belly and thighs, she gazed dazedly around. She sat statuelike while the surprise of land colors stunned eyes used to the dazzle of the sea. The beach sand actually looked as pink as the enameled insides of shells scattered at her feet; crimson and white lilies speckled a stretch of sea oats before the line of green cedar trees. Blue-and-white herons fished along the shoreline by the ruin of their boat, and a row of pointy-leafed bushes with fire-red flowers grew in abundance just beyond the windswept beach. A cerulean sky with egg yolk of sun dazzled overhead.

Still, she sat unmoving, as if the sea's battering had left her as unconscious as Alex. But then he moaned and pressed his face against her stomach as though she were the softest, safest pillow in his Baltimore bed, moving one arm to encircle her waist. She jolted alert at his instinctive reaching out for her. This place might look like paradise, but they needed food, water and shelter. He was ill and hurt. She had much to do.

"Alex. Alex, can you hear me?" she implored, repeating her fruitless appeal from last night. His forehead felt even hotter and clammier. Surely this sun would dry and warm him. "Alex, it's Brett. We're safe. Alex, I love you so much. We're somewhere, but I don't know where and I need you!"

Amazingly his eyes slitted open, and she shaded them against the slant of sun. Each bristle of his week-old beard glinted bluish in the intense light. "Brett," he rasped.

Her heart leaped. "Yes, yes. We're here, my dearest. Somewhere on dry land. I think your ankle's broken, so I'll have to go look for water on my own. You stay right here and rest. The boat's on the shore all broken—" She spilled out a torrent of thoughts before she realized he wasn't really listening or responding. She laid him gently back to kneel over him and thrust her face close to his. "Alex, do you understand what I said?"

His distracted gaze snagged hers at last. "You mean," he muttered, seizing her wrist with an iron grip, "the *Free Spirit*'s broken on the shore? Did Giles or Kelsey burn her? Did you spy with them to take my ship?"

She sucked in a gasp as if he'd hit her in the stomach. Surely he was just delirious. His head bruise or his fever spoke. He couldn't still believe that, couldn't mean that! She had to find water to get his fever down.

"No, Alex, listen to me. The *Free Spirit*'s fine. We'll get her back someday. And I didn't help the British. I love you. I'm going to help you.''

But she needn't have explained. He was raving about Baltimore and fighting back with his ships. He wasn't looking at her, but his grip on her wrist was fierce. As she loosened his fingers, she talked calmly to him. The tears she was too exhausted to cry echoed in her voice. At least, she thought, when he released her and lay back, apparently exhausted, on the sand, he wouldn't go wandering off in his delirium on that swollen, discolored ankle. She stood, shook out her tattered skirts. She had to find water and food, and care for Alex.

She pressed her hands to her head to clear her fuzzy brain. Alex had told her the other day that there were no freshwater streams and rivers in the Bermudas, if that's where they were. But it rained frequently, he'd said. There was no drinking water on the beach, but perhaps if she went inland...

She surveyed the place they'd landed. Tall cedar trees, juniper shrubs, squat palmetto palms and trees dangling strange gourds separated the beach from deeper forests and fields inland. It all looked uninhabited, but were there wild animals? She had no choice but to plunge in and find out before the last remnants of her strength were gone.

She took four of the largest mollusk shells she could find to carry water back. If the halves of their rum keg had washed in, she didn't have time to search for them now. She carried a large piece of driftwood as a protective club. Reluctantly she left Alex behind and set out. Her heart pounding, she scuffed big X's in the sand to mark her trail, until the soil became less gritty and she was forced to rely on landmarks. When she saw dried, hollow gourds under a big calabash tree, she discarded her shells and carried the gourds to put water in.

The forest deepened and the sea scents gave way to spicy odors of vibrant oleander, heady cedar and crisp pine. Every few weary yards, she looked back and all around. She even surveyed the sky. Surely the birds found fresh water somewhere inland. If only she could follow their sky paths. She lifted her club and spun to face each crackle or whisper of forest. Then she heard the other sound.

She whirled, her heart thudding. Clasping the gourds to her belly in a loop of skirt, she held her club aloft and ready. A low grunt, a guttural cry! She pressed back against a soaring tree with dark, lacquered leaves. Footsteps in the pine needles! She screamed as a large wild boar snorted and seemed to run straight for her, but he veered off just three yards away and plunged down a little knoll in the opposite direction.

Knees shaking, blood pounding, she leaned against the tree and cried soundlessly. She, Brett Benton from civilized London, was lost on some pagan, forsaken island. Alex, hurt and ill, needed water, needed her to come back. And his fevered words showed he still thought, deep in his heart, that she might be a British spy who had caused the loss of his beloved ship! She slid down the rough tree bark to sit and sob dry tears. She had no home; she had deserted England, and America didn't want her anymore than Alex did. She loved him desperately and he'd never said one thing about love. He was a proud, independent man and she'd forced him to wed her when he didn't even care enough to love her. He'd charge off on his own just like that wild boar when he got back to Baltimore—and she'd be just as alone as ever, just like this—

Her head jerked up. She squelched her strangling panic and hysteria. That wild boar! He had to drink fresh water somewhere and he couldn't fly like the birds to find it. Water for herself and Alex, surely somewhere close!

She got to her feet and stalked in the direction the animal had fled. Down a little scrubby ravine thick with hibiscus, she squinted nervously at the sky to watch the direction of the slanting sun. She didn't want to just go in circles and not be able to get back. It was so leafy, cool and solemn there, so alien and silent to ears accustomed to the crash and pound of waves and surf.

She found herself on a little rock ledge littered with dark green hibiscus leaves and speckled, colored ones from the croton plants clinging in the ridges above. And there, her next step wet her nearly ruined slipper in a cool, leaf-covered puddle of rainwater.

She gasped and knelt to skim off the leaves. Her gourds and club clattered to splash the shallow ponds about her everywhere. She scooped up a handful of the delicious, clear, cool liquid. "Slowly, drink slowly, even if you are in desperate need," Alex had said. Alex! She had to find her way back to him, then perhaps even come here before nightfall again. She had to wash him, wash herself! She drank slow swallows and splashed her face and arms again and again in the precious nectar. She looked around and found deeper puddles of water, then, beyond, a shallow rock pond as big as a Kensington Park fountain. Through a little gap in the rocks, she saw spindly-legged birds and the stout pig that had frightened her, nosing off leaves to share the puddle for a drink. Trembling with excitement and relief, she ducked her gourds to fill them gurgling full and headed back for Alex.

Alex's eyes followed Brett everywhere, though she was too busy to note it. Where the beach met the line of cedars and palmettos, they had stretched their canvas tarpaulin and woven the stick sides of their crude lean-to with palmetto fronds to cut the sun and wind. The tarpaulin and the tinderbox, which Alex had wedged into the hem of the tarpaulin, were the only things Brett had salvaged from the shore besides the bashed-in boat itself—which was too far gone for much but firewood. His ankle had not been broken, but the wrenching sprain was slow to heal, and even after a week was still painful. His fever had left after three days of her nursing, and the discolored swelling of his head contusion had finally gone down under Brett's ministrations. For five days he'd felt as weak as a babe and she had done all the work. Brett Benton Sanborn had been his very salvation.

These past two days he'd regained his strength on the thin raw strips of tunny she'd forced down him all week and the other fish they cooked in abundance over their fire. Palmetto berries, turtle eggs roasted in the ashes, tart limes, crabs and sea urchin roe had not only helped to keep them going, but filled both of them out after their ocean ordeal.

She, especially, had filled out beautifully, he noted with more than approval. A good week of land food and her lush body had bloomed like the sweet oleander blossom on their private little island chain in the glistening sea. His avid gaze followed her approach up the beach. Now, since she'd done such a good job of feeding him, his other hungers had returned.

She looked, he thought, completely stunning. He would never have imagined when they'd first met what a goddess hid under Miss Benton's prim exterior. Her loosed, shoulder-blade-length chestnut hair glimmered gold and garnet in the sun. Her tattered green gown revealed the sleek slants and curves of limbs, flat belly, rounded hips and full breasts. Her skin, even on her face, was toasted golden, accenting her balanced, classic features. Her dove-gray eyes, fringed heavily with thick, gilded lashes, were deep and utterly disturbing.

He could not keep his eyes off her. When he'd been ill, she'd been both nurse and comforter to him, but now that he had greatly recovered, she had become more reserved again. No more stroking of his forehead to soothe the fever or massaging of his leg and arm muscles to ease their ache. She no longer hummed to him while she thought he slept, or recited endless reams of Wordsworth's poetry or Bible verses while he drifted off to sleep. His pillow was the flat, hard ground now, not her curvy, soft lap. Blue blazes, he wanted and needed more! But he owed her his life, and she deserved a gentlemanly husband, not the savage lover she made him feel right now.

"And what goodies are you offering for luncheon today, ma'am?" he inquired breezily as she stooped to enter their little lean-to. She was holding her skirt up, cradling something close to her pelvis, apparently unaware that her tattered skirts flaunted both shapely knee and sweet thigh.

"Better than luncheon at the Fountain Inn and the Prince Regent's Carlton House put together!" she boasted, and her musical laughter caressed his ears.

He recalled with a sharp twinge of desire that she hadn't even seemed to know how to laugh when she'd first come to Baltimore, but now... She fell to her knees beside his sleeping mat, which she'd woven from palmetto fronds over layers of grass. A dozen oddly shaped yellow fruits tumbled out from her skirt between them.

"Are these the things you called paw-paws?" she asked.

"They are indeed!" he declared, and bathed her in a warm smile at another of her little victories for their survival. "Where did you find them? I thought we might have to live only on those tart limes and sour palmetto berries for fruit."

"They're really luscious and delicious, Alex!"

She went on to tell him exactly where in her little realm of discovery she'd found the paw-paw trees, but he hardly heard her. *She* was what looked luscious and delicious to him. Her eyes glistened with health and pride. She emanated warmth and passion. She was entrancing, gilded with beauty and overwhelmingly desirable. He tried to stem his need just to seize her in his arms. But dammit, she *had* chosen to be his wife, forced him to a marriage that gave him all kinds of rights!

"Umm, they're good and sweet," she murmured as she bit into a golden paw-paw. Juice glazed her full lower lip and she licked it with pink tip of tongue. She extended one to him. To her surprise, he gently clasped her wrist to bring it all the way to his mouth, then licked down and between her sticky fingers instead of eating the fruit. She froze, mesmerized, then tried to tug back while he gently tightened his grip.

"I guess I'm starved for something good and sweet besides the fruit," he whispered with a helpless shrug as their eyes snagged and held.

She didn't move, though her heart danced a rapid tattoo in her breast. His look and tone and touch were rawly, deliberately seductive. Yet this past week, he'd given no hint that he expected them to resume their so-called forced honeymoon, as he'd termed it bitterly more than once before. When she didn't pull her hand back again, he finally bit into the fruit she held, then released her wrist.

"You're feeling all back...to normal then," she managed. His eyes devoured her. She knew that if she wasn't careful, she'd make a fool of herself once again by blurting out that she loved him, when it was blatantly clear to her his needs had always been of another sort. This past week she had thought and thought about their predicament and their relationship. She'd intentionally exhausted herself improving the little castaway world they shared so that when she lay down near him at night she would not ache and yearn for his arms around her. But the stronger her body got after their ordeal, the weaker her resolve became that she not embarrass herself again by clinging to him. If he so much as touched her the way he used to—or even just kept watching her with those narrowed blue eyes and his unique flare of nostrils one more minute—she would be no better off than the poor women like her mother and Sally Windsor whose men left them when the tumbling and baby planting were over.

She ignored his look of chagrin as she squirmed back on her hips and quickly gathered the spilled paw-paws. Still on her knees, she stretched up to put them on the hanging food shelf that she'd rigged with a board and vines. "Crab marinated in lime juice and sea-urchin roe for dinner," she told him brightly, desperate to change the subject. "And then we can take another little walk on the sand to strengthen that ankle. But I'd better go once more for water before it gets dark, so I'll just get my gourds and vines and be back soon."

"Brett," he interrupted her chatter, "believe me, I'd chase you if I could, but my ankle won't be up to it for a few days yet. And I'm much too well to pretend I need another hand bath like the lovely ones you gave me to get my fever down—"

He let the implication hang between them. Her gaze slammed into his across the tiny space of shady lean-to. Despite the perpetual blush of sun on her face, she felt her skin go hot at the thoughts he deliberately invoked. She knew she'd awakened him when she'd shaved him for the first time with fish oil and the dagger she'd found in his boot. But she hadn't realized he was awake when she'd peeled his tattered breeches and boots off to wash even the white, private stretches of his ebony hair-flecked skin, as well as the bronze expanses. She had been certain he'd been delirious or asleep the times she cooled his naked body with water both from her rock pool and the heart of the palmetto palm. Surely he could not know how she had lingered admiringly, even awe-struck, over his muscles, powerfully sleek even in his help-lessness—over every handsome inch of him.

Like a coward, she said only, "I know you're quite capable of your own baths now. And you don't need to chase me. I'll get you whatever you want—water, food, another shell neck-lace—" she plunged on.

His eyes swept over her, lingering on her bare, brown legs, her waist and the thrust of her breasts against the fraying green cloth of her bodice. "But what I want, Brett Benton Sanborn," he went on, "is you in my arms, so what's the nurse's remedy for that?"

"How do I know you really mean it?" she demanded, sud-denly angrier with herself than with him. She didn't mean to play his puppet, as other women had before her! Supposed wife or not, she didn't intend to do everything he wanted now, only to be cast aside later, or even to leave of her own accord, as Simone had!

"Haven't you noticed by now," he countered, his voice slow and low, "that there's a way to tell if a man means it?" Brazenly he crooked his good leg and settled his right arm heavily on it, while his injured leg sprawled straight out to-ward her on the ground. She bit her lower lip and forced her saucer-wide eyes up to his face again. The proof of his desire for her was blatantly obvious against the tight stretch of his tattered gray kid breeches, which she'd laundered herself on the rocks the other day. "I always thought it most unfair," he went on, "that there's no precise way for a man to so easily discern desire on the woman's part by just looking."

When she darted her arms across her chest to hide the nubs of nipples straining against her worn garments, she saw him actually bite back a laugh, as if he read her mind. "But you see, sweetheart," he went on, "taut-tipped breasts could be from the sea breeze. I'm talking about something comparable to the way I show I mean it.''

"Well, since we're talking so immodestly," she shot back at him, "it's hardly fair that men can tell so easily when a woman's a virgin and she can't tell the same about him." That did split his face into a broad grin, the monster, but it was too late to take back what she'd blurted out now.

"I agree. Perhaps men and women are even then. But you know, when a woman's a virgin, the loving is not usually half as wonderful as when she's not and has a little more tender tutoring. You don't believe me?" he continued when she shook her head. Keeping his weight off his foot, he slid over toward her.

"It's not that I don't believe you or want to find out—as very well you know, with your snide smile, Alexander Sanborn!" Everything she'd been agonizing about the past week spilled out before she could stop it. "It's only that I regret forcing you to wed me, since you obviously had no desire for that at least, and I think loyalty has to go together with passion!" Her fervent declaration echoed Simone's last advice to her and she knew it.

He looked surprised, then angry. He reached for her, but she darted back with a quicker move of her hips than he could manage with his tender ankle. She scrambled off the mat, out of the hut, then bent back to look in just outside the doorway.

"I admit I love you, Alex, and to me that means wanting you, too. But I realize you don't love me. And I know it won't do your Yankee pride and your precious business a bit of good to be wed to an Englishwoman you still think might be a spy!" She walked backward on reluctant, shaky legs. "I'll go get the water now," she called back over her shoulder as she turned and ran. "I'll only be about half an hour!"

"Brett, come back here!" he shouted, but she ignored him. "Brett!" He smacked a hard fist on his sleeping mat, and sand flew. The woman had turned him inside out one way or the other since the day he'd met her, he fumed. She was stubborn, pushy and maddening! But she was also bold, beautiful and so very, very—damn—necessary in his life! With a curse aimed more at himself than her, he shoved his sleeping mat right over next to hers. Then, on his cedar wood crutch, he hobbled grumbling down to the beach to look for sea urchins for dinner.

That night after a delicious meal had filled their bellies, they had gone for a slow walk and then gazed in silence at the stars sprinkled overhead like diamonds on black velvet. But the camp fire had settled to smoldering silver ashes, and she had claimed a weariness she did not completely feel. In their leafy lean-to, she lay alert, tense, closer beside him than usual, since he had boldly pushed their sleeping mats side by side and she hadn't had the nerve to put them back. All evening he had been charming, accommodating, thoughtful and maddeningly admiring. He had called her "sweetheart" as if he meant it, but only given her a light peck on the lips before he had rolled on his back next to her in the sable darkness. She could hear him breathing deeply now, but she knew well from these weeks of being by his side that he was not asleep. She jumped when he spoke so close.

"Sweetheart?"

"What?"

"I'm sorry if I was too pushy earlier."

She bit her lower lip a moment. Her heart thrilled. She knew he wanted something and what that something was. And though she desired him desperately, too, she steeled herself not to just cave in to him.

"I'm the one who's been pushy, Alex," she told him, struggling to keep her voice from quavering. "You always seemed just—well, 'pully.'"

He chuckled low. She heard him roll onto his side, facing her. She held her breath. "I'd like to pull you right over here, sweet Brett, but I won't. I suppose that under normal circumstances back in Baltimore we'd probably be arguing. I've got to remember that these past two weeks we've been through so much that you've been forced to be kind and tender to me."

"That's not true! I wasn't forced. It's only that I didn't want to force you—after our marriage and all."

"Does 'and all' mean our lovemaking in that little first mate's cabin when I was so angry and panicked I couldn't think straight? I was rough and nasty, Brett, but I swear to you, I won't be if you'll let me touch you again."

She began to tremble. The sea breeze, nerves, her desperate need and love for him all jumbled together to send shivers up and down her skin. His hand slid slowly from the darkness to find and clasp her wrist. He linked his big fingers through her slender ones to make one hand. "I won't ever, ever be that way again, Brett," he repeated. His big body emanated heat to her in the dark; his raspy voice rustled her hair. "Let me love you gently, any way you want, sweetheart. Just let me love you!"

It was the word she had longed to hear, but did that mean he really loved her? Suddenly all her agonizing over it didn't matter. She loved him and that was that. And they were married, really married, or at least would be until they got back to Baltimore. Surely she could fight him there if he claimed coercion from the enemy. And she could show him how much she cared, maybe even have conceived a child by then to make the name Sanborn and Son a reality again!

"You said—" her voice came to him a silver whisper "—you would love me any way I want. I just want you to keep me. Other than that, I'm not sure what I want—"

He rolled closer on his elbow now, so that their bodies touched lightly, full length. His rugged, handsome face shimmered in the surrounding darkness. "Then let me show you everything I know and you can decide what you want. But for the fact that this ankle's going to keep me from getting on top of your beautiful, golden body the way I want right now, that starry sky's the limit for us out here!"

Her body trembled against his even as she laughed, half delighted and half astounded at his boast. When her arms encircled his strong neck, he rolled them over until she lay facing him on his other side, her back pressed gently to their woven wall. They kissed until their quickened breathing matched the crash of waves on the beach. Tenderly, reverently, his hands removed those remnants of their garments that the sea had spared them.

Enveloped by sweet breezes and deep night, they explored and stroked each other. Little nips and licks and kisses followed. His hands became lost in her bounteous tresses, seemed to go everywhere! Emboldened, she slid her palm over his big shoulders and down his upper arms and arched back. She molded her hands to his chest muscles and snared her fingers in the curly, resilient hair she found there. She laughingly imitated his arousal of her by flicking her tongue across his tiny nipples, and when she heard and felt him gasp in surprise, she became wilder yet along the length of him. She only learned there was a point of passion beyond which he could not endure when his hands seized her hips and he lifted her up and astride him to pierce her with his power.

"Oh! Oh, Alex!"

"Just until my ankle strengthens, but it's so good!"

"I know. I didn't know, but it is!" She cupped her palms on his hard shoulders to support herself. When she bent to meet his lips, her hair trailed tantalizingly along his face and neck.

"You said you've always been pushy, my beautiful love. Push now and see what happens!"

She did. And pulled. And held to him and kissed him and found that what he had promised was indeed true. Loving did get even better than wonderful with experience. They drowned in her hair, which spilled over them, and in their rapture of each other. The May night was long, but for them, lovers again and again and again, hardly long enough.

They had indeed found paradise, Brett thought repeatedly the next week. Surely there was no serpent hidden anywhere to ruin this perfection. As his ankle healed, they explored their Eden and named the animals, just as Adam and Eve had: Henny the plumed heron, who fussed over everything like Henny Featherstone at home; Todd the cavorting tern, who reminded them of little Todd Miles; Quinby the wild boar, for the brute Quinby Marsh. They held hands, laughed, pelted each other with the hibiscus blossoms that she wove each day for a living necklace. They walked nearly naked on the beach and splashed totally nude in the biggest rock pool in the pine forest ravine. They named regions and parts of their island, which they dubbed "Castaway." They wrote each other love notes in the sand, which only had to be redone more elaborately and explicitly when the tides encroached to ruin them. They spent long nights talking of nothing and of everything between bouts of passionate lovemaking. She taught him poetry and he described all the places in Spain and Italy he'd seen before returning home to oversee Sanborn's with his father. She had never felt more happy, more vibrant, more feminine, more alive.

Though he still used a walking stick, they began to explore farther down their little chain of islands, which they called "The Un-United States," always keeping a lookout for sails or signs of human habitation. But, other than the barren, bleached ruins of various wrecked ships, there was nothing. When the tide was low, they island-hopped on a raft Alex made from boards of their battered longboat.

One morning, two islands down, they discovered a world of platinum coral rocks, sculpted into a private grotto and hidden by ferns, where rainwater was trapped in even larger pools than those on Castaway. Beyond the seaward cleft in the grotto glittered jeweled water in bands of lavender, pale green and sparkling sapphire.

"It's like heaven," she whispered, awed. "We'll name this island Paradise."

"If I wasn't hoping to start out to find St. George's Town next week, we'd move here," he told her.

Suddenly, she resented his mentioning they ever had to leave. Her grip on his hand tightened and she pulled his arm possessively against her side. He saw her frown. "Let's get in and cool off," he said only.

Gingerly she lifted off her ragged-hemmed skirt, which came barely to her knees now. Over her ruined bodice she always wore a necklace of hibiscus blossoms for modesty's sake. Modesty, she mused—a great joke, considering the way they'd played and worked and loved naked together as if they were merely different parts of the same body.

He dived in with a booming splash, while she hesitated. The water was crystalline clear. She could see his brown body, strong and angular, knifing through it in a burst of silver bubbles. Below him golden brain coral and lilac fan coral edged the deep, rocky bottom. Little fish with vibrant parrot tails shimmered in the depths. Alex surfaced hooting and splashing. As she stood there naked in this stunning place while his eyes dared her, she thought of the old, stoic, sad Brett Benton who never had any excitement in her life. But this was Brett Sanborn, in love and loving, she thought happily, and she jumped in beside him, laughing at the upward explosion of water she created.

They floated, laughed, tickled, and bounced their voices off the overhanging iridescent rainbow walls, gone wavy in the reflection of slanting sun on their water. He gave her her first real swimming lesson, then demanded payment in what he termed "those long, hot kisses." He treaded water, holding her up facing him, his big hands splayed on her ribs just under her breasts. She kissed him, meaning it to be just a teasing peck. But he tasted so clean and fresh and wonderful that she darted a tongue out just as he'd taught her forever ago in distant Baltimore.

She skimmed his lips, savored their inner sleekness. Her tongue touched his, then darted and slid in little stroking waves in a swimming lesson of another kind. He still held her up in the gentle waves they made together, but his thumbs moved over the underswell of her breasts and flicked back and forth against her pointed pink nipples to enhance the long, devouring kiss.

She broke away at last. "Mmm—can't breathe."

"Who needs to breathe when we have all this?"

He pulled her back to him and stroked her again, lower along her hips, then dipped a quick hand between her thighs. That other woman who had once been such a foreign visitor to her body now seemed totally at home, the woman who danced and laughed and loved Alex Sanborn, body and soul. Now she smiled and floated away on her back teasingly, until he separated her trim ankles and reeled her in toward him. But she caught him by wrapping her legs around his chest. He paddled harder to keep afloat. His breathing deepened.

"Brett, let's get out."

"No, I like it."

"You'll like it better where I can get a foot down, I promise!"

She had to admit she loved her power over him when he wanted her so much. But it only made her want to give him anything he asked. She laughed deep in her throat in pure joy and held to him as he hurried them out onto the little ledge. He lifted her, then laid her down on their scattered garments. She thought for a moment that he meant to enter her instantly when he spread her legs again and pressed close. She was fully ready for him, but he hesitated, poised over her on his elbows, his face so intent.

"Brett, I love you so much! I never knew I could need a woman this much. And I don't mean just this way."

Tears of rapturous joy flooded her eyes to make his brown face shimmer, before she blinked to further drench her soaked lashes. At this moment, in this beautiful spot, this precious man was all hers. And he wanted her. Best of all life's gifts, he loved her!

"I love you, too, my Alex! So much. When I think how we used to fight—"

"Shh! And may again someday. But if we do, we'll always make up—just like this—and forget about everything and everyone else."

She did forget about all else out there that wasn't part of their little paradise. Nothing, nothing could ever hurt or separate them again. It would always be like this! She soared above rational thought. He slid heavily inside her and caressed, stroked, teased, and then, when she urged him on with her own fervent little circles of wild hips, he exploded into her to fill her body and her heart.

* * *

They had lain naked in each other's arms but a few minutes, before Alex reluctantly pulled her gown up over her. "We'd better head back, or the tide will make it hard to get out, sweetheart."

"Mmm. I wouldn't mind spending eternity here."

"Come on. We'll pass through again in a day or so when we're provisioned and on our way to find St. George's Town."

They did not linger to glance back. Nothing could improve on what they had shared there today. They shaded their eyes as they stepped out into the glare of afternoon sun on the beach. And stood facing four bearded men with pistols drawn.

She stifled a scream when Alex gave a tiny warning squeeze of her hand. They had hoped for rescuers, but these men looked so unkempt, so threatening with their guns and leering eyes.

Alex tugged her slightly behind him, then faced them with hands on hips in a bold stance. "Good afternoon, gentlemen," he declared, his voice calm but strong. "You gave my wife and me a start there."

"Seein' what you two been up to, can't imagine why," the biggest of the men said, and guffawed and spit into the sand at Alex's feet. "This here's one a the outer islands in my domain, see?" he declared, and waved the pistol nearly in Alex's face. "And fancy women in these parts is few and far between, so's I know you'll be real willing to share. You two look real ragged, but we can spot real high and mighties when we see 'em, right, boys?"

"All we're asking is safe passage to St. George's Town. There'll be a fat reward for you there," Alex said, his voice maddeningly calm to Brett's ears. But she saw his back muscles flex and stiffen as if in warning.

"Rich folks, a real fine duke and duchess. He calls the likes of us wreckers 'gentlymen,' too, eh, boys?" The hulking blond man laughed and the other three joined in raucously.

Brett peered around Alex's shoulder and squinted into the sun to see the spokesman better. His greasy yellow hair was crudely sheared and tied back in a long tail with a sash of dirty crimson China silk that was also wrapped around his head. His brown eyes were sharp; his swarthy cheeks bore a single white slash that also puckered his thin lower lip. He had crooked teeth and a smashed, flat nose, and he talked with a nasal twang. Although he was almost as tall as Alex, he hunched his massive shoulders as if he were leaning or ready to spring forward. He wore an old, bright, red-stained British officer's coat and much jewelry, both women's and men's. Brett stepped closer to Alex's back when she felt the men's eyes creep over her again.

"An' what's the duchess have to say then?" he goaded.

"My husband has said it all," she declared, fighting to keep her voice calm. "We want safe passage to St. George's Town and you'll be glad you did. Our friends know our boat has put into this area, and they're no doubt searching for us this very moment."

"Ay, fancy British talkin' from a fancy, high and mighty wench. I told you, boys! All right, no more jabberin'. Let's just tie up the mouthy duke here and get us on back 'fore the tide shifts," the leader ordered his men. "It ain't every day that Lucifer Flyte, King of the Bermudas Wreckers, finds hisself two real nice fancy slaves to serve him at table or whatever—and the duchess here in my bed."

Suddenly Alex moved. He shoved Brett back and took a swing at the first man who reached for her, then grabbed for the man's gun. Lucifer shot his gun at Alex's feet, then swung it at him. Alex ducked, but the pistol he struggled for hit the sand. As Brett made a lightning-quick move to retrieve it, three of them pounced on Alex. He went down while Lucifer himself stepped on the pistol in the sand that she'd grabbed for. He yanked her up and pinned her against the coral ledge, his gun pressed under her upraised chin. She tried to see what they did to Alex as she heard the sounds of them tying, then kicking him into submission.

"I like slaves with spirit, specially females," the brute told Brett. When she started to beg for Alex, he jammed the hot muzzle of the gun harder against her chin. His breath this close reeked of garlic. He trailed a heavy finger down her arched throat and between her breasts as he spoke. "See, the tide waits for no man. And we're hopin' for a real nice prize wreck real soon. Else, I'd just haul you back inside and take up where the duke left off between those sweet thighs, hmm. But I gotta nice bed in a nice house back on Devil's Isle all cozy for the likes of you, Duchess!"

"Sure, Lucifer," one of his men said. "If'n Devona don't slit this un's pretty throat first!"

"Jez shut your trap! I rule Devona and not the other way round!" Lucifer exploded with a kick and hawking spit at the man.

Brett gasped with disbelief as Lucifer yanked her past Alex's prone body and down the beach in the opposite direction from their little island. It seemed so dear and distant now. She tasted the bitter bile of stark fear in her throat.

The wreckers had a longboat shoved up on the sand. They dragged the bound Alex behind her. She tried to turn back to catch his eye, but when he called out to her not to be afraid, one man kicked him hard again. Lucifer Flyte shoved her ahead of him into the prow of the longboat to block her view and leered at her as his men shoved off and bent hard over their oars into the incoming tide.

Fourteen

Brett counted eight one story, rough-board houses of sprawling irregular shapes and sizes behind the low sand dunes on the wreckers' island. On various keys and beaches along the way she had noted the battered skeletons of vessels in various states of decay, and here she saw many more. Despite her pleas and Alex's repeated offers of ransom money, their captors dragged them out of the boat and off in different directions. Lucifer took Brett and the other three hauled Alex off like a wild animal bound for the slaughter. Mongrel dogs yipped at Brett's heels and a few dirty children ran along shouting questions, until Lucifer kicked at the dogs and ordered the children off. They disappeared instantly to leave only adults, both men and women, bent over packing crates. Lucifer shoved Brett through the door of the largest house at the center of the village.

It was dim inside, and despite her plight, the delicious smell of cooking from somewhere out in back jabbed her empty stomach. The main room was crowded with heavy, carved furniture, chairs, settees, sideboards and tables of various styles. The walls were littered with silver and brass candelabras and gilt-framed paintings of unknown people and places, all hung haphazardly. Thick Turkish rugs lay randomly three to four deep, making walking unsteady. Two open doorways led to rooms in the back of the cluttered house. The large

Jacobean dinner table by the only seaside window flaunted crystal and Georgian silver worthy of the Prince Regent's table. Six crimson velvet, high-backed chairs awaited diners. At Lucifer's approach, two thin girls clad in old gowns far too big for them stopped setting the table and scurried back against the wall to just stare.

"Git on with yer work!" Lucifer bellowed, and gave Brett a poke in the back. He pulled her into a bedchamber with various gilded mirrors surrounding a huge, carved four-poster. She was about to rake her fingernails down his cruel face and flee, when she noticed there were others in the room. A small, copper-haired baby lay kicking chubby, bare legs on the green brocade counterpane of the bed and a woman with flaming red hair and pale, oval face jumped up from primping before a mirrored dressing table to rattle the array of cut-glass bottles there.

"Got a real lady to serve you, Queenie. Talks real proper, jus' like you always wanted," he announced grandly, and shoved Brett toward the startled woman. "A duchess, an' she won't deny it if she knows what's what," he added with another sharp poke between Brett's shoulder blades.

The woman seemed very young—perhaps only sixteen or seventeen. Her voluptuous breasts were brazenly displayed in a tightly laced golden gown with an old-fashioned stomacher cut so low her beige nipples actually peeked through the tawdry lace. Her eyes were green, her face strangely gentle and sweet, considering her surroundings and companions. She wrung her graceful, ruby-and-pearl-ringed hands as she spoke.

"A real duchess?" she asked in a low pitched, awed voice. Her face lit like a child's. "From England? Blessed to make thy acquaintance, a course," she told Brett with a quick dip of knees that, Brett realized, was meant to be a curtsy. The woman looked imploringly at Lucifer again. "That is, I am blessed if she wilt be my servant and not thine, Lucifer."

"Hell, I said so, didn't I?"

"Why wouldst a duchess serve me of her own accord?"

Queenie asked warily, still addressing Lucifer as if he had all the world's answers.

"You stupid wench!" Lucifer bellowed, and gave Brett another shove in Queenie's direction. "'Cause I got her husband locked up at Gowers'! She'll behave real nice if she don't want him sliced in little pieces, see? I'll be back for dinner in an hour an' you just see she's settled down and waitin' table. An' get her in something nice!" he bellowed as the baby on the bed began to cry at his vocal explosions. "An' see if between the two of you, you can keep that brat quiet, or out she goes to some nursemaid, I told you. I'm sick of her cryin' when you're s'posed to keep me happy at night! An' I want her weaned, I said. Those nice teats of yours are mine and no other's, specially to feed some whelp who prob'ly ain't mine!"

Brett stared aghast at that tirade as the red-haired woman's pale green eyes filled with tears, though her lower lip set hard as if in smothered defiance. Brett prayed she'd display more backbone than was apparent. As far as she could tell so far, this Queenie might be her only hope to rescue Alex.

With another shove, which bounced Brett into the woman, Lucifer Flyte breathed a sigh of relief and realized Queenie did, too. She hoped desperately that as this full-bodied red-head was Lucifer's woman, she herself would be able to escape his bed, despite his threats. And if this woman was in awe of a real duchess and stupid enough to believe Lucifer's claim she was one, how far would such a charade get her?

"The baby has hair like yours," Brett ventured in the awkward silence when they were alone. "A lovely child. I'm sorry Mr. Flyte doesn't like her. He sounds as if he might actually hurt her if you can't get her away from here. I know if I were a mother, I'd be awfully worried about that."

Queenie nodded, wide-eyed, and Brett wondered if the woman was dim-witted. But when she proudly told Brett all about the thrill of birthing the child three months ago, she realized the woman was only terrified witless around Lucifer. Her loving mother's voice instantly calmed the child. "She hath the name Rebecca. Lucifer's she is, but he wilt not accept her, since he hath begotten no others," she explained. "He saith I was secret handmaiden to another."

Brett puzzled at her strange, stilted pattern of speech, but over the next hour the entire story of Queenie, whose real name was Devona Nye, tumbled out from the girl, who was by no means dim-witted. When she was one year old, Devona and her mother, Mary Sarah Nye, were on the British ship *Providence*, which was lured onto the reef. That was nearly sixteen years earlier. To save Devona's life, her mother was forced to become mistress—or handmaiden, as Devona called it—to Captain Bart, the leader of the wrecker band. But ten years ago Lucifer Flyte killed him in a challenge and took over. Lucifer marooned her mother and those most loyal to Captain Bart on some sandbar far off the coast that the tide would cover. When Devona turned fifteen, she caught Lucifer's eye and had been his main handmaiden ever since.

"His *main* handmaiden?" Brett asked as she piled Devona's hair on her head in elaborate curls and twists, fastening it with gold filigreed pins. "He has other handmaidens besides you?" she managed shakily when Devona just frowned into the mirror and pouted her full lips to rouge them with her finger.

Devona shrugged helplessly but managed a wan little smile at Brett's handiwork. She thanked her profusely, then finally explained, "Lucifer is patriarch here, thou knowest, and full of wrath. 'Thou shalt not kill' meaneth naught to Lucifer. And hast thou not heard, even Abraham led men in battle and possessed handmaidens."

Brett shuddered at the realization of how morally confused Devona was by this life. Not only was she quoting the Bible blindly to apply it to this hellhole, but she seemed to be trying to speak like it. "I'll wager you learned to read from the Bible, didn't you?" she asked as she fastened an emerald necklace around Devona's slender neck. If the girl read the Bible, maybe she would at least exhibit some Christian mercy to someone in desperate need. Brett considered working very hard to please Devona and then begging her for help, but she knew she didn't have time for all that. Not after what Lucifer had threatened outside the coral grotto and the way he'd eyed her in the longboat.

"My mother taught me to read from the Bible," Devona told her proudly. "That be almost all I remember about her, save that she wast very beautiful with red hair. But Lucifer burned the Bible, curse him. I did find another in a wreck last year, only the front part called Genesis, and as water-soaked as Noah's flood. But I got Rebecca's name from it." The girl turned and looked up at Brett. "Please never tell him I cursed his name. And I thought British ladies must all talk as those do in the Bible. But if thou art a duchess, thou doth not talk that way."

"I imagine British nobility used to years ago during King James's reign, but not now, Devona. Besides, it's always been one's willingness to be kind to others and help those in need that makes a real lady—a queen such as Lucifer calls you. And my heart is so heavy now that my husband, the duke, is a prisoner. I worry for his safety, just as you do for your beautiful, helpless little Rebecca."

Devona's pale brow furrowed as she pondered that. "I shall pray for your husband, but if Lucifer decreeth it, so be it. I dare not gainsay Lucifer, lest he harm Rebecca."

At that, Brett sensed her own defeat. The girl no doubt resented Lucifer's treatment of her, but feared for herself and the baby too much ever to help a prisoner. If Devona lived like this with a man who had as good as murdered her mother, what chance did a stranger who begged her help have?

From a leather-tooled sea chest at the foot of the bed, Devona dragged a jade-green satin gown and thrust it at Brett. "He shalt beat us both if we prepareth not for supper," she said. "Mayhap in the future I shalt just repeat the words thou—I mean you—say, and renounce the old way of speaking. When we gain riches from more ships and Lucifer and I journey far to England as he promised, I must talk right!"

Brett hurried into the jade-green gown. It had long, tight sleeves edged in faded lace and heavy full skirts with no petticoats to hold them up. The velvet-edged neckline was very broad and square, but at least, unlike Devona's, it covered her breasts. Devona produced a black velvet ribbon to tie her hair back. Brett washed her face and hands in a porcelain washbowl with painted Chinese figures of birds, then hurried out into the main room in Devona's wake to face Lucifer again.

Serving Lucifer Flyte and three of his cronies at the table went from bad dream to nightmare. Brett worked alone, as the two skinny girls setting the table had disappeared. Still, she managed to filch food for herself to gain some strength, each time she carried a dish in from the outdoor kitchen, even under the watchful eye of a sullen cook. She dared to ask the old woman which house was Gowers', but the sour thing wouldn't even talk but to grunt orders. Devona sat aloof at the opposite end of the table from Lucifer, picking at her stew and buttered bread while the three men gulped their food, guzzled rum, talked only to each other and belched.

Brett noticed, however, that one of the three guests, a man called Clancey, seemed more reticent and polite. At least he didn't spout profanity or ogle her like the other men, and his hint of a jaunty Irish brogue had charm. Clancey tried more than once to draw poor Devona into conversations on proper topics, and while the other men soon demolished them, Brett noted how Devona's usually downcast eyes lifted to shine in gratitude toward Clancey. He was short and stocky with sandy hair and a pleasant face sprinkled with freckles, and had walked to the table with a pronounced limp. He was also fairly wily, as he and Devona both looked away from each other when Lucifer glanced over or addressed him.

But Brett had her own immediate worries. Whenever she got in range of Lucifer's hands, he pinched her bottom or fondled her breasts, even when Devona shot him pained stares down the length of table.

"That Spanish ship you promised me's long overdue, Stubbs," Lucifer groused to the fat man on his right over yet another goblet of rum. "We had big lanterns on longboats out from shore every night this week, hopin' she'd miss the channel and run her belly on the reef."

"Gold as well as goods on her, I heard in St. George's," the man named Jess grunted. "Naw, she's due. You'll get her." He swigged his rum, while his greedy eyes watched Brett in her corner until she lowered her defiant gaze. Rubbish, it wasn't worth the risk to challenge these demons with a hateful stare.

"Hell, we'll get her all right," Lucifer assured them all. "Takin' Duchess here's a real good omen today," he boasted as Brett hurried over to refill their goblets before they had to ask again.

If they would only get dead drunk, she had a chance, she thought as she sloshed his rim full. But they seemed like bottomless pits. Their already obnoxious behavior hardly worsened a bit from it, she thought, until Lucifer cracked her bottom so hard she almost fell onto the table.

Brett's first instinct was to brain him with the pitcher, but her eyes fastened on his other big hand, playing with a small dirk he'd picked his crooked teeth with. Stubbs and Jess roared with laughter at her obvious chagrin. Then Jess belched and said, "Sure hope she's part of the sweets you done promised us tonight, Lucifer. Don't call you King of Devil's Isle for nothing, considering the way you entertain at table when we're out from St. George's!"

Brett backed quickly into the corner and Devona's eyes met hers before they darted back to Clancey, who cleared his throat before he spoke. "I really think that with Miss Devona here and all, we could show a little more respect for womankind," he began.

"Respect!" Stubbs hooted. "For womankind!"

Lucifer just grinned tightly and flipped his dirk into the tabletop again and again to chew the polished oak surface to bits.

Brett was sure now that Devona didn't have the backbone to help her. And Clancey obviously had little influence with these men. How she'd love to get her fingers on that dirk in Lucifer's hand! Maybe she could hide a carving knife when she went back out to the kitchen. But just when she was certain she had a plan, things crashed out of control again.

"You go on in to bed now, Queenie," Lucifer ordered Devona. "Tend the brat, as I want her real quiet when I come in tonight or it's quits for her in this house. Me and the men got business now. And Duchess," he said when Brett moved quickly to stand behind Devona's chair, "Queenie's gonna do without your services for a bit, as we need them here *real bad*."

Jess and Stubbs snickered, while Clancey looked absolutely stricken. Brett's skin crawled with foreboding as they all eyed her.

Devona stood slowly and shook out her skirts. "Duchess vowed to tell me about London tonight, Lucifer. She promised," she protested quietly.

"Later, woman! She'll be here tomorrow and the next day, too! Git now!" he bellowed, and without another backward glance at the distraught Brett, Devona went in and slammed the door.

Brett stood back in the growing shadows away from the table, with its single lantern, while the men haggled prices for pirated contraband to be carted to St. George's Town tomorrow. From fragments of speech she overheard, she gathered that this island must be connected to the main one by a land bridge at certain times of the day and that St. George's must be four hours off by horse. Four hours from freedom! If only she could rescue Alex and they could be on their way, she agonized. And this Clancey McFee was an importer in St. George's who sold or shipped Lucifer's pirated goods from a warehouse on the dock. Her hopes plummeted further. Even Clancey was in this with them then, so she was doomed. Still, she gleaned that Clancey had arrived here today with four big horse-drawn carts. If only she could sneak out to locate the horses!

"Duchess! Rum!" Lucifer shouted, and banged his goblet on the table again, though she'd just filled it.

Her hands trembled and she spilled some when he threw his arm around her hips and pulled her against the arm of his chair. "Spirited and real high and mighty, this one is," he assured his cronies. She kept her eyes down and gave him no provocation to do more. "Thought you three might like to watch and take a turn at her when I'm done tonight," he said, and belched. "Gotta break the new ones in good and thorough!"

Brett gasped. He couldn't mean that! Not with Devona and his child in the next room and Brett's husband in another house nearby! She would die before she'd let this foul bastard touch her that way. Her frightened gaze snagged Clancey's, but he glanced quickly away.

"Don't look too spirited to me," fat Stubbs observed. "Let's haul her outside and see if you can prove it."

"For the love of heaven, just wait a minute," Clancey protested with both palms held up. "I'm in this because I had to be at first and now because Lucifer's got the goods on me, but that doesn't include forcing unwilling females."

"Hell, ain't we all proper now?" Lucifer challenged. "I s'pose you'd like a turn at the little whore in my bedroom, who'd be willin' enough with a gentyman like you, huh?" His voice came deadly low, so that for the first time they had to strain to hear him.

"That's not true, Lucifer," Clancey argued. "Devona's loyal to you."

Lucifer grappled Brett even closer to his side, though she pushed steadily at him with her elbows to keep from tumbling across his lap. "An' I tell you, Clancey McFee, if I ever thought diff'rent for one minute, you'd be the first one I'd make buzzard bait. But if you can't stomach the little party I'm offerin' with the duchess here tonight, jez make sure you're not in the palace with Devona while I'm out. Now, lookee here, boys, let's just sample the sweets—"

When he hooked a hand in the front of Brett's bodice to rip it down, she heaved her rum pitcher in his face. All hell broke loose. She yanked away from his grasp as he roared in anger. But that soon changed to delight when Stubbs shoved the protesting Clancey out the front door. The three men turned on Brett, stalking her into a corner. She threw a Chinese porcelain vase at them and then another, while they lurched at her, snatching at her skirt, taunting her with lewd promises. Jess grabbed a handful of sleeve and yanked her nearly off her feet in his unsuccessful attempt to strip her bodice down. She heard her heavy skirt tear as someone pulled at it. She screamed Devona's name once, before Lucifer leaped at her and dragged her outside by both wrists.

As if she weighed nothing, he pulled her toward the beach while her legs and hips dragged a long mark in the sand as if a big serpent had crawled that way. They passed a shoreside line of the bonfires built to lure hapless ships onto the reef to plunder. He pulled her around a sand dune speckled with blowing sea oats. Clancey was not in sight, but the other two men loped along expectantly at Lucifer's side.

Alex, she thought despairingly—how she needed, wanted Alex! Lucifer dropped her on her back. Three leering faces instantly bent over her. She tried to kick, but someone grabbed her legs. She threw sand as she fought, but six hands pinned her down. Probing fingers plunged into her gown to free her breasts. She sobbed in great silent gasps as Lucifer ordered her legs spread while he stood to fumble with his breeches. She fought to make her mind a blank, for something to focus on, some beautiful, precious place to hide away in her thoughts. She would run to her and Alex's little palmetto lean-to on their island called Castaway, where they had been so happy! She would hide there until this agony was over.

She wasn't sure she'd really heard the words at first when a man's voice shouted, "Lucifer, Lucifer, for the love of heaven, stop!" Clancey! It was Clancey! "Look, just beyond the reef! That's gotta be it! See those lights? And you can pick out a big-bellied sail if you squint."

Hands released her. "Hell, but if it ain't!" Lucifer crowed, and slapped Clancey on his back. "We'll settle with this little scrapper after the plunder, boys. Clancey, keep an eye on her, and if she 'scapes, you're bird meat. I gotta get these shore fires stoked up!"

Lucifer tore off bellowing, with the other two in his wake, as Clancey McFee helped Brett to her feet. "I'm real, real sorry," he told her. "But at least I came—you know, in time." His earnest face shone pale in the reflected light of flaring fires. "The ship saved you, not me, though I wanted to," he added.

She turned her back to compose her garments and herself. Her teeth chattered in the cold wash of fear, but now was her chance with this man. "I'm very grateful," she said, wheeling back to face him. "I could tell you're not like the rest of them. The only thing is, if I can't free my husband and escape, the same thing will happen tomorrow. You're an importer in St. George's. If you could only help us get there, it would be worth a great deal to you, as well as us. My husband and I own a large American shipping firm called Sanborn's and—"

"For the love of heaven," Clancey exploded. "The man Lucifer's got in chains at Gowers' is Alex Sanborn!"

Brett gripped his wrist. "Yes, yes! Do you know him? Please, we need your help!"

He shook his sandy head even while he pulled back from her grasp. "No, it's not that I know him. Just a few days ago a British naval ship put in to St. George's with word Alexander Sanborn was a criminal against the crown, escaped and dangerous. There's a three-hundred-pound reward on his head, living or dead!"

Brett sucked in a breath and pressed her hands to her mouth. She'd blundered badly to tell this man who Alex was. Lucifer would kill him, send his corpse to town to collect the money.

"What ship was it?" she managed. "Not a big frigate called the *Raven's Wing*?"

He shook his head. "Some sloop that goes back and forth from the blockade to St. George's real regular for navy supplies. There's no money on your head, Mrs. Sanborn, but you're wanted, too. There's even a likeness of the two of you tacked up in King's Square and one on the State House. I recognize you now that I think of it. There's no way I can help you when I can't even help myself, so don't go askin' again. I won't tell Lucifer what I know, but he'll be finding out himself soon enough, Mrs. Sanborn, that he will, I'm afraid. You'd best come on with me now before someone wonders what we're doing out here.''

They walked slowly, as his limp was pronounced on the soft sand. All sorts of possibilities bombarded Brett's stunned brain. Overcome Clancey, run off to hide in the chaos of their trying to snag the poor, doomed vessel that was now within her sight, almost on the reef. Run back to the house to beg Devona for help while Lucifer was busy with the wreck— That was it, Devona!

''I have no other hope but you, Clancey McFee,'' she told him hurriedly as he led her out from behind the sand dune. ''I believe you're a good man. I'm begging you to help me because you know I'm doomed here—as doomed as poor Devona. I know you want to help her, and I do, too.''

He turned to face her, and his hand on her elbow tightened. ''Devona! Don't mention her in the same breath with me around here!''

''She deserves better than Lucifer,'' Brett went on, ''but she'll never leave without her child, even with a kind and gentle man she obviously admires. She told me that devil Lucifer doesn't even think Rebecca is his, and I heard him threaten the child. Don't you think Devona would give anything to get away from here if she could take Rebecca, too, and have a real chance at freedom? Alex and I could take them back to Baltimore, where Lucifer would never find them. We could send the authorities back here from St. George's to arrest these criminals. You could go to Baltimore with us, too.'' Her impassioned voice flowed on. ''And with Alex Sanborn's help, if you free him, we can all make it together. You have access to the horses, and these people are all so busy now,'' she concluded with a sweep of her free hand at the scene.

Around them, the wreckers ran everywhere. Brett stared aghast at the demonic dance within pools of light and darkness. Some manned longboats, which others shoved off the sand in a hubbub of noise and movement. Women and children hurried toward the shore with long, hooked pikes. The strongest men bent their backs like oxen to turn two huge winches with braided rope cables that snaked out into the sea itself. And there, chained both wrist and ankle, Alex bent to help his captors rotate one huge winch.

"Alex!" she cried, and tried to run to him, before Clancey jerked her back.

"For the love of heaven, are you crazy?" He threatened with a hard shake. "What a woman, bold and daring one minute and emotional and stupid the next. Now keep your mouth shut!"

To her dismay, he tied her wrists to a post in the center of the village, ignoring her tirade of pleas. When he said no more, she strained her eyes to see Alex forty feet or so off as he came around, around turning the winch. When she looked back for Clancey, he was gone.

At that moment, in a terrible, grinding crash, the big vessel impaled herself on the reef. Everyone stopped to gaze seaward, and the wreckers' shrill cheers drowned Brett's cry. The line of lights on the great ship tilted, then turned askew, as she lurched, helpless, in the inky sea. Time blurred for Brett as she watched the cavorting inferno all around her. Flames leaped from beach fires and silhouetted darting figures waiting for their bounty to float in. The men at the winches forced Alex to turn harder as longboats and floating crates were hauled in from the deep and pounced on by wreckers on the sand. Cheer after cheer went up as women poled in booty and pried the wet casings away. Piles of goods grew upon the sand by the fires. The longboats themselves began to come back in, only to disgorge their loot and set right out again. Only then did Brett realize that no passengers or crew were being landed. And it was only then that she gave up all hope for her and Alex.

They were actually leaving the people on that vessel to sink with it! Of course, then the victims would take their tale of wreckers and plunder with them to their watery graves. But if Lucifer's band did that and cheered all the while, she and Alex were as good as dead! Soon enough one of those returning longboats would be Lucifer's. He would see her tied there like a sacrifice waiting for the brutal celebration he had promised her, while Alex was chained eternally to that wheel. Her stunned, tear-glazed face reflected all the churning horror she felt inside.

Finally, the voice she feared most pierced her ears. "Gold coins here! Spanish pieces of eight thick as bean soup!" Lucifer's voice bellowed through the din.

The cry went up and spread from the shore like wildfire. "Gold coins! Gold! Gold!"

The wreckers shouted and streamed toward the glittering display on the shore. Brett's legs shook, and she leaned against the pole. Now was her chance to shout her love to Alex at least. She turned to find him. He hadn't seen her. He stood looking shoreward, too, still chained to the winch the others had deserted. She gave a little involuntary scream as a knife flashed before her eyes. She gasped, turned. Clancey! Clancey cutting her free!

"I knew you weren't like them!" she told him through a sob as he separated her wrist ties.

"I had to wait for them to leave," he muttered. Fear on his face shone stark in reflected crimson light. "Devona and the baby are waiting at the horses. Help me get your husband then. No time to rid him of those chains!"

They tore to Alex's side and hacked away the single wooden catch holding his chains to the winch wheel. His eyes smiled into Brett's from an exhausted face caked with sweat and dirt. "I knew my Brett would find a way if I couldn't," he murmured.

"This is Clancey and he's going to help," was all she got out before she and the limping Clancey half dragged, half carried the heavy, shackled man away from the screaming, cavorting mass on the shore.

"Don't know how he'll ever ride," Clancey panted. "No time to get those chains off his ankles."

"I'll put him over my horse ahead of me on his stomach until we're out of here. We are taking all the horses so they can't follow?" she asked.

Clancey only nodded in amazement at the bold aplomb of this stunning, wild-haired woman who had been so limp with helpless tears a moment ago. And even thrown over Brett's horse on his belly, while his chains dragged barely off the ground, Alex actually dared to grin in pride at his wonderful woman—his wife.

The four horses with five souls fleeing Lucifer's kingdom plunged into the sable black of the humid Bermuda night.

Fifteen

The horses' flying hooves scattered sand. Soon the narrow cart-wide path turned to crushed coral that twisted white-faced in the moonlight ahead of them. But even in the depth of shadow, Clancey seemed to know the way. He rode first, holding the baby. Devona came next on a horse he led. She had obviously never ridden before, but she stuck on with determination, bending low to grip the animal's neck. Brett fought to sit upright with Alex's weight across her lap while she held the reins of the last horse. These animals were hardly fine-bred trotters, and their flanks soon became slick with sweat. After ten minutes of frenzied ride, Clancey slowed and held up a ghostly hand in the dark.

"Why haltest thou?" Devona cried. "Go on! He wilt catch us."

Clancey came back beside her wheezing horse. "There's nothing he can catch us on, Devona, 'less he gets in a boat tomorrow and goes round to St. George's. But I can hide us there. I vowed to protect you with my very life, you and Rebecca, too. Besides, we've got to knock those chains off Mr. Sanborn, and I'm not sure how."

"Any big rock," Alex grunted. "Soon. This horse is tiring already. Brett, let's switch to the other."

Devona fussed and jostled the baby in her arms at the delay while Clancey dismounted and helped Brett hoist Alex on the fresher horse. It gave Brett and Alex their first moment of conversation, and she told him in quick sentences of the price on his head, of their likenesses displayed in St. George's public places.

"Damn that greedy, vengeful bastard!" Alex clipped out. She didn't have to wonder whom he meant. "Let's go, Clancey, my friend," he said from his awkward position draped over the broad withers of the animal. "I've got all sorts of scores to settle." Brett hooked one hand to steady him at the waist of his breeches and they were off.

They rode on through a gloomy cedar forest whose thick growth formed an arched ceiling over their narrow lane. Then sand again, and the crash of distant breakers on the breeze. "A narrow inlet with a sandbar ahead," Clancey called back. "This time of tide, the horses won't go more than fetlock deep!"

The baby began to cry and Devona did, too. The sturdy horses sloshed through the rippling water and clambered up on dry land again. "Tucker Town's next," Clancey called back to them with a pat on Devona's shoulder. "I've thought of a place there we can stop to get the chains off."

They walked the horses through the little town, all of them glancing right and left into the shadows between white-washed, slate-roofed houses, as if Lucifer would leap out at them. Tucker Town, on the shore of broad Castle Harbor, consisted of small, one-and-a-half-story fishermen's houses, each with old whalebone jaws from the whaling heydays over the doorways.

"I have friends down here at Cedar Hill," Clancey called out just beyond the little settlement. At the end of a short lane, he dismounted to pound on a door. A light flared inside, "Clancey McFee here, Gerald, in need of your help!"

A bleary-eyed man opened the door and shone the lantern on them. "Folks rescued from the wreckers out on Devil's Isle," Clancey told him. "Just a bit of food, for the love of heaven, and something to knock off a man's chains, and we'll be on our way."

Brett helped Alex slide off. She saw a gray-haired woman

behind the man Gerald. "Sure they're not hot on your tail, boy?" Gerald asked.

Clancey shook his head. "No way they can find us till St. George's Town, I swear it."

Waiting in the dark, Alex lifted his chained arms over Brett's head to embrace her. Wearily, gladly, they leaned against each other, their lips meeting in a brief kiss. And then she helped him clank up the steps into the house.

In a half hour the men had Alex's wrist and ankle chains off, but they decided the manacles themselves would take too long, even though they would give him away later as some sort of escaped prisoner. They had to be in town by daybreak, Clancey kept saying over Devona's murmuring to the fussy baby.

"But I heard you say just four hours before," Brett put in. "And with the horses—"

Clancey shook his head across the table over the hasty repast of bread, cheese and bananas the old woman had laid out for them. "You see, Mrs. San—Brett, I mean," he said, aware anyone from St. George's might have heard that name now, "low tide's not good for the ferry and we have no choice but to take it onto St. George's island. We'll barely make dawn as is."

"And Lucifer shalt be waiting there to wreak vengeance on our heads!" Devona whispered, wide-eyed, as if to herself.

Brett's eyes met Alex's and held. For them the town meant more than the threat of Lucifer. British troops who had been in contact with Dalton Kelsey, a price on Alex's head. Could they even trust Clancey once he had Alex in town within reach of three hundred pounds' quick coin? He was going to have to give up all he'd worked for to flee with Devona; a sum of cash such as that might prove irresistible.

Despite the food, Brett was shaky with spent emotion and exhaustion. So much had happened today that it seemed ages since they'd left their little sleeping mats on Castaway. She leaned her head gratefully on Alex's shoulder when he put his metal-braceleted arm around her. Old Gerald had given him a worn fisherman's shirt, but the sleeves on it were hardly long enough to cover his wrist irons.

"You've been so wonderful," he whispered to her as Clancey and Devona spoke with their hosts. "He didn't really hurt you, did he, that bastard Lucifer?"

Her eyes filled with tired tears. "He tried. But Clancey came along and helped there, too."

Alex leaned across the table to grasp Clancey's shoulder. "You've saved our lives and my wife's honor today, Clancey. And I'm telling you and Devona right now, I'll do anything I can to return the favor. You're both welcome to come back with us to Baltimore. I can use a good, honest man who knows the import business."

"Even if he's been in tight with the wreckers?" Clancey asked as Devona smiled at last.

"He never wouldst have done Lucifer's bidding had his brother's life not been at stake," Devona spoke up. "Lucifer abducted his brother to force Clancey's help when they were new off the ship from Dublin. And when his brother died helping unload a sinking ship, Lucifer yet held Clancey captive by threatening to expose him."

"Rubbish, that would have been the pot calling the kettle black!" Brett exploded, and sat straight up in Alex's embrace.

"A strong lady, but she doesn't understand," their old host Gerald put in. He shook his head at Clancey. "Doesn't know the fear that band of men out there on no-man's-land can spread. No one crosses the Devil's Isle wreckers and lives to tell it."

Devona began to cry again and insisted they leave. Brett took a last look around the little limestone-and-cedar haven. But it was filled with wavering shadows and the raised stone hearth was cold and dark. Soon they were out into the black, blowing night on the road to St. George's again.

Clancey's private ferry did take them precious time, even though they didn't stop to wake his usual ferrymen. Alex and Clancey worked the oars, while Brett held all four horses and Devona nursed the baby again. Lilac dawn tinted the eastern sky by the time they pounded along toward the town again. Here, orange bougainvillea and fragrant frangipani edged many hedges and stone fences, and the hilly town of white, sun-struck buildings lay before them, offering both its shelter—and its danger.

"I shalt die before ever he takes me back!" Devona vowed again, and clutched her little leather bag to her, which she'd cradled all the way as if it were a second baby.

Brett assumed she'd had the foresight to put her jewel collection in there, but she hadn't asked.

"We're all in this together," Brett assured the frightened girl as they slowed their lathered horses to a walk. They dared not clatter by the slow-moving carts toting goods to morning markets up ahead. The less they did to call attention to themselves, the better. On the ferry they had laid plans to hide out in Clancey's warehouse until they could find an outward-bound vessel. It was illegal to be heading for America from British-held Bermuda, but Alex, if he could go unrecognized, might spot an American captain he trusted. Or the money Clancey had hidden at the warehouse might buy the truth of an unlawful destination from some blockade runner.

"I'm proud of you, Brett," Alex whispered again as they entered the town. But he looked worried. He kept his head uncharacteristically down, though his eyes darted here and there through his thick brows as he spoke. "I wouldn't wish for anyone else in the world beside me right now than the woman I love."

To stem the tears those words evoked and buck him up, she said only, "I should hope not. Simone would never consent to go about in tattered gowns the way I have these past few weeks, and that simpering snip Claudine Cantrell would insist on checking every move she made with her prune-faced mother."

Alex shouted a laugh that made both Clancey and Devona jump and look back. It was the last joy they were to have that day.

They funneled into town with the market crowd but noted a cluster of red-coated British soldiers up ahead on Water

Street, which Clancey had promised them that would take them straight to his brick warehouse on the docks. So they turned hastily left onto Duke of York Street, only to jog again up Queen Street when they saw more soldiers just ahead.

"Something's doing, that's sure," Clancey hissed. "We'd best not take the horses across the square. Get off, we'll leave them here. They're not the only things I'll be forfeiting to get us safely out of Bermuda!"

They left the horses in a narrow lane and followed Clancey through a graveyard thick with crooked, whitewashed stones. He opened the back door to the white limestone church and motioned them inside. Coolness wafted over them. "First time the likes of this good Cath'lic's been in St. Peter's Episcopal, but it leads straight to King's Square," he whispered.

Inside, it was silent and deserted. Brett wished they could stay forever. The walls held memorials to townspeople, just as the churches in England did. For the first time in months she thought she was homesick for London, then she realized she longed only for peace and sanctuary in the midst of all this danger. They hurried under the tall, three-tiered cedar pulpit by the cedar altar set strangely at the side of the pews. She and Alex held hands tightly. Would they ever make it back to Baltimore to be wed properly in an American church someday? she wondered. Would Alex ever want to—would he still want her once they were back in his own territory of anti-British Baltimore, where he at least was safe?

"If we get separated for any reason, my warehouse is the second to the east across the square, with 'Fitzmarlin and Clancey' on it bold as brass," Clancey told them. "There's bins of Lucifer's loot inside to hide behind. Let's go then."

The stark sunlight in the square shattered their eyes as they emerged from the cool depths of St. Peter's. They walked nonchalantly down a pyramid of gray stone steps and started across the bustling square. Alex kept his shirt-sleeved arm across his lower face as if wiping his nose. Near the cedar stocks and pillory, which stood empty now, they spotted the post with the drawings of them tacked to it among other decrees and notices. Brett's hair was pulled straight back and she had a prim, sour visage. Alex looked as vicious as a pirate.

It hit her then, even as they hurried by: that was just the way she would have drawn herself and Alex when they'd first met. But now, they had merged somehow on common ground. He had plumbed the depths of her smothered passions. And she had somewhat tamed the beast in him through learning to really see the kind, loving man beneath the pride and anger. It made her believe no one would ever recognize them from those pictures Dalton Kelsey had ordered drawn, and she walked with firmer steps as they hurried in the side door to the warehouse.

"My workers will be here at eight and I'm going to send them home by telling them today's shipment will be late," Clancey said as he hustled them into a far corner behind stacked crates. "As soon as we have the place to ourselves, one or the other of us will have to venture out on the docks to see about passage."

Time dragged by. They heard his workers arrive, then leave. Clancey and Alex finally cut Alex's manacles off his wrists and ankles. Clancey brought them water and two guns. Devona trembled, and the baby evidently sensed her terror and refused to be nursed or comforted. Brett took turns bouncing and walking the child back and forth, back and forth. Clancey went out on the docks, then returned with a broad smile on his freckled face.

"A blockade runner bound for Philadelphia, leaving in hours! The captain will give us passage for my contribution of cargo, as he's not full yet. For the love of heaven, I think it will be real proper if Lucifer's goods pay our passage out of here!" he said, gloating. "Best stay back here now and keep quiet. His men will arrive in a few minutes for the goods!"

They congratulated one another and celebrated with the hot cinnamon pastries he'd brought them. Nothing had ever tasted so sweet and wonderful to Brett. They were as good as home! Alex's mother and sister lived in Philadelphia. She would meet them before they headed back to Baltimore. Everyone but the fussy baby seemed to sense deliverance. The usually circumspect Clancey even kissed Devona soundly on her pale cheek before he went to greet the workmen who would load the goods on the American ship. But, hidden back behind the bales and boxes of goods, the little celebration came to a screeching halt when they heard the next words.

"You Clancey McFee?"

"I am, lieutenant," Clancey replied shakily, yelling the man's title much too loudly.

"Word is a chestnut-haired woman was seen entering here hours ago. Said to resemble the British woman whose likeness is posted in the square. Of course, you can't trust rumor, but best we have a look."

Brett's heart fell. She seized Alex's wrist in a crushing grip; a frown petrified his face. "I—for the love of heaven, I don't know—who you mean," Clancey stuttered. "I've been away, gone away for a day or so, you see."

"Orders from high up in the fleet. Shoot the man she's with, but fetch the woman back. Seems she's real important to someone and worth a good promotion if we find her. Unfortunately the old drunk who spotted her didn't think to mention it until now. Search the premises, men."

"Really, there's no one here—" Clancey shouted. "You see, we're not working today." Alex's and Brett's eyes locked as the baby began to fuss. Desperately Devona thrust her nipple at the child.

"How many men?" Brett mouthed to Alex, who peeked around the stack of cases with a pistol in each hand.

"Four, I think. Five total," Alex whispered. "Too many to handle the way they're spread out."

The baby wailed and Devona stuck her finger in its mouth. "We'll all get caught this way, Alex," Brett whispered. "But if I step out there so they can see me, you could get them all together while I distract them."

"No. You've done enough. I'll get them one at a time," he ordered, and pushed her back.

But it was the only way she could see. She was not going

back to Dalton Kelsey while these Brits shot Alex! And there was Devona, desperate, and this fussing baby who would soon announce their presence to the entire waterfront! So Brett just walked away from Alex and out the other side of the narrow, piled aisle.

When the first soldier saw her, her heart pounded so hard she thought drums heralded her approach. "Lieutenant! Down here!" the man shouted. "A chestnut-haired woman!"

She strolled quickly out into a wider area to draw them away from Alex and Devona. "Oh, British soldiers!" she gushed, and clapped her hands in apparent relief. "I'm so glad you've found me. I've been abducted from my fiancé, Commander Dalton Kelsey, and then shipwrecked. I walked into town and hid in this man's warehouse, but I don't want to get him in trouble! I assure you, Commander Kelsey will be so happy to have me safely returned!"

All five soldiers surrounded her now. She was so nervous she actually counted them twice as if she were an idiot. What was taking Alex so long? Surely he must have understood what she was doing and would follow up with her plan. If these men escorted her out into the square, they were doomed!

Even as Alex stepped up behind the men and handed Clancey one of the guns, her clever, deceitful words riled him. Would he never be rid of that bastard Kelsey? She sounded so damned convincing. Damn, he had no doubt Kelsey would love to have her back! Despite all they'd shared, he was still madly jealous. What if Brett found Kelsey attractive? She had allowed the bastard to court her, after all. Here was her chance to return to him. He knew better, of course, as she rattled on at the jubilant soldiers while he and Clancey approached from behind. But the jealousy ate at his insides over this.

"Hold it right there, officers," his voice rang out clearly. "The first one to go for a weapon's a dead man."

The lieutenant sputtered with shamefaced rage and the others merely looked dogged. Brett lifted the men's weapons and tied them foot and wrist while Clancey and Alex held the guns, and Alex silently scolded himself for doubting her one moment. They gagged the men with their own sashes, then dragged them back behind various stacks of goods.

Within the hour, sailors arrived to cart off goods for the American vessel, which, right now, Clancey said, was flying a neutral Spanish flag. From boxes of goods belonging to shipwrecked souls, they all selected clothes and personal items for the voyage. Brett noted that Devona was right at home pawing through the booty, but it all made her own skin crawl. They disguised themselves as best they could and headed out just before four in the afternoon, which was the time set for the vessel to sail if she was to clear the harbor by nightfall. So far, no one had evidently noticed the disappearance of the little cadre of soldiers.

Dressed like British sailors, Clancey and Alex led the way, jostling each other with canvas bags over each shoulder as if they were in their cups. Devona and Brett came just behind. In the folds of her gray cloak, Brett held little Rebecca, who had gone to sleep in her arms at last. Devona cradled her precious leather bag. The women walked close to the brick warehouses, shoulder to shoulder, along the dock. How good and solid the ships looked to Brett, but she mourned the abducted *Free Spirit* all over again.

Alex and Clancey turned unsteadily up the gangplank. The three-masted vessel, called the *Golden Eagle* bustled with activity to cast off. Men were aloft in the yards and riggings. Brett savored anew the pungent aroma of pitch and fresh paint. She lifted her eyes to the very top of the mainmast to watch a sailor dangle there.

And then Devona screamed.

Lucifer Flyte and two other men blocked the women's entry to the gangplank. Two more emerged from the dockside crowd as Alex and Clancey ditched their gear and thundered back down the plank.

Chaos erupted. Alex and Clancey took on the men closest to Brett and Devona. Lucifer leaped at Devona. Like a wild woman, she bit and clawed at him, while Brett stood helplessly with the baby. The other man tried to yank the child from her, but she kicked at him, then turned away to thrust the child into an old man's arms, just before her attacker came at her again.

She ducked to elude his grasp, and at that moment Alex exploded at him to rain fists into his jaw and belly. He doubled over; Alex shoved him off the dock with a splash and turned to help Clancey, whose bad leg hindered him. His man had him down now. Brett watched in horror as the scene jumped and blurred before her eyes. Lucifer, holding the writhing Devona by one arm, pointed a gun toward the prostrate Clancey, holding it out stiff armed. Alex lunged toward him, but Brett knew he would be too late. She screamed, too, as she waited for the blast of the gun point-blank at Clancey's chest. Behind him, one of Lucifer's men aimed at Alex's vaulting body.

But when the crack of gun came, it was Lucifer who slumped in midair. He hit the dock like a toppled tree. Devona stood with the gun she'd drawn from her little leather bag. Lucifer lay very still as a shiny crimson stain spread from under him on the dock. His three men stood frozen a moment, staring like everyone else. Then they ran. Brett took the baby back from the old man. She hurried over to the frozen Devona, who still gaped, fish mouthed, at Lucifer.

"Those men escaping and this one lying here!" Alex's voice rang out to the crowd. "They're wreckers from Devil's Isle, and they've got a huge cache of gold coins out there that they just took off a Spanish vessel they wrecked on the reef."

Several people in the crowd pounded off after the fleeing men. Some pounced on Lucifer's corpse to check for gold. Alex hustled Clancey, the stunned Devona and Brett with little Rebecca up the gangplank as the crowd pulled Lucifer's boots off.

"Justice is mine, saith the Lord," the glassy-eyed Devona kept repeating. "But I had to save Rebecca. It was my duty to kill him or myself."

"You saved Clancey's life. We all understand. No one blames you. We have to go now, Devona," Brett told her, and helped her up on the deck while Alex pried the gun from her clawlike grasp.

When Alex found he knew the captain, they were literally welcomed with open arms. The sailors in the rigging had had their entertainment for the day and cheered wildly as the ship cast off, leaving the picked-over, bloody corpse of Lucifer Flyte lying on the dock until someone rolled it off into the waves. Clancey carried the raving Devona down below, then came up to fetch Rebecca. Brett and Alex stood together as the ship came about. They only moved back from the rail when they saw the dockside flood with miniature crimson British uniforms raising tiny fists toward the departing ship. But by then the canvas of the *Eagle* had bellied out with sea wind away from St. George's Town.

Brett, Alex and Clancey sat at the table in the captain's cabin after supper that night. Brett cuddled the baby as Devona lay, wide-eyed as if in a stupor, in the bunk, staring at the ceiling. Her passionate tirade about killing Lucifer, the father of her child, had stilled at last, but she looked at no one and would not eat or speak. Clancey, slumped over his elbows, looked stunned, too.

"The cronies Lucifer brought to catch us will hurry back to Devil's Isle and fight to take his place," Clancey muttered. "Vultures picking over the dead they themselves kill, that's all they are. No matter how Devona is right now, I'm glad we got her and the child away."

"You did the right thing for them and yourself, Clancey," Alex assured him. "And I wouldn't be surprised if the lure of gold doesn't turn that waterfront crowd into a bunch of avenging angels against those wreckers as a sense of justice never has."

Clancey nodded. "The lure of gold," he repeated. "Despite what I managed to bring with me, I'll have to find a job in America to support us—especially if Devona gets better and will wed me."

"I meant it about a position for you at Sanborn's," Alex told him. "We owe you a great deal. Truth is, we need a bookkeeper we can trust right away."

Clancey's dour face lit. "I kept all my own books. Though,

for the love of heaven," he admitted sheepishly, "I'd never have shown them to anyone since it was all illegal contraband. Lucifer would have slit my throat if I'd crossed him."

"I promise you, Brett and I won't be quite that severe," Alex said, but his smile was for Brett, at his side.

"You two as equal partners," Clancey murmured, his voice awed. "It's hard to believe at first—until I got to know Mrs. Sanborn."

"It was hard for me to believe at first," Alex said with a squeeze of Brett's shoulders.

"But with war fever so high there," Clancey went on, "and the threat of Baltimore actually being captured by this Commander Kelsey you told me about—it must be very hard for the townsfolk to accept her there. Her being British, and all," he finished lamely.

Brett's and Alex's gazes collided. So simply had Clancey laid bare the heart of their fear for the future. They passed over it to keep Clancey's—and their own—spirits up. But later that night, after they'd made hot love in their wide canvas hammock in a cubbyhole of a stateroom, Clancey's observation echoed back to haunt Brett.

She lay awake, her cheek on Alex's naked chest, listening to his steady heartbeat. The ship's captain had told them Napoléon had been sent into exile to some barren island called Elba. Now that the war in Europe was over, all Wellington's British "invincible" troops had been sent to the blockade fleet to win the American war once and for all. An attack on British-hating Baltimore might threaten the Sanborn partnership she'd worked so hard for, as well as the partnership of their tenuous marriage. Whenever anyone so much as mentioned Dalton Kelsey, smoke flared from Alex's nostrils. She had to find a way to earn Baltimore's trust and respect and prove herself to Alex once and for all! Now that she had so much, there was much to lose. Suddenly panicked, she cuddled closer to Alex in the slightly swaying hammock, reassured by the warmth and strength she felt from him.

"Don't fret about Devona." His voice came quiet, but she

still jumped. "She's fragile compared to you, but she'll make it."

"I thought you were asleep. I was just thinking over all that's happened."

"Mmm. You seem to have a real penchant for leaving bound, gagged, furious British soldiers in your wake. I hope you'll keep that up if your countrymen come calling on Baltimore."

She lifted on one elbow. "Alex, I want to be at your side, whatever happens. Promise me!"

He pulled her slightly up along his body so that their faces almost touched. In the wan wash of starlight through the single porthole, they stared eye to luminous eye. Ever so gently, he kissed the tip of her nose. "If they actually attack, we'll have to see how things go, sweetheart. But right now, all of me's aching to touch all of you all over again."

Swept away by his passion and her love, she let him escape that promise for now. But as she clung to his swaying body on the rocking ship in this unsteady world, she vowed to hold to her tremulous dream for their future just as hard.

Sixteen

~~~oⒼⒼo~~~

Baltimore braced for battle with the British. Everywhere around Brett on Hampstead Hill above the town and harbor, citizens worked feverishly on makeshift defenses. Three weeks ago, the English army of "invincibles" that had defeated Napoléon, had burned Washington, the capital itself. Even now, rumors said, President Madison and his wife, Dolly, were hunted refugees on the back roads of the nation, while British troops rampaged at will along the Potomac. Alexandria's warehouses had been thoroughly looted. The fleet loaded with troops had been sighted passing Annapolis. Everyone knew that Baltimore, "that nest of pirates" the British hated the most of all, would be next.

In the six weeks that Brett had lived in Baltimore as Mrs. Alexander Sanborn, she had come to love the city with a new and special feeling. Their ship had returned easily from Bermuda to Philadelphia. The British fleet and army were massing to take key coastal cities, so the northern blockade had loosened. They had spent just one night with Alex's mother, and briefly met his sister's family. Brett was not certain which had shocked them more, his British wife or his obsession with personally settling the score with one of the British commanders.

They had been remarried in a small, private ceremony at Zion Lutheran. But lately, as the British wreaked their havoc

on America, things seemed to have gone tense and sour between them. Brett had barely seen Alex except when he tumbled exhausted into bed. She kept busy, too. She oversaw the
packing of warehouse goods to withstand attack. She made
certain Sanborn's dependent families, like the Mileses and
now the heavily pregnant Sally Windsor and her children,
were cared for. With old Molly's help, she ran Sanborn
House. She tried to coax Devona from her continued despon-
dency while Clancey helped Alex all he could. And now she
was determined to help in the drive to make Baltimore de-
fensible.

"The coffee smells wonderful, Molly," she told the old
housekeeper. Brett handed the excited servant boy, Clemmie,
the first cup to try from the huge copper kettle simmering
over the fire. "I just hope these Baltimore patriots think so,
too, considering who's going to help serve it to them."

"I told you now, this sure 'nough a fool idea after what
that rabble done to you in the market. These folks wilder than
wild to fight the British lately," Molly muttered with a roll
of dark eyes. "An' I mean *any* British, that sure!"

Brett was determined not to dwell on her assault by the so-
called brave Baltimoreans while even women stood by to
watch. She was Mrs. Alexander Sanborn now, she assured
herself. She longed to—she had to—be one of them to show
Alex she was completely on America's side. The Committee
of Vigilance and Safety had issued pleas for shovels, picks,
wheelbarrows, wagons and horses to help build these makeshift earthworks and gun batteries. Brett had been certain Sanborn's contributed to that. But when the committee let it be
known that food and drink were desperately needed for the
workers, Brett had taken two huge sacks of the best coffee
beans from the warehouse and had them ground. With Molly
and young Clemmie, who had moped about since Simone had
left, she had come up here to serve the Baltimoreans herself.

Shaking her turbaned head, Molly loaded her tray with the
full, steaming china cups and carted them off. Clemmie and
Brett took other trays in different directions. Brett walked
along the brow of the sickle-shaped hilltop that overlooked

the inner harbor. Everyone knew that if the British landing forces could take this key site or if the fleet could get close enough in to blast Fort McHenry into submission, the city would be burned like Washington and raped like Alexandria.

Alex and Clancey had spent yesterday here before General Armistead requested their help at Fort McHenry. Around Brett, activity still bustled everywhere. Under a threatening gray sky, men had rifle pits dug waist deep. Shop owners and lawyers bent their silk-shirted backs next to rowdy roustabouts and burly blacksmiths. Freed Negroes in bandanas dug next to bankers still in top hats. Ahead of her, teams of requisitioned carriage horses hauled cannon up the hill. Carpenters and shipwrights manhandled heavy timbers meant for masts to roll the big guns into position. The air was alive with the whack of hammers. A muted fife-and-drum rendition of "Yankee Doodle" floated up the hill from draft militia learning to shoot volleys below. She passed women from all positions in life, some with children, handing out rolls, apples, or other food.

Her tray was heavy and her arms shook by the time she faced the first group of dirty men unloading cannon balls from a vegetable cart. "Good hot coffee to perk you up!" she told them with a hopeful smile as she extended the tray.

Only one young boy reached for a cup right away. The other sweating, burly workers just frowned and glared. She recognized one of the men who had blocked her from her carriage that day in the marketplace while the others attacked her. Her arms shook even more, and not from the weight of the tray.

"Watch that brew, boys," one grunted. "Might be Brit witch poison."

"Heard Sanborn was fool enough to marry you," a man muttered, while another actually dared to knock the cup out of the boy's hands, splattering him with hot coffee. The man's eyes went accusingly over her as if attempting an explanation of why a fine Baltimorean would wed a low Brit. Perhaps to see her swelled with child, Brett thought, and colored. Alex *had* been forced to marry her, after all. And she had indeed missed her monthly flow, but had told no one her suspicions that she might be pregnant yet. One way or the other, these people would believe the worst of her. Sharp resentment sliced through her. These Baltimore brutes never gave her a chance!

In answer to their rude perusals and mutterings, she stared down the man who'd knocked the cup from the boy and lifted her tray toward him. "Baltimore coffee from someone who has known Britain, but is now on Baltimore's side, however unfairly her individual citizens act. Really knowing the enemy and then *choosing* the American's side—that's more than I can say for most of you," she challenged.

Suddenly she feared they would tip the tray back at her or smack her with clods of that red soil. The memory of her degradation in the marketplace shook her resolve again. But she stood her ground, looking from one to the other, while her arms shook so hard the coffee swayed and sloshed.

Then another woman's voice cut in. "This here's a real good lady! Better'n the likes of you bullies by far! I'm real proud to know her, but maybe you all don't deserve to!"

Brett's glance darted sideways. It was Lissa Miles, blue eyes flashing, hands on slender hips. What a transformation from the pale, sad wretch she'd first met!

"Me and my children been saved by what she done for us when we dint do a thing to deserve it," Lissa plunged on. "You louts aren't fit to clean her shoes! She cares for people whether they're down and out, like I was, or not. I'll just fetch a bunch of women and children over here to help her if the likes of you be wanting another fight with the weaker sex of Baltimore, or Britain, too!"

Lissa and Brett exchanged taut, nervous glances as Lissa reached over to hand around coffee cups. One man stepped forward to take the tray. "Thank you," Brett told him with a smile, though she blinked back tears. "You're all doing a wonderful job out here under trying circumstances." Slowly she wiped her sweaty palms on the big apron she'd borrowed from Molly.

"Thanks to you, too, Mrs. Sanborn."

"Real good coffee, ma'am."

"The best—Mrs. Sanborn's Baltimore imported," a gruff voice added.

On Brett's many trips with the coffee tray that day, other women came up to help her. And the roustabouts and shippers of Baltimore alike took cups of coffee from Brett Benton Sanborn's own hands, in gestures of acceptance that brought tears of joy to her eyes. Now—finally—she felt as if her new home had taken her in.

Church services on Sunday, September 11, 1814, were interrupted by the boom of three warning cannon shots from the town green. Congregations emptied the churches to hear the news that the British fleet had crept clear up the Patapsco River. And they already knew that the remnants of the American fleet were bottled up or at the bottom of the Atlantic. The few sleek, lightly armed privateering vessels that remained were no match for heavy bomb and rocket ships. The fledgling War Department in Washington lay in ashes. Baltimore was on its own.

By noon, Charles Street in front of Sanborn House was a river of refugees surging northward. Carts, wagons, carriages, horses, their own feet—those who did not volunteer to fight were running.

"Cowards!" Brett cursed as from Devona's front bedroom window she watched the frenzied exodus. Devona sat in a rocking chair near the low-burning hearth, holding little Rebecca but not moving otherwise. But at Brett's verbal explosion, the red-haired woman's pale green eyes lifted. The past few days she responded if spoken to directly, but still had not offered a thing on her own.

"Sometimes it taketh more courage to flee than stay," Devona whispered.

Brett spun to face her, thrilled she'd said anything. "Of course, but not to desert Baltimore. It was different for you, Devona. Won't you come downstairs with me for supper now? The men will be back soon. It would do wonders for

Clancey if you were out of this room—to hear you talking again.''

But Devona just shook her head once more as her face shifted back to that distant look that even Clancey's dedication and the baby's charming antics could not penetrate. Brett had almost decided to insist Devona accompany her, when she heard a voice amid the hubbub outside that shocked her. Old Henny? She squinted out the window again. Henny Featherstone hadn't been out of her home next door for decades!

Brett tore downstairs and out onto the lawn. Carting her husband's old musket and waving a banner embroidered Not Self, but Country! Henny stood in the middle of the street, trying to halt the onslaught. Brett ran out, ducked around snorting horses and darted ahead of a large, lumbering wagon loaded with youngsters.

''Henny! Get off the street. You'll be hurt in this crush!''

''Turning tail to run, all of them! The British are coming! Now's the time to fight! Even you're staying, Brett. You tell them!''

''Not here, Henny!'' Brett grabbed the old woman's arm and took the heavy, long-muzzled musket she'd been waving with the flag. ''Come on! You can tell them from the lawn!''

''Not one of them worthy of the men who died to make them free from the British! Not one with backbone to put country before self!'' Henny raved as Brett hauled her haphazardly out of the rolling flow of people. A fine barouche with two prancing bays almost knocked them down. A whip flicked close to Brett's face as it glanced off the lathered flank of the animal nearest her. Brett yanked Henny back from the crunching wheels just in time and, startled, glared up at the pompous Claudine Cantrell and her wrinkled mother.

''Out of our way, traitoress!'' Claudine cried, and pointed the riding whip at Brett. ''Staying to help your British friends when they burn this city?'' she goaded.

''Staying to fight them!'' Brett yelled up at her, tempted to actually fire the old musket at the witch and her fist-shaking mother. ''It's the traitors who are leaving, so good riddance!''

Claudine flicked her whip out again. Brett lifted the musket to block the lash. It coiled itself around the barrel. She yanked, and Claudine spilled half out of the carriage before her screeching mother hauled her back in by her skirts. A big wagon behind them cracked the back of their carriage to jolt them both, while the driver behind cursed and screamed.

The whip still clinging to the musket, Brett turned her back and hustled Henny across their lawns. "George Washington is spinning in his grave at this display of cowardice! Spinning!" the old woman declared. "Our second War for Independence against the redcoats and they're running like rats. I even saw that bastard Quinby Marsh and his sour wife in that shameful retreat!"

Surprised, Brett spun to face Henny. "But he's got ships and warehouses just like Sanborn's. And he's running?" Raw fear slammed into her stomach like a fist. She didn't care that the bully Marsh and his wife, who had egged on her assault at the marketplace were fleeing; but that someone who had a lifetime's fortune to lose believed Baltimore was doomed devastated her. Brett fought down her fear. She had many things to do. Alex was due home, and he'd not see her waver!

"Henny, since you're out of your house, I'll send over for Glenda and you'll stay with us. Now don't argue. With the men away all the time, I'll need someone good with guns in case the enemy comes calling."

That seemed to pacify the old woman and she nodded proudly. "Just like the old days! I owe those redcoat devils for many a good American life," she assured Brett, and went in at a sprightly clip at her side.

It was nearly an hour later when the men came in, exhausted and dirty, to report on progress of preparing Fort McHenry. They gobbled food and Clancey went up to see Devona before they started back. Alex tugged Brett into the library for a private moment. He leaned back to close the door behind them. "Brett, it's going to be a long siege out there when they try to take the fort. We've done all we can. I'm trusting you to oversee things here and at the warehouse, but

if the bastards use those long-range bombs and rockets, you're
to stay off the waterfront, out of their way."

He looked harder, thinner and frazzled to her, almost as he
had during their siege against other great odds, adrift at sea.
She felt instantly tender toward him despite his brusqueness
of late. She knew he faced the loss of everything he held
dear; she only hoped he feared losing her half that much. And
if the British ever captured him, he was as good as dead.
Since Dalton Kelsey had sent word to distant Bermuda, he
would surely find and hang him here.

"If worse should come to worse, Brett," Alex was saying,
his voice stern, "I want you to head north to my mother in
Philadelphia. I won't have you ever falling into that son of a
bitch's hands again!"

"I'm not running like those cowards out there! There's so
much to do here!"

He seized her shoulders and shook her hard. "Blue blazes,
you'll do as I say for once! You'll listen to me for the first
time since I've known you!"

"Rubbish, Alex Sanborn, and you know it!" she shot back.

In response, he kissed her so hard her neck snapped back.
He laced one big hand in her thick chestnut hair to hold her
lips to his, and she matched his searing kiss and hard caress.
Their lips parted, tongues darted and plunged. She pressed
her full breasts to his hard chest. He clamped her hips and
thighs to his in his desperation. These past few days that he
had worked and slept at Fort McHenry he'd missed her terribly, though it galled him. Now that he was back in Baltimore, he couldn't escape the fact that the man he still thought
of as her fiancé was to blame for the rape of his precious *Free
Spirit* and the looming destruction of his entire life! Damn,
there was no time to think of this now. He could heard Clancey's voice raised in the hall just outside. They had to go
back to wait, to fight, maybe to die. Still, he longed to push
her down on the thick carpet and hike up her skirts to take
his leave of her by demonstrating how completely she was
his!

She knew she clung desperately. She couldn't bear to let

him go. She should be with him, helping him, even at Fort McHenry. There were a few women out there, he'd admitted, officers' wives. She and Alex were partners in business and marriage—shouldn't they be partners facing this ultimate danger, too? And how she wanted to tell him that she thought she was with child, that there was another reason to preserve Sanborn and Son now. But he was leaving. She had no intention of sharing such news when he was on his way out the door without her again. It was an occasion that should be celebrated together.

Clancey's voice. Clancey banging on the door. They stood shakily apart, breathing hard. Their eyes devoured each other as if to memorize each inch of flesh. Then, with a low curse, Alex spun away and opened the door.

"Alex! Brett!" Clancey gasped out. "Kit O'Malley's brought Sally Windsor here, and she's—for the love of heaven, she's going to have that baby real soon!"

They dashed out to where old Molly was directing the warehouse foreman, Kit O'Malley, and another man to assist the groaning woman upstairs. Alex helped, while Brett darted up just behind. As they laid her in the room directly across from Devona's, Brett shouted over the banister to Henny and Molly, "Go boil water or something! I'm relying on you two to help. I've never birthed a baby, never even seen it."

"I have," the quiet voice came from just behind her.

Brett wheeled to see Devona watching from the door of her room.

"It was the most blessed experience of my life, even though Rebecca's father stayed away and cursed me all the while."

Brett trembled with joy and excitement. It was the first time since Devona had shot Lucifer on the St. George's Town dock that she'd walked anywhere of her own accord. "Sally's without the baby's father right now, too," Brett said. "I know she'd appreciate your help, and I will, also."

Devona nodded and moved closer to put her arms around Brett's shoulders. "Justice hath been done in my life, and I accept that," the girl said quietly. "Now I pray it shall be done in yours."

But Sally's labor and Devona's change of heart were not the only shocks that day. After assuring Sally that Devona would help, Brett hurried downstairs to oversee preparations. It was then that she heard Kit O'Malley tell Alex, "'Fraid y'all donating those two brigs to sink for the harbor blockade's not the only sacrifice y'all be making in ships, boss. Word is, out on Sparrows Point lookouts spotted a frigate flying Commander Kelsey's ensign and the vessel was towing the *Free Spirit*. And her decks are widened to take more guns, boss."

Brett gasped. Alex turned to see her. Their eyes locked. "Then one way or the other, I've no choice but to destroy her, too," he said. "Kelsey's not going to use *my* ship to fire on *my* city no matter what I have to do!" He started at a good clip for the back door, with the limping Clancey in his wake.

"Alex!" Brett cried. "Alex, wait!"

Clancey went on ahead to get their horses, while Alex halted at the back door. He did not turn to face her. "Blue blazes, I thought he told you he wouldn't convert the *Spirit* to take their big cannon," he spit back over his shoulder.

"Can I help it if he's changed his mind? And you can't destroy her, Alex. Sinking the other ships at the harbor's mouth to keep the fleet out, that's one thing, but not the *Spirit*. She's special. She's our future. We'll save her, get her back."

He turned at last. His angry face looked carved from granite. "Will *we*?" he challenged, his voice brutally cold. "Maybe our *we* has been doomed from the start! Take care of Sally. I just hope your past 'intimate associate,' Commander Kelsey, hasn't murdered her new baby's father, along with everything else he's destroyed!"

"Alex—" she called, but he strode to his horse and mounted without another look back. Her eyes filled with helpless tears as she watched him clatter off for Fort McHenry.

Three days later Alex and Clancey stood in the southeast bastion of Fort McHenry. Alex squinted through his spyglass at his clipper ship, still tethered to the larger thirty-gun frigate, *Raven's Wing*. Even through the roiling smoke of battle, he could pick out the *Spirit*'s rakish slant of masts and her sleek decks, which had indeed been widened to take more guns than the six she'd had originally. And, of course, there was the bold figurehead painted to look like Brett. You might know that bastard Kelsey had kept that. So far the *Spirit* hadn't fired a shot; Alex couldn't even tell if the vessel was well manned. But the fact that the British had possession of his beloved ship ate at his insides like acid, and he thought again of his plan to destroy that which he loved.

"Damn them, Clancey!" he spit out. "Damn them all to hell!"

For more than twenty-four hours, the red brick and green sod, pentagonal-shaped fort had shuddered under the heavy assault of British bombs, mortars and rockets. From the entire fleet of fifty vessels, sixteen of the lighter draft ships had sailed close enough through the Patapsco shoals to assault the fort. If Fort McHenry fell, the city she protected was next. And the old American guns didn't have the range to hit the ships that blasted the fort like a big, sitting duck.

Around Alex and Clancey, the fort's defenders huddled under the double onslaught of bombardment and weather. Torrents flooded the ditches; men stood ankle deep in mud. Gun platforms were awash like decks of ships. The gunners spread their jackets over boxes of flannel cartridges to protect them while they waited for the fleet to edge forward within their range. Pickets hunched their shoulders in the deluge, and, like the fort and helpless city, endured.

Below them the fleet had all sail stowed and looked like a dense forest of tree trunks mouthing smoke and fire from their roots. Destruction rained from the skies. Alex and Clancey ducked instinctively as yet one more mortar shell screamed to splinters in the parade ground within the walls, then rent itself to death in a cluster of crashes. Another gout of smoke erupted from one of the five snout-nosed bomb vessels. Four to five bombs were always aloft at one time; this hit shook the earth to leave thick clouds above craters, reddish, foul-smelling hot gasses and a path of whirling iron fragments. The next one went slightly long, and on its way down just missed the huge American flag hanging defiantly over the fort.

"Twenty yards north and they'll get the powder magazine," Alex muttered. "It's not bomb proof, even with those ten-feet-thick walls. We'll have to stay to help move all the powder.

Chilled and damp, Clancey gripped his elbows with his hands and stamped his feet in a puddle. "If General Armistead doesn't need us after that, you're going then?"

Alex shook his head, and water flew off his chin despite his hat. "Not until it gets dark. But I will burn her, if I can get aboard and start a fire in this rain." He thought suddenly of the traitor Giles Cutler and his sickness with fire. Blue blazes, he could actually use the bastard now.

He squinted toward the harbor again. Kelsey was evidently saving the *Spirit* with the lighter vessels so that they could move in like vultures for the final kill. Already, Kelsey's *Raven's Wing* and the frigate flying Admiral Cochran's flag had sent shots into the nearest targets.

He burned for revenge against Dalton Kelsey for so many things, he admitted to himself as he and Clancey walked the outer walls. The Lord's justice, Devona would call it. But he was also bombarded by feelings for Brett in the midst of real bombs all around. He had been cruel to ride off from her without another backward glance—without what might be a final kiss. He had hurt Brett when he loved her, and he felt a pain for it as intense as of the one he felt when he contemplated destroying his beloved clipper ship.

He stepped inside the next roofed watchtower and fumbled in his breast-coat pocket for the note he'd written hurriedly in General Armistead's quarters earlier. He read it again, oblivious to the next barrage of bombs, which made Clancey jump and duck:

My beloved wife, Brett,
I cannot help what I must do about the *Spirit*. Great risk,

I know, but as necessary to me as being an American—
and as necessary as loving you. I just wanted to take this
last chance to tell you how much I have admired you—
and for some of the things I've fought hardest against.
Your courage, goodness, honesty, your fierce loyalties—
I could not have loved you so completely any other way.
Whatever happens now, I trust that you will go on as
before with Sanborn and Son. At first I wanted you to
have none of what I loved—now I trust you with it all.
You've won many friends, including the hearts of the
stubborn Baltimoreans. Nothing can stop my beautiful
Brett over the years.

> Love forever to my bold sweetheart,
> Alex.

He refolded the note and wrapped it in the bit of waterproof
lining he'd cut from his cartridge pouch. With Clancey right
behind him, he ran down the slick stone steps. The two of
them darted across the parade ground, peering skyward for
the next swooping arc of shrieking black doom. Men in a mix
of tattered uniforms or in motley, mud-speckled civilian dress
hunkered down here and there in trenches and bunkers.

"I'm going to give this note to a friend on the southwest
bastion," he shouted to Clancey over the din. "Daniel Dills,
another shipper. He goes back and forth into the city with
communications and can get this to Brett. Then I'm going to
see the general again about letting me take a few men after
dark to fire the *Spirit* and somehow sail her into Kelsey's
ship."

"I'm with you," Clancey told him, though he could barely
keep up in the mud with his bad leg.

Alex's hand grasped the man's shoulder. "No, Clancey.
Brett would need you at Sanborn's if something happened to
me. And then there's Devona. Now that she's better, she'll
marry you."

"For the love of heaven, Alex, you above all people know

a man's got to do what he's got to do! And Devona would never marry me if I came back without you, anyway!''

Alex smiled grimly and nodded. "Then it's you, Mason Finch and me. But first let's see Daniel about this note to Brett.''

Commander Dalton Kelsey snorted a pinch of tobacco from his gilded, enameled snuffbox, then sneezed in unison with the latest bomb launch from the *Volcano*, which lay just off his flagship's port bow. By damn, but he hoped that bomb found a few more Yank dogs to fry! Still, he had no choice but to take the risk he'd summoned his men to hear orders on. He wanted Alex Sanborn dead, and he had to get his hands on Brett before anyone else high-ranking could protect her when they took this town.

The three-week-old *Baltimore Patriot* rag sheet of a newspaper he'd come by during the sack of Annapolis had bragged about how privateering patriot Alexander Sanborn and his British bride had returned triumphant from the jaws of the blockade. So they were both here! Since the bait of their sleek little clipper hadn't lured them out, he had no choice but to recall the guards off it and go in after them himself.

Of course, he'd convinced Admiral Cochran his motives were much more military than that. Besides, he'd told Cochran, with the maps that turncoat Giles Cutler had sent him months ago, he could easily locate the string of major warehouses ashore and set them on fire, thereby planting fear in the hearts of Baltimore's defenders. A careful, wary landing party of eight trained Royal Marines, led by Commander Kelsey himself, should have no trouble getting there and back, with or without two captives.

"Men," he addressed his hand-picked Royal Marines when they were all assembled, at attention as he always required, "a change of duty is in order." Several of them had smudges on the white belts or yellow facings of their scarlet jackets, so he glowered pointedly their way. No good to let demands slide even in battle, but he chose, this once, to go on without either reprimand or chastisement.

"You may now consider yourselves an elite, covert landing party. I intend to explode a few select warehouses in the inner harbor, thereby creating the diversion of havoc and panic ashore. At nine this evening, we will be covered by a cessation of fire to make the Yanks relax their vigilance. Later there will be a ten-minute burst of fire to draw possible attention from our landing, followed by quiet. They'll believe we have stopped for the night, when we're only beginning ashore."

He rocked proudly back on his heels at his recitation of this perfect plan. "And then at precisely one o'clock after midnight, or at my signal before, our ships will open up with everything they have. By damn, along with our diversion, no doubt that will do the craven Yank dogs in! There will be no mercy extended, as there was in Annapolis or even that sordid little excuse for a capital we torched a few weeks ago. When we take Baltimore, Merry-land," he joked snidely, but plunged on when no one laughed, "every house, every picket fence will be burned to the ground to teach this rebel nation a lesson once and for all!"

He paused again to encourage the few cheers, which then crescendoed. He nodded, and they ceased as if on cue. "Lieutenant Gage will issue captured Yank civilian garb to wear in case we're spotted. Best to check it for fleas and lice, eh? Each man will carry extra shot and powder, and some will tote other gear. You will row me in a gig through that primitive blockade of sunken ships they've attempted out there that keeps us from sailing right in." He cleared his throat. "Assemble at dusk, and by dawn's early light, I promise you, men, we'll have what we deserve! I swear to you I'll eat breakfast at the best house on Charles Street before we loot it and burn it—or I'll eat breakfast in hell!"

They roared rather too heartily at that as they filed out. It made his heart swell, too, but not with patriotism or pride. No, by damn, his heart swelled with raw hatred—and with the need to get Brett in his hands. And Brett's promise of her great-uncle's papers, the papers that could mean the end of his career!

He strode over and gazed out the open porthole at the chaos of belching smoke above the distant, star-shaped fort. Their oversize, pompous American banner dared to still flaunt its broad-striped and starred face through the streaks of bloodred rockets. He spit out the porthole and yelled for Lieutenant Gage to help him change.

Seventeen

At the Sanborn and Son offices, Brett held a lantern before her as she climbed the stairs from the office to the accounting loft, but then gutted it out to comply with the city blackout. She wore her warm dark green redingote over her gown and boots; nerves and the dampness from the rain had chilled her all day. Out the row of windows toward the harbor she could see the rocket's red glare through the darkness over Fort McHenry, two miles away. Not knowing if Alex was safe was worse than the continual reverberations of shelling. Two endless days while buildings shuddered and windows rattled. Shells grumped as they hit or missed targets, and the air around her throbbed worse than her head. She was afraid for Alex and Baltimore, and she could not shake the feeling that something dreadful—even beyond this war on their very doorstep—was going to happen tonight.

She felt her way to the tall stool where Giles Cutler had first taught her the Sanborn accounting system, so different from the one at the Liverpool orphanage. How distant and dull that other life of hers in England seemed now. Alex and America had changed her life—for the better until this battle for Baltimore. In the weeks before the British came, she in turn had taught Clancey all she knew about Sanborn accounting. And other good things had happened lately. Sally had borne to her husband, Josh—God protect him whatever Dal-

ton Kelsey had done with him—a lovely daughter she'd insisted on naming Brett. Devona was herself again and
couldn't wait to tell Clancey she would marry him. If Clancey, like Alex, came back.

Brett heaved a huge sigh. It was nearly nine o'clock. Would
this barrage go on forever? Alex had told her to stay away
from the warehouse if the British used bombs and rockets.
She had decided she should oversee things here this evening,
but she'd best go home. No use taking more risks than necessary, or he'd rant and rave again about her *never* obeying
him. A wistful little smile lifted the corners of her lips. He
was wrong about the "never," though she'd managed to be
as stiff-necked as he since she'd set foot in Baltimore. But
love and a purpose in life could transform anyone. Sharing
herself with Alex had made her less needlessly aggressive,
more able to accept her own beauty and purpose in life. How
wrong her mother had been to make her feel plain and unwanted as a child. Her child would always have better!

"Mrs. Sanborn? Y'all up there, ma'am?"

"Yes, Kit! I'm coming right down to go home!"

She fastened the frogs on her redingote and pulled up its
hood against the rain. Kit O'Malley, who had detested her for
being British and a woman when she'd first arrived, was now
a great help. "I can't thank you enough for all you've done,
Kit," she called to him from halfway down the stairs. "Did
you fix the pulley on that elevator in the warehouse?"

The big, bearlike man stood waiting for her by the front
door, cap in hand. "No, ma'am. It's real dangerous, too. That
one frayed rope holding the platform up—it's like it's on a
hairspring. But it'll have to wait. We're so shorthanded now.
I told the guards to keep out from under it."

"That's fine. We all have other worries now. You aren't
riding back out to Fort McHenry through that inferno in this
rain and dark, are you?"

"Thought I would, ma'am," he said simply. "I can dodge
the bombs on just a two-mile ride. Besides, listen."

She listened, and realized the scream and thump of bombs
had stopped. The silence was stunning. They looked at each

other, straining to hear, hardly breathing. There was no sound except the patter of rain. "What could it mean? Are they giving up?" she asked.

"No one's giving up, ma'am. It's a fight to the death. But it's sure a good time for me to go. The two guards here'll make rounds all night. I told them, no sleeping and stay out from under that platform! If I can, ma'am, I'll be back tomorrow, less'n they put me on a gun or such out there at the fort."

She smiled at him and nodded proudly at the simple boldness of this brazen breed of Baltimorean. She would be proud to fight or live side by side with them the rest of her life. She understood them now. Not London gentlemen at all, but different. Real men carving out real lives in a brash new land. "You've been wonderful, Kit. I'll go outside with you," she said, and turned the wick down on the lantern on the floor.

The rain still fell, though it seemed to have lightened, too. Kit pulled both horses under the narrow shelter of the doorway where she waited. Suddenly a form lurched at her from the darkness. She gasped. Kit jumped forward to slam the man against the building. "Tom Irwin, what are you doing here? It's that stupid bastard the boss sacked for trying to kill y'all at the warehouse last spring, ma'am," Kit cracked out, and slammed the man once more into the brick building.

"Not kill, jus' scare 'way," the man protested. He sounded very drunk. "Damn Brits—an' I was right."

"Don't hurt him, Kit. What is it you want here, Mr. Irwin? You must realize this is not a good time to come skulking about in the dark," Brett said, and stepped closer around Kit's hulking shoulder to peer at the man's gaunt, rain-glazed face. Tom Irwin reeked of cheap whiskey.

"He didn't jus' sack me, you know. Beat me up bad, too, Mr. Sanborn did. Hell of a temper. Well, we're even now."

"What do you mean?" Brett demanded. "What are you saying?"

"He means nothing," Kit put in, and shook the man again.

"Wait!" Brett said. Her heart thudded to match the increased patter of rain on cobblestones and brick. "It's more."

"Y'all can't trust the likes of scum like this, ma'am," Kit insisted. "Sanborn's never should've hired a drunken sot!"

"Tell me, Mr. Irwin," she insisted. "What do you mean?"

"Bomb hit the southwest bastion out at the fort. I was there," he went on, gesturing grandly. "Heard three Baltimore shippers got themselves kilt. And I seen Mr. Sanborn and his new man, Clancey, there, talking to Mr. Dills just 'fore it hit. Blood, bodies all over."

"Alex! Alex is hurt?" Brett cried.

"Hurt, dead. Don't rightly know. Guess you'll jus' have to wait an' wonder. Jus' like I did about where my next meal was coming from after Alex Sanborn give me the toss, eh?"

"You bastard!" Kit roared as he landed two quick blows on the man's jaw.

"Kit, no!" She grabbed his arm to stop him. "He's drunk! He could be lying."

"Revenge, he's good at that," Kit admitted, and backed off. They watched Tom Irwin slide heavily down the wall to sit hard in a puddle.

Brett fought to keep the panic down, the tears back. Somehow she mustered the sanity to send Kit on his way to the fort with the promise that he would get word back about Alex somehow. Then she sat on her horse in the dark silent street for long minutes, as rain ran down her nose and chin and neck. The drunk had lumbered off into the shadows. It might be hours before she would know about Alex, she realized. She'd promised him she'd stay at the house if the enemy used bombs and rockets, but things were so achingly silent now. The fort was only two miles away. She had to know, to see him. What if he was injured, fatally perhaps? She had to be with him, tell him he was everything in her life. Almost instinctively, she pointed her horse's head in the direction of the fort instead of home.

The quiet was eerie as she pounded out of town. Afraid her horse would slip or break a leg, she soon slowed to a walk. Supply wagons and marching troops, meager as they were, had churned the dirt road to mire. Halfway to the fort, she began to pass ghostly white tents and crude shelters of rain-sopped blankets where men had camped until the shooting started and they had fled inside the fort. She knew a long rail fence would begin soon along the road and then a plank bridge to cross before the guarded tunnel entrance in the long brick wall. Surely she would reach it soon, she told herself. Then the skies over her head exploded.

Blasts of sound and light deafened and dazzled her. The horse shied. Brett grabbed for its wet neck to stay mounted. Rockets, incendiary shells. Fiery fingers in the sky fell like flaming fence posts all around. Air thundered, earth shook. She'd been crazy to believe the British had stopped. She'd never make the fort through that curtain of fire surrounding it! Mortars shrieked across the path behind her, too. Panicked, she veered off the road in the only direction that seemed safer, toward the water just before the barricade of sunken American ships.

The horse thudded along in a panic of its own. Brett grabbed the reins to slow the terrified animal. As soon as it quivered to a halt she dismounted, slipped nearly to her ankles in brackish mud. A blast exploded close by and the horse reared, nearly striking her with flying front hooves. Brett fell back; the horse yanked. The reins went free and the mare tore wildly off into the darkness toward the city.

Stunned, Brett sat still a moment before scrambling to her feet. The skies were silent again, as if the past few horrible minutes had been mere nightmare. She shook out her ruined skirts and wiped her muddy hands on her redingote. Not a light shone from the city, as that would give the British a target if they somehow broke through the barricade of sunken ships. What should she do now? It was about a mile to the fort from there and a mile back, she thought. She had to know Alex was all right. Resolutely she started toward the fort.

Each stride forward she slipped a little back. She had only gone several yards, when she heard muffled oars and men's whispers. She clasped her hands to her breasts, held her breath in expectation. These must be men patrolling the barricade to be certain the enemy did not break through. She should probably call out to them so no one mistook her for a Brit. Then, despite her terror and dismay, she almost laughed at that thought: she saw herself as an American now! Alex had once told her she must choose, and on this terrible night, she knew she had.

She halted when she heard a crunch of prow on the shore, squinted through the gloom and patter of rain. Yes, a gig of men patrolling the barricade, perhaps almost ten of them. She moved closer. They wore dark civilian garb; one even wore the distinctive jacket of the Baltimore Light Infantry. "Hello," she called. "Please don't shoot. I'm Mrs. Alex Sanborn and my horse just threw me."

In silhouette, she saw several musket barrels. One man scrambled up the slippery bank to see her face. "By damn," a British voice she knew only too well clipped out, "tonight the Fates are on *my* side!"

She screamed and started to run, but the attempt was fruitless. He slipped, but she did, too, sprawled on her hands and knees as he dragged her to her feet.

"My dear girl," Dalton Kelsey began, then snickered in her frightened, stunned face, "we simply must stop meeting this way."

He grabbed a fistful of her loosed wet hair and bent her head brutally back to study her. His face leered at her, ghostly gray in the pale light. The move tilted her hips and thighs hard into his and she felt the press of his sword and big knife.

"So you're mine completely at last! I'm so pleased you're coming along, as we're going calling in Baltimore!

When they saw she would not help them at any cost, they tied her hands behind her and a sash around her mouth. They hustled her along with them at a fast pace. She saw they carried several powder kegs under oilcloth and a sack of coiled rope she soon guessed were fuses. Kelsey slapped her on both cheeks when she balked as they reached the edge of town. But she realized he did not need her help, anyway. Twice he consulted a map in a quickly flaring match, then led his men directly to the line of dockside warehouses.

Kelsey yanked her against him under the Sanborn and Son sign swinging in the wind. He pulled her head back again by her hair as if he delighted in her squirming. "Sorry about the slaps, my dear, but war's war. By damn, but you've been sadly misled to put yourself on the other side. I destroy anyone in my path when it's war."

She stiffened in his grasp. She *would* hold herself aloof from him despite his power over her. Desperate, she kicked out at Kelsey and caught his shin with the toe of her boot.

He shoved her hard against the brick wall, almost where Kit had hit the drunk Tom Irwin earlier. He pinned her bound wrists up into the middle of her back, and her cheek scraped the rough, wet brick. "Three of you go in and shoot anyone inside," he ordered his men brusquely.

She heard someone actually turn a key in the lock! More of Giles Cutler's heritage of treachery! Three men bustled in. Silence, then several muted shots. Kelsey dragged her inside.

Brett's frightened, wide eyes above her gag took it all in. Eight large armed men besides Kelsey. She must find a way to stop them. Explosions here and the entire waterfront could go up with it, perhaps the whole city, too. She'd heard them say the fleet meant to begin the attack on the fort again. The stops and starts tonight had been meant merely to cover this mission.

"Shall we lay the fuses, Commander? You said you wanted this building to go up before the others."

"No, I've changed my mind. One of you guard the door and the rest of you take the other two places and lay the fuses there first. Then report back to tell me all's ready."

Brett's stomach fell as the soldiers obeyed instantly. So he wanted time with her alone. He dragged her into Kit O'Malley's tiny corner office with desk and chair. The two guards had evidently been playing cards there. She assumed they'd been shot but didn't see their bodies. Kelsey raked the cards to the floor. He shoved her into the chair, then rifled the desk to lift out pen and paper.

"By damn, so Yank dogs do know how to write. I wasn't sure," he muttered, and laughed harshly. "Now, my dear," he said as he perched on the corner of the desk and swung a booted leg, "I'm going to spell out my orders for you before I take that gag off. You always did have too sharp a tongue and quick a mouth for me." He chuckled again. "Though, I tell you, Brett, if we had time tonight, I'd let you put that tongue to good use for me. War—and watching the enemy get what it deserves—always did make me randy as a goat. But now to business," he said, leaning over to gloat in her face. To her dismay he began to unhook the front of her redingote as he talked, purposefully shoving it back off and down her shoulders to bare her sopped, disheveled gown and heaving breasts to his stare.

"I've long admired your uncle, my dear. I find now that you've deserted the British cause and his memory, I rather fancy having his memorabilia—his papers and such, a whim I'm sure you'll honor as you will anything I ask tonight."

Brett tried to ignore his hands. He slipped the shoulders of her blue gown down her arms to lower her neckline until the top swell of her breasts was fully exposed. "And so," he went maddeningly on as her mind raced for an escape, "you, sweet Brett, are going to sign over the right to all his goods to me. If you do so, I will spare this warehouse and the *Free Spirit* in the conflagration to come. There," he said with a final tug at her plunging neckline. "By damn, I never knew how much promise your body held. Sad that it took that lecherous Yank dog Sanborn to bring out all this passion. You may say he took you by force off my vessel at sea, but I saw the way you looked at him, my dear."

She shuddered as he tugged the neckline just to the tops of her nipples, then sat back to study her again. She didn't trust him, but she had no choice but to sign. He had wanted Great-uncle Charles's things all along? But why? Surely not admiration. There was little remaining but the few medals the Admiralty had left her and the papers she had never really perused. But Dalton would have to untie her hands if she agreed to sign. She could throw the inkwell or something! Saucer-eyed, she nodded her agreement.

He watched her avidly while she wrote the words he dictated, then signed her name Brett Ann Benton Sanborn. He took the inkwell away instantly, but when he sanded the paper from the shaker, she saw her chance. Quick as a cat she flipped the sand from the paper at him and fled for the main room of the warehouse. He cursed, yelled for his man. They had her quickly trapped between them in an aisle of piled goods. If they were just nearer the broken pulley she could see up ahead, she could have loosed the frayed rope and brought it down on their heads!

But Kelsey dragged her back to the desk and slammed her on her back across it while he pressed on top of her. "Go get the others now!" he clipped out to one of his gawking men. "By damn, we'll blow this place up first, with this wild little bitch in it!"

She heard the soldier run out. Dalton thrust his knee, spreading her legs while keeping them pinned against the sharp edge. She breathed hard, willing herself not to fight back just yet. She must garner her strength, wait for the moment to kick him. She dared not make another abortive move. His breath scalded her face; one hand groped at her breasts.

"I should have known all along," a loud, deep voice said.

Kelsey jerked against her. He covered her mouth with fast fingers as he lifted his head. "Sanborn!" he gasped.

Brett breathed a sigh of relief. Alex, alive and well! She struggled to see around Dalton's shoulder where he still lay against her. A wet, disheveled and furious Alex, with a gaping Clancey and Mason Finch behind him!

"Let her up or I'll blow your head off, Kelsey," Alex demanded. "I'll see she gets what she deserves for this deceit, but tonight, you're first!"

She tried to talk, to tell Alex that the other British soldiers would be right back, but Kelsey's hand gripped her face so hard, he puckered her cheeks and mouth. "Give it up, Sanborn," Kelsey dared. "You'll never be certain your wife's not the British spy I sent months ago, so you don't deserve to be on the winning side anyway."

Brett saw the hurt on Alex's rugged face war with his desperate desire for revenge. She tried to cry out again. Alex leaped forward to tear Dalton off her just as a British voice cried out, "Every man jack of you but the commander, hands in the air!"

It all happened at once. Someone fired. Mason Finch went down holding his shoulder. Kelsey released Brett and she screamed. Her eyes met Alex's; he gasped in surprise as he saw her face for the first time. One of the British soldiers slammed a musket butt into Clancey's skull and he crumpled. Alex Sanborn stood facing eight British soldiers, while Kelsey yanked Brett back into his arms behind him.

"Dalton, please stop your men!" Brett pleaded, certain a bullet or gun butt would strike Alex next.

Kelsey shoved her back down in the chair. "Quiet! Hold his arms, men! And someone hold this woman!"

She was pinned to her chair by hard hands on her shoulders as Kelsey taunted the furious Alex as one burly man held his arms and another pointed a gun right at him. "Your lovely little British wife here, Sanborn, has just signed over her rights to your rather sadly depleted business you know," he lied. "At least it will be depleted when we get done exploding this warehouse and pillaging your house on—Charles Street, I believe it is—in the city," Kelsey goaded. Before Alex's narrowed eyes he flashed the document she'd written and signed. "You do recognize the signature as the one she wrote on your so-called wedding day, do you not, Yank dog?"

"Alex, it isn't—" she got out before her guard clamped a big hand over her mouth. She bit down hard and tasted blood, but she barely cared when he howled and yanked his hand back from her teeth.

"Hang this man immediately in the name of the Crown!" Kelsey barked out, pointing at the stunned Alex. "He's cheated British justice and me before. And bring our little informer along to watch!"

Six men dragged the struggling Alex down the middle aisle past the limp bodies of Mason Finch and Clancey, to throw a rope over an iron hook dangling from the ceiling. They tied his hands behind his back. Brett screamed until Kelsey had her gagged again. She fought her burly captor, but he easily dragged her along, too. This was not happening, she thought. And Alex looking at her, believing Dalton had spoken the truth. He had to believe her this once! She had to tell him she carried his child, that Sanborn and Son must go on!

"No blindfold needed," Kelsey commented coldly as her guard pulled Brett to face the terrible scene. "Let the dog see what he's losing—what is mine that he tried to take before. And hurry. We've much to do before the firing commences from the harbor again."

Brett watched in horror as one man tried a big noose in the dangling rope. Her eyes slammed into Alex's. She tried to shake her head to tell him Kelsey had lied. His eyes, sharp and bold as ever, took in her disheveled gown, her loosed hair, then seemed to touch her bruised face like the softest caress. She knew then he believed her and not Kelsey. But the tragedy was, she was losing him forever all the same.

"She came out to meet us on the riverbank when we landed, Sanborn," Kelsey's taunting voice plunged on. "And I'm taking her with me when this place goes up in flames, with your dead body inside of it! Your passionate widow with her legs spread for me in my bed while your city burns. Just think of it!"

As the men surrounded Alex to shove the noose around his neck and tighten it, Brett saw clearly what she had to do to stop them. Except Alex also stood under the heavy planked elevator that hung by just one defective cord. If Alex could only move a few steps. If she could just reach the frayed rope that Kit had showed her earlier, give it a yank, surely the elevator would slam down onto those under it. But her own arms were still held. And her own countrymen were going to hang the only man she would ever love.

She slumped in her guard's arm. "The woman's fainted, commander."

"Too bad," she heard Kelsey say.

Her guard lifted the gag from her mouth, but left her sprawled on the floor otherwise untouched.

"By damn, men, get on with it! All eight of you, hoist him!" Kelsey shouted.

Through squinted eyes, Brett watched the eight men hasten to follow orders. They shoved Alex a few steps out from the elevator landing so that he was directly beneath the iron hook, then stepped back to hoist him. Now all the men save Alex and Kelsey were in the path of the elevator. Quick as lightning, Brett scrambled up to yank at the frayed rope on the wall. Two of the men shouted and pointed at her, but no one looked upward or moved. Dalton shrieked as the big planked platform careened down on his men like one of their own thudding bombs!

In the chaos, Alex lunged farther away, fell in the attempt. The soldiers crumpled to a moaning mass of mingled arms and legs pinned under the platform. Brett sprang for a gun and lifted it chest high at the stunned Kelsey. The noose still around Alex's neck, his hands bound, he got to his knees behind Kelsey.

"You deceitful, traitorous little bitch!" Kelsey ground out. "Your uncle would never forgive you for this! By damn, you've ruined it all now! Come on, British to British, give me the gun now." His voice turned to crooning as he stalked her. "I know you won't shoot your uncle's old friend. He was almost my uncle, too, you know, brought me along the way he did you. It was his fondest wish we should marry."

Brett almost felt as if she stood apart and watched the dreadful scene. The flow of his words over and around her chilled her to her core. Her finger trembled on the trigger of the pistol. "Poor old man, Brett, give me the gun for him. Poor Uncle Charles, lying there with his head bashed in by the fireplace poker, so he—" Dalton went on, his voice almost mesmerizing.

Brett gasped and jerked alert. "The poker! No one knows that's what the intruder hit him with! The authorities said to keep that a secret until the man was caught and questioned! His papers! There's something terrible about you in his papers! You—it was you!"

Dalton yanked his knife from his belt. It flashed out as her gun went off, the bullet striking him in the groin. He doubled over in pain just as Alex butted into him from behind. The man flopped down belly first on his own knife, shuddered, then lay still.

Brett threw herself against Alex where he knelt on the floor. She held him close, then took his own knife to slice his wrist bonds. He stood and pulled her to her feet. He kissed her hard, then cupped her chin in his big trembling hand. "The bastard shouldn't have slapped you, scraped your cheek and dragged you through the mud if he wanted me to believe him again," he said. "But even without that, I knew in my heart that my Brett only defied me to help. He's dead, Brett," he told her when she darted a look down. "From now on we make all big decisions together. Go check on Mason and Clancey," he told her. "We've got a lot to do."

In the next hour, they summoned the city officials to the warehouse and got help for Clancey and Mason. Alex was sad to report that his friend Daniel Dills had died with two Baltimore patriots out at Fort McHenry in a hit on the southwest bastion just after Alex had delivered a note for Dills to take to Brett. He told her what the lost note said, and she hugged him wordlessly in gratitude and love. Brett had her way: the *Free Spirit* would be saved and not sacrificed! Since Alex knew that the *Raven's Wing* now had no commander, he had not even taken the equipment to start a fire on the *Spirit*, for which he had come to the warehouse. Now, with Brett's help, Alex was convinced he could get them on the clipper ship to sail her away from the British.

"You're certain Kelsey took those men he had with him from guarding our ship?" Alex asked her again as they rode together on his big stallion back out toward the harbor. The bombardment had begun again at one o'clock, just as Brett had predicted, so they stuck to the dark, distant shoreline.

"Yes," she assured him. "And I overheard them say that if Kelsey didn't send up his blue flare when the warehouses were ready to be exploded, the ships were to resume firing without him, just as they have."

"You do make a charming, daring spy, after all, Mrs. Sanborn," Alex yelled back over his shoulder through another distant burst of shells and rockets. "I'm just glad you're on my side and that Commander Kelsey liked to brag. Word is another British high-up, General Ross, was killed by a sniper. Now that Admiral Cochran must realize Kelsey's diversion has gone wrong, maybe it will shake him up to get his fleet out of here. The old Satan learned the hard way yesterday that if they get any closer to the fort than they have, we've got guns to answer back!"

That bold American tone she loved! She had never felt closer to Alex, or more alive. He had believed in her even when he had found her pinned under Dalton Kelsey in his warehouse in the heart of Baltimore! She almost blurted out she was with child, but she couldn't risk his not taking her aboard the *Free Spirit* at the last minute. He needed her, and finally he was acting as if he knew it. After all, they had gone over their plan all the way out here. He hardly had time to get anyone else's help who knew and loved the ship the way she did!

They tethered the horse to a tree and located the gig the British landing party had left, right where Brett had said it was. "Adrift at sea again together," she called excitedly to Alex as he shoved them off.

"Quiet! Blue blazes, just row, Sanborn! Sound carries on the water and they might hear us," he roared, then grinned as another deafening barrage bellowed overhead that could drown out even a brass band.

"Rubbish, Mr. Sanborn!" she retorted with an answering grin. They were together and she was now totally unafraid, she marveled. He had told her how wrong he had been ever to shut her out of any aspect of his life. Whatever happened to the two of them now—to the three of them, she thought, and pressed a hand to her still flat belly just before she took her pair of oars to help row—she had everything she'd ever dreamed of.

The choppy water reflected the bombs bursting in air all the way to the ship, but the vessels firing seemed a good ways off, and their courage quickened. Alex mounted the swaying rope ladder over the side of the clipper first, then gave her the come-ahead sign. He pulled her up over the side and hugged her in silent jubilation on the deck. The *Free Spirit* seemed a deserted ghost ship to Brett, untouched but for the additional mounted cannons on her widened decks. But the vessel shuddered as if to echo the blasts from the other ships.

Brett stayed up on deck by the wheelhouse, both pistols drawn, while Alex searched for possible Royal Marines below. Her nerves screamed as she waited for what seemed forever. But he'd told her to stay there until he came back up, and she intended, this once, to obey. Her stomach churned as each blast of bloodred rockets etched the fort against roiling smoke. At least if they still fired on Fort McHenry it could not have fallen, Brett reasoned to buck herself up. A hint of dawn's early light shimmered on the rim of horizon before Alex finally came back up on deck.

Brett squinted to see. He had another man with him, a thin graying man he half supported with his arm around his shoulders. She gasped. Joshua Windsor! "Josh!" She hugged them both hard. "Sally will be so thrilled. She's just had her baby!"

"I heard," he said. "And named her Brett for a bold Baltimore shipper I know. And I heard I'm to steer this big wooden baby out of here. I told you you'd get her back if you were patient, Alex. She was even too beautiful for that fiend Kelsey to ruin."

There was so much to tell, but they were silent as Alex sawed through the two big ropes that tethered the clipper a short distance from the *Raven's Wing*. Suddenly the sixteen British ships fell silent. "What is it?" Brett whispered. "Another diversion?"

"Unless McHenry's fallen at last," Alex said grimly. He squinted through the misty dawn toward the fort. "Our flag's so big," he said, almost to himself. "If the fort stands, we should be able to see the flag."

But there was no time to gawk. Brett helped Alex hoist sail, while Josh brought the ship about. Even with just one mainsail up to catch the early dawn breeze, the clipper pivoted like a dancer. They leaped away from the British fleet straight for the protection of Ferry Bar. Standing near the wheelhouse with Alex, Brett looked back to behold the most beautiful sight she had ever seen. The fleet, intent not on them but on its own failure, was fluttering pennants in the rigging, the pennants that, she had learned years before from Great-uncle Charles, meant retreat. The three of them whooped and screamed and hugged one another. Alex and Brett cried and kissed, while Josh shouted at them for more sail until they ran fore to unfurl more canvas.

As the new sail bellied out, they smiled into each other's eyes. They clasped hands, then looked back in unison toward Baltimore. In the first glimmer of new day, Fort McHenry lay battered but not broken. The future lay ahead of them beautiful and free. At last Brett told Alex her good news about Sanborn and Son. Tears filled his eyes as he hugged her hard to him. Over the fort, the big American flag gleamed like a patch of rainbow in the morning sky.

Epilogue

The Sanborn and Son heir surprised everyone by being an heiress, when Miranda Simone Sanborn was born eight months after the Battle of Baltimore. Although Alex had been adamant that a surgeon be in attendance, Brett had also insisted that old Henny Featherstone and the young and very able new town midwife, Devona McFee, be with her all the time. After the delivery, the portly surgeon washed his hands down the hall, then returned to the Sanborn's spacious master suite to check on mother and child. He found the mother looking amazingly lovely for a woman who had just survived her first labor. Her beautiful gold-red hair was fanned out over her pillow to wreath her happy face as she nursed her new daughter. Her two friends stood arm and arm, all smiles, at the foot of the bed. As tired as he was and as little as he'd actually done there with the stubborn women in the way, he couldn't help smiling at the scene himself.

Brett glanced up when he approached the bed. "Oh, Dr. Rowan, I thought it would be Alex."

"Seen hundreds of Baltimore babies in my time," the doctor went on as he took his leave, "but never one quite that pretty."

"As a new thrilled mother, I'm believing every word you say, Dr. Rowan," Brett called after him with a wan smile as she gently stroked Miranda's golden lamb's-down head.

"Yes," she whispered to the tiny-fisted child, who had fallen asleep on her breast, "you are so beautiful. And your mother's always going to let you know that, even if you get tall and gangly when you grow up. Just look what can happen in your life if you stick to your guns, my little darling."

She glanced toward the door. No Alex yet. Surely he wasn't that disappointed that Miranda was not an Alex the younger. Henny Featherstone came over to plump her pillow and Devona just kept beaming from the foot of the bed. "Now Rebecca shall have a real fine friend to grow up with," Devona declared.

"Another strong woman to face the future, just like her mother," Henny put in, much to Brett's surprise at her mention of the future. "Can't muddle about too much in the past even at my age. Laws, I'm proud to see a bit of America's future."

"And I'm proud Miranda's going to have a wonderful second grandmother right next door, as well as in Philadelphia, Henny," Brett assured her, and the old woman's eyes glazed with tears.

But where was Alex?

Suddenly they heard a thump, thump down the hall, as if a giant were climbing the stairs. Henny craned her neck and Devona rushed to the door. When Brett heard Devona gasp, she cradled her fragile daughter even closer to her. Devona motioned to Henny and they both stepped out into the hall. Brett started as Alex stumbled in the door, his arms laden, and Devona closed the door to leave them alone. He was lugging the big, double swinging sign from the Sanborn and Son offices, which he leaned on the foot of the bed before approaching in awe.

It had only been one night, but he looked as if he hadn't slept in weeks. His rugged face was drawn, his eyes bleary. But when he saw his wife and daughter, his gaze gleamed and he broke into a huge smile. "She's gorgeous," he breathed, and actually wiped a tear from his cheek with a big, shaky finger. "Just like her mother."

"There will be plenty of time for sons," Brett put in quickly, shifting the baby so he could see more of her.

"Imagine," he said, the old hint of tease back in his voice as he bent closer, "two of you to deal with. And, my sweetheart, when I heard it was a girl, I wanted you to know—" he kissed her lips, then darted off to lift the heavy, bulky sign "—blue blazes, Brett, I wanted you to know you and any children we have are perfect to me. Look, what do you think? I meant to ask you first, as we confer on all things about the business now, but…" His hopeful voice trailed off as he pivoted the sign so Brett could see it.

The painting of their bold sailing ship, the *Free Spirit*, was still on the sign, but the Sanborn and Son name under it had been replaced with shiny new dark-blue lettering edged in gold. The Sanborn Family it read now, and on the second sign dangling below, Alex, Brett, Miranda.

"See," he told her proudly, "there's room for other names, but if not, all that matters is that the three of us are together."

He leaned the sign against the foot of the bed once more and sat gingerly on the edge next to Brett's hip to examine the wonder of the child they had made. He kissed Brett again, slowly and tenderly, then, at her urging, took his new daughter in his arms. "Maybe the name of our new shipping empire should be 'Sanborn and all the happiness and love in the world,'" he said, his voice ragged.

"That's what Miranda and her father have brought to me," Brett said, stroking the tiny cheek with one finger.

"And long before Miranda, that's what you brought to me," he told Brett. "And we won't ever argue again," he added with a broad grin.

Brett held tightly to his free hands as she said, "But I meant to tell you that the lettering on the sign would show up much better if it were in white and red—you know, like the star spangled banner—with some gold stars around the edges of the sign to call more attention to it, too."

Over their sleeping daughter, their gazes held, and they laughed quietly together.

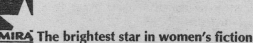

New York Times Bestselling Author

REBECCA BRANDEWYNE

FOR GOOD OR FOR EVIL— THE INSIDE STORY...

The noble Hampton family, with its legacy of sin and scandal, suffers the ultimate tragedy: the ruthless murder of one of its own.

There are only two people who can unravel the case—

JAKE SERINGO is the cynical cop who grew up on the mean streets of life;

CLAIRE CONNELLY is the beautiful but aloof broadcast journalist.

They'd parted years ago on explosive terms—now they are on the trail of a bizarre and shocking family secret that could topple a dynasty.

GLORY SEEKERS

The search begins at your favorite retail outlet in June 1997.

 MIRA The brightest star in women's fiction

MRBGS

National Bestselling Author

JoANN ROSS

does it again with

NO REGRETS

Molly chose God, Lena searched for love and Tessa
wanted fame. Three sisters, torn apart by tragedy,
chose different paths...until fate and one man
reunited them. But when tragedy strikes again,
can the surviving sisters choose happiness...with
no regrets?

Available July 1997 at your favorite retail outlet.

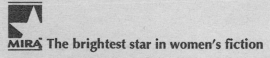

New York Times Bestselling Authors

JENNIFER BLAKE
JANET DAILEY
ELIZABETH GAGE

Three *New York Times* bestselling authors bring you three
very sensuous, contemporary love stories—all centered
around one magical night!

It is a warm, spring night and masquerading as legendary
lovers, the elite of New Orleans society have come to
celebrate the twenty-fifth anniversary of the Duchaise
masquerade ball. But amidst the beauty, music and revelry,
some of the world's most legendary lovers are in trouble....

Come midnight at this year's Duchaise ball, passion and
scandal will be...

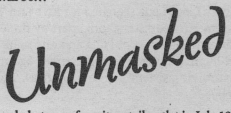

Unmasked

Revealed at your favorite retail outlet in July 1997.